Elizabeth Drummond hails fr[...]
stint in New York (when she [...]
Carrie Bradshaw) now work[...]
home in Essex. *The House Sitte*[...]

𝕏 x.com/lizzythebrit

Also by Elizabeth Drummond

The Reunion

THE HOUSE SITTER

ELIZABETH DRUMMOND

One More Chapter
a division of HarperCollins*Publishers*
1 London Bridge Street
London SE1 9GF
www.harpercollins.co.uk
HarperCollins*Publishers*
Macken House, 39/40 Mayor Street Upper,
Dublin 1, D01 C9W8

1

This paperback edition 2024
First published in Great Britain in ebook format
by HarperCollins*Publishers* 2024
Copyright © Elizabeth Drummond 2024
Elizabeth Drummond asserts the moral right to be identified
as the author of this work

A catalogue record of this book is available from the British Library

ISBN: 978-0-00-852008-3

This novel is entirely a work of fiction. The names, characters and incidents portrayed in it are the work of the author's imagination. Any resemblance to actual persons, living or dead, events or localities is entirely coincidental.

Printed and bound in the UK using 100% Renewable Electricity
by CPI Group (UK) Ltd

All rights reserved. No part of this publication may be reproduced, stored in a retrieval system, or transmitted, in any form or by any means, electronic, mechanical, photocopying, recording or otherwise, without the prior permission of the publishers.

For Mum and Dad

Prologue

Pippa Munro waited; her impatient gaze fixed upon the hilly road that wended its way up from Hurst Bridge towards where she stood. Her boyfriend's car was nowhere in sight. A light summer breeze kissed her sweaty, sticky skin as she looked out across her hometown, eyes roving over the narrow, flint-walled lanes and tapestry of meadows that were as familiar to Pippa as her own face. Behind her, the magnificence that was Squires House loomed proudly, the old, wisteria-draped brick luminous in the light of the sun. The evening was approaching, but the sun was still high enough to cast a heavenly glow upon the town she felt lucky enough to call home. She knew and loved every inch of this small Yorkshire town. She might have been only seventeen years old, but Pippa was already certain that there was nowhere as perfect as Hurst Bridge anywhere else in the world.

"Where is he?" she muttered. Alex was going to miss her big moment when she got to claim her prize! It wasn't often

Pippa got to visit Squires – the most beautiful house in Yorkshire in her opinion – and yet here she was wasting precious seconds standing outside waiting for her boyfriend.

Something hit the back of Pippa's head and landed by her feet; a dried twig lobbed by none other than her cousin Frankie. "Any sign of Alex?" he asked as he ambled through the gates to stand by her side. He smelled of toffee and sun-cream.

"Not as yet," Pippa admitted.

Frankie's pale eyes, so like her own, twinkled behind his thick-framed glasses. Merely a few months older than Pippa, he had the same unruly dark hair and slight frame. But for his lack of freckles, they could almost have been mistaken for twins at first glance. "What's keeping him?"

"Dunno." Pippa's love for Alex swelled protectively. "He said he'd be here." She checked her phone for the millionth time but there were still no texts or calls from her boyfriend of one year. From behind her she could hear the raucous chatter of the town's residents as they milled around the old house's stunning gardens. Somewhere amongst them were her parents, no doubt enjoying old Mrs Allen's home-brewed cider as they nattered to their neighbours and gossiped about Trudy Squires's latest designer outfit.

"I can't believe he missed your glorious victory." Frankie tutted. "He knew what it meant to you to win."

"It's not that big a deal," Pippa fibbed because to her, it kind of was. "Just a cheap medal. And I'm sure there's a good reason he didn't make the fair."

Hurst Bridge's annual Summer Fair was Pippa's favourite time of year. Every July, the town's green filled up with food vans and stalls selling the most delicious food, as well as artisans who travelled from miles around to hawk jewellery, pottery and candles of unbelievable quality, and there was always live music. If this weren't enough, the fair culminated in a series of Wheelbarrow Races, where teams of two navigated tracks of varying difficulty taking turns pushing each other in wheelbarrows. Bragging rights were the ultimate goal, not to mention a laughably tiny medal for all victors. Most thrillingly, that very day Pippa and her best friend Mae had won the teenagers' race – no mean feat in the warmth of the afternoon sun. Frankie had been their enthusiastic supporter, as evidenced by the enormous sign he'd created for them and waved devotedly the entire time.

Currently, the traditional post-fair celebrations were in full swing, held as usual in the impressive grounds of Squires House. Outside the great iron gates of which Pippa was currently standing. And waiting. Still.

"I stink," Mae Grant announced as she approached. She slung a lanky arm across Pippa's shoulders, her cropped rusty-coloured hair sticking up in spikes. The pungent smell of fresh sweat assaulted Pippa's nose and she elbowed Mae good-naturedly.

"Yuck. Off me. Now."

Mae giggled and hugged Pippa even tighter. "Hate to break it you, you hardly smell like roses right now." She exhaled and flapped a hand in a futile effort to cool her flushed cheeks. "Whew! Does anyone mind if I take myself back down to the green and throw myself in the pond?"

"The ducks might have an opinion on that," Pippa smirked.

"I'll fight 'em off." Mae shrugged.

"I'd be more worried about drinking in all that delicious rat shit," Frankie drawled. "Can't beat a bit of Leptospirosis on a summer's day."

Pippa squealed in revulsion. "I'll pass on a dip in the pond, thanks."

Mae nudged her. "I take it Alex isn't here yet?"

Pippa shook her head. "I'm a bit worried he's been in an accident, that he's hurt."

"He won't be, I'm sure." Mae frowned. "What makes you say that?"

"He's not here," Pippa answered. "He said he would be. He promised. Why else wouldn't he be here but because of something dead serious?"

"I bet he'll be fine," Mae said hurriedly. "Have you called him?"

"A couple of times," Pippa said. She met her best friend's eye and sighed. "I'm sure he'll be all right. I'm probably being daft." She sniffed her armpit and wrinkled her nose. "On second thoughts though, probably just as well he's not here. Yuck."

"He's a farmer," Frankie said. "He'll have smelled worse."

"Oh, be still my heart." Mae stretched her arms into the air. "But why are we standing around here when the party is back there?" She thumbed behind her. "This is my last year of doing the races, we should make the most of it!"

Pippa arched a disbelieving eyebrow. "Your last race? Really? Ever?"

"Well, dunno. Probably," Mae said. "The minute my A Levels finish next summer, I'm off to India. Who knows when, or if, I'll be back."

Pippa and Frankie exchanged mournful glances. Although Mae had been expressing her wanderlust tendencies for years, her imminent departure felt as though it had come far too soon. Pippa wasn't sure she was ready for goodbye. After all, Mae had been her best friend since nursery school. "You'll be back." Pippa gestured around her. "How can you say goodbye to this forever?"

"This town isn't going anywhere. It'll be exactly the same quiet little corner of the moors until the end of time." Mae shrugged coolly, but her eyes shone with affection. "It's you idiots I'll miss the most."

"And that's all we ask," Frankie said, a tremble betraying the lightness of his tone.

Pippa looped arms with her cousin and he squeezed her gently. She knew he loved the town as much as she did. Pippa couldn't imagine leaving it forever. Travels and holidays were all well and good, but this was *home*.

"Don't get me wrong, Hurst Bridge is great." Mae's voice deepened with sincerity. "But I've got adventures to have before I work out what I do with the rest of my life. Come on Pip, don't be so serious." Mae grabbed her hands. "Run away with me."

Pippa squeezed her best friend's hands. "I said I'd join you in Goa for a bit," she said.

"For, like, a week!" Mae pouted. "I'm telling you,

Rajasthan will be amazing. And then Nepal … come on, you must want to see Nepal?"

"Of course I do," Pippa said. "Problem is, I can only afford a week away. I flipped a coin and Goa it is."

"Get a job out there if you need more money, I'm going to!" Mae said. "Waitressing, cleaning … whatever. The way I see it, we won't be this young and free for the rest of our lives, so let's have an adventure."

"Pip, you must have monster savings," Frankie chimed in. "You've worked your arse off this past year."

Pippa shrugged modestly as she thought of her healthy savings account. She'd worked at the local coffee shop every moment she'd got this past year, as well as providing maths tutoring to some of the local primary school children. Although she was portioning a little of the money to meet Mae in Goa, she had plans for the rest of it. They might not be as exotic as Mae's, but to Pippa, they were an adventure of a different kind. "Alex and I are going halves on a new car, remember? So what I don't spend on travelling with Mae goes into that."

Mae folded her arms. "Oh, right. You're still doing that then."

Pippa bit her lip. Alex and Mae had never really gelled, although they just about tolerated each other. It bothered her that two of her favourite people didn't get along, but as far as Pippa was concerned, they'd better start learning how to, fast. Pippa had known Alex Goodman was The One from their first kiss at the tender age of sixteen.

"Yes," she said, unable to hide the annoyance from her voice. "Cars are expensive, we both drive … so it makes sense to go halves on a new car together." Alex's father, Ted, owned one of the largest farms in the region and was ready to step down from the running of it as soon as his son felt able to take over. "We'll need one for what we have planned. Alex's banger is, like, a death trap."

Mae's eyes widened. "I get it. You'll need a car that's road-safe if you're both to become titans of the agricultural world. But halves? Isn't it more like 80/20, with you putting up the 80?"

Pippa ignored her. The details didn't matter, did they? They might be young, but Pippa and Alex were in agreement; they were in this together. Pippa had one more school year left, after which she was set to take an accountancy course in order to learn all she could about the financial side of running a business. Alex, being older than Pippa, had already completed his first year at agricultural college in Bradford. Once they had both graduated, the pair of them would train alongside Ted with the aim of taking over Goodman's Farm and develop the business to new levels. It did mean they would have to take care of Ted in his old age, but Pippa didn't mind. The Goodmans were part of her family now, and with her parents already murmuring about retiring abroad one day, it made sense. She just wished Mae and Frankie could see it the way she did. "There's so much potential in Goodman's Farm. Alex thinks he can expand it to be way more successful than it is now."

"Which is great." Frankie leaned forward. His dark curls obscured his glasses and he pushed them out of the way with long, elegant fingers. "For *him*."

"And me." Pippa felt her face grow hot.

"I know that you love Hurst Bridge and want to stay here for the rest of your life. But like Mae says, you've got time to figure that out," Frankie said. "I mean, running a farm? Really?"

"Yes!" Pippa tutted. Goodman's was a huge farm, with over two hundred acres of land, some of which was dedicated to cattle, but several acres had become unused due to Ted's declining health. The farm needed a lot of work to make it more profitable and Pippa had a whole heap of ideas but knew that without the right education to hone her business skills she would be no use. "It may seem lame to you, but I can't wait to get started." Why couldn't Mae and Frankie believe that? Everything about what she had with Alex felt natural, felt right. They'd get married at some point, of that Pippa had no doubt, but there was no rush. First, they had to ensure the success of the farm and make it an empire. The most successful farm in Yorkshire, if not England. Together. They were a team. For life. "And you know, once we've established a business, we'll be able to see the world as a family. That's what I want."

"I guess that's why you've been spending all your time with the Goodmans," Mae muttered.

Frankie suddenly started inspecting his nails closely, but Pippa didn't miss the quick glance he and Mae shared.

"Not *all* my time," Pippa grumbled.

"If Alex is the future King of Hurst Bridge, then where is he?" Mae asked. "Shouldn't he have been in the races? Lording it up with the Squires family? He should at least have been watching."

"He was going to be here," Pippa said, although now she thought about it, maybe she wasn't remembering things correctly. He'd said something about needing to get his car fixed yet again and that he'd try to stop by afterwards. But then his last text had said something about him going to grab a burger at a new place in Sheffield with a couple of friends from college before coming back to Hurst Bridge. "He must have been waylaid, is all."

"Shame." Mae yawned and stretched her lanky frame. A DIY tattoo of a star constellation peeked out under the hem of her T-shirt.

"He's busy, all right?" Pippa was getting seriously fed up with having to defend her relationship. "Not everyone can swan off abroad, Mae. He has responsibilities to his dad, and I want to be part of that."

Mae sighed. "I'm only thinking of you."

"Yeah well, maybe concentrate on your own life for a change," Pippa snapped. Mae's eyes narrowed mutinously.

Frankie leapt into action. "Okay, okay." He raised his hands. "Let's not fight. We're happy for you, Pip. Aren't we? Mae?" Mae elicited a savage grunt and Frankie tutted. "Come on you two, let's get back in there." He stuck his thumb at the grand old house behind him. "Vincent Squires throws the most epic post-fair parties and we're out here missing everything."

Pippa had to admit defeat. Alex would get here when he got here. No sense in missing out on all the fun in the meantime. Frankie was right; Vincent Squires knew how to throw a party. He may have been over eighty, but he ran his estate with the vigour of a man half his age, largely thanks to his trusted estate manager, Grantham. His only son Carmichael was proving to be less useful at estate management and more proficient at driving very expensive cars. Nonetheless, it had been a tradition for decades that the Squires family would host the post-fair celebrations and Wheelbarrow Race prize-giving for the people of Hurst Bridge every year.

Pippa had always loved the events at the stunning old house; and what's more, she envied the eighteen-year-old Squires twins for having been able to spend their childhoods here. Behind tall, intricate gates was a long, cypress-lined driveway that ended in a neat, rose-bordered circle, offset by a low, bricked building that housed the family cars. The house itself was at least three hundred years old, made of weathered Yorkshire brick and draped with wisteria, set amidst rolling acres of immaculate lawns and, thrillingly, a maze, albeit a small one. It was the beating heart of the little town. Despite all Pippa's years of attending the races, she had never lost the feeling of adoration that washed over her whenever she looked upon the old house. What must it be like to call a place like that home?

As the trio headed down the long drive, Pippa's battered phone buzzed. Pulling it out, she saw a text from Alex.

Popped to the pub with Dave and Ollie. Will meet you after prizes?

Disappointed that her boyfriend wouldn't be around to see her receive her medal, Pippa texted back.

What happened to the car?

It'll survive another month maybe. Let's get shopping soon! X

Sighing, Pippa shoved her phone back in the pocket of her shorts. At least she'd get to see Alex later, but it seemed to her that if he had time to hang about with Dave and Ollie, he had time to come to the fair.

Mae clocked Pippa's face. "Alex not coming?"

"He'll be along in a while," Pippa replied stonily.

Mae thinned her lips. "It's a shame he's not here to see you claim victory," she said. "We trained super hard for it."

"Yeah, he knows, and he's really proud," Pippa lied smoothly. She wished Alex had at least asked about how the race went, given that Pippa wasn't overly athletic at the best of times. It was a big achievement for her. But then the sounds of happy revelry became too loud to ignore and her irritation melted away. The friends made their way round to the back of the house, where lush acres of garden sloped gently towards the open moorland. There, in prime position on the lawn, was a little stage area, where a local band were playing a sweet, jazzy standard that fit perfectly with the happy mood of the crowd milling around the lawns with drinks in hand.

Frankie gripped Pippa's arm. "Is that Wolfie Squires?"

Mae and Pippa almost threw their necks out in their haste to follow Frankie's gaze. Beside the stage, with folded arms and a sulky expression, stood a tall, lean lad with a mass of wheat-blond hair, who clearly wanted to be anywhere but here. An equally tall girl with the same sharp features lingered by him, engrossed in her phone.

"Here, we have the lesser-spotted adolescent Squires Junior with his twin counterpart," Mae whispered in a bad imitation of a nature documentary. "Although his normal habitat is titting about in posho private schools down south, he can occasionally be observed stinking up the atmosphere of Hurst Bridge."

"He can be identified by his razor-sharp taste in tailoring and quintessentially *louche* posture," Frankie chimed in, with a far snootier sounding voice than Mae's although he was less successful in fighting off his giggles. "Do not attempt to approach, however, as he will almost certainly look down his nose and freeze you with his ice-cold stare."

"Why is he here?" Pippa wondered aloud. "He never comes home." It was kind of like spotting a celebrity. The Squires twins had attended the local primary school for exactly one week before their father Carmichael had whipped them out and sent the pair of them to boarding schools down south, much to the dismay of Carmichael's parents Vincent and Trudy. The whole town had been abuzz with the rumour that Carmichael felt the local school didn't offer the right calibre of student for his children to socialise with. In other words, it wasn't fancy enough. Which was stupid, because Hurst Bridge had one of the finest primary schools in the county. People bought houses in the town and surrounding areas in the hope of sending their kids to it. But then, Carmichael Squires didn't seem as enamoured with Hurst Bridge to the extent his father was. Everyone knew it and by the looks of it, his kids felt the same.

"Wolfie doesn't look very happy about being here," Mae observed. Wolfie's sister, Emilia, on the other hand, was now chattering happily to friends and enjoying a glass of punch.

"No," Pippa agreed.

Although there was no way he could hear her voice above the din of the crowd, Wolfie lifted his head and met her gaze head-on. His eyes were like headlamps, enormous, cobalt-blue and bright. They bored right into hers with what seemed a cold arrogance, just as Frankie had joked. It instantly riled her. "Come on," she sniffed. "Mrs. Squires is handing out apple cakes."

After the medals were awarded, the stage was cleared away and the band played on for everyone's entertainment. Older guests started waltzing sedately around the lawns together, against the backdrop of the luminescent evening sky over the moors. Pippa and her friends sat on the grass, gorging on homemade apple cake and lemonade, giggling and ribbing each other whilst the afternoon fast became evening.

"Pip, love?" Eileen Munro headed over, a little wobbly from a glut of cider and sunshine. "You coming home for your tea?"

"Nah, I'll go to Mae's," Pippa told her mother. Alex still hadn't shown himself and she needed her friends.

"Is Sandy okay with that, Mae?" Eileen asked.

"It's fine with my mum, Mrs Munro," Mae assured her.

"Right you are," Eileen said. "Pip, text me when you're on your way home."

"Yes, Mum." Pippa flapped an embarrassed hand at her.

Eileen blew her a kiss then scurried back to Pippa's dad, who was loudly regaling some of their neighbours with stories about his fishing exploits.

"Just to be clear," Mae said as soon as Eileen was out of earshot. "Tea is frozen pizza and some of Sandy's premium vodka because she is working until midnight." She nudged Frankie. "You're invited too."

"I should bloody hope so," he said.

Pippa stood, her tummy already grumbling in anticipation of the pizza, despite the vast quantity of apple cakes she'd gorged on. "Right, going to nip to the loo." As generous as Vincent Squires was with his land, he drew the line at allowing people inside his home. Pippa was desperate to see the interior of the house. Rumours of its lavish furnishings abounded, tales of diamond chandeliers and silken wallpapers. But alas, in her time of need, Pippa had to make do with using a Portaloo, one of several that Vincent had hired and set up at one side of the garden by the entrance to the maze.

After she was done with the facilities, Pippa made to head back to her friends, but stopped. There, from the maze, she heard classical music. Specifically, piano music. Had Vincent Squires laid on some entertainment obscurely tucked away in the centre of the maze? Surely, if he had, he'd have said something when handing out the prizes. Could it be some special treasure hunt of sorts?

"Hello?" Pippa took a few steps in. The music was definitely coming from somewhere in the maze. Fortunately, it wasn't a large one, and it took her only a minute to reach the heart. "Oh." In the centre of the maze was a small lawn with immaculately kept rosebushes that kicked out an intense fragrance and there, lounging on a lichen-coated bench, was Wolfie. In his hand was a portable stereo and it was from this that the music emanated. At the sight of her, he glowered and turned down the volume.

"Can I help you?" Traces of Yorkshire thrummed through his accent, but there was a plummy quality that spoke directly to his elite education.

"Sorry, I heard the music and got curious." Pippa was taken aback by his rudeness. His family opened up their gardens to the people of Hurst Bridge every year; it couldn't have been a huge shock to see her there.

Wolfie fingered the buttons on the stereo. The balmy evening light cast shadows across the angles of his lean jaw. If he weren't so bloody moody, he'd be extremely handsome, Pippa decided. "I came here for some peace," he told her.

"Peace?" He was more than moody, Pippa thought; he was downright miserable. How could anyone not enjoy the Summer Fair?

"Yup." He didn't elaborate.

Pippa was bemused. What an odd thing to say. Yes, the fair meant the town got busy, but that was to be expected because Hurst Bridge had one of the finest Summer Fairs, like, ever. Something that the Squires family had had a significant role in creating.

"Why are you home then?" Pippa asked hotly. "If this place is such a nightmare."

A savage smile twisted his face. "School is over."

"I suppose you're going to university in September," Pippa said. "Far away from here, like."

"I am going far away from this place, that's for damn sure." His hands, large and capable, returned to fiddling with the stereo.

Pippa sensed he was done with conversation – not that he was any good at it – and turned to leave. Then she stopped. How could someone with their own *maze* be such a misery? And why he thought it was appropriate to turn his nose up at everything around him, she didn't know. "You don't know how lucky you are."

Wolfie looked up at Pippa sharply, clasping the radio to his chest. "Excuse me?"

She hadn't expected such a visceral reaction. "Why are you being such a dick?"

"A *dick?*" Amusement played across Wolfie's face.

"Acting like everything about your life is so terrible." Pippa's cheeks burned. Maybe it wasn't good etiquette to call your host's son a dick, but Wolfie's attitude was seriously the worst. "Stop trying to be too cool for school. We live in a really nice town."

"Ha! Too cool—!" Wolfie spluttered a laugh. "I don't think I've ever been accused of that before."

Pippa wasn't done. "And your house! God, I'd *love* to live in a place like Squires. You are so lucky."

Wolfie suddenly went deathly still, his mirth vanishing. "Yes." He looked down at the stereo in his hands, long fingers tightening around it. "Yes, I am." The volume of the music crept back up and Pippa got the feeling she was very much dismissed.

Chapter One

THIRTEEN YEARS LATER

Pippa closed the laptop with a groan. It had been a mammoth task balancing the last month's incomings and outgoings, but she had a handle on it, finally. Not the most thrilling way to spend a Friday night, but of late it had become the norm, such was the mania of her working week. Even so, it was satisfying to see her ideas yielding decent returns. Hiring out the orchard for events had been as lucrative as her projections had suggested and her negotiations with the cattle feed supplier had resulted in some serious savings. Pippa grinned, satisfaction thrumming through her veins. It had been a good, if tiring, day. And maybe, just maybe, it was about to get better. She looked down at her currently bare ring finger and let out an exuberant little squeal.

Alex had been up to something; Pippa knew it. She'd

caught him with his 'secret' face a few times – the face he pulled when he was planning something – and any time she tried to engage him in any farm-related matters, he seemed more distracted than usual. There'd been some loaded comments recently about a 'new future' and 'next steps'. Not only that, but as he left the house that morning, he'd told her they had some important things to discuss when he got home. Excitement coursed through Pippa's veins as she imagined what that might mean. Pippa allowed herself to dream. The early years of running the farm had been brutal – far beyond anything she'd imagined in the heady, idealistic early days of their relationship. Although the farm was always busy, back then the margins had been narrow to the point of skirting disaster. The first few years post-college had seen every penny earned going back into the business and any dreams Pippa'd had of marrying and starting a family had to be postponed. But Pippa had gleefully agreed to this, throwing herself into carving out their shared dream.

The truth was that, over a decade later, their efforts had paid off, and no one knew that better than Pippa. The farm was very successful and had been for some time now. Pippa considered the accounts she'd just reviewed; they were in a better position than they could ever have dreamed. Surely now they could take a moment to relax and enjoy their success? Maybe even take that extended holiday they'd idly discussed a few times? Perhaps as a honeymoon? Pippa wasn't sure, but she suspected Alex might be of the same mind. And so, she'd taken precious time out of her day to file and paint her nails – just in case.

She allowed herself a brief twirl around the kitchen in her new and now favourite dress; a calf-length white cotton number with a tiered, floaty hem and a neckline that made her feel like a bosomy heroine from a Regency drama. Hidden boning pulled in her waist and pushed up her chest, whilst the gathered sleeves had a rather sexy way of slipping off her shoulders to reveal the creamy, freckled skin underneath. Fashion had never been Pippa's strong suit, but she'd spied the dress in the window of a boutique when running errands in town the week before. It was unlike her to make such an investment in her style but, in that moment, it had seemed essential to her wellbeing. She hoped Alex would enjoy her in it as much as she loved to wear it. What's more, she hoped the sight of her in a white dress would prompt him to ask the question she'd been waiting for all this time.

"Have you gone off your rocker or summat?" Ted's voice startled Pippa and she stopped twirling with a jolt. Alex's father stood in the doorway, dressed in his usual ancient corduroy trousers and donkey jacket, dark eyes bristling from under bushy white eyebrows.

"Just having a stretch!" Pippa unconvincingly waved her arms around and quickly changed the subject. "What are you up to?"

"Hmm." Ted grunted. "Out."

"Are you sure?" Pippa glanced out of the kitchen window into the March evening. "It's below ten degrees out there."

"I'll be fine." Ted's glare dared her to contradict him. "I'm having tea with the darts team."

"I see." Not for the first time, Pippa observed that no matter Ted's ailment, he always rallied enough strength to down a few whiskies with the chaps from the darts team.

"So, if you can collect me around ten-thirty, that'd be great." Ted shuffled his legs. "My knees can't take these chilly winds."

"You can't get a taxi back?" Pippa fought a wave of annoyance. If this evening went the way she hoped, breaking off to collect a whisky-sodden old man would certainly put a dampener on things.

"A taxi?" Ted's chin wobbled. "Not at them prices! I'll text you when I'm ready. Oh, and I need to go to the consultant's earlier on Thursday," he went on. "Can't be doing with these 4pm appointments, they're too tiring. Before 11am, that'd suit me."

"I'll see what I can do," Pippa replied, knowing full well there wasn't anything she could do. It was tough to get any appointments with this particular geriatric consultant so they had to take what they could get.

"Hmm." Ted grunted suspiciously and Pippa clenched her fists at the show of ingratitude. He was old, she reminded herself, and it must be scary dealing with so much illness. Diabetes, osteoporosis ... the impact of decades of hard outdoor graft had resulted in what felt like handfuls of daily medication and myriad appointments with a revolving cohort of consultants. She'd be grumpy too! Still, an occasional thank you would be nice. "I'll be off then," Ted said and with one final nod, he shuffled out.

"Call me if you need anything!" Pippa shouted after

him, only to be answered by the slamming door. She let out a deep breath. Ted was ornery; everyone said it. But over the years, Pippa had noted his helplessness was usually carefully timed to suit him. Like, tonight, he was well enough to tackle the chilly evening to have a night out, but God forbid he take himself down to the pharmacy by himself or attend a check-up solo. She did wish Alex could play a larger role in Ted's care. He always seemed to have a diary clash, even for last month's colonoscopy, which Ted had been particularly anxious about. Honestly, talking to Ted about his gastric trials and tribulations had been excruciating to say the least. Pippa sighed. Alex simply had to participate more in the daily grind of his father's care. She was genuinely happy to do her part and help, but juggling all the responsibilities was tough. And this was *before* children!

Rising from the kitchen table, Pippa stretched, wincing at the crick in her neck. The house was always cold. No matter what tricks Pippa came up with, the house remained riddled with draughts. She reached for her cardigan, her tummy tilting when she heard the front door creak open.

"Only me!" Alex called.

"In the kitchen." Pippa tried to keep her voice level, as if she wasn't wondering which of Alex's pockets the engagement ring was hiding in.

"There she is." Alex's broad shoulders filled the doorway and those dark eyes twinkled knowingly. "Another day of running the flippin' world!"

"Yup." Pippa's heart felt bigger just at the sight of him.

His smile was as rakish as ever, cheeky with promise and as sexy as the first moment she'd laid eyes on him. His long-lashed eyes twinkled at her like they always did, as if he was letting her and only her in on the biggest secrets life had to offer. She even loved the way Alex walked, a wide-legged swagger that spoke of his deep-rooted confidence in all areas of life. "How was the auction?" Alex had been over to Hull to check out a bankruptcy auction in the hopes of scoring a bargain. Pippa had drawn up a list of items they could use, along with suggested maximum bids.

"Ugh. A waste of time, really." He slung his jacket over a chair and raked his hands through his neat dark hair. "It all looked so tatty. Ended up leaving a few minutes in and having a late lunch with Graham Cafferky – you remember him from school?"

"Yeah … barely." As Alex prattled on about the steak he'd eaten, Pippa wished she hadn't wasted all that time drawing up a wish list of bids. One of the lot items was a trailer listed for a steal of a price that would have been really useful. "The stuff looked to be good nick in the catalogue. Are you sure it was that bad? Like, did you stay long enough to be sure?"

"I was there, wasn't I?" He said with a frown. "And I'm telling you it was pointless. Rubbish."

"Okay." Pippa sighed with disappointment. "You should have called. Maybe I could have joined you for lunch." They so rarely got to socialise together anymore outside of work. It didn't seem fair that some old school friend she hadn't thought of in years got the chance to share in a delicious steak with Alex whilst she slaved over boring accounts.

"I'm sorry, love," Alex said lightly. "You're so right. It was all very last minute. Besides, I knew you'd be busy, as ever. Dad okay?"

"Yes," she replied. "Although he wants to change his doctor's appointment next week."

"He does hate those late afternoon sessions," Alex said with a wince.

"Well, tough." Pippa opened the mug cupboard. "It's me that has to take him and I say it's fine."

Alex looked around. "Is he here?"

Pippa shook her head. "You missed him by seconds. He's having pie and mash with the darts gang right now. Do you think you could pick him up around ten?"

"I'm beat!" Alex yawned. "Been driving all day it feels like. Don't suppose you could do it?"

Pippa eyed the closed laptop, thinking of the books she'd balanced that day. "I'm pretty tired too," she said. "But I suppose I could pop out to get him. He's just down the road, after all."

"What would I do without you?" Alex scooted up behind her and nuzzled her neck, the prickle of his stubble making her shiver in delight. It had been a long time since they'd had quality alone time and she was thankful Ted was out of the house. Maybe tonight they could finally have something more satisfying than an exhausted quickie in silence. At night, it was very difficult making love to the soundtrack of Ted's cacophonous snoring and there was never any opportunity during the daytime. As Pippa returned Alex's kisses, she caught sight of his jacket hanging on the chair. Was it her imagination or was that left pocket looking a bit bulky? Could there be a ring-box stashed in there? Alex pulled away and patted her bum. "I'm gasping, love. You couldn't make us a cuppa?"

"The slave driving never stops." Pippa reluctantly stepped out of his arms and turned on the kettle. "Anyway, speaking of parents, Mum was wondering when we could go and visit."

Alex blinked. "She was? Did she say when?"

Pippa shrugged. "Whenever we can fit it in. They're easy." Guilt gnawed at her. It had been more than six months since she'd spent quality time with her parents.

"Planes to Florida are expensive." Alex pulled a face. "When are they next coming here?"

"Not sure. But remember, they were here at the end of summer," Pippa said. "They can't always come to us; we have to make the effort for them too."

"They were the ones who chose to retire abroad," Alex said, pursing his lips.

She tutted. Yes, tickets were expensive, and it would mean taking time away from the farm, but it was always worth it. "It's my parents," she said. "Besides, they'll—" Pippa bit her tongue. She'd almost blurted out that they would want to congratulate them on the engagement, but that would have been massively presumptuous. Alex was looking expectantly at her. "They've missed us," she said instead.

"We'll see." Alex nodded at the laptop. "Did you manage the wages?"

"Of course," Pippa replied. "But about Mum and Dad, are—"

Alex grabbed her hand. "Let's talk about it tomorrow." He ran his lips across her knuckles. "You look gorgeous. What's this dress?"

"It's new." Pippa posed with her hands on hips. "Like it?"

"Yeah! I mean, you do look like you're off to milk cows in some random TV show." He waggled his eyebrows at her breasts. "But in a sexy way."

"Perve." Pippa giggled and reached into the overhead cupboards for teacups. "I love it."

Alex looped his arms around her waist from behind. "So do I! You know I don't know anything about style. You're always beautiful to me, no matter what. Even when waist deep in cow shit."

"You have such a way with words," Pippa murmured as she poured boiling water into the cups and dropped in the tea bags.

"Forgive me?"

Pippa sighed indulgently. "This time."

"Good." Alex nuzzled her neck again. "Because I've got a surprise for you."

Pippa dropped a soggy teabag. Was this it? Finally? "Okay." She acted cool as she finished making their drinks, but the anticipation was rendering her almost breathless.

"Come on, sit." Alex plonked the teacups on the table, then pulled out her chair. Once they were settled, he leaned forward, filling her head with his familiar scent of the outdoors and fabric softener. He took her hand, rough fingers twining with hers. "It's been a mad few years, hasn't it?" he said.

"It has." Pippa's innards jumped like fireworks.

"And I'm so proud about how we've overhauled this place. We're a great team." His grip tightened on hers.

"I was thinking the same just earlier," Pippa said happily.

Alex's hand strayed towards his jacket pocket. Pippa gulped. Was this it? "I've had a revelation," he went on, his hand stilling. "I realised after what we've accomplished here, we can do anything we want."

"I completely agree." Pippa nodded eagerly, as if the movement of her head could urge his hand to continue its progress into the pocket.

His dimpled smile, so freckled and familiar, stretched wide. "I knew you would. So … how about an entirely new adventure?"

Pippa loved that he believed their future was an adventure. Because it was, wasn't it? Marriage, kids, new business ideas … unchartered territory that they could tackle together. "I'm listening..."

"I mean, I'm thirty-one now. I know what I want." Alex rubbed the back of her hand.

Pippa took a shaking breath. This was it. It had to be. She was so glad she'd worn her lovely new dress for this moment.

"I want excitement. I want the new, the interesting." Alex's handsome face broke into a broad grin. "I want the biggest challenges and I only want to share them with you."

Pippa thought she might cry with joy. "You know I want that too."

Alex smoothed an errant strand of her wavy hair away from her face. "Darling, beautiful, Pip."

"Alex." Anticipation surged like a wave desperate to crest.

Alex grinned excitedly and leaned in. Pippa tensed, ready. "You know how Mick Dunstan came round last month?"

Pippa's excitement stalled like a busted engine. Had she mis-heard? Why on earth was Alex talking about Mick? Mick Dunstan owned vast hectares of farmland and was probably the wealthiest farmer in Yorkshire, if not the Northeast. What did that man have to do with a marriage proposal?

"Mick?" she repeated, just to ensure she had heard Alex correctly.

"Yeah, Mick Dunstan." Alex spoke as if it were the most obvious conversational segue on earth.

"Right. Sure. Mick," Pippa said faintly.

"Well, he and I got to talking." Alex squeezed her hand tightly.

"About weddings?" Pippa blurted.

"Wed—?" Alex shook his head in bewilderment. "Pip, no. What? He's buying the farm!"

Pippa blinked. It was as if her ears were blocked with treacle, because surely, she couldn't have heard those words coming from Alex's mouth. "Which farm?"

"My farm." Alex looked around him. "This place."

Pippa rocked back in her chair. "You ... you sold this

place? Are you—?" Her mouth was suddenly dry, and she took a deep gulp of tea, not caring at the heat scorching her mouth. Something was very wrong. "Is this some kind of joke?"

Alex's mouth puckered. "No, Pip. I'd never joke about something so important."

"But we never…" Pippa's brain churned. They'd never once discussed that option, not even as a hypothetical. She had the sensation of fault lines yawning open beneath her, of the world rearranging itself without her permission. "We didn't talk about this."

"What's there to talk about?" Alex demanded. "It's *my* farm. Pip." He searched her eyes. "It's a deal worth over a million and a half quid."

Pippa struggled to concentrate. What did money matter when compared to their entire future? The farm was where their kids were going to grow up, where she would grow old and play with her grandchildren. "I don't … I'm sorry … I'm struggling to understand." She cast her gaze to where her hand sat atop his, primed to receive a diamond ring she now understood wasn't coming and maybe never would.

He took a big swig of his tea. "Mick made a stellar offer for the house, the land, the livestock. I took my time to consider it, but really, what's there to think about?"

"What's there to think about?" Pippa echoed, gulping back tears. "This is my – our – home."

"Come on, Pip." Alex held his hands out to her, as if he could manually dissemble the disagreement before him. "Don't be unreasonable. We always said we'd build this place up. Expand it. What's the point of that if not to profit and reinvest?"

"Unreasonable?!" Pippa scrambled to make sense. He was talking as if their many, many conversations about the future had never taken place, as if she had dreamed Goodman's farm was to be her forever home. "You think I'm unreasonable for reacting this way? Alex, you've just dropped the biggest bombshell of my life on me and what, I'm supposed to just accept it without question?"

"Doesn't feel like you're giving this idea a fair shot, no," Alex replied.

"Why didn't we discuss this? Why didn't you talk to me about it before deciding anything?" she demanded.

"We're talking now, aren't we?" Alex's eyes were wide and beguiling.

Pippa was unmoored, as if lost at sea with no land in sight. She cast about for rationality. "What about your dad? This has been in his family for generations. It's his home too."

"Finn's taking him in and Dad's on board with that," Alex said. His younger brother and wife lived the other side of town with their baby boy, Dylan.

Pippa suddenly felt very cold, and it had nothing to do with the ancient farmhouse's poor insulation. "You've already discussed this with Ted?"

Alex frowned. "Of course."

"Your dad already knows." It wasn't a question. Pippa felt sick. Ted had been standing in that doorway making demands on her only moments ago. The man had known what was in store for her and hadn't shown a shred of consideration. Hadn't thought to mention it. Like his son, he'd not deemed her input as valid. "Have ... is this final?"

"Yep, since this morning. I signed the papers on the way to the auction!" Alex swigged his tea, eyebrows jumping. "I thought you'd appreciate the efficiency."

Pippa stared at him hollowly. So that was the real reason he didn't take the auction seriously. "You've thought of everything, haven't you?"

Alex gulped. "I mean, yeah. Haven't I?"

"Everything except me," she said sadly. "You didn't factor me in at all. Didn't think to run it by me in any way, shape or form."

Alex shook his head. "I thought you'd like the surprise! But I *did* think about you, Pip. When Mick made the offer, I knew I couldn't just sell up without a plan. You would hate that."

I already hate everything about this, Pippa thought miserably. "Oh, so there is a plan? What might that be?"

Alex finally delved into his jacket pocket, fished something out. "Well, now the sale is agreed, I'm currently in conversation with estate agents down in Kent. Here." He lobbed something across the table at her.

Hands shaking, Pippa picked it up and unfolded it. It was a brochure advertising a space that clearly used to be a small retail park, ripe for development. Pippa flicked through it. The first page showed a concrete forecourt with decrepit shopfronts and a carpark overrun with weeds. "This?" she whispered. "You want to leave the farm ... leave Hurst Bridge ... for ... this?"

"This is a *retail park!*" he said with misguided reverence.

"It's a dream! Use your imagination. It's right off the motorway, great location. Just needs jazzing up, new retailers inviting in... We can expand it to have eateries, maybe even a cinema. There are no limits!"

Right off the motorway? Pippa had no desire to live by a motorway when all she'd known was rolling green moorlands. "Why?"

"Why *not*?" He gestured broadly. "I've never loved the farm, not the way Dad did, and he understands why I'm doing this," Alex said quietly. "The big question is, do you?"

Pippa jolted, lifting her eyes to his. "You never loved the farm?"

He shifted. "Well, in the sense it's where I grew up ... of course I do. But I want more than this, Pip. That's what I've realised. I think we can do more. Better."

"Better," Pippa repeated, nauseated. "I never knew this life wasn't good enough for you."

"That's not what I'm saying." Alex's voice had the hastiness of a man who knew things were getting away from him.

Pippa worried the brochure in her hands, fingers brushing over the creases again and again. What an idiot she was. Running around like a daft loon in a fancy dress, thinking her man was going to propose when in actual fact he was casting around for a more exciting life. And she'd not the faintest idea.

Pippa stood, head swimming. She ran her hands over the battered kitchen worktop, her fingers finding the ancient grooves in the surface, carved from generations of

Goodmans living and working here. She loved this old farm. The way the air smelled – manure and heather and earth – was as familiar as her own face. When the sun shone the milking sheds would trap the golden light in the courtyard, casting the farm in a glow unlike anywhere else in the world. And Pippa loved to spend time in the fields, watching the vast cow herd peacefully go about their business. It was always a soothing distraction from the pressures of her work.

"I can't believe you've done this," Pippa muttered. Bile rose up in her. "I need … I need time. I need air." Head swimming, she bolted from the kitchen, pulling her phone from her pocket. With Alex crying out for her to return, she ran out of the front door, hitting speed dial.

"Hey, Pip!" Frankie's warm voice sent a rush of reassurance through her, but when she couldn't reply for the heavy, breathless sobs, his concern was instant. "What's happened?"

"I—" Words stuck in Pippa's throat.

"Do you need me to come and get you?" he demanded. "Where are you?"

Shivering in the March evening, Pippa could hear Alex lumbering through the house towards her and she suddenly realised she couldn't look at her love's face, not right now.

"I'll come to you," she choked.

"I've got wine," he said immediately. "Get to Strikers and order a cab. I'll call Mae." Pippa nodded; the local taxi firm was at the end of their road and Frankie's home in Sheffield was just a half an hour drive away. "I can't hear you when you nod!" Frankie added.

"I'm coming," she croaked.

"Pip!" Alex blundered through the front door. "Please!"

She backed away, his beautiful face a blur through tears. "Don't," she said. "Don't follow me." Then she turned and ran.

Chapter Two

"Kent?!" Frankie practically yelped his disdain. Pippa had escaped to her cousin's flat, a chic new-build just off West Street in Sheffield. Large windows overlooked the skate park, which was now quiet in the encroaching night. The lights of the many bars and restaurants glowed, highlighting the happy revellers still thronging the streets. Pippa envied their seemingly carefree lives as she nursed her enormous glass of red wine. All they had to worry about was having a good time and not the impending implosion of a life carefully built with love and attention over many, many years. Pippa drooped her head against the kitchen table and Mae stroked her hair affectionately. Her friend had abandoned her work at Hurst Bridge's only pub, The Hand and Flower – perks of being the landlady – and raced to be with Pippa the moment she got the emergency call from Frankie.

"I don't understand." Mae waved her hands, bangles

clanking. "You say he's never once mentioned Kent until now?"

"Never!" Pippa declared. "Not a sausage."

"But I thought you were getting engaged?" Frankie said.

"Well, I mean, so did I. At least I hoped." Pippa sniffed. "It was time. We'd always said that we'd get the farm up and running first; that had to come before we could consider marriage. So, I waited. We've surpassed our wildest dreams and now...!" She threw her hands up, causing wine to slosh onto the kitchen table. "Kent! Fucking Kent!"

"Shh." Frankie swooped in to wipe up the spillage. "Theo is from Kent."

"Oh." Despite her agony, Pippa couldn't resist exchanging a knowing look with Mae. "Is he now?" Frankie's astonishingly handsome flatmate was in his room, apparently engaged in an epic boss-level battle on his PlayStation.

"Don't say it like that." Frankie coloured. "I'm merely trying to be polite. The man has only recently moved to Yorkshire so let's not slag off Kent too loudly now, please?"

"What, in case he takes his fine self back there?" Mae's joke earned a stern glare.

"He's been your flatmate for how long now?" Pippa asked.

"Seven weeks," Frankie answered, suddenly very focused on wringing out his dishcloth.

"And you've fancied him for how long?" Mae went on, with a cheeky glint in her eye.

Frankie opened his mouth to protest but then stopped,

rolled his eyes. "Six weeks and six days." He stopped cleaning and reached for his wine. "I bumped into him coming out of the shower the day after he moved in. He had just a towel around his waist, and I fell for him so hard I think I gave myself a hernia."

"Oh my God, that's so cheesy," Pippa laughed despite herself. "Has Theo been taking tips from *Easy Pick-ups Out of Lazy Romcoms*?"

Frankie gaped with faux outrage. "Give over, it wasn't intentional. He was just getting out of the shower!"

"If you say so," Pippa sniggered into her wine. "Can't believe you fell for that one."

"What a shame that he's from Kent," Mae added. "Because now, we're all in agreement that Kent is the seventh circle of hell. Unfortunately Frankie, thanks to Alex, you can't date anyone from that county without us questioning your morals."

Frankie sighed. "With abs like his, my morals and standards are up for debate."

"Kent's lovely, no question," Pippa interjected. "But I don't want to live there. What do I do?" Frankie and Mae studiously avoided making eye contact with her. "What?"

"Mm-mmn." Mae shook her head. "I'm not going to say it." Pippa stared at her in confusion.

Frankie pouted. "Oh, what? Come on, don't make me say it."

"Nope." Mae topped up her wine. "This is a cousin thing."

Pippa fought to keep her cool. "For Christ's sake, you

two! I have a boyfriend playing mind games with me, I don't need any more!"

Frankie sighed. "Okay fine, it's just …"

"We think this might be a good thing!" Mae blurted.

"Alex breaking my heart?" Pippa said. "The possible end of my relationship? You think it might be good?"

"We don't mean it like that," Frankie soothed. "But maybe having some space would be beneficial. Work out who you are without Alex."

Bewilderment carved a hollow in Pippa's gut. "You think I don't know who I am?"

"Alex takes all your focus!" Mae cried. "You've practically blended into one person. You run the farm, care for Ted, manage all the staff... It's like you're Alex's lackey, not his life partner! No wonder this has blindsided you."

"I'm not his *lackey*." Pippa's heart churned with a mix of self-pity and shock. Mae couldn't be right. Could she? "That's an awful thing to say."

"What Mae means"—Frankie shot Mae a baleful glance—"is that maybe you've been so focussed on the plan you and Alex came up with, you've forgotten to focus on, well, on you and Alex."

"So now it's my fault?" Pippa said. "I've been a shit, work-obsessed girlfriend, is that it?"

"No, no, no," Frankie assured her. "You've been amazing to Alex. Problem is, you've been so consumed with the farm, I worry you don't take time for yourself. Like, for example, when was your last holiday? When did you last leave the country?"

Pippa gaped. "Okay, so now I'm a workaholic *xenophobe?*"

"You know that's not what we're saying," Frankie told her. Pippa did know that, deep down. She knew that they spoke out of love, but every word lanced like a dagger and it was hard to cope with that in her vulnerable state.

"We hardly see you," Mae said. "Weeks go by and it's all hurried texts, ten-minute calls… You do realise this is the first time you and I have hung out in two months even though we live three miles apart?"

"Farms are demanding," Pippa defended herself.

"You know we understand that," Mae said. "We grew up in Hurst Bridge too, we know all about farm life. But you have staff now. You could take a break now and then. Enjoy life."

Pippa paused. Wasn't that what she'd been thinking of late? Shame burned her cheeks. Was she really in that bad of a rut?

"Do you even know how to be *you* without him?" Mae went on, her voice soft. "I get it, you love Alex and want to marry him, but babe, is he as committed to you as he is to being the next big business mogul?"

"We've been together since we were kids." Pippa's voice was clogged with red wine and emotion. "If he wasn't committed, then what the hell has he been doing all these years?"

"I'm not saying he doesn't love you," Mae said hurriedly. "But—"

"There's no ring!" Frankie interrupted. "He keeps moving the goalposts. At first it was decided you'd get married after the farm was up and running after Ted's retirement. Then he decided that once he could hire a deputy manager to take away some responsibilities he could commit to a marriage, and how long did it take for you to fill that role? Then everything had to wait until after the orchard business was launched..." Frankie slid into the chair next to her. "You seemed happy enough with all the farm stuff – and killing it, by the way, dead proud of you – so we didn't say anything, but I can't deny we've been worried."

"That farm would be a wasteland without you," Mae hiccupped. "You literally saved it."

"And if you went to Kent, I'm sure you'd save that place too," Frankie added kindly.

"I don't want to go to Kent." Of that, Pippa was as sure as anything. As certain as she was that she loved Alex, she was also convinced that Kent was not for her. But what did that mean for her relationship? Surely, her love for Alex surpassed mere geography? Yet the thought of settling down anywhere other than Hurst Bridge was so alien it made her head spin.

"You said Kent was a done deal though," Frankie murmured.

"It is. It's happening." Pippa gulped. "For sure."

"Maybe not," Mae said encouragingly. "Maybe there's time to discuss it? Cancel the sale? Or at least, come up with an alternative plan?"

"I don't think so," Pippa said sadly. She thought back to the resolution in Alex's face. "I think this project is more important to him than ... anything. More important than me."

"I'm so sorry." Frankie reached for her hand. "I don't know what to say other than I think Alex has done a really shitty thing and I pledge to hate him forever if that's what you require."

Just then, the kitchen door opened and Theo shuffled through, yawning. Dressed comfortably in sweatpants and a tight vest, he gave the friends a lazy grin. "Evening," he said as he pulled a tumbler out of a cupboard.

"Hi." Pippa couldn't believe the perfection of his arms. Those biceps! She stole a glance at Frankie, who was gazing at his flatmate with stars in his eyes.

"Nice to see you again, Pippa." Theo filled his glass with water. "Hey, you live in Hurst Bridge, right?" When Pippa nodded, Theo smiled. "There's that gorgeous old house there," he said. "Squires?"

"That's right," Pippa said. "How do you know about it?"

"Driven past it a few times," Theo said. "Lots of important conservation sites around Hurst Bridge."

"Theo's an ecologist," Frankie said proudly.

"You think Squires is gorgeous now, you should have seen it in its heyday." Mae swirled her wine glass. "We used to go up there for all sorts of events. Really was the heart of the town."

"Not anymore," Frankie muttered, and Theo raised an eyebrow.

"What happened to the house?" he asked.

"Nothing major. It just isn't what it used to be," Mae answered. She'd have said more but Frankie butted in.

"Old man Squires died is what happened." Frankie was clearly thrilled to be in the spotlight of Theo's attention. "And his son, Carmichael, just wasn't as bothered about the house or the town, so he never opened his home up to the people. All the traditional events just ... stopped without the support of the Squires family. Then Carmichael's kids naffed off as soon as they were old enough."

"That's right, Emilia married some toff in Cumbria and popped out a bunch of kids. Trudy moved over to be with her when Carmichael died," Mae added, shrugging when Frankie and Pippa looked at her in surprise that she knew so much. "What? It's all on Facebook if you know where to look!"

"I thought you said Facebook was the tool of the patriarchal elite," Frankie said impishly. "Didn't you call it Faeces-book for a while?"

"Consider me happily oppressed," Mae tutted. "The thing is, as a business owner I have to use it. Anyway, Wolfie – Emilia's twin brother – lit out of town at eighteen and we haven't seen him since." Her eyebrows lifted. "Oh, by the way, did you hear about Grantham?" Mae explained for Theo's sake: "He was the caretaker at Squires."

Pippa had fond memories of the wiry Yorkshireman, one of those men who always seemed elderly no matter his age.

Frankie said, "Yeah, I heard his wife was ill. What was it again?"

Mae's brightly painted lips curved downwards. "Parkinsons, I think."

"It's so sad," Pippa said. News of Joan's diagnosis had travelled fast around Hurst Bridge. Grantham was dedicated to his wife and from what she could remember, the pair of them were practically second parents to the Squires kids.

"That's terrible," Theo remarked politely.

"Anyway!" Frankie threw up his hands. "I'm sure Theo doesn't want to hear about the misfortunes of people he doesn't even know."

"It's okay." Theo smiled and it was devastating. "I like hearing about your life."

Frankie's face turned molten red. His mouth flapped open then shut. "Umm."

Mae clutched Frankie's arm. "I think what Frankie wants to say is he'd love to tell you more about it some time."

"Yes, any time." Frankie gulped audibly. "But not now." He gestured vaguely towards Pippa. "Crisis mode."

"Oh, of course! Say no more." Theo gracefully excused himself but not without one last affectionate glance at Frankie. The moment his bedroom door was closed, Frankie puddled into his kitchen chair as the girls made smacking kissy sounds.

"You two are a disgrace," he snarled into his wine.

"He's seriously hot," Mae giggled.

"And so obviously into you," Pippa said, enjoying the attention being diverted from her car-crash of a life.

"Because dating your flatmate is such a good idea, isn't it?" Frankie snarked. "Anyway. Enough about me and the hottest man to ever walk the face of the earth. Pip, what are you going to do?"

"I don't know," Pippa replied. "And that's what scares me."

"Well, we're here for you, whatever you decide." Mae knocked back another mouthful of wine then winked. "But if you do end up moving to Kent, I'm disowning you."

Several hours later, Pippa disembarked tipsily from her taxi, wincing at the forty quid fare. Her fault for staying at Frankie's for longer than planned but spending time in the loving company of her cousin and best friend was like an embrace she never wanted to end. If anything, they were proof positive that she couldn't leave Yorkshire. She trudged down the path to the farmhouse she and Alex had called home for almost ten years. How could the man who supposedly loved her ask her to leave them behind?

The house was dark as Pippa let herself in. She could hear Ted's thunderous snoring coming from upstairs. Once the wave of relief that Alex had remembered to collect his father had passed, she checked the fridge for Ted's medication. It was there but running low and she made a mental note to check the prescription. Then it hit her, where *was* Alex? Surely, he'd heard her come in? She flicked the kettle on and guzzled a pint of water but when she sat at the kitchen table with a mug of decaffeinated tea, he still hadn't shown himself. She was wondering whether to check their bedroom when she saw the envelope on her laptop.

Pippa pushed the mug away and moved to the other end of the table to pick up the envelope. An encroaching numbness began to spread as, with shaking fingers, she pulled out a single sheaf of paper – Alex had insisted upon having his own letterheaded notepaper – and gazed uncomprehendingly at the achingly familiar spiky handwriting.

Pippa,
 I'm staying in a hotel in the city tonight to give you space.
 I'm sorry.
 Best, Alex.

Pippa dropped to her knees and howled.

Chapter Three

The morning dawned grey and misty as Pippa wearily turned the kettle on for what felt like the hundredth time. Sleep had been elusive, her bed vast and cold without Alex's reassuring bulk next to her. She'd even attempted to sleep on the couch but a broken heart and a fuzzy head from the red wine round Frankie's left her wide-eyed all night long – something multiple camomile teas hadn't changed.

With sunrise came the Head Labourers, Helen and Des, their chatter permeating through the windows with the morning light. Pippa roused herself from her daze, wondering if Alex would show up that day. His note had left no instruction as to any responsibilities he might need her to assume in his absence and so, like many mornings, Pippa did what needed to be done. She unlocked the milking shed for Helen, who started setting the equipment up, as Des readied to guide the herds in stages to be milked. Once the milking routine was underway, Pippa measured out Ted's medication ready for when he woke up, then made a start on breakfast. Pancakes, she decided, with plenty of honey and fruit. She needed the sugar. But as she began to assemble the ingredients for the batter, she heard Ted shuffling around upstairs and realised it wasn't fair to eat so lavishly in front of a diabetic. Sausages it was then, and she headed to the fridge. But there were none to be found – she'd bought an entire pack a few days ago. Had they all been eaten? She was investigating the depths of the fridge when she heard Alex's voice.

"Hi."

She turned to face him. In contrast to her sleep-deprived self, Alex looked relatively rested. "Hi," she said dully.

"How are you?" His voice was polite, like a stranger's.

"I've been better," she said.

"I'm sorry." He nodded to the kettle. "Shall I make us coffee?"

Pippa was certain she consisted of 99% caffeine at this point but agreed, for the sake of having something to focus on. Alex fetched cups and measured out coffee.

"Did you sleep?" he asked.

"No," she admitted. How she wished she looked more dignified. Having such a pivotal conversation in her sweatpants and misshapen Metallica T-shirt was hardly helping her feelings of total inadequacy and confusion. "You?"

He shrugged. "Only a little. But some space was probably just what we needed, right?"

Pippa regarded him stonily. "Actually, I think talking it out is what we needed."

"You're the one who ran off to Frankie's," Alex reminded her gently as he handed her a coffee. "We could have done all the talking you needed last night."

"Can you blame me for taking some time out to gather my thoughts?" Pippa accepted the proffered mug, even as her stomach churned in protest at the sight of it. "You'd just blown up my entire life."

"That's not what I did," Alex protested as they took seats at the kitchen table. "I've been racking my brains all night. I know it's a big thing to drop on you. And I am sorry for that."

Pippa blinked back relief-fuelled tears. "So, you understand?"

Alex cupped her face. "Completely."

Pippa exhaled. "God, you really scared me! I thought I was going mad last night!"

"Oh, love." Alex kissed the tip of her nose and love flooded Pippa's exhausted system. It was going to be okay.

"So, what now?" she asked, leaning into his touch.

"What do you mean?"

"The sale," Pippa replied. "Surely... I mean, now you understand my point of view, you're going to cancel it, right?"

Alex's face contorted with a frustrated pain. "No, Pip. The sale's still happening. I'm sorry about the way I told you, but I'm still doing this. I mean, *we* are. Right?"

Pippa leaned away from him, that blessed relief draining fast. "No, not right."

Alex visibly fought irritation, his cheeks pinking with the effort. "God, Pip. Stop being so stubborn! It's a brilliant opportunity and you won't even consider it. At least discuss it with me like we always do when we have a big decision to make!"

Riled by the hypocrisy of what Alex had just said, Pippa slammed her mug down, blurting, "I thought you were going to propose to me last night."

"Propose?" Alex went visibly pale. "Why would you think that?"

Pippa lifted a hand. It was as if the world had braked to a sudden halt, but Pippa was still hurtling forward. It was dizzying and she knew the only way to make it stop was to be completely truthful. "It's time ... I mean, it felt like it was time," she said shakily. "We've talked about it so much over the years, the when, and the how. Like you said, we discussed the big decisions. We said that once the orchard hiring business was up and running, we could think about marriage and kids an—"

"Whoa." Alex shook his head. "I thought those chats were, like, you know, hypothetical. You know, what with the business being so full on."

"Well, they weren't!" Pippa fought tears that burned her exhausted eyes. "Not to me." Her mind worked at great speed, reliving every conversation they'd ever had. Was it possible she'd misunderstood Alex's intent for the future? She'd been so driven, so focused on following the roadmap they'd set for themselves, it hadn't occurred to her that Alex had diverted to a different course. But then again, had the signs always been there? What she'd seen as compromise and commitment on her part, Mae and Frankie had seen as capitulation. *His lackey*, they'd said. There had been discussions about the future alright, but each time the final call had been Alex's.

"Pip. Love." Alex intoned wearily. "I thought you understood."

Pippa looked at Alex through tear-misted eyes and it was like seeing him through a new lens. It was one thing to sell the farm out from under her, but another to act like that had been their shared vision all along, when he must have known damn well it wasn't. How many times had they planned and plotted? The decision to delay a wedding and babies so they could get the farm to where it needed to be hadn't been hers alone. And to think that she would leave her hometown for what looked like a grimy concrete hellhole was preposterous. "How could you do this?"

"I thought you'd relish the challenge, to be honest," he said haughtily. "Your parents are living the retirement dream in Florida, Frankie busy working in Sheffield and Mae's all wrapped up in the pub ... there's plenty of reasons to leave. Hurst Bridge isn't the centre of the bloody earth!"

"I know it's not." God, he made her sound like some inbred hick too scared to leave the borders of her hometown. Which wasn't true in the slightest. Pippa had always envisioned taking time out to see the world when it made sense, of having adventures with her own little family one day. But those dreams didn't change the fact that as exciting as the world was, nothing, but nothing, beat home. "And this is definitely a done deal with Mick?" Fresh pain lanced her heart when he nodded confirmation. "So, what does that mean for us?"

Alex's eyes widened. "Well, I presumed ... I mean, I just thought that you'd come with me. Work your magic like you did on this place."

The coffee mug shook in Pippa's hands. "It wasn't magic, Alex." It had been her hard work that had seen the farm's yields increase year-on-year; her sacrifices that had kept the lights on, the staff employed and the cattle fed. She'd only endured this because she felt she was building something that would benefit not just her but the town she loved so much. A business that she could share with her kids. "You presumed," she went on, "without asking."

Alex's brow furrowed. "It's my farm," he said. "My decision."

Pippa's body felt limp, as if she might fold to the floor. "*Your* farm," she said.

He went very still. "Yes."

"And the fact it's my home, where I've dedicated all my time and effort means, what? Nothing?" She gulped back tears. "Did I not even warrant asking? Do I mean that little to you?"

He paled, jamming his hands in his pockets. "I'm sorry you see it that way. I just did what I thought was best for us."

It was as if he wasn't hearing what she was saying. How much plainer could she make it? "I don't want to leave."

"For God's sake!" Alex leapt out of his chair. "Do you not see what a prime opportunity this is? Did you even read the brochure?"

Pippa nodded. He'd helpfully left the brochure next to

the letter and she'd perused the document until her eyes were too sore to focus. "I did."

"And?"

Now he asks me my opinion, Pippa thought. "It's risky. Without solid contacts in the right industries, you'll be starting from scratch without much leverage. I also noticed that there's not enough information on business rates and—"

"And what?" Alex demanded. "It's not *cosy* enough? Not Yorkshire enough? Too far out of your comfort zone?"

Pippa was aghast. He was treating her like an ignorant stranger, not his life partner. "How can you talk to me like this?"

Alex threw his hands up. "How can *you* not appreciate the opportunity? We have a real chance to enter the big leagues of business here, make serious money. A name for ourselves!" He exhaled, cheeks puffing. "I thought this would be the perfect project for you."

"I had the perfect project," Pippa said, her voice cracking. "I had *you*. We had each other and I thought that was enough." What made her heart hurt was that it clearly hadn't been enough for Alex.

"Look." He folded his arms. "The deal is done. You might not want to move to Kent, but..." He lifted his chin, eyes reddening. "You can't stay here. So, what's it going to be?"

Chapter Four

Two months later

"Are you serious?" Frankie slammed his front door behind him and surveyed the scene. Pippa was prostrate on his couch in almost exactly the position she'd been in when he'd set off for work that morning almost five hours ago.

Pippa grunted but didn't move.

"Are you wearing my sweatpants again?" Frankie headed to the fridge and pulled out Tupperware. As he decanted last night's leftover pasta onto a plate, Pippa thought about the fact that he had been eating lunch at home more often of late. Initially, she'd thought it was so he could spend an extra half an hour or so with her, but increasingly, it occurred to Pippa that Frankie was starting to genuinely worry about her.

"Maybe." She rolled to her side and yawned. Despite the fact she spent a lot of time lying in front of the telly, she was exhausted all the time. Adrift. Since she and Alex had split, she had no job, no home, no purpose. She'd had plenty of time to work out what she wanted to do, but it seemed all she was capable of since the breakup was mindless, painful existence. Even sleep was beyond her.

"There's no maybe about it." Frankie pointed at her. "Mine."

Pippa huffed. "Fine. Yes. I love them! They're perfect for watching Loose Women," she said. "Massive pockets that I can fit snacks into."

Frankie's eyes fluttered as he fought to remain calm. "They're cashmere, Pippa." She rubbed the fabric between her fingers with a sceptical expression and he tutted. "Okay fine, cashmere blend. They still cost a bomb."

Pippa nodded. "So, you're telling me that I shouldn't hoard bourbon biscuits in them?"

Frankie slid his pasta into the microwave. "I'd rather you didn't!"

"Jeez, chill. I'm just pulling your leg." She stood and stretched.

"Good."

"What's your stance on digestives?" Pippa ducked as Frankie lobbed a tea towel at her. The towel sailed over her head and landed on her Monstera, which had been unceremoniously shoved in the corner next to the standing lamp. "Mind my plant!"

"I swear that thing grows a foot a night," Frankie said. "I wouldn't be surprised if it's actually a Triffid. I bet I'll wake up one night to find it sucking my brains out through my nose or something."

Pippa retrieved the kitchen towel and patted the plant's leaves. "Don't be so dramatic."

"Seriously, though." The microwave pinged and Frankie brought his reheated pasta to the table. "You and the scary plant have been crashing for, like, weeks now. Have you heard from Alex? At all?"

Pippa hesitated. The truth was, no, she hadn't. Not since he'd loaded up a hire truck mere days after their showdown and headed down south. Even the mention of his name was like someone reaching down her neck, pulling out her heart and tearing into it with ragged teeth. Pippa felt the loss of Alex down to her bones. Frankie didn't need her to explain that, though. He knew.

"Say no more." Her cousin twirled his fork at her. "I'm sorry, love."

"No, *I'm* sorry." Pippa sat next to him and picked an olive off his plate. "I've crashed here for free like a massive slob and I'm totally cramping your style with Theo."

"Hey." Frankie patted her hand. "Nothing's happening with Theo anyway. I'm a gormless mess whenever he's around. Besides, I'm always going to be here for you. Remember when I broke up with Cal? You took care of me then. Literally fed me and bathed me." When Pippa wrinkled her nose, he shuddered. "I know, we said we wouldn't mention that again. But you saved me, like you always do. I owe you."

"Thanks." Then Pippa noticed an uncertainty tugging at her cousin's face. "But...?"

Frankie chewed contemplatively. "You know I love you."

Pippa smiled and nodded. She knew that more than anything else in the world and she always had. "Back atcha."

Frankie took a deep breath. "Not to sound like a totally unsympathetic twat but I was hoping you might find a job. Help me out a bit. It's just ... bills and that. Plus, you're costing me a fortune in biscuits at the moment."

Mortified, Pippa buried her face in her hands. "You're right, I'm sorry."

Frankie's eyes bulged. "Like I say, I'm here for you! But it's been a couple of months now of boxsets and couch time. Might be good for you too."

Pippa wanted to crawl into a hole and remain there for many years. It wasn't that she hadn't tried to find work in the immediate aftermath of the split. Panicked by the notion of no home and no income, she'd applied to varying roles that she thought might do, but nothing had come of those efforts. Her role at Goodman's Farm had been so fluid, her salary kind of all over the place, that recruiters didn't know what to do with her. Besides, very few jobs actually appealed. It galled Pippa that she'd essentially run a million pound plus business like a pro for years but hadn't even thought to formalise her title or create a CV. She'd placed her destiny solely in the hands of Alex and he'd abused that trust. After the sixth or seventh rejection, she'd admitted defeat and essentially adopted Frankie's sweatpants as her own.

"I'll try." Her voice was small.

"I had a thought," Frankie went on. "Why not speak to Mick Dunstan? I mean, who knows the farm formerly known as Goodman's better than you? You could be an invaluable source of support for him."

"I bet he's fully staffed," she said instantly.

"Maybe, maybe not," Frankie chastised. "But if he needs a little help with something, maybe that could ease you back into the workplace?"

"You really think I should try?"

"I do," Frankie affirmed.

Pippa felt her pulse pick up pace. Frankie was right. It was a no-brainer to ask Mick for work. Although, subconsciously, Pippa knew why she hadn't approached Mick, why she'd avoided Hurst Bridge completely since Alex left. The humiliation of the break-up had been too hard to bear. Everyone had known her as Alex's girl for years and everyone also knew why she was no longer with him. She couldn't bear the pity, the curious stares. Staying in Sheffield with Frankie had been a refuge from that. But she couldn't avoid Hurst Bridge forever. Pippa knew for Frankie's sake she had to do as he suggested.

Dropping a kiss on her cousin's head, she hurried to his bedroom where he'd allotted a bit of wardrobe and drawer space for some of her clothes. The rest languished in suitcases in the corner of his room. Peeling off Frankie's clothes, she pulled on her trusted 'smart' dress, a simple wool shift she'd picked up from a charity shop. It had been a steal, considering it was vintage Jaeger. The deep navy made her skin glow and her pale eyes pop. As she shoved her feet into comfortably ancient loafers she yelled out to Frankie. "Can I use the car?"

"You're going *now*?" Frankie said, as she barrelled through the flat to look for her handbag.

"Why not?" Pippa ran fingers through her tangled waves to create some semblance of style. "No time like the present." She knew if she didn't ride this wave of intent now, she'd never leave the couch.

Frankie smiled indulgently. "I've missed this Pippa."

"Which Pippa?"

"The go-getter," he said, as he unhooked his car fob from his tangle of keys. "The grafter."

"Thanks." Somewhere deep down, a small flame of purpose flickered, warming her soul. She had to admit it was good to be doing something other than wallowing in despair. Besides, it was clear that she had to earn money and fast, if only as a mark of respect towards Frankie. She grabbed the car keys. "Wish me luck!"

"You don't need it!" he called after her as she hurtled out of the door.

Half an hour later, Pippa pulled up outside Dunstan's Farm and took a deep breath, casting a glance around. Driving through Hurst Bridge hadn't been as bad as expected. Despite the still-fresh sting of humiliation of Alex's betrayal, she was overwhelmed with longing as she drove down the familiar and lovely streets. Hiding out on Frankie's couch, immersed in boxsets of reality TV, had only masked just how much she missed her hometown. Driving down the old little lanes had unearthed the true pain at her absence from it. The sweet, freshly mowed green was resplendent in the sunshine, the cleanly swept pavements and the picturesque Yorkshire stone houses looking idyllic as ever. Sheffield was a fun city and God knows she loved her cousin, but this town was Pippa's home. She just needed to find a way back, to be able to hold her head high, and a job at Dunstan's could be just the ticket.

Pippa got out of the car. From what she knew about farmers, it was 50/50 whether Mick would stop to take a proper lunch. Now he'd just acquired the extra acres from Goodman's, it was possible he had too much work to do so. But when she rapped on the door to the enormous cottage, it was Mick himself who answered the door.

"Pippa!" His smile was broad, much like the man himself. He was solid, with beefy arms and salt-and-pepper curls receding from a florid, sun-baked face. "It is Pippa, isn't it? Alex's lass?"

"Yes, I am Pippa but no, n-not his lass anymore," Pippa stammered. "Alex left."

"Oh." Mick frowned. "Actually, I did hear something about that. I'm sorry. He had big plans for the both of you, as I recall."

"Well." Pippa shrugged. "The less said about that the better."

"Right." To his credit, Mick didn't push her for details. He invited her in and offered tea. "Don't mind me as I finish my lunch, will you? Must rush out to the top fields in a few."

"I won't take up too much time." Pippa gratefully accepted a cup of tea. It gave her something to do with her hands. Mick resumed attacking a half-eaten tuna sandwich, his kind eyes fixed upon her face. It hit Pippa that she hadn't even worked out how to ask for what she wanted, she'd just rushed out here unprepared. Most unlike her. Nonetheless, she took a deep breath and launched. "As you know, I was a key player in the business development for Goodman's Farm. I oversaw a profit growth averaging around 7% year on year. Thanks to me, the margins—" She stopped as Mick lifted a polite hand.

He swallowed, washing down his sandwich with a swig of tea. "Sorry, love, are you after a job?"

"Big time." Pippa nodded. "Alex kind of left me high and dry."

"Oh, goodness." Mick put his mug down.

Pippa's wave of desperation began to crest. "Please, I could really help you align your interests now you've acquired Goodman's Farm. No one knows it better than I do."

"It's land, love." Mick smiled at her. "Cattle. And with all due respect to you, I know land and cattle."

"But surely I could help," Pippa said, keenly aware her tone was akin to begging. "There must be something I can do. Taxes? I'm dead good at payroll, anything to do with HMRC."

"I'm sorry," Mick said. "I do a lot of that myself. And the wife takes care of the rest." His eyebrows drew together as he regarded her. He picked up his sandwich. "I wish I could help. But part of the reason I've done so well is that I run a lean team and we're fully staffed. Honestly, if I had a space, it'd be all yours." Sharp incisors tore into fresh bread and Pippa's tummy growled. "Hang on!" Mick's words were muffled by sandwich, and he swallowed quickly. "If you're looking for a job, I might know of something."

Pippa exhaled in relief. "You do?"

"But not here," Mick said. "Squires is looking for a caretaker. A housesitter, if you know what I mean."

Pippa was thrown. "Squires?" But then she remembered what Mae had said recently about Grantham, and how his wife was ill. He was probably not able to fulfil his usual duties and if the house was sitting empty, then his absence would pose a problem. No doubt the place was full of valuables that would need protecting until one of the family was able to take up residence.

"Yup." Mick sucked mayonnaise off his thumb. "I saw Grantham in town the other day and he mentioned it. Want me to put in a good word?"

Chapter Five

A couple of days after the fruitless job hunt at Mick's, Pippa found herself back in Hurst Bridge, but this time she was visiting Squires. It had been years since she'd seen the house this close. Her last visit had been at the last Wheelbarrow Race the town had hosted. She'd been twenty-one that year, freshly graduated from her accountancy and business courses. Alex had finished college the year before and was already learning the ropes to become the new head of Goodman's Farm, far too busy to run the races with her and as Mae had been wandering Cambodia at the time with Frankie, Pippa had had to make do with being a mere spectator of the races. Vincent Squires had been visibly weak after a stroke six months before, even though his smile could have been seen from space. Due to his father's condition, Carmichael had picked up the reins of the fair organisation with minimal enthusiasm, yet Pippa still recalled a sun-drenched, happy day. Vincent had died only weeks after, and it seemed the appetite for the Summer

Fair had left with him, as there had never been another fair in Hurst Bridge since.

The spring sun presided over a cloudless sky and the town of Hurst Bridge basked in its warmth. As Pippa approached from the Sheffield Road, modern boxy dwellings gave way to the old farmhand cottages that formed the heart of the town. All of them were picturesque little buildings of grey stone with well-tended gardens and rambling flower bushes that were set back from the road. There was the old primary school, now surrounded by forbidding iron fences that hadn't been there in Pippa's day. She grew closer to the green and the few shops Hurst Bridge boasted came into view. There was the corner shop that had become a SPAR, surrounded by a few more stores that were recent additions to the town; an Instagram-ready hair salon, a sophisticated-looking coffee shop and a chemist that proudly advertised high-end cosmetics. She continued past the green, the centre of the little town with its picturesque duck pond and majestic oaks that lined the promenade cutting through it. In the far corner, Pippa could see the playground she'd frequented as a child and a few yards from that, the ancient pub she'd had her first beer in at thirteen, now owned by Mae, who'd infused the lovely old pub with her trademark style and excellent IPAs from all over the world.

Pippa drove on through the town, dozy in the spring warmth. As the road began to ascend out of the valley, the houses began to thin out. Just there, set off the road and almost hidden by a cluster of pines was the little house Pippa had grown up in. As her parents were living the retirement dream in Florida, Pippa wondered who lived there now, and if they had kids who went to the local school. She caught a flash of warm yellow light emanating from what had been the Munros's dining room and she experienced a pang of unexpected nostalgia. Her life had been so simple back then; her future bright and welcoming.

Suddenly the road curved and became steep. On one side the edge fell away sharply, stretching down to a narrow valley with moorland peaks on the other side. Dots of fluffy sheep were studded like chess pieces in the patchwork of heather and drywall whilst an occasional bird of prey lazily swooped through the clear blue sky. It was a sight that never failed to take Pippa's breath away. And then, like a sentry guarding the town against the wildness beyond it, was Squires House. It resided on a corner of the winding pass, the forbidding grey stone laced through with ivy that once had been dutifully pared back but was now running rampant, obscuring windows and choking roof tiles. The once lush wisteria was nowhere to be seen.

Pippa eased up to the tall wrought-iron gates, almost delicate with their curlicues and monogrammed decoration. She pulled on the brake and got out of the car, stretching. Behind the gates, the drive extended to the house, but no one was there. She frowned. The call with Grantham had been a little vague and she wasn't sure if she was meeting him or someone else. Could Trudy or one of the twins have travelled to meet her? All Pippa knew for certain was that she was here to discuss a housesitting gig that was to last a minimum of two months but may extend to six. There was minimal pay, but food was included and, of course, lodging.

Pippa would just be grateful to get out from under Frankie's feet. The sexual tension between him and Theo was so palpable you could practically taste it. How the two of them hadn't got it together was beyond her reckoning, but she suspected her presence had something to do with it. She checked her outfit. It was a favourite one to cope with the heat, a long linen dress with a square neck and a discreet floral pattern. It looked reasonably professional but ensured she wouldn't boil in the heat of the midday sun.

A burst of crackle to Pippa's right startled her. An intercom! Slick and metallic, it looked out of place next to the old perimeter wall of lichen coated stone.

"Hello?" The voice wasn't Grantham's; it was younger. Haughty.

"Pippa Munro. Here for an interview?"

There was silence for a few seconds, then a high-pitched buzz. The gates creaked open, and Pippa hopped back into Frankie's Micra – because of course, the car Pippa used to drive had been in Alex's name, for reasons she couldn't recall. Soon, she was parking up right outside the garage block that possibly had been stables once upon a time, with fading double doors secured by rusting locks. She slid out of the car, barely able to believe where she was. The house was resplendent in the bright light, despite the aggressive ivy and the extensive lichen peppering the lintels.

As Pippa locked the car, she couldn't help but notice the sweeping driveway was pock-marked by weeds and the once pristine edges uneven with thistles. She walked towards the front door, clocking the dandelions clustered around the entrance, the obvious crack marring the bottom doorstep. The building was no less beautiful for these little flaws of course, but she felt a small seed of sadness take root inside her at the notion this gracious house wasn't looking its best.

Reeling with excited curiosity about what lay beyond the front door, Pippa lifted her hand to knock. Before she could even touch the door however, it flew open to reveal a man so tall and muscular he practically filled the doorway. He blinked rapidly at the sight of her, and Pippa felt a jolt of recognition.

"Why, you're ... Wolfie Squires!" The blond boy from the maze all those years ago had grown. And how. His face was still lean, with those high cheekbones and electric-blue eyes but now a thin silver scar bisected his chin, barely visible until it caught the light. When his eyes met hers, Pippa had a bizarre urge to reach out to the door frame for support. The sudden feeling was nameless, yet fleeting, like momentarily peering over the edge of a vast cliff and pulling back with fear at the depth of the fall. As someone who had spent the past two months mired in the monotone flatness of heartbreak, Pippa couldn't help but wonder if Wolfie had experienced the same sensation too, such was the profoundness of it to her.

Wolfie's lips parted, but then he merely blurted "You're late, Pippa Munro."

It was a far ruder greeting than Pippa had expected. She straightened her shoulders, pushing aside her nonsensical reaction to his presence and glanced down at her watch to see that it was only three minutes past the appointed meeting time. Surely, he couldn't be so anally punctual that a three-minute delay rendered him that blunt? "Actually, I did arrive on time. I was, however, outside the gates for a while waiting to be let in." Wolfie remained silent and Pippa took a deep breath. She needed this job, and it wouldn't do to upset her potential boss. "Apologies for any inconvenience," she added through gritted teeth.

"Come on through." He whirled away and Pippa followed, shutting the door behind her.

"Wow." Pippa stopped in her tracks to take in the grandeur of the house. She hugged herself, scarcely able to believe she was finally getting to see inside. The entrance hall was long and wide, both floor and walls panelled with dark wood. The high ceiling had a chandelier suspended from it, swathed in an enormous dust sheet, but from where Pippa stood, she could see the swell of crystals through gaps in the fabric and she remembered a teenaged Mae insisting the Squires family had imported all their chandeliers from France. It had seemed preposterous at the time but right now Pippa believed it utterly. To her right was what appeared to be another wood-panelled room with a huge banquet table, also hidden under a swathe of fabric. Despite the dust and the tarps, the grandeur of the space was no less dimmed. Although, Pippa thought as she coughed, they could do with opening some windows. There was a pervasive musty smell that she could practically feel attaching itself to her clothes.

"Come along." Wolfie was striding to the left into what looked like a library. The room was dim and many of the shelves were empty, but some books still lingered, shabby and alone. In one corner a piano lurked under a thick cover, the curved lower legs just visible. Wolfie led her to a pair of large leather wingback chairs that faced each other in front of an elaborately tiled fireplace. "Please, be seated."

Pippa did as she was told, her heart racing unreasonably as Wolfie brushed past her to sit opposite. Once seated, he reached over to a small walnut side table at his elbow for a notebook and wire-rimmed glasses. He put on the glasses and whipped open the book. As he did so, Pippa compared him to that sulky boy she'd encountered in the maze all those years ago. He still retained that elegance he'd had even as a teenager, now dressed in sharp navy trousers and a crisp white shirt he wore unbuttoned at the neck. Pippa's eyes drifted to the hollow at the base of his throat; the suggestion of clavicle that drew her attention to thick muscles bunching the fabric of his shirt. Everything about him spoke of a regimented attention to detail. His hair was immaculate, his nails trimmed and buffed. Even his aftershave smelled zesty and expensive. In comparison, Pippa felt very shabby in her old dress, clamping her arms to her sides in case her deodorant failed to do its job on this incredibly warm day. As Wolfie leafed to a clean page in his notebook, Pippa felt the need to fill the awkward silence. She gestured at the piano.

"Do you play?" she asked.

Wolfie's eyes flicked to the instrument. Was it her imagination or did they soften a touch? "I so rarely get the chance." His tone suggested he wasn't about to elaborate on that point and Pippa sensed she should wait for him to take the lead. So she merely smiled politely as Wolfie raised his head and regarded her for a few long seconds, running a ponderous thumb over his bottom lip. It took every ounce of willpower Pippa possessed not to follow the thumb's journey over those pink, sensuous lips. *Get a grip*, she told herself. It was like she'd forgotten all sense of how to behave around attractive people now that she was single.

Eventually, Wolfie cleared his throat, creaking the spine of the notebook. "Right. As you know, we need someone to watch over the house for a few months whilst Grantham deals with his ... personal life." His accent hadn't entirely lost the broadness typical of their home county, but there was still that intimidating briskness to his words Ella remembered from all those years ago. "The house has some valuables that we want watching and we don't want any uninvited guests squatting here. I swing by from time to time when I have business in the area, but my work takes me away from here a lot."

"Do you find it hard being away from home so much?" Pippa asked politely.

Wolfie's eyes darkened. Pippa's stomach did a loop-the-loop in response. "Let me be clear," he said. "This place is not my home."

"You grew up here," Pippa said, confused.

"I grew up here," he concurred. "But I do not consider it my home."

"Because you spent a lot of time at boarding school?" she asked.

A sickly smile crossed Wolfie's face, vanishing almost as soon as it appeared. "Let's just say it's useful as a base when I have business around this part of the country, but the place I live when not working is just outside of London."

Pippa had never heard such an awkward way to describe home. Yet she could tell by his shuttered expression that this topic was taboo, so she nodded as if the matter was entirely clear and decided to change the subject. "I see. What is your business, out of interest?"

"Security consultant." Wolfie leaned back, resting his ankle on his knee. "I advise corporations, high-net-worth individuals and such on their security detail. Whether that's travel protocols, armed transportation or IT infrastructure, I help them find their vulnerabilities and shore them up."

The role sounded a little dull to Pippa, however it was interesting to see how much Wolfie relaxed now that they had moved away from discussing the matter of home. "Is it dangerous?"

Wolfie tapped his chin. "Occasionally I come up against people of questionable moral character." His full lips quirked. "But I can handle myself."

"I bet you can," Pippa said, realising too late that her reply sounded somewhat lascivious, when she'd been aiming for politely complimentary. Wolfie, to his credit, didn't react. He merely fixed those electric eyes on hers. "That is to say," Pippa gabbled. "It sounds like an important job."

"It's a living," he drawled. "Anyway. Like I said, I'm not here often enough to guarantee Squires' security, and alarm systems can only do so much. We relied on Grantham heavily to keep the house in good nick. Now he has some distractions in his personal life, it's incumbent upon me to find a solution."

Pippa hid her disquiet at his choice of words. Poor

Grantham was losing the love of his life to a vicious disease and here was Wolfie Squires acting like it was a huge inconvenience to him. Although Pippa very much wanted to give the man a piece of her mind, she bit her tongue. She needed this job. "I understand," was all she could say.

"The thing is, it's not simply a question of residing in the house to ensure security," Wolfie went on. "This place is old, as is a lot of the furniture that remains. Everything needs care and attention. Maintenance." Just as Pippa was panicking about her lack of comprehensive DIY skills, Wolfie clarified. "All quite basic tasks in nature. Much of the furniture is antique and needs regular polishing. Ditto some silver. We have rugs and curtains that need beating and hoovering, so on and so forth. Plants watering, floors sweeping. The details are all in here. It's Grantham's Bible, basically." He leaned over to the little table next to him and poked a thick binder that up until that moment, Pippa hadn't noticed.

"I see." Pippa fervently hoped she wouldn't have to do anything too high-profile like cleaning chandeliers or precious antiques. That was a far cry from balancing books and mucking out cowsheds. "That's a lot of care and attention," she added with a gulp.

"It is," Wolfie agreed dispassionately. "Of course, lodging is provided, as well as a very basic salary, as I'm sure you discussed with Grantham, to compensate for some of the special care that the contents of this house require. We also cover food. You would need to save your receipts for Grantham; and he'll swing by when he can to provide refunds." His electric eyes bored into hers. "We won't pay for alcohol or cigarettes, to be clear."

"O-okay." Pippa hadn't expected them to and was nonplussed by the fact he felt the need to impress that fact so strongly.

Wolfie's gaze flicked down to his notebook. "I understand that you have been working as a…" He narrowed his eyes. "A farm manager? I'm sorry, it's not quite clear."

Pippa flushed, cursing inwardly for the umpteenth time that she hadn't ever thought to formalise her role at the farm. Still, she squared back her shoulders and forced the most professional smile she could muster. "Actually, it was kind of a fluid situation." She cringed at how strained her voice was. "I was essentially a business development manager, but yes, I pitched in wherever I was needed. Whether that was helping with milking the herd, negotiating suppliers or setting up an event space for hire. It was over two hundred acres with various income streams. Not an easy job but I … I loved it." She felt her throat begin to close with emotion, but she forged on, determined. "I guess I simply used my skills where I … ah … I could."

If Wolfie noticed her stutter at the end he didn't remark on it. He nodded. "Seems like you ran the place. You're moving on – why?"

Pippa hesitated, unsure if she could discuss Alex without bawling. "It's not easy to talk about."

Wolfie ran a thumb over his lip again. "Then tell me what you find easy to say."

Pippa exhaled shakily. What was easy about her life

right now? But there was something about Wolfie's calmness that encouraged her to at least try and talk about it. She smoothed her dress over her knees. "My boyfriend owns the farm. Well, my ex-boyfriend. I mean ... he *owned* it. Past tense. Because he sold it. And now, because my parents emigrated to Florida, I'm without a home and also a job. And a boyfriend." For a horrifying moment, she felt tears threaten and she stared intently at her knuckles, white as they gripped the fabric of her dress. *Don't cry*, she berated herself. Wolfie didn't seem like the type of person who tolerated displays of demonstrable emotions. To her surprise, he didn't appear perturbed. He merely lowered his leg to a neutral sitting position and leaned forward, his forearms leaning on his thighs.

"I'm sorry for your trouble," he said eventually. His face was impassive but not unkind. He was sitting so closely to her she could feel the warmth radiating off him and when Pippa finally felt able to control her tears and look him in the eye, she was totally unprepared for the swooping sensation in her stomach that accompanied the gesture.

"Thanks," she whispered.

Wolfie took a breath and turned his face away. "Let me show you the living quarters." He jumped up and strode off towards the sweeping staircase and Pippa trotted after him in an effort to keep up. Their feet clattered against the hardwood stairs, and soon they emerged onto a gallery-style landing. Large rectangular patches denoted where pictures must have hung and a few remained, covered in thick hessian sheets. As Wolfie peeled off down a hallway, it struck Pippa just how quiet the house was, the way their movements echoed. No laughter greeted them, not even the sound of a radio or TV. The house was utterly lifeless.

"Here." Wolfie gestured to a room. "This is where you would sleep."

"Wow," Pippa gushed for the second time. She'd been expecting a little garret in the servants' quarters, not this. The room was huge, with a bay window looking out across the varied landscape of moorland and crags dotted with swathes of heather rippling in the summer breeze. The furniture was simple but elegant: a four-poster bed, a wardrobe and drawers, as well as an overstuffed armchair positioned to take in the view.

"Bathroom next door," Wolfie said. "Water pressure here is non-existent so expect your showers to be fleeting at best." As if on cue there was a cranking noise from the walls and Wolfie huffed. "The pipes like to announce their presence from time to time."

"This room is gorgeous." Pippa ran her hands along the crisp white bedlinens. The mattress felt perfectly firm too. But then something occurred to her. "You're talking as if I've got the job. Is there no one else to interview?"

Wolfie smiled briefly, like a sunbeam piercing dense fog. "You presume we've been inundated with applications."

"I don't know what I thought." Pippa didn't have vast experience of applying for jobs, but from her recent attempts, there often was competition for any role worth having.

He regarded her for a long moment. His eyes really were the most stunning shade of blue and being in their full beam felt like an interrogation. "We've not had any other applications," he said eventually.

"Seriously?" Pippa was incredulous. From her brief research into housesitting, she knew it was a popular pastime and she would have bet that a house like Squires was a desirable gig.

"Seriously." He looked away.

"Why?"

Wolfie's eyes widened. "The, er, responsibilities demanded, maybe? Not sure. It was a relief to see you had applied."

"Right." Pippa didn't care that Wolfie was basically admitting that he was desperate, because essentially, she was desperate too.

"What are you thinking?" he asked.

What was she thinking? Pippa stifled a hysterical giggle, because she was thinking that right now, she should be down on Goodman's Farm, managing the wages. The new calves would be getting bigger by the day, something that she should be there to witness. She should be calling the feed supplier to haggle on the next quarter's orders. And in that other life, she and Alex should be planning a wedding, a future together. She swallowed.

"I think ... I'm in if you'll have me," she said.

"Oh, yes." His mouth quirked. "Do you think you can handle Squires?"

Pippa lifted her chin. The blunt truth was that she had to. Being homeless, she didn't have a choice. Besides, Alex had put her through hell, hadn't he? And she'd survived, right? Watching over a house would be a doddle. "Not a problem."

"Great," Wolfie said. "If you have any issues, you can always give Grantham a buzz in the first instance." He turned to walk but paused, pointing down the hall to the door at the end. "By the way, I stay in that room just down the hall when I visit. I tend to it myself, so you won't need to do anything in there."

"Of course." Pippa flushed at the very idea that she'd enter his room. If Wolfie noticed her discomfort, he didn't show it. Instead, he headed off to the stairs again, loping down quickly. Pippa hurried after him. He stopped in the entrance hall, looking down at her.

"When can you start?" he asked.

"Almost immediately," Pippa said. "I'm crashing at my cousin's. I'm sure he'll be happy for me to get out from under his feet."

Wolfie nodded curtly. "That's good to know. My schedule is packed, and I don't have much time to get this done, so I need someone here I can trust." He folded his arms, swallowed visibly. "Can I trust you, Pippa Munro?"

There was a rawness in his words that made Pippa start. Wolfie's eyes bored into hers and she straightened her spine. Some inner cognition told her it was deeply important that Wolfie believed he could trust her. "You can trust me," she said.

Wolfie's mouth twitched in what might have been a smile on anyone else. "Great." His warm palm enveloped hers in a handshake that was firm and commanding. As their skin made contact, Pippa felt once more as if she were about to step off a high ledge into a vast, groundless void. Her stomach jumped, her breath caught and so she kept her eyes on Wolfie's collar. She didn't know what would happen in that moment if she met his gaze, but she was certain that she wasn't ready for it.

"Right, okay, you're happy for me to move in immediately?" Pippa asked, her voice scratchy.

"Absolutely," he replied. "Grantham will call you, confirm the move-in date and you can give him your particulars, your bank details." A shrill ringing filled the air. He pulled his phone out of his pocket and rolled his eyes. "I must take this call. Are you all right to see yourself out?" And with that, he started the call, barked, "Wolfie Squires," and powered off back into the library, leaving Pippa alone in the huge hallway, wondering what on earth she'd let herself in for.

Chapter Six

"You know you can still back out," Frankie muttered as he gazed up at Squires. "Stay at mine for a bit longer, babe, seriously." They were in his Micra, parked on the sweeping driveway of Squires. His little car was loaded down with all Pippa's worldly possessions as well as a rather squashed Mae on the backseat. The pair of them had kindly helped to load up the car and accompanied her on the drive over to Squires to help her settle in. They'd both claimed they wanted only to be helpful, but Pippa suspected they didn't want to miss the chance to nosy around the grand old house.

"Don't be like that!" Pippa said. "It's *Squires*! Don't you think it's exciting I get to live in a house like this?"

"I mean, maybe, once upon a time," Mae chimed from the back seat. "It's such a mess now."

Frankie winced in agreement. "It looks so ... unloved. Does it even have power? Water?"

"Yes?" Pippa hadn't even thought to check what other

facilities it had. She'd just assumed. "Well, it has to if I'm to live there, right?"

Frankie grimaced and hopped out of the car. "Here's hoping." He popped open the boot and heaved out Pippa's suitcases. Pippa helped Mae extricate herself from the backseat before unloading the items she'd been sharing her space with: a blender, a bag of thick coats and the Monstera plant. As Pippa's meagre belongings piled up on the driveway, she reflected on how little she had to show for a life she'd thought completely set only a few months ago. She truly had been fully immersed in Alex, to the point where she'd almost reached the age of thirty and now had nothing meaningful left. It struck her that she was something of a blank space, one that had once been so full of everything Alex. And as Mae grappled with the largest suitcase, Pippa realised even her wardrobe choices were Alex and Goodman Farm-centric: sensible, practical workwear and slightly smarter outfits for meetings with suppliers and the like. She'd never considered her style before because she'd never had to. Her work, her love, that was all that had mattered. Now it was all gone. Fresh tears sprang into her eyes.

Mae caught Pippa's expression and paused her wrestle with the suitcase. "Hey." She dropped the luggage and wrapped her arms around Pippa. "Everything will be okay. You'll see."

Pippa was mortified. She'd thought she'd done all the crying possible over the past couple of months. "How?" she croaked. "How has my life come to this?"

"No, no, no." Frankie hurried over and enveloped them both in a hug. "Come on, love."

"We're really proud of you," Mae murmured into Pippa's hair. "This must be really hard but you're doing so well."

"Listen," Frankie ordered, and Pippa looked at him. "I know you can make this work. You've had a bad break-up—"

"—an epically bad one at that!" Mae chimed in.

"You're flailing," Frankie went on. "You're struggling. And sure, you've ended up doing some form of legalised squatting in this ... pile of bricks." He gestured vaguely at the house. "And yes, your bank account is in need of a serious cash injection."

Pippa wiped her eyes. "I'm waiting for the moment this becomes motivational."

Frankie was deadpan. "No, that's the end of my speech, I just wanted you to be aware of how shite your life is." When Pippa laughed, he broke into a smile. "Kidding. All I can say is you are, like, the strongest person I know. You're going through a bad patch, that's all. You're heartbroken and that's the kind of pain that takes a long time to work through. But you'll get there. Take it from me, you know I know something about suffering pain in this place."

Pippa was touched. "Frankie. What you went through ... losing Uncle Jack? That doesn't even compare to a break-up."

"It's different, sure." Frankie levelled her with his pale eyes, so like hers. "But pain is pain."

"I appreciate you saying that, but—"

"Look, my dad died, and it was shit. Yeah." Frankie batted off the harrowing experience of his teen years with a stern shake of the head. "I had good people around me, who saw me through it and out the other side. I also learned something valuable about how precious life can be. All I'm saying is, sometimes the worst thing that happens to you, in a weird way, can also be the best." He jutted his chin out defiantly then picked up Pippa's Monstera, not even complaining when the enormous leaves completely blocked his face. "So, let's get you moved into this mouldering pile of bricks and see where life takes you."

As the friends struggled towards the house, loaded with all of Pippa's stuff, the front door opened, and an elderly man peered out. Pippa couldn't help but smile. Grantham hadn't really changed much since her childhood. Still favouring braces and work boots with his tweed suit, he had the same sprinkling of fluffy white hair haloed around his bald head.

"Pippa?" he said, stretching his hand out when she nodded. "Grantham."

"Oh, I know." Pippa hurried to shake his hand and introduced her friends. "I remember you. Used to see you around a lot during the Summer Fairs."

"Crikey, that's going back some years. Here." Grantham took the plant from Frankie, somehow managing to position it on his hip so that the leaves didn't obscure his face. "Let me help." The old caretaker led them into the house.

Frankie and Mae followed through to the hallway, where they promptly skidded to a halt, open-mouthed with awe. Pippa felt a curious sense of pride at their reaction.

After all, she got to live in this grand, if crumbling, mansion. But then Mae's nose crinkled.

"Oh," she said. "That's ... a smell."

"Are you sure there aren't mice?" Frankie asked, casting a suspicious glance around him. "Because it smells awfully mousey around here."

"It's a building hundreds of years old," Pippa whispered theatrically. "I'll bet there are mice *dynasties*."

"Rats too," Grantham added mischievously. "Although granted that's more since the organic lot set up next door."

"Organic lot?" Pippa repeated. She vaguely recalled that some kind of smallholding business had set up right next door to Squires and had acquired land from them, but it was all very recent, and the owners weren't from Hurst Bridge. Her workload had been so intense in the past few months of her time at Goodman's Farm that she hadn't been able to introduce herself.

"Yes. Lovely couple!" Grantham said. "Their main business is organic pork, but they keep chickens as well. Beehives too, if I'm not mistaken and a cracking berry patch. Got to say, I have noticed a few more rodent droppings since they set up shop."

Pippa was aware of Frankie's overt cringing, and she moved to put him out of her eyeline. "Well, I'll keep an eye out for any lost rodents," she said.

"Good. Anyway, how about a tour?" Grantham suggested.

"Yes please!" Mae replied emphatically.

Once they'd lugged Pippa's belongings upstairs, Grantham started the tour. Even though Pippa had seen much of the house already, she tagged along. Frankie gasped as they went into the master bathroom. It was almost as big as his flat, with neat tiling and an ancient-looking shower over an enormous freestanding bath. "The water is a bit temperamental in this place," Grantham advised. "The shower will either give you a feeble trickle or blast you into oblivion, with any guess as to what temperature you'll get. But you get clean anyhow. And the pipes do rattle somewhat." He cast a worried glance around the room. "If you hear them getting particularly rambunctious, let me know."

Mae was swooning over the bathtub. "I'd love one of these," she crooned, practically hugging the thing. "I'd literally sell my soul."

"That bath has cleaned four generations of Squires," Grantham commented. "A fair few of the dogs too! The amount of mud those creatures collected …" he chuckled ruefully. "And they did love to roll in fox poo." Mae jerked away from the bath with a grimace.

Grantham led them back downstairs to the kitchen, a long, low-ceilinged room with white walls and sections of exposed brick. A battered pine table crowded with mismatched chairs took up one side of the space and at the top of the room was a huge fireplace stained with what must have been centuries of soot, but now a well-used Aga filled the hearth. Grantham pointed at a fridge in the corner. "We have some basics like milk and teabags in already, but you'll need to stock up for your meals, for which we will reimburse you. Not alcohol, of course."

Pippa was distracted by the big window positioned

over the sink, which offered a view of the hills so stunning it blew her mind. She could easily imagine residents over the years standing where she stood now, gazing out across the scenery. And whilst the people had changed, the hills had not. They had endured. She'd wager those wending drywalls were older than the house. Love and gratitude for the town she called home surged through her. How could Alex have left this? Left her? Grantham cleared his throat, and she snapped back to the present.

"Yes, Wolfie said that already. About the booze." Pippa briefly entertained the notion that they were concerned about her drinking to forget her sudden and enforced spinsterhood. Such was the curse of living in a small town, it wouldn't surprise her.

"Although, speaking of alcohol." Grantham's eyebrows wagged as he led them to a small oak door tucked away in the corner. "Let me show you something pretty groovy." He twisted the heavy handle and opened it to reveal a short flight of stone steps. They descended into a cool and musty cellar space.

Pippa took a moment to let her eyes adjust to the dim light. She had never seen so much wine in her life! The small stone room was lined with floor-to-ceiling racks and every slot was filled with a bottle, some more dusty than others.

"Carmichael was an avid wine fanatic, and this is probably the only room in the house that is in perfect condition as a result." Grantham lifted a Bordeaux and displayed it like a sommelier. "Look at that. 1961.

Carmichael bought this as an anniversary present for his wife."

"And they didn't drink it?" Pippa was mystified.

"Oh no!" Grantham chortled, reverently sliding the bottle back into place. "He got it at auction; he knew its value."

"Think I'd have preferred a nice pair of earrings for an anniversary present," Mae said.

"Yeah, bit tight to give a bottle of wine to someone and not let them drink it," Frankie added.

"Well, this is an expensive collection," the caretaker said stiffly. "Carmichael was a real enthusiast and, now that he's gone, this is almost like a lasting memorial to him. He was adamant it remained in the family after he passed." Was it Pippa's imagination or did Grantham grimace at the notion? His capable smile soon returned, however. "I just did a bottle rotation, so you won't need to for some time."

"Rotation? You rotate the bottles?" Pippa was dumbfounded. It was strange enough that even in death Carmichael wanted to keep more wine than a healthy person could drink locked away, let alone that the wine had to be cared for to the extent Grantham described.

"Yes. Keeps the corks moist." Grantham regarded her seriously. "Imperative, that. Come along. More to see."

They went back up the steps into the kitchen. Blinking in the light, they headed through to the huge dining room. A covered table and chairs took central position with what appeared to be large sideboards taking up each wall. "You won't spend much time in here," Grantham predicted, "only when the furniture needs some polishing. That's a sizeable job, I warn you." He then led the gang through to what appeared to be a family room. It was larger than the dining room, lined with huge windows and here, yet again, most of the furniture was covered, aside from a squishy sofa adorned with throws and an ancient-looking TV propped opposite it. "It gets the main channels does that," Grantham said, patting the top of the TV.

Pippa exchanged alarmed glances with her cousin. What did Grantham mean, the 'main channels'? "Do you have Sky? Netflix?" She feared the answer. After all, the television set appeared so old it probably belonged in a museum. Pippa had relied on her trashy TV shows to keep her going during the dark days post break-up and wasn't sure she could go without them cold turkey.

"Oh, nothing quite so fancy," he replied, and Pippa's mood plummeted. "The BBC of course, and you might get one or two of the others if the weather behaves itself." He saw her stricken expression and smiled reassuringly. "Not to worry, we've got Internet – I saw to that – although it's tempestuous at the best of times. Doesn't like to work on Sundays and it's sluggish most mornings. But the lady of the house never minded and Wolfie brings his own router when he's here, so we've left it as is."

"It's not too late to change your mind!" Frankie whispered theatrically to Pippa.

"Oh, give over!" Grantham tutted. "As I said, we've never had much need of the internet. There's always too much to be done. I suppose that sounds unthinkable to your generation."

"It'll take some getting used to," Pippa said

diplomatically as she took a deep breath. It might be a good thing to have limited access to TV and Internet. It could give her time to think, to rebuild. She'd largely stayed away from social media since becoming single, terrified of exposing herself to the well-meaning intrusions of her online friends. The questions, the curiosity. Her mind flashed to the pathetic pile of possessions she'd brought with her and the urge to lose herself in a marathon of Real Housewives hit like a wave.

"Come on, you need to see the gardens," Grantham said kindly. Pushing the wallowing sensations down, Pippa followed him through the house. They walked to the kitchen and out through the back door. Pippa held her breath, only to let it out in a disappointed huff. The vast acres of neat green lawns were gone. The garden was a decent size to be sure, but a decent size for a modest three bed semi, not a huge, old mansion. Instead, there was a new perimeter fence which annexed off much of the former grounds.

"I didn't realise they'd sold off so much!" Pippa exclaimed.

"They made a practical decision," Grantham confirmed gruffly. "With Carmichael dead and Trudy down south, these gardens became a burden." He sighed. "Beautiful though they were."

Pippa sensed Grantham was sad about the family parcelling off the land, so she didn't say anything further, but Mae did.

"Well, I'd like to meet the Johnsons," she said. "Their

honey is the best I've ever had. And I've had swamp honey from Georgia. I know good honey."

Grantham looked utterly bewildered, and Frankie patted his shoulder. "Our friend Mae is very well travelled. She doesn't really like to talk about it, in case you hadn't noticed."

A comically outraged Mae elbowed Frankie in the side. "Oi, shut your— Oh, look, is that them?" She pointed across the fence where two men could be seen, heaving around what looked like aluminium siding.

"Yes!" Grantham said. "Come on, I'll introduce you."

The trio followed Grantham over to the fence. Pippa could barely see over it but was able to smile a greeting to the guys that ambled over.

"Patrick and Todd Johnson, meet Pippa Munro." Grantham pointed. Patrick was tall, husky, with sandy hair and kind, deep-set eyes. Todd was smaller than his husband, but well-built, with a pristinely smooth bald head and a friendly grin. They made a handsome couple, dressed in worn workwear and boots.

"Hello. Are you the new housesitter?" Patrick leant over the fence to shake her hand.

Todd followed suit then smiled at Grantham. "We're gonna miss you."

"Don't be daft," Grantham said. "I'm only down the road. I'm hardly going to the moon."

"It's nice to meet you," Pippa said, arm aching from stretching it over the fence. "I thought I knew everyone in this town, so it's a novelty to meet new people!"

Patrick grinned. "We're not *that* new," he said. "It's already been well over a year."

"What brings you here, Pippa?" Todd asked. "I hear you used to work at Goodman's?"

"Work there?" Frankie exclaimed. "You mean, ran it like a boss!"

"Well, yes, I *used* to." She flushed. That was the thing about Hurst Bridge. Everyone knew everyone and word travelled fast. She had hoped that due to the Johnsons being relative newcomers to the village that she wouldn't have to explain her situation, but as Todd and Pat exchanged a subtle glance of knowing, Pippa burned with humiliation.

Mae breezed in. "Mae Grant," she said. "I own The Hand and Flower, on the green?"

Todd's face brightened. "Yes, I know it. Great pub."

"Thanks!" Mae glowed. "I bought it a few years ago once I returned from traveling ... sometimes I wonder why!" But the proud grin on her face gave away her happiness. Mae loved that pub. "Anyway, I hear you have pigs?" Mae shot Pippa a small smile and Pippa thanked every God in existence for Mae's amazing powers of deflection.

"Yup," Todd said, beaming. "We used to be based out in Derbyshire but our land was sold out from under us to developers and so we had to uproot, set up here. We specialise in pork, but we also have a berry patch and a little chicken run and—"

"Their eggs are the best I've ever had," Grantham interrupted.

Todd beamed his thanks. "And of course, our special beehives."

"The beehives that were a pet project," Patrick said, somewhat ruefully, "became something a bit more substantial."

"Honey is so fashionable; we'd have been mad not to invest!" Todd said somewhat defensively. "People like honey and they'll pay for the good stuff. Even *you* can't deny it's lucrative." He leaned conspiratorially towards Mae. "We sell it at Whole Foods now."

Pippa was hugely impressed. "That's great! Exclusively?"

"For now," Todd said modestly. "But we're looking for further opportunities. Sometimes we have too much work to cope, but this is our dream."

"Beats pushing papers around." Patrick pretended to yawn. "I mean, look at my office now." He gestured behind him. "I love it. Even in the pissing rain. There's nowhere we'd rather be."

Pippa could only nod in agreement. They were her sort of people.

"Yes," Todd agreed. "And, oh, Juniper!" He looked down at his feet and there was a massive snort. Intrigued, Pippa and her friends craned their necks to follow Todd's gaze and there, rooting around Todd's feet, was a huge ginger pig with bristly hair and large ears. "Don't mind Juniper," Todd said. "Just on her daily perambulation."

"She's supposed to be in her pen," Patrick said. "Plenty of perambulation space there."

"Can she help it if she's curious and likes to break out?"

Todd shot back. He bent down to caress the pig's face. "You're a queen is what you are."

"She's a Tamworth," Patrick said to Pippa. "Rare." At Pippa's confused look, he hurried to explain. "We don't rear her for pork. She's more like a pet. We're hoping to breed from her but—"

"But she's a wanderer with no interest in settling down." Todd finished for him, scratching the animal's head. It seemed to Pippa that she purred.

"She's a madam," Patrick said acidly. "And Todd indulges her too much."

"She's lovely," Pippa concluded.

"I do like you," Todd told Pippa with a grin. "Look, we'd best get Juniper back safe so we can get on with our work. So lovely to meet you all."

And with a wave, the men walked off, bickering lovingly about the pig, whom Pippa swore looked over her shoulder with a smirk.

"I think that's as good a time as any to leave you to it," Grantham said. "Wolfie might be by later this week, he told me to say."

"Okay." For want of anything else, Pippa asked, "Will he be coming from far away? I know he has to travel a lot with work."

"I think he's working over in Harrogate today," Grantham said, tapping his chin in thought. "Some big client. Then off to Poland for a couple of days."

"Well, that sounds suitably mysterious," Frankie remarked. "He must be the most elusive part-time resident of this town."

"He's very good at what he does," Grantham said, and Pippa detected a note of pride in his voice. "It's not surprising, given his army experience and everything."

Frankie grimaced. "He was in the army?"

"Yes. He signed up straight out of school; saw some serious action. It was a scary time and his parents …" He thinned his lips. "Well, I'm just right glad he came home in one piece."

Pippa flashed back to the maze, that summer when she encountered an eighteen-year-old Wolfie alone, listening to music. She remembered he'd said he'd be going far away. Perhaps that's how he came by the scar on his chin. Somehow, she couldn't reconcile the chaos of war with the restrained, serious man she'd met with recently. He was so buttoned-up, kind of rude at times too. What on earth had he endured during his service? His army experiences couldn't be the only reason he acted the way he did. After all, he'd been pretty obnoxious towards her that time they'd met in the maze and that was before he'd enlisted.

Once in the kitchen, Grantham fished in his pocket and handed over a weighty ring of keys. "These are now yours," he said solemnly. As Pippa took the keys from him, she noticed a certain reluctance on his part to let go. The old man's eyes moistened, although he tried to hide it. Pippa understood. He was being forced by circumstance to relinquish something that had meant a great deal for much of his life. She knew exactly how that felt.

"I'll take care of them," she promised softly.

Grantham nodded gruffly. "Any emergencies, just call me, but otherwise…" He trailed off, lost.

"I'll try not to bother you," Pippa said. The binder of instructions he'd created was pretty comprehensive, after all. Grantham took his leave and then it was just Mae and Frankie.

"Promise you'll call me if you change your mind." Frankie's lip wobbled.

"Hey, I'll be fine." Pippa hugged him. "Ooh, now I'm gone you have no excuse not to make a move on Theo."

Frankie paled. "Oh God, you're right."

Mae pulled Pippa into a tight embrace. "I hate to think of you rattling around this place alone," she said. "Call me anytime."

"As much as I am looking forward to getting my sweatpants back, I will miss you." Frankie sniffed. "Who am I going to watch old episodes of the Kardashians with?"

"For God's sake, I'm not dying!" Pippa laughed. "We can still do everything we did before, I just won't be taking up space on your couch or eating your biscuits all the time."

Frankie rolled his eyes good-naturedly and dropped a kiss on her forehead. "Love you. See you soon."

As Frankie and Mae got into the car and left, Pippa forced herself to wave them off with an optimistic smile. But as soon as Frankie's car disappeared from sight, foreboding crept in. Pippa leaned against the heavy front door and looked down at the fat binder in her hands, then to the cold, empty space around her.

"What on earth have I done?" Her voice echoed around the hall with no reply.

Pippa Munro was utterly alone.

Chapter Seven

The morning was dark, with a sliver of new sun kissing the horizon. But that didn't stop Todd and Pat's sprightly cockerel from greeting the day with great enthusiasm.

"Jesus Christ." Pippa buried her head under the pillows, but to no avail. The thick goose down was no match for the determined bird's shrieks. After several minutes of praying to all the gods for the damn creature to be silent, Pippa finally looked at her phone and uttered more curses; 5am! Pippa hadn't seen this time since she'd moved out of the farm, and she'd grown quite fond of a lie-in. Gingerly, she stuck a leg out of the covers and immediately retracted it; despite summer being around the corner, the house remained an icebox, and she could swear a draft had grazed her skin. It was probably unbearable to live here in winter. Diving under the cover with her phone, Pippa tried to block out the noise and the chill by browsing social media, but the reception was woeful and the Wi-Fi seemed determined to move at the slowest pace imaginable. Gnashing her teeth, Pippa stuck her arm out of the covers and waved the phone around to see if a small change in altitude helped. But the blue progress bar advanced at its own snail's pace, and eventually she gave up.

Disgruntled, Pippa tossed the covers back. There was no denying it; she was awake. Braving the icy air, she darted to the bathroom to chance a shower. Thankfully the pressure was decent and the temperature warm, although the pipes did make an awful racket. Pippa washed quickly, not entirely confident that the plumbing wouldn't crash down around her ears if she didn't.

Once finished, teeth chattering, she dressed in sweatpants and an oversized hoodie, shoving freezing feet into fluffy socks and slippers.

"Coffee," she told herself. She creaked open the door and emerged into the hallway. What few windows there were, were covered in heavy drapes, rendering the hallway unnaturally dark. Pippa was able to make her way downstairs whereupon she drew the curtains to allow daylight in. With each drape she opened, the pale morning light reminded her just how empty the place was. Pippa shivered. There was all manner of nooks and crannies for someone to hide in. "Don't be silly," she chastised herself. "You're entirely alone."

Still, Pippa did another check to ensure the front door was locked before she ventured into the kitchen, trying not to get lost in staring at the vast bleakness of the darkened moors beyond the kitchen window. How had it come to this? She was alone in this freezing, albeit stunning place, with the ghost of her romantic past miles away, living his supposed dream without her. It was so far removed from what she'd ever imagined for her life as she approached the age of thirty.

The kettle boiled and as she stirred the coffee, she looked around the kitchen, noting small cracks in the window. She frowned; no wonder the place was so bloody cold! Wrapping her fingers around her hot mug, Pippa trailed around the house, catching sight of her pale form in the occasional mirror or reflective surface, pale and solitary like a lonely ghost. It did nothing to improve her mood, nor did it make the house appear any more favourable. In the uninterrupted coolness of the early morning, Pippa could clearly see every flaw, every point of neglect. Not a single room had a window that wasn't damaged and despite the protective covers over the furniture that remained, she could see glimpses of cracked leather or leaking stuffing. More than one room smelled faintly of damp. Floorboards creaked at every turn and when she finally slumped wearily on the sofa in front of the ancient TV, Pippa found herself swallowing tears. Sadness oozed from every pore of this fine house and what was more, it was contagious.

This was not the house she remembered. Although she'd never so much as crossed the threshold until this point, she'd always viewed Squires as a beacon of perfect happiness, of aspiration. Now, it was an abandoned relic, something once so revered yet not even worthy of proper care and attention anymore. Many lives had been lived here; the house probably had its fair share of love stories and family triumphs to tell. But all that significance was just abandoned, and for what?

It wasn't too long before Pippa's stomach woke up and demanded satisfaction. She went to the kitchen, glad of distraction from her contemplation of the poor old house. There was some bread and margarine amongst the basics Grantham had left her, so she had toast as she watched the sun rise over the moors.

Once properly dressed in a comfortable, knitted dress, Pippa drew up a shopping list to be tackled later that day. Then, she approached the binder where she'd left it in the library.

Was it her imagination or had it grown fatter since her interview with Wolfie? She settled in one of the leather chairs, realising it must be the one that Wolfie had sat in when they met. Traces of his scent still lingered, and she chose to ignore the tingles that that realisation sent through her.

The house required a lot of attention for one so empty. The furniture needed regular polishing – but only with an organic, homemade solution that Pippa was expected to prepare herself. She was to water the flower beds front and back daily, as well as beat various curtains, carpets and rugs regularly. There were rat traps to check, windows to wash, floors to vacuum, all in addition to general daily cleaning. Pippa exhaled deeply; she really had underestimated the level of responsibility this role demanded. But Pippa knew she could manage it; after all, she'd run an entire farm, hadn't she? Time passed quickly as she studied the instruction book, working out how best to organise the tasks in a way that was practical. It was oddly soothing, using her skills to create the most efficient of systems, and for a moment, everything else fell away. All the sadness, the heartache, the pain... Work truly was a balm.

When Pippa finally lifted her head from her task, her neck was stiff and her back ached. Warm shafts of sun pierced through the library window and so, with a fortifying mug of tea, she strolled outside. The morning mists had rolled back, and the sun shone from an azure sky. Despite the sunshine and the chorus of birds welcoming the new day, the grounds still made for a depressing sight. The many rolling acres of emerald lawns were no more, with what looked like merely three or four acres remaining. The grass was neatly mown but the once resplendent shrubbery and flowerbeds were long gone, replaced by mournfully empty patches of soil. As Pippa followed what used to be – from memory – a staggeringly beautiful rose bush, now a sad, bloomless shrub, something at the rear of the garden caught her eye – a tall hedge, with some kind of vine criss-crossing it. Pippa walked over to inspect it further. There was a gap, she could see that now, and the hedge stretched several metres either side of it.

"The maze!" Pippa laughed in delight. Although Grantham had done a good job of keeping the lawn to an, albeit spartan level of neatness, maintaining the maze had clearly defeated him. The path leading into the maze was overgrown, with the flowering vines crawling all over it. She took a few steps in, trying to compare it with what she remembered from the day she met Wolfie. It smelled different; dank and abandoned. Yet there was something vital underneath that scent, a sense of promise. Rampant weeds choked the life out of the maze hedges, with many thriving in the dappled shade. Foxgloves in varying jewel tones dotted the path around her as well as patches of a small, sweet purple flower and varying types of ferns cluttering the once neatly delineated pathway that Pippa had walked down all those years ago. Despite the neglect, it was strangely peaceful inside the little maze. The outside world had fallen away; Pippa couldn't even hear birdsong from where she stood. With every step she crushed greenery, releasing a verdant scent.

Her heart ached at the sadness of it. Even in its current state of disrepair, this maze was a real little sanctuary, and she felt a surge of anger towards Wolfie Squires for letting such a haven descend to this level. His dismissive attitude, his continuing absence … why couldn't he respect the gift that he had? Why did some people choose to run away from things that could bring great joy?

"The grass isn't always greener!" Pippa cried out, realising only seconds later that she had actually spoken out loud. Tears pricked. The maze answered her anguish with a crushing silence as if shocked by the presence of a loud, emotional woman when it had been forgotten for so long. She allowed herself a few indulgent sobs. How could she not? How bad did things have to be for a perfectly healthy, otherwise normal woman to identify emotionally with a maze, of all things?

Pippa's stomach grumbled, reminding her that a breakfast of toast wasn't sufficient for a broken heart, and that she needed supplies. Swiping at her tears, she turned on her heel and headed back into the house.

A little later, Pippa strode out of the SPAR shop, satisfied by her purchases, even if she'd been waylaid by about five well-meaning customers enquiring after her welfare. She waved farewell to Mrs Mayhew behind the till, who was mouthing *Have a good day* so frantically that Pippa worried the woman's dentures would slip out. As Pippa walked along to the green, it occurred to her that she needed shampoo, given that she couldn't steal Frankie's anymore and she'd forgotten to get some at the supermarket. The chemist was yards away, so she scurried in.

And ran smack into Ted Goodman. He was being escorted by Julie, Alex's sister-in-law. A busy woman with rampant curls and curious eyes magnified by over-sized glasses, she blinked down at Pippa with awkward surprise.

"Pip!" Julie said, strangled. "Nice to ... er, how are you?"

Pippa cleared her throat. "I'm well thanks, Julie." The lie was surprisingly easy to tell, given that she'd been weeping in a maze by herself just over an hour ago. "You?"

"Oh." Julie lips flattened minutely but then she gestured down at Ted. "All good. We just popped out for a walk and to pick up Ted's medication."

"Hi, Ted." Pippa turned her eyes to the man who at one point she'd considered a surrogate father. He'd once echoed the same sentiment after a few too many sherries one New Year. Funny how that seemed to have fallen by the wayside now Alex was gone.

"Pip," Ted harrumphed at her.

"How have you been?" she said stiffly.

"Fine," he said, balefully. "Luckily, Finn and Julie took me in. *They're* taking care of me." The barb in his tone was unmistakable, but Pippa wasn't going to rise to it. Ted was an old man in pain, no matter how churlish he might behave.

"I'm glad you've settled in," she said calmly.

"Aye, no thanks to you," he snarled.

Pippa was dumbstruck. It seemed like Ted was insinuating that she was the one who had abandoned him. Cheeks burning, she tried to reply calmly: "Ted, I'm sure it must have been a shock to have to leave your home but Alex—"

"Pff." Ted flapped a wobbly hand. "I haven't heard a peep from you since the split."

Nor I you, Pippa thought. Ted might be old, but he had her phone number. Knew how to send an email even. But he was right, she could have reached out. "I'm sorry," she croaked. "I should have at least—"

"I'm a sickly man, in case you hadn't noticed," Ted went on as if she hadn't said anything. "To lose you both like that hurt me right bad, it did."

"I'm sorry," Pippa repeated, although she was a little bewildered. Why was Ted taking it all out on her? "Though Alex was the one who left. It must be some comfort that he made sure you were taken care of. He didn't just walk out on you."

"I know that!" Ted snapped. "I'm not happy about the way he did what he did, however, I suppose he consulted me to a degree. But you? You left Hurst Bridge without a word."

"Oh." Pippa felt very small. She'd been so consumed by her own heartbreak that she hadn't even thought about how the split would affect Ted; whether the old man would miss her. But then, she supposed, she'd been his de facto daughter-in-law for over a decade, as well as his main caregiver.

"Yeah, *oh*." Ted bristled. "And this one means well." He gestured at Julie, whose lips thinned to the point of invisibility. "Thing is, she has the baby. It's hard for me to get the care sometimes."

Julie looked like she might cry. "Now Ted, I think that's very unfair."

"Sorry," Ted grouched. "I don't mean…" His shoulders sagged and his rheumy eyes watered. "It's hard, that's all." His attention trailed off and he looked deliberately away from the two women as if to gather his composure. Pippa understood. Ted had never coped well with change, and she did regret how she'd handled her departure from his life. But looking at the way he spoke to Julie and the new lines of tiredness around the woman's eyes, Pippa experienced an unexpected wave of relief. Relief that she didn't need to run around after an often-cantankerous old man and his myriad medical needs – needs his son had had no interest in meeting.

"I understand," she said softly. Alex ending their relationship had effectively also ended Pippa's obligation to Ted, but she had a strong suspicion that pointing that out would lead nowhere.

Ted merely grunted and craned his neck even further away. Pippa fought the urge to sigh. As much as she felt sorry for him, why didn't he care about Pippa's heartbreak? Where was her sympathy and support?

"Pippa?" Mrs Allen appeared at her elbow, reeking as she aways did of her famous cider. Frankie used to joke that Mrs Allen was actually one thousand years old but was pickled and preserved just like her various alcoholic concoctions. "It is you!" Her wrinkled face beamed. "How are you? Not seen you around for months now. I hear you've moved into Squires!"

Pippa's smile was forced. Yet another sign that the jungle drums still beat wildly in Hurst Bridge. "Yes, I'm looking after the place for a bit."

"Of course." Mrs Allen's chin wobbled. "I understand Grantham has had to step away. Poor Joan. I took her some of my plum cake the other day."

"How did she seem?" Julie asked.

"Fair to middling," Mrs Allen said with a hopeful smile. "She's not the best of patients, though. Still got a twinkle in her eye. We have a rota for visits. Do you want to be put on it?"

"Of course!" Julie beamed. "I'll take the baby; she might like that."

"Wonderful." Mrs Allen's eyes alighted on Ted, and she beamed almost gleefully. The woman may have been a pillar of the community, but she never missed an opportunity for gossip. "Why, Ted Goodman!" she went on. "How are you getting on?"

"I'm alive." Ted narrowed his eyes at the woman.

"And Alexander...?" Mrs Allen sounded so innocent, but her eyes darted eagerly between the three of them.

"He's doing grand," Ted told her gruffly.

"We were all so shocked when we heard you'd split up," Mrs Allen said to Pippa. "I said to my John, I said, I cannot believe Alex Goodman let that one go."

Pippa's cheeks heated. "Yeah. Well."

"I mean!" Mrs Allen threw her hands up. "I thought you'd be getting married. I was looking out blanket patterns to knit for your babies!"

Pippa was horrified to feel tears forming again. "That would have been nice," she choked. Julie regarded Pippa with some pity, which made Pippa feel even worse.

Ted snorted. "Alex? Marry! He's too obsessed with making money for that."

Mrs Allen's eyebrows almost disappeared into her hairline, so shocked was she. "Nay, he's the marrying kind. Isn't he?"

"Meh," Ted replied gruffly. "A dad knows these things about his boy. Alex wanted financial domination more than anything else. Not to be tied down with domestics, a wife and screaming kids." Julie's jaw dropped, and she glanced guiltily at Pippa.

"He gave me quite the opposite impression," Pippa's voice splintered.

"Oh my." Mrs Allen laid a sympathetic hand on Pippa's arm.

"Pip, come on," Julie said tenderly. "Ted doesn't mean that... You had Alex's heart; you really did. We all could see that. He just, I dunno, got his head turned by his ambition."

"An ambition I fuelled," Pippa said sharply.

"No, now come on," Ted growled. "He worked hard, always has."

"Thing is Ted, so did I!" Pippa snapped. "But was *Alex* also getting up at 2am to help you to the bathroom? When did he last fill your prescription or wait on hold with your consultant whilst filing tax returns?" Yes, Alex had left the grunt work all to her.

"Let's all calm down," Julie suggested.

But Julie's platitudes fell flat. Shampoo forgotten, Pippa mumbled her goodbyes and staggered out onto the street. It had been hard enough seeing Ted again, but to learn that even Ted knew Alex maybe never intended to marry her was a knock she hadn't seen coming. Fury coursed through her body as she marched back to Squires. She'd run that farm and created a profitable business all in the name of her future with Alex. And he'd let her! Like a fucking lord, and she his serf. He'd sat back as she did the lion's share of the work, including the care of his father, which was clearly beneath him, only to reap the rewards by himself.

As she charged down the road, she had the alarming sensation of all eyes on her, of gossips whispering behind her back. Suddenly desperate for the peaceful solitude of Squires, Pippa lowered her head and hurried as fast as she could back to the lonely old house she now called home.

Chapter Eight

"I heard there were quite a to-do between you and Ted Goodman t'other day," Grantham's voice rasped down the phone at her.

"What of it?" Pippa muttered.

She was still sore from the revelations, her heart aching even though several days had passed since her encounter with Ted. *This* was why she had been so nervous about coming back to Hurst Bridge. As much as she loved her hometown, the reality of small-town life had hit her square in the face, because everyone knew that Ted Goodman had delivered some home truths to his son's ex-girlfriend. According to Mae, it had been the main topic of conversation at the pub every night that past week. However, the truth had almost certainly been distorted, as there had been some rumblings that Pippa had perhaps tried to kill Ted. Or Alex. It was unclear, but Mae had put them right on just who exactly was the true villain of the piece. Mrs Allen had clearly been hard at work spreading the gossip of the events she'd witnessed first-hand. Although Pippa had thrown herself into the routine of housesitting to distract herself, the anger still burned.

"I wondered if you were okay," Grantham said. "I hear you took off in quite a mood."

"A mood?" Pippa repeated harshly. "Well, if you found out the man you once wanted to marry had no real intention of ever doing so and only wanted you to help him make money, wouldn't you be a tad annoyed?"

There was a ponderous silence. "Aye," Grantham replied eventually.

Pippa knew she was probably being a bit dramatic, but she also believed she had every right to her feelings. Alex couldn't have faked everything in their relationship in the name of ambition, she knew that. But their relationship had clearly suited him very well professionally and over the many years they'd been together, that aspect had taken precedence. No wonder things had felt stale. "I'm sorry," she said. "I don't mean to take this out on you." Especially given what he was going through.

"Don't you worry," Grantham said mildly. "That lad always did strike me as a bit feckless. Besides, you can text or call me anytime you need anything. I'm not dead yet and it's a nice distraction from other things. Now, how are you finding Squires?"

Touched by his concern given everything he had going on, Pippa reassured him. "I think I have an understanding of how to manage my responsibilities," she said. "I also went and had a look at the old maze."

"It's in a sorry state, isn't it?" Grantham said, dispirited.

"I did my best, but the bindweed is just running riot. In the end, Wolfie said to focus on maintaining the house and just keeping the lawn bare and neat. Joan loved that maze but ... well, you've seen it."

"Why don't I have a go at tidying it up?" Pippa wasn't sure why she suggested such a thing, but she hated to hear the defeat in Grantham's voice.

"Done much gardening, have you?" he said, clearly amused.

"Not much." Pippa shrugged. Gardening had been something her mother had always encouraged, and whilst Pippa had been willing to help her with various tasks around their garden, it wasn't something she knew much about. "How hard can it be?"

"You did hear me mention bindweed?" Grantham chuckled. "But if you want to have a go, be my guest. You noticed the tool shed?"

Pippa told him that she had, and Grantham explained the equipment they kept. "Did my best to maintain it all but ... well, it's old. Have a look for yourself. It's the small brass key on the ring."

"I'll check it out," Pippa said. Surely a little bit of weeding wasn't beyond her?

"Have at it," Grantham replied. "There might even be some books on gardening left over in the library, if you want to do some research."

A little later, once Pippa had completed the day's vacuuming and silverware polish, she ventured out to the shed to examine the tools Grantham had described. The door was stiff, the handle leaving flakes of rust on her hands, but she finally managed to wrench it open. Looking around, she shuddered. The corners of the shed were thick with dense cobwebs and when she pulled the cord by the door to turn on the ancient bulb, Pippa was certain she heard *things* scuttling away. It was a small shed, with a tiny rectangular window, sagging workbench and several gardening implements hung on the walls. They at least looked well cared for, if ancient, and Pippa felt a twinge of emotion at the thought of Grantham toiling away to take care of tools that surely he was getting too elderly to lift. Also hung up was a wheelbarrow and Pippa wondered if it had ever participated in the races. It looked like it might be old enough.

On one of the pegs, Pippa saw a set of shears. They seemed to be still quite sharp and so she took them down, taken aback by their weight. She hefted them determinedly over her shoulder and headed over to the maze, intending to hack through some of the thick vines that crisscrossed the little hedges. But mere minutes into her task, Pippa came to understand Grantham's amusement. The slim vines were sinewy and the shears not quite sharp enough to slice through easily. It took several hacks to cut through each bit. There were so many of them too; it would take days to clear them all. But she could have a go, couldn't she? Bit by bit, she could hack away these awful vine things, kill them at the root and hopefully that would allow the maze hedges to return to full health. Pippa had also seen a ride-on mower stored under a tarp next to the shed, so perhaps once the vines were cleared, she could have a go at mowing the unkempt maze pathways. Some of the foxgloves would have to go, but there were some lovely clumps growing along the base of some of the hedges; they could stay and add some much-needed colour.

Pippa chopped through a gathering of vines, then dropped the shears and pulled at the ones she had cut. She pulled. And pulled. But instead of coming away from the hedge with a pleasing flourish, the vines dug in. They went on and on, tangling in other vines and then plunging into the soil below to what was sure to be a complex root system. It didn't take Pippa long to realise she could cut all day; there was no way she could clear these weeds by herself, let alone work out how to untangle them all from each other.

"It's like a fucking Rubik's Cube of weeds!" Pippa cursed, throwing the shears down. She was hot, possibly a little sunburnt already, and her arms covered with sap. She needed a strong drink and a trashy box-set marathon, immediately.

"A Rubik's Cube of weeds?" Wolfie's unexpected voice from behind startled her. She stumbled, catching her ankle on the dropped shears, but then a strong hand gripped her upper arm and righted her. A smooth, expensive scent filled her head. "You do have a way with words, Pippa Munro."

Blushing hotly, Pippa disengaged herself from Wolfie's clasp. "Thanks for the save," she muttered. Wolfie looked exceptionally smart in navy trousers and a fitted shirt, open at the neck. That luxurious blond hair fell artfully over his high forehead as his blue eyes sparkled with amusement. In her comfy, bobbled leggings and sap-spattered skin, she must have looked a complete fright.

"You know, you don't need to tidy up the maze," Wolfie said gently. "It's not in the binder for a reason; it's too big a job."

"I thought it would please Grantham," Pippa said defensively. "He said Joan used to love it."

"Yes." Wolfie's eyebrows furrowed. "That's true. She did, once upon a time. I forgot." He raised his eyebrows. "You do know that's bindweed you're trying to hack through though?"

"Yes," Pippa said haughtily, deciding not to mention that she only knew that thanks to Grantham. "I didn't realise you were a gardener?"

"I'm not." A shoulder bounced lazily. "But Grantham practically raised me. I wouldn't be doing him justice if I couldn't recognise an invasive species or two. Anyway. That weed is a menace."

"I'm just learning that." Pippa picked up the shears. "I'll come up with something to stamp it out. Where have you been this week?"

Wolfie stifled a yawn. "Flew back from Poland this morning. Early flight as I had an appointment to make."

"Sounds tiring. You must be glad to be home." Pippa knew she'd made a mistake the moment the words left her mouth. Wolfie's gaze hardened.

"Home? No, I'm actually here to show this guy around." Wolfie gestured behind him to where a gentleman in a flannel shirt and jeans paced, holding a shiny black camera.

"A photographer?" Pippa was confused.

"Nothing gets past you, does it?" Wolfie smiled tightly.

"You pay me to keep my eyes on the place." Pippa used

two fingers to point at her eyes and then at the photographer. "Witness me in action. Why is he here?"

"Believe it or not, he's taking pictures."

"I can see that," Pippa said dryly.

"Well, it is part of the normal process when selling a house," he said. "Buyers do like to see images of the property they're about to drop huge amounts of money on." He went on to say something else about the property market, but Pippa didn't clearly hear it. Selling? Wolfie was selling Squires?

"Why?" she blurted.

Wolfie stopped mid-sentence. "Why am I selling?" Pippa nodded. "Oh. Um. Well, the house is mine. So I suppose the answer would be, because I can?"

Pippa stared at him. Was he mad? "But this is your family home," she said. "Does Emilia know?"

"My sister doesn't care," he said calmly. "She lives a wonderful life with her rich husband far away from here and besides, in the grand patriarchal tradition of old families, the house belongs solely to me. Em gets Mother's diamonds."

"I see." Pippa gazed up at the beautiful house, resplendent in the afternoon sun. "But ... won't you miss it?"

"I'm barely here enough to miss it," he smirked. "Or hadn't you noticed?"

"To be fair, I only started working here this past week," she said.

"It's time," he said. "Besides, this place ... needs more attention than I give it." Wolfie's words sounded laboured, as if discussing Squires gave him actual, physical pain. He shook himself. "That's why your role was tentatively set at two to six months," he went on. "Plenty of time for a sale to proceed, whilst making sure the house stays safe." He nodded at the maze. "Which is why I wouldn't bother with that. Chances are, it'll get razed with the rest of this heap." Wolfie smiled down at her, the summer sun blazing through his golden hair. "Have a good day, Pippa Munro." With that, he strolled away, acting for all the world as if he hadn't just dropped the almightiest of truth grenades on Pippa's head.

Chapter Nine

"Are you sure he meant that?" Eileen Munro quivered down the phone. "Razed? As in..."

"Wolfie Squires would like nothing less than to sell to someone who'd tear this house down to the ground," Pippa told her mother, forking wilted spinach into her mouth. It was lunchtime on a Monday, just a week after Wolfie had revealed his plans for Squires. The listing had been live for only a few days and already there was a viewing lined up later that afternoon. Wolfie had been in Geneva since she had last seen him, sending the most abrupt of text messages to confirm the sale going live. The news had leant an odd significance to Pippa's chores. Every time she swept the floors or cleaned the windows, Pippa wondered if it was to be the last time, if some dramatic, super-fast sale would take place overnight and she would have to say her goodbyes before breakfast. She hoped the new owner would keep the building standing. Pippa couldn't bear the thought of someone callously tearing down this place without any inkling of its specialness.

"They can't do that, surely!" Eileen said. "Isn't it listed?"

"Nope." Pippa had checked. She'd told herself it was idle curiosity and not desperate sadness when she'd typed the search terms into Google. The house had crept under her skin already and no mistake. She'd always admired it, but now she felt a protectiveness taking root. The high ceilings, the epic views ... plus there was such a peaceful energy blooming from underneath all the neglect. Only a dimwit could overlook all that. And Wolfie Squires didn't strike Pippa as a dimwit.

"Well, I hope his lordship will be there to show the buyers around," Eileen said with indignation. "Fancy going to all this trouble to get you in only to sell out from underneath you."

"It *is* his place." Pippa spoke automatically but she did wonder where Wolfie was, and if indeed it was to be him showing the potential buyer around. Because Pippa knew if it was to be her, she'd have to fight the urge to kick the buyers out of the house. "I'm sure he'll be here. At least, I presume he will be."

"He's away a lot." Eileen was not impressed. "His poor mother."

"I don't think they're that close," Pippa said. "Like ... literally. Geographically. Trudy's in Cumbria. Miles away."

"Have you heard from Alex?" Eileen ventured, her voice trembling. Despite it being almost three months since the break-up, Pippa's mother was not coping well with the development. "Are you sure you don't want to give him a call? Maybe go and see him? It's been long enough now for you both to cool down."

"Cool down? It wasn't merely a bad argument, Mum. We split up!" Pippa tutted. "You do understand what he did to me, don't you?"

"Yes," Eileen said. "And I appreciate how you must be feeling but…"

"How I feel is betrayed. Abandoned. Humiliated. Need I go on? Why would I go back to someone who made me feel like that?" Pippa's lunch churned in her stomach, and she pushed her plate away. It made getting over Alex that much harder when her mother kept bringing him up like this every time they spoke.

"I get that," Eileen said. "But you were together for over a decade. I thought he'd be in our family forever. Give me grandkids." She sniffed, blew her nose.

Pippa sighed, relenting. "I understand that this is hard on you too," she said. "And that you thought he'd be your son one day. But we didn't know Alex as well as we thought we did. At least, *I* didn't." Although Pippa knew she was definitely the injured party, guilt twinged. If she'd not been so stubborn, if she'd just given Kent a go, maybe grandbabies would still be on the cards and Eileen would be less upset.

"I'm sure I'll get used to it," Eileen assured her. "But I don't like the thought of you spending so much time alone in that big old house. You know, you could come out here for a bit. Let me look after you."

"We'll see," Pippa hedged. Being spoilt with love sounded incredibly tempting, but Florida was not her type of place. Hot and sticky, with far too many alligators per square metre for her liking. How her parents could prefer it over Hurst Bridge she didn't know. Besides, plane tickets were not cheap.

"At least let me send you a few quid," Eileen went on. "To tide you over."

"Mum, no," Pippa said firmly. "I'm managing fine. Taking a beat, figuring out my next steps."

"You'd best get a wriggle on with that," Eileen fretted. "Squires may well be sold any day now and you'll be homeless again. Are you sure I can't send you—"

"Mum, please! I'll be fine." Pippa clocked the time, relieved that she had a reason to hang up. "I've got to get on, there's a few more tasks to be done this afternoon."

"Right you are." Eileen blew kisses down the phone. "Hang on a sec. Your dad's here. He's off fishing today with Ivan from next door. Here you go, Pete, I'll put it on speaker. It's Pip."

"Hi love." Her dad's voice boomed down the phone. "You looking after yourself?"

"Yes and—" At that moment the gate buzzer loudly interrupted. "Shit."

"Language!" Eileen crowed.

"Sorry, but I think that must be the buyers." Pippa hurriedly shoved her dirty lunch plate into a cupboard to wash later. "They're early." She pulled the phone away from her ear and looked at the screen. No messages from Wolfie. Where was he? "Wolfie isn't here. I guess I'll have to ask them to wait."

"Tell them the place is haunted." Pete Munro giggled

down the line like a schoolboy. "Or, better yet, tell them it's got a rodent infestation. That'll put them right off buying."

"Don't give her ideas, Pete," Eileen admonished.

"You're a menace, Dad," Pippa said with a laugh.

"What's the saying? Don't let the bastards grind you down," Pete said. "I'm sorry about the house, pet. Wish there was something we could do."

In that moment, Pippa really wanted a hug. She made do with blowing a kiss down the phone. "Thanks."

"Call us later," her mum said, love softening her voice.

Pippa promised to do so, then hung up, chuckling at her dad's suggestions for scuppering the sale. She hurried to the door and pressed the button for the gate intercom. "Yes?"

"Hi. We're here to meet a Mr Wolfie Squires?" A male voice boomed down out of the speaker. "Toby Hartnell, *Top Stay Hotels*."

Pippa's heart sank as she recognised the name of a well-known budget hotel chain. "You have an appointment?"

"Yes. We're a little early," Toby answered. "I do hope that's okay."

Pippa briefly wondered if she could just ignore them in the hope they would go away, but obedience won out and she pushed the buzzer. "Come in." She unlocked the front door and leaned against the frame, watching as the old iron gates creaked open. Her phone buzzed with a text message full of kisses from her mum and her heart squeezed. Being an only child had its drawbacks, particularly when it came to the issue of grandchildren. Guilt started to prickle her tear ducts and Pippa hastily shoved the phone in her pocket, watching as an impossibly shiny Mercedes rolled its way through the gates and down the driveway, coming to a halt in front of the house. Out popped a very smartly dressed man and woman, brandishing sleek briefcases and calculated expressions.

The man reached Pippa first, handing her his business card, a bright turquoise rectangle that read *Top Stay Hotels* and underneath was the name *Toby Hartnell, VP Property & Acquisitions*.

"Toby, pleasure to meet you!" The man beamed down at her; he was all long limbs and balletic movements, with scant strands of red hair gelled back across a freckled scalp. "Allow me to introduce my colleague, Steffany."

The woman marched powerfully over. She had a rigid helmet of glossy brunette hair and violent pink lipstick that made even the most professional of smiles appear slightly shark-like. Steffany handed over her own card that denoted her as VP of Branding at *Top Stay Hotels*.

Pippa took the cards out of politeness but in truth wanted to tear them to shreds. Toby and Steffany didn't have the first clue about Squires. Or Hurst Bridge, for that matter. What kind of people looked at this building, this view, and thought 'budget hotel'? "Welcome," she said automatically.

"Sorry, you are?" Toby asked.

"Pippa Munro," she said.

"Do you live here?" Toby asked, eyebrows furrowing. "We were told this house was ... well, abandoned, for all intents and purposes."

Pippa swallowed. Yes, Squires *had* been abandoned, by the people who were meant to love it. She made an effort to pull herself together. "I'm watching over the place," she said eventually. "You're here to—"

"We're considering buying it, yes," Steffany interrupted, her eyes roaming all over the house. "Tell me, is the plot south-facing?"

Before Pippa could say anything in response, the roar of an engine drowned her thoughts. The iron gates swung open again, and a sleek motorbike powered down the drive, gravel dust flying in its wake. The bike screeched to a halt; the kickstand was slammed down. The rider flung his long legs over the bike and dismounted, pulling his helmet off in one fluid motion. Pippa gaped as Wolfie shook sweat-dampened hair off his flushed face.

"Sorry I'm late," Wolfie declared. "Nightmare traffic." His leathers creaked as he strode towards them, hand outstretched. "Wolfie Squires."

"N–no problem," Toby stammered as he shook Wolfie's hand. "Toby Hartnell, pleasure."

"You aren't late." Steffany practically threw herself forward to grab Wolfie's hand. "We're early. Steffany Wilkinson. Call me Stef."

"Pleasure to meet you," Wolfie said, in a tone far removed from such emotion. He turned to Pippa, his expression unreadable.

"Hello, Pippa Munro."

"Hello." She wondered why he insisted on calling her by her full name all the time. Was it a thing privately educated people did? Or maybe he was just being professional in his treatment of her. After all, she was his employee. Oddly enough, propriety was the furthest thing from her mind at that moment. The sight of him in clingy leathers confirmed what she'd suspected at the interview; the man really was in great shape. But she couldn't let that startle her. The *Top Stay* guests might be thrown by Wolfie's dramatic and somewhat ravishing entrance, but Pippa wasn't going to let her inner churn show. "Welcome home."

Again, Wolfie stiffened at the mere mention of the word home. What was it about Squires?

"I won't be here long," Wolfie said, curtly. "I never am." He turned to Call-Me-Stef and Toby. "After you?"

The trio entered the house and Pippa stepped back to allow them in, shutting the door with a heavy heart. Toby made a rapid beeline for the piano in the library, his hands already running all over it by the time Pippa had entered the room.

"Do you play?" Toby asked Wolfie as he approached.

"A little," Wolfie said. "I er – used to be quite into it when I was young." Pippa remembered the lonely boy with the radio, the way he'd clung to it like a life raft.

"Not anymore, then?" Stef asked, smiling so hard at Wolfie it looked painful.

Wolfie grimaced. "I had that drummed out of me, I guess you could say. Let me show you the views round the back. After all, that's what you'll be interested in." Pippa wondered what on earth he meant by having it drummed out.

"As long as the view isn't of the town," Steffany cracked. "I mean, it's hardly the most exciting place in the world."

Pippa rolled her eyes. Yes, Hurst Bridge was quiet but that was part of its charm – the peace it afforded the residents. It didn't make it boring or not worth anyone's time. Reminders of the day Alex left suddenly cascaded into Pippa's mind, stealing her breath. She leaned against the doorway, trying to calm herself. Would there ever be a day when something didn't trigger painful memories?

"Are you okay?" It was Toby, regarding Pippa concernedly.

"I'm fine." Pippa hadn't realised that she was staring into space with tear-filled eyes. "It's just..." She inhaled slowly, very aware that Wolfie and Steffany were looking at her as if she were crazy. "Hurst Bridge is a lovely place," she said eventually. "I think it can surprise people, if they'd just give it a chance."

Steffany merely allowed her a sceptical smirk and turned away. Wolfie regarded Pippa for a long second, before dismissing her with a soft, "That'll be all."

"They're selling Squires?" Mae's face twisted with disappointment.

"Yup." Pippa gulped back her coffee. Once Steffany and Toby departed, Pippa placed a desperate call to her best friend, and they escaped to the café on the green, which was imaginatively called 'The Café On The Green'. It had been recently renovated, with chic white tiles and retro artwork adorning the walls. Large Edison bulbs hung from the ceiling, casting a warm glow over the numerous customers, who flocked to the place for the generously sized coffees and delicious cakes.

"But to who?" Mae asked.

"Heard of *Top Stay*?" Pippa said.

Mae groaned. "Yeah, the budget hotels? I've stayed in loads of them."

"Well, perhaps that's what we will have instead of Squires," Pippa growled. "They were viewing today."

"That sucks." Mae tapped into her phone. "Come on, does *this* look like it belongs in Hurst Bridge?" She showed her screen to Pippa, having pulled up the hotel's website to reveal the latest build in Nottingham. It showed a solid cube with utilitarian white windows and a large cement car park. Inside, the décor matched the colour scheme of Toby and Steffany's business cards. Pippa couldn't imagine getting a good night's sleep in a room with vivid turquoise walls. Mae was right; it wasn't the sort of building that would fit in in Hurst Bridge.

"This is so bloody typical," Pippa sighed. "My ex sells my life out from under me so I move into the house of dreams, only to have that sold out from under me too."

"I know," Mae said, frowning. "That place *is* falling apart, though. Looks like the Squires family hasn't invested any time or money in it for years. Did Wolfie say why he's selling?"

"Not really. He basically said because he could," Pippa replied.

Mae thought of something. "Maybe they're skint and that's why they're selling up?"

Pippa frowned. The house *was* on the tatty side. But the Squires family were insanely wealthy. Weren't they? "Like I said, not sure. He's been deliberately vague."

"I bet that's it." Mae took a swig of her mocha. "I mean, Carmichael was dead flashy, wasn't he? You saw that wine cellar. And remember the cars? I'll bet he frittered every penny away."

Pippa nodded. Carmichael used to speed around the village in a variety of swanky vehicles. There was a custom Range Rover that had been a favourite and Pippa also recalled a vintage Jaguar as well as several Mercedes in varying shades. She hadn't seen any sign of those vehicles in the garage, so either they were being stored elsewhere or they had been sold off. "How sad," she said. "I wonder how Trudy is managing if that's the case."

Mae shrugged. "Does it really matter at the end of the day? No business of ours."

"You're right. I need to focus on where I go when I'm made homeless for like, the second time this year." Pippa lolled her head back and flapped her arms. "What am I going to do? Oh!" Her arm had caught someone walking past her chair.

"Pip?" Finn Goodman stood next to her, for it was he that Pippa had snagged with her flailing arms. Alex's little brother was the last person she'd wanted to see at that moment or, indeed, at any moment. Mainly because he looked almost exactly like Alex, just with lighter hair and a lot more freckles. Even that faintest notion of familiarity lanced her like a blade.

"Hi, Finn." Pippa wearily got to her feet and accepted his offer of a hug. It did seem like the mature thing to do, seeing as she'd known him for much of his life. "How's university life?"

"Great, thank you," he said. Finn lectured on horticulture at Sheffield Hallam, where Julie also worked. "How are you?"

"Ah, you know." Pippa's face hurt from all the fake smiling, but she was damned if she'd let Finn see her crack. Losing her cool in front of Ted had been bad enough. "Getting on with life."

"I never got to say how sorry I am," he said. "It's so weird. You were like my sister. And now you're not."

His words stung and Pippa bit her lip. "It is what it is." Then, because she wanted to pick at the scab, asked, "Have you heard from him?"

"Yup." Finn scratched his neck. "You know Al, not one for detail but seems like he's doing great. Busy. Every time I call him, he's rushing from one meeting to another, barely able to stop and chat." Finn smiled bashfully. "So it must be going well, right?"

Finn's sweet optimism was like a barb piercing her skin. "Then I'm happy for him." Anger bubbled up from the wound. "Breaking my heart was obviously worth it."

Finn paled. "Pips, I'm sorry, I didn't mean..." He cleared his throat. "I know it's been hard. Especially with my dad being ... well, Dad."

"Yeah, he went off at me." Pippa's cheeks burned with the memory.

"I heard. You know, he's hurting too," Finn said. "I think he misses Alex. More than he thought he would."

"At least Alex consulted Ted before he blew up our relationship," Pippa sniped. "He didn't afford me that courtesy."

Finn looked troubled. "I know Alex didn't handle things between you well, but I'm sure if you call him—"

Pippa lifted a hand to halt his speech. "Me? Call *him*?"

Mae chimed in. "Don't think so!"

"Why would I do that?" Pippa added.

Finn shifted, as if he might bolt. But his wavering gaze met Pippa's fierce one and then he relented. "He just seems sad is all," Finn said. "I think he might be lonely. I mean, he doesn't know anyone down there, does he?"

"Well, he should have thought about that before he decided to throw our relationship away like it meant nothing," Pippa said, barely able to breathe at the audacity. Alex was suffering, so, what, she had to run after him and fix things? "He'll have to take care of that problem by himself."

Finn lifted his hands. "All he wanted was to build something exciting with you and you said no."

Pippa gritted her teeth. "I *was* building something exciting with him. Or so I thought. Problem was, it wasn't good enough for Alex."

"I'm merely speaking up for my brother," Finn said, resignedly.

Pippa barked a painful laugh. What happened to speaking up for *her*, the woman who'd once been like his sister? But the strength of fraternal devotion in Finn's eyes was all too obvious and it pained Pippa to see it. He'd chosen his side and although it hurt, Pippa understood it. Blood came first. "I'd best go. I'm late for…" She realised she was late for literally nothing apart from cleaning a house that didn't even belong to her. And that was all Alex's fault.

Mae sensed the storm brewing inside Pippa and swooped in. "Yeah, let's go. I need to get back to the pub anyway."

Pippa left the café in a blur, hardly aware of Mae's guiding hand on her elbow. The world outside was harsh and bright, her stomach a jangled mess. Some wretched part of her ached at the thought of Alex miserable alone, but mostly she burned with the unfairness of it all. The Goodmans were closing ranks around Alex and whilst it was understandable, Pippa couldn't help but feel left in the cold, isolated from people she'd once known as family.

Mae fumed in solidarity, power walking so fast that Pippa could barely keep up. "You'd think Alex would have the decency to make a cock-up of his life after what he did to you."

"Mae, wait." Pippa wrenched her arm away. "Am I crazy? I mean, was I a terrible girlfriend?"

Mae halted, grabbing Pippa by the upper arms. "You're crazy if you think you weren't an *amazing* girlfriend," she said. "Ted Goodman's probably only alive still because of you." Following Pippa's sceptical stare, Mae conceded. "Okay, maybe that's a slight exaggeration. But surely now you can see what Frankie and I were getting at all these years: your entire life was built around Alex. I mean, he could barely get out of bed without your help." She arched a wicked eyebrow. "I'd put money on that selfish git crashing and burning spectacularly before the year is out."

"Aww." Pippa tilted her head. "That's sweet. Do you really think so?"

"Yes, and I don't care what Finn says." Mae nodded sombrely. "Alex will be destitute without you."

Pippa leaned in for a hug. "Thank you. You're the best."

Mae wrapped her arms around Pippa and chuckled. "I try."

Pippa peered up at her best friend. "Do you think maybe all his hair will fall out too? And his balls shrink to the size of peas?"

Mae squeezed her tightly. "If there's any justice in this world."

Chapter Ten

A couple of days passed without incident, for which Pippa was grateful. The shock of Ted's outburst and the looming house sale combined with Finn's revelations had left her shaken. But there was something about the honest demands of housework that wiped her anxiety clear, and Pippa welcomed it. Despite the many flaws of the house, its charm remained intact, and Pippa took comfort from the fact that she was the lucky person who got to spend her time surrounded by it. It was a lonely existence however, aside from a friendly wave over the fence every now and again from Todd and Pat. Mae and Frankie were in constant contact, but their lives were demanding enough without running around after her.

There was no sign of Wolfie since the *Top Stay* visit and Pippa had to admit she was a little relieved. Wolfie Squires carried himself like a leashed storm; full of power but with the vaguest threat that an inner tempest might breach the barricade of regal calm. He was the opposite of Alex, who could set a room at ease with one of his broad, welcoming smiles. Wolfie was a different breed altogether, one Pippa had no clue how to navigate.

But she had to put all that out of her mind. It was Saturday, and the morning sky was a perfect shade of pale blue that would no doubt deepen as the day got warmer. Pippa had made sure to water all the garden plants thoroughly, taking some extra time to pull out the pesky weeds that bothered the once pristine driveway. It was sweaty work, but worth it when the front of the house looked a tiny bit more refined as a result. A part of her itched to tackle the garden properly, particularly the maze, but the binder had spoken, and the next task beckoned: polishing the dining set. Despite being protected under plastic, the glorious old wooden table and matching chairs still needed attention. The instructions in the binder were very clear and somewhat laborious. Although Pippa wasn't overly familiar with the intricacies of polishing antiques, she presumed there were various specialist products with which to do it. But such products were not acceptable at Squires, oh no. The binder insisted upon an 'organic approach' using an olive oil and white wine vinegar concoction which had to be mixed freshly and stirred frequently to maintain the right consistency. The resulting solution was a stinky gloop that made her gag, soaking into her skin and making her cuticles sting. But Pippa craved the solace that the labour brought her and so she set to work, gently rubbing the mixture into the wood and filling her nose with its acidic scent.

Even though she had to concentrate on bringing the

wood to a high shine, every so often Finn's words about Alex danced across her brain. Each time they did, Pippa poured that heartbreak into her task, the muscles in her arms aching with the effort. The spindled legs of the table were particularly tricky with all the ins and outs of the intricate carvings and more than once, she ended up flicking homemade polish over her hair and face.

When the gate buzzer rang, she was surprised to find that not only had she been working on the great table for over an hour, but that she'd managed to polish most of the wood. Not only that, but her efforts had also yielded a deep shine as if the table was not in fact squillions of years old. It looked beautiful. A warm nugget of satisfaction took root within her and suddenly the matching chairs waiting for the polish treatment didn't seem like such a terrible task. She hurried to the door, smiling when Todd announced his presence.

"Todd!" She had opened the door before he made it down the drive. "How lovely to see you. Come on in!"

"Thank you." Todd stepped in and his face transformed as he took in the surroundings. "Gosh, this place is so beautiful."

Pippa sighed in agreement. "Isn't it? Shame it's getting sold." Todd's expression turned from awestruck to concerned. Pippa filled him in about the visit from *Top Stay* and Todd's jaw dropped.

"A hotel? Here?" he said. "This is *awful*. And construction work next to my farm? The bees will abandon ship. Juniper ... well, Juniper will no doubt revel in the chaos because that's what she does. But the others?

Pigs are so sensitive. It could really damage our operations."

"You never know, maybe if you complain loudly enough, that will stop the sale," Pippa said brightly, although something about Wolfie's careful, controlled nature told her such complaints would be unfounded, legally speaking.

"I'll look into it." Todd sniffed. "Are you ... are you covered in vinegar?"

"Urgh. Sorry. A homemade cleaning solution." Pippa grimaced. She did stink. "I'd best crack on so I can finish up and shower. Can I help you with anything?"

"Of course, the reason I came round." Todd laughed at himself. "Juniper's escaped, I think she's in your garden. Can I pop through and get her?"

"By all means." Pippa led him through to the back door. "You know, next time, if it's easier, just hop over the fence."

"Grantham let me do that," Todd admitted. "But given that you're living here alone, I didn't think you'd want a man you barely know strolling about the garden."

Pippa was touched by his consideration. She opened the door to the garden and sure enough, Juniper was gambolling around like a giddy puppy, albeit a 500-pound one with uneven teeth. Todd loped out to the garden, pulling a collar from his pocket.

"Come on now, lovey." He clicked his teeth. "Let's get." Juniper was snuffling in the ground. She had clearly found something delicious growing there and was not in the mood to move. Todd clipped the collar on and added a leash. "Wilbur will be missing you."

Juniper rolled her eyes; Pippa was certain of it. "Who's Wilbur?"

"Her paramour," Todd replied, rolling the r's. Then he huffed. "Well, he wishes. We're hoping they breed but no luck so far."

"Juniper has a boyfriend?" Pippa said. "That's so cute!"

"Don't get too excited. He's a lazy sack of shit," Todd replied. "He sleeps approximately twenty-three hours of the day and suffice to say that does not do it for Juniper."

Pippa laughed, hard. "Juniper wants more from life. Can't blame her."

"I can definitely relate!" Todd chuckled. "I left my steady, well-paid job in marketing to wander around the moors picking wild garlic and looking after wayward swine. Maybe *Juniper* is my soulmate and not Pat."

"Wilbur has some competition then," Pippa said. "I take it we won't be expecting piglets any time soon?"

"Unless Wilbur develops a personality or performs some grand romantic gesture, I don't think we'll have any luck. I can see the disgust in her eyes when she looks at him." Todd shrugged. "Tams are endangered, so I was really hoping she'd throw him a bone."

"Poor Juniper." Pippa could barely stop laughing enough to get the words out. "Nice to know I'm not the only one with a disastrous love life."

"Disaster is the word," Todd affirmed. "Every time I see her, she looks up at me as if to say *you expect me to shag that?* No wonder she broke free." He looked down at his pig. "Come on. Home." He tugged at the leash, but the pig was immovable, like a rock. Juniper's stubborn expression combined with Todd's ineffectual attempts to move her had Pippa laughing hard to the point of weakness. When Juniper nonchalantly let out an enormous fart, Pippa thought she might collapse in hysterics and so she reached out a hand to steady herself, but instead of the wall, she hit warm, firm muscle. Startled, she turned.

"What's going on here?" Wolfie had snuck up behind her at some point in the conversation. He was in running gear, all of which was clinging to his sweat-soaked body. His rumpled blond locks were damp and sticking to his head. This, coupled with exertion flushed cheeks made him look younger, less severe.

"Where did you spring from?" Pippa was agog. She hadn't seen him since the *Top Stay* visit, yet here he was as if he'd never left. Wolfie glared down at her, lips parted as if taken aback by her impertinence. Pippa swallowed, forcing a polite smile. "I mean, hi." He smelled, overwhelmingly, of the outdoors.

"Got in a little while ago and went straight for a run." Wolfie glanced down at his smart watch.

"I've been here all day!" Pippa was perplexed. She hadn't even realised he was back. "When was that? Are you some kind of ninja?"

"It's a big house," he said with a small smile. "I was in and out. Wanted to get into the hills." He gesticulated towards Clough Hill, which was clearly visible from the garden.

Pippa looked over the moorland to the hill. A destination for avid hikers, although it wasn't too far from

Squires, it was at least a three-mile trek and incredibly steep in places. "You ran up *there*?"

Wolfie swigged water from a bottle he was carrying. "Yup," he said, as if it were no big deal. "Tell me, Pippa Munro, why is there a gigantic pig tearing up my garden?"

"Sorry about that!" Todd called from where he was still trying to convince Juniper to abandon her rooting. "I'll have her next door as soon as she takes the brakes off."

Wolfie gave him a long, somewhat bemused stare then nodded slowly, looking back down at Pippa.

"I have a visitor this afternoon. Another potential buyer. Okay?"

"Of course." Pippa wondered why he even cared to ask her opinion on the matter. With another brusque nod, Wolfie headed into the house. Pippa turned back to watch Todd's efforts, but she no longer wanted to laugh. Wolfie's brief appearance had left her jangled with curiosity. She couldn't work out if he was rude or shy or arrogant, or all of the above. The not knowing made her simultaneously want to drill him with questions whilst also staying clear of the man. It was then that Pippa realised she was still coated in the homemade cleaning solution, and she wanted to scream. She must have looked – and smelled – like a total fool. No wonder he scarpered off.

"So I finally get a good look at the elusive man of the house," Todd remarked, panting heavily from his exertions with Juniper.

"You've never met?" Pippa asked. "But you've been here ages now."

Todd shrugged. "We only ever spoke to Grantham.

Wolfie, we would spy from afar on rare occasions, like some kind of celebrity." He raised his eyebrows. "He looks good in shorts."

"Can't say I noticed," Pippa said airily, although inwardly she agreed wholeheartedly.

"Give over! You have eyes, don't you?" Todd shot back.

"Shut up!" Pippa squeaked. She glanced back into the house, relieved Wolfie was nowhere in sight to hear this. Even a simple joke about the appeal of a man who wasn't Alex made her insides wobble. "He's technically my boss. Also, like, my landlord. Please stop being inappropriate."

"All in good fun. You're single, he's ... well." Todd waggled his eyebrows. "Who knows what his deal is, but I didn't see a ring on that finger."

The mere suggestion of wedding rings sent Pippa hurtling down a cesspit of self-pity in 0.2 seconds, straight to the parallel universe where a different Pippa Munro was planning a long-awaited wedding to her long-term love and looking forward to the most idyllic future. Pippa hated that version of herself. And as for Wolfie, well he was sure to have some kind of well-heeled, Miss World type girlfriend squirreled away somewhere down south. No wonder he didn't want to be in Hurst Bridge any more than he had to be. Pippa hugged herself in an attempt to keep her emotions in check, but her distress didn't escape Todd's attention. He quickly sobered.

"Hey." Todd tilted his head. "You all right?"

"I'm fine." Pippa took a deep breath then shook her head. "Actually, no I'm not, not really. Bad break-up. A long story."

"We all have them," Todd murmured. "Feel free to share with me if ever you're inclined." He flashed a kind smile. "Believe me, no judgement."

Affection surged through Pippa. "Thank you."

Juniper gave a sudden tug on her lead, forcing Todd into a stumble and breaking the moment of burgeoning friendship. "Great, now she decides to move." He dug his heels in and regained control of the determined pig. "I need to get her home. Will you be okay?"

"I will be," Pippa said firmly. She had no choice in that, after all.

"Call me if you need anything," Todd said. "My number's on the noticeboard in the kitchen." Touched by his kindness, Pippa promised she would.

Once she'd escorted Todd and Juniper off the premises, Pippa looked down at herself. Her skin was sticky, coated in foul-smelling cleaning solution and even though she was desperate to shower, there were more chairs to clean, plus she had rattraps to check. Pippa decided that once those messy chores were complete, she would treat herself to a bath. Maybe a gin and tonic to go with it. Just then, her mobile's ringtone faintly called to her from her room. Something in her gut lurched; could it be Alex? Cursing herself for leaving her phone unattended for so long, Pippa sprinted up the stairs.

What would she say to Alex if he called?

Did she even want him to call?

Arriving on the landing, Pippa skidded round the corner, wishing she could move quicker. Surely the caller would give up soon and—she hurtled headlong into something warm, firm and wet, her forehead making contact with something decidedly pointy.

"Argh!" Pippa's yelp was matched by someone else's pained cry. Clutching her aching head, Pippa looked up.

Wolfie stood before her, massaging his elbow. Pippa opened her mouth to apologise but the sight of him stole all the words from her vocabulary. He was practically naked, soaking wet from the shower with a fluffy towel knotted around his narrow hips. The man looked as if he'd been hewn from marble, with drops of water clinging to well-defined abs. His chest was taut and lightly tanned, with some kind of an inscription tattooed across firm pectoral muscles. A slim trail of hair teased a path down below the edge of the towel and Pippa was momentarily seized by a sudden curiosity about where it led. She tried not to stare, but the last time she'd been this close to a man this naked had been months ago and as much as she'd loved Alex, not once had the sight of him undressed unravelled her like this.

"Where's the fire?" Wolfie muttered, wincing as he rubbed his elbow. "And God, how hard is your head?"

It was taking all of Pippa's effort to keep her eyes on the man's face. "Sorry," she squeaked.

"Is your head all right?" he asked. "We banged pretty hard just then."

Pippa snorted with nervous laughter at the unintended pun, instantly regretting it as Wolfie's face darkened with apparent irritation. Flushing, she waved a hand. "I'm fine," she said, even as she realised she might develop an unsightly bruise. "My fault."

"Yes, it was." Wolfie hitched his towel up, perhaps suddenly aware he was almost nude in the presence of a woman he barely knew. "I don't think anything's broken though."

"Only my dignity," Pippa said with a groan. "Sorry, again."

"Don't mention it, Pippa Munro." And with that, Wolfie loped off to his room. Pippa was unable to do anything apart from stand clutching her aching forehead and watch him leave.

"What *is* it with the full name?" Pippa murmured to herself. As soon as Wolfie closed his door behind him, the paralysis in her legs lifted and she scurried to her room and slammed the door shut, leaning against it so she could catch her breath. Her heart was still thudding with an unfamiliar adrenaline, her skin tingling.

Unbidden, Pippa had an image of reaching out to Wolfie's perfect chest, of licking drops of water from his body. She wondered how his skin would taste, what it would be like to feel his lips on hers, his hands in her hair. Desire unfurled within her, and she welcomed it like a long-lost friend as it snaked its way up her body. Her nipples stiffened and she clenched her legs together, crying out for release.

Mortified, Pippa took a deep breath then let it out. Lust had been absent from her life for so long it felt almost alien. Heartbreak had been her most constant companion and having gone through precisely one major break-up in her life, Pippa was a stranger to what lay beyond a broken heart. She hadn't even considered fostering an attraction to another man, least of all someone who was both her boss and landlord in one. She shook her head, forcing the roiling emotions back down. Leaving Alex had taken every ounce of strength and dignity from her, and she would be damned before she threw away whatever progress she'd made since then by mooning over a man with whom she had no business getting involved. Even if he did look like *that* when clad only in a wet towel. She checked her phone and tutted – it looked like a spam call. Relief and disappointment both curdled in her stomach at the fact it wasn't Alex. She shoved the phone in her pocket.

Pippa poked her head out of her bedroom door and looked towards Wolfie's room. The door was shut, but she could see shadows moving through the little gap at the bottom of his door. Good. If he was shut away in there, he couldn't pop up and bother her with his inconvenient handsomeness as she worked. Besides, she had chairs to polish and rattraps to check. She took a quick glance in the mirror on the wall; her eyes were bright, her cheeks flushed.

"Get over it," she told herself. "He's just a man."

With that said, she headed downstairs and made short work of the remaining chairs. Once done, Pippa made her way to the cellar where the bulk of the rattraps were. Opening the door, she fought off a distasteful shudder. Although she had no fear of rodents, she had no desire to encounter any, dead or otherwise.

Pippa crossed her fingers as she entered the cellar. Fortunately, she soon discovered that the traps were empty but there was one that looked broken, the spring hanging off it. The bait was also gone, so Pippa could only assume that some wily creature had managed to outsmart the trap. Somewhat relieved, Pippa decided to take the trap out to see if she could fix it. Mindful of the dust and the fact that a rat could possibly have crawled all over it, she found a hessian sack in the corner and scooped the trap up into it. As she worked, there was a rattling in the walls. The pipes. She presumed it was the aftermath of Wolfie's shower, and the memory of him half-naked in the corridor popped treacherously into her mind yet again.

"Stop it, brain!" Pippa ordered. "We've discussed this." Determinedly, she twisted the neck of the sack as if it were the lifeline feeding lusty daydreams to her mind. "No more."

Just then, something skittered in the corner of the cellar, startling Pippa from her illicit reverie. She forced herself to check each corner of the space, relieved to see there were no rats in sight. Whatever critter made that noise had mercifully vanished and she decided to make her escape before the creature returned.

Pippa emerged into the kitchen blinking, the sunlight pouring through the windows a shock after the darkness of the cellar. She sneezed and rubbed her eyes, groaning when her hands came away smeared with dust. Pippa hurried to the sink and splashed her face with water, sighing with relief as the itchiness in her eyes subsided. She reached out to the right, but the towel rod was empty.

"Oh, for fuck's sake!" She had been positive there had been a hand towel there that morning when she'd washed up her coffee cup. Just then, a warm hand grabbed hers.

Fright stole her breath but then she recognised a familiar and expensive scent. A towel was placed in her hand.

Once Pippa had dried her face, she opened her eyes. Wolfie stood inches away, watching her with the smallest of smiles and dressed in a fitted shirt and jeans, his hair still a little dark from the shower. Beside him was a man Pippa had never seen before. The visitor was decked out in a crumpled beige linen suit, a magenta dress scarf trying valiantly to add an edge of maverick swagger to the ensemble but failing miserably.

"Thanks." Pippa lifted the towel.

"No problem," Wolfie said. "You looked like you needed a hand."

"Yeah. It's the ... the..." Pippa sneezed again, then looked down at herself. She was coated in dust; the sack must have been lying in the cellar for years. "Sorry."

"How's the head?" Wolfie asked.

"It's okay," she assured him. His concerned eyes were a spotlight and Pippa wasn't sure if she wanted to be under it.

"Hi there!" The visitor stepped forward, craning around Wolfie to catch Pippa's eye. His oddly bright red lips were curved in a leery grin. "Lou Donnelly."

Glad to be jarred away from Wolfie's intensity, Pippa forced a polite smile Lou's way. "Hi."

The man beamed, puffing out his chest. "You might have heard of me. Lou's Burgers? Looking to expand into more locations."

"Oh, I see." Her heart sank at the concept that Squires could become a burger place. This chain in particular seemed to be popping up everywhere across Yorkshire. Questionable recipes and even more questionable ethics when it came to where they sourced their ingredients. Yet weirdly popular for some unfathomable reason. "I'm Pippa."

"Pippa is kind of a custodian, if you will," Wolfie explained. "Keeps an eye on the place for me as I don't have a permanent base here. Fixes snags and such."

"I imagine a place like this has plenty of snags," Lou sympathised. "I can see why you'd want to sell." His eyes drifted down to the sack at her feet. "What you got there?"

"Rat trap." As soon as Pippa answered, Lou recoiled.

"Rats?" The restauranteur exclaimed. "I can't have rats. Do you have a rat problem here? That's an absolute no-no."

Wolfie's mouth opened and closed, and Pippa realised this wasn't a question he could answer easily without being sure he was truthful. He wasn't here enough and clearly wasn't the type of man to easily lie about such an issue. Her father's cheeky suggestion ran through her mind and Pippa saw an opportunity.

"We do have to put an awful lot of traps down," she said, affecting a meek expression. "Takes a great deal of effort to keep up with them all."

"From my experience, I can assure you that we don't have any kind of rat problem." Wolfie practically snarled at the man.

"Does that mean you want me to stop putting out the traps?" Pippa asked Wolfie innocently.

Wolfie gaped. "No, I— Well, they should—" He took a deep breath. "Can we discuss this in private a little later?"

He smiled down at Lou who looked positively irked. "Come along. Let me show you the grounds. Absolutely stunning views for a dining terrace." And, shooting a fiery glance at Pippa, he led the man away.

Trying not to laugh, Pippa heaved the sack out of the front door and round to the side of the house where the bins were tucked away and she disposed of the broken trap. On returning to the house, she reached for the door and was almost bowled over by an irate Lou Donnelly.

"I'm an epicurean, Mr. Squires. A gourmet!" Lou waved his arms in the air. "I cannot seriously consider building my latest outpost on a site where the current owner can't even be honest about his rat situation!"

Wolfie's eyes took on a murderous hue. With a voice loaded with menace, he shot back, "Like I said, we don't have a rat problem."

"Then what are those droppings?" Lou gestured back towards the house.

Wolfie gritted his teeth. "We are in the countryside. You do tend to find droppings here and there."

"I'm a restauranteur," Lou yelled. "I know my shit and that is definitely rodent in nature."

Wolfie sighed. "Again, countryside?"

Lou shook his head defiantly. "I'm not comfortable with that volume of shit, thanks."

Wolfie stretched out his hands. "If you could just—"

"No, I won't *just*." Lou shook his head fervently and backed away to his car, a low-slung Maserati in lurid green. "This isn't it. Not for me." And without so much as a goodbye, he slid behind the wheel and gunned the engine ostentatiously, all the while eying Wolfie balefully.

As the car screeched off the property, Wolfie propped his hands on his hips and spun slowly on his heel to look at Pippa. "Mind telling me what that little act was about?"

"What do you mean?" Pippa did her best to look affronted.

"You know we don't have a rat problem," he said.

"To be fair, I never said we did," she replied truthfully. "I just said we have a lot of traps."

"Grantham keeps a few around the place and in the wine cellar as a precaution," Wolfie snapped, although he clearly wasn't certain. "That's hardly a lot."

"Well, I've never lived in a house with even one trap," Pippa said. "So just one trap to me is a lot."

"Didn't you work on a farm?" Wolfie said, eyes blazing. "How can you be so clueless about rats?"

"How can *you* be so clueless about your own home?" Pippa retorted.

Wolfie went rigid. "I know what I need to know," he said. "And I know I need to sell it."

"Don't you even feel a little bit sad about that though?" she asked.

"You don't know what you're talking about," he shot back. "Let me tell you something, you're just like everyone else in Hurst Bridge. All you see is a beautiful house and the way my father flaunted his wealth. But that's not everything." He swallowed and, for a moment, Wolfie Squires looked hauntingly, achingly sad. "You have no idea."

Pippa reached out and touched his arm. She knew something about deception. About homes being not what they seemed. "So tell me."

Wolfie stilled. His gaze landed upon where her hand touched him and then strayed to her mouth. Unthinkingly, Pippa licked her lips. That one act, small as it was, changed something in the man before her. His eyes narrowed in on her mouth and she could feel the tension radiating off his powerful body as his breath hitched. She was assaulted by a sudden urge to reach up and rake her fingers through his hair, to put her lips to his neck to see how he would taste there.

Zing!

Pippa's phone's ludicrous chirp went off, because of course it did. The air eased; their breathing slowed. Wolfie stepped back murmuring something vaguely regretful and Pippa reached into her pocket, grimacing an apology she wasn't sure was needed. It was a picture of her father proudly holding a fat, silvery fish about a foot long.

"Sorry, it's my dad," she murmured.

Your dad caught himself a largemouth bass! her mother's text read. *His biggest ever catch. He insisted I send this to you and to let you know he put it right back in the water.*

"My dad's such a goof," Pippa said with a laugh. *Congrats to Dad*, she messaged back with a smile.

When she looked back up, Wolfie had gone.

Chapter Eleven

The next few days were ferociously busy. Pippa found that beating all the rugs and curtains took an entire day and the amount of silverware that needed looking after was crazy. She'd spent an entire morning carefully cleaning each piece, wondering why on earth anyone needed five different kinds of soup spoon. But it was Friday at last and although her job wasn't exactly the typical nine-to-five, it had been a challenging week. The emotional upheaval of finding out about the sale, plus the tumult of being in Wolfie's orbit, had really taken it out of her. Everything about him inspired a curiosity in her that bordered on alarming. It was clear that under that thick layer of dour superiority was a well of vulnerability and emotion, but he struggled to show it, even in his own home, and Pippa couldn't help but wonder what held him back.

She'd paused for lunch – tuna mayo sandwiches the size of her head, so hungry was she – then, as she made herself a cup of tea, she looked out of the kitchen window and there in the garden was Juniper. The pig was rooting around in the same spot as the last time she'd broken into the garden.

Laughing to herself, Pippa headed outside.

"Juniper!" she called. "This isn't your garden."

The pig gave her a disdainful look and then resumed her foraging.

"What have you found?"

Juniper snorted in response.

"Come on."

The pig now had a fancy red collar around her neck, with a tag, just like a dog. *Juniper Sunbeam*, it read. Pippa tugged at the collar to encourage her to move. Juniper chewed something green and eyed Pippa. She gave the collar another tug, but Juniper couldn't care less.

"Juniper, you need to go home!"

She tried to nudge the pig but at the last moment Juniper moved and Pippa slipped, landing hard on her backside. Juniper munched on, unbothered.

"All right there, neighbour?" Todd called from over the fence.

"Come and get your girl!" Pippa cried back. Her trousers were covered in mud and as she struggled to her feet, she saw that Juniper had rooted up what looked like a turnip.

Todd vaulted over the fence and jogged over. He saw the churned garden and grimaced. "Sorry," he said. "Juniper is a champion forager."

"I think you need to feed her more," Pippa remarked. "She was not letting me get in the way of whatever it is she's found here."

Todd inspected the ground, nudging it with his feet. "Looks like an old vegetable patch," he said.

"Oh that's right. They did use to grow veg here," Pippa recalled. She had a vague memory of a fenced-off area covered with netting. "In fact, yes, I think one year Joan grew so many tomatoes she made Bloody Mary cocktails with them for the Summer Fair."

"A shame it's gone to ruin then," Todd said as he wrestled with Juniper.

"It'll probably get paved over at this rate," Pippa said mournfully.

"I can't bear the thought of some awful business taking over this beautiful place," Todd said. "How are the viewings going?"

Pippa frowned. "I don't know. Although, I did manage to put off this restaurant guy by making out that we had rats."

Todd pulled a face. "You have rats?"

"No more than your average old property. I just made him think we had like, an infestation or something," Pippa corrected gently.

Todd laughed. "Genius." A wily expression crept across his face. "Shame you can't make every buyer think that."

Pippa's face flamed. "The man of the house didn't appreciate me saying it, but yeah, wish I could put off all buyers so easily. Maybe Wolfie would reconsider if he got no takers?"

"It's not a bad idea, you know," Todd agreed. He tapped his chin. "Maybe I can help you?"

"How?"

"Dunno." Todd grinned wickedly. "But I'll have a think. There must be *something* I can do. You know, like, be the neighbour from hell."

"You'd do that?" Pippa asked.

"For Juniper, of course I would." Todd patted Pippa's shoulder. "And you, I suppose."

"I appreciate that," Pippa said. "Do you fancy a tea?"

"Wish I could." Todd started to lead Juniper back towards the farm. "But I have a busy afternoon. Rain check?"

Once Todd had left, Pippa inspected the damage Juniper had wreaked. She had churned up a corner of bumpy grass at the opposite side of the garden that backed into the perimeter fence. Todd was right; the pig had unearthed a long-neglected vegetable patch. Remembering the many attempts by her mother to involve her in gardening, Pippa crouched down to try and work out what was still growing here, surviving through the neglect. Juniper had clearly found turnips and if Pippa wasn't mistaken, she could see some small potatoes that had been unearthed during the pig's rampage. On the other side of the patch, she recognised raspberry plants; although struggling, they had a few little berries developing and just under the soil were loose canes. Close inspection of the large leafy plants at the back revealed some courgettes hiding underneath and next to them were what looked like peas. Idly, Pippa pulled up some dandelions and some other weeds, combing her nails through the soil to make sure she'd removed all the roots. It was unexpectedly soothing; the feeling of dirt sifting past her skin, the fresh air caressing her as the gentle sun beamed down. The birdsong was riotous and, before Pippa knew it, she'd cleared a large area of weeds away, leaving the remains of the surviving plants. Bliss cascaded through Pippa as she sat back on her heels. She laughed at herself; all she'd done was pull up a few weeds! But the patch looked neat now and was it her imagination or did the plants look a little happier for it? As she inspected the leaves for bugs, Pippa realised there could be a nice project here for her. She'd never had time to get into gardening – her mum would be thrilled – and now seemed the perfect opportunity. Yes, perhaps in her spare time she could work on growing veg and tidying up the maze. Keeping busy was definitely the antidote to the sickness Alex had created.

Pippa's phone blipped. It was Mae.

Let me in!

Her heart lifting at the thought of a surprise visit from Mae, Pippa hurried to the door and pressed the buzzer for the gates. Seconds later, Mae was strolling through the front door alongside a shiny-cheeked woman with pigtails and red-framed glasses.

"Erin?" Pippa cried, grabbing her for a hug. "I thought you were still teaching in Vietnam?"

Her old school friend squealed in excitement. "I got back a few weeks ago!"

"Not long after you and Alex imploded," Mae added.

Erin's face screwed up in sympathy. "I heard all about that. I'm so sorry. I've been meaning to reach out, but I've been desperately job hunting and I wasn't sure whether you were ready to get out and see people."

"That's okay," Pippa said. "I *was* kind of a recluse for a while."

Mae rolled her eyes. "Kind of? There were successive sweatpants," she said to Erin. "You were best off out of it."

Erin pushed her bottom lip out. "Poor thing. Break-ups suck. Hao and I split up, and three days later I was booking my flight back home. And now, you're looking at Hurst Bridge Primary's new Deputy Head!"

"No way!" Pippa gushed. "Huge congrats. You're going to be amazing! I know it."

"I think this catch-up would go down much better with a brew." Mae beamed at Pippa. "Kettle?"

Soon they were huddled around the table, drinking tea and scarfing chocolate biscuits that Mae had produced from her string bag.

"Now, we have ulterior motives for being here," Mae said after the initial catch-up. "We have a favour to ask of you."

"Oh?" Pippa was intrigued.

"Yeah." Erin cleared her throat. "As Deputy Head of the primary school, I'm heading up any fundraising and my first project as a newly minted employee is to raise money to fix the roof."

"The roof?" Pippa repeated. "That sounds like a big undertaking."

"We need about eight grand," Erin said. "It really is big. Give me a collection for new books or pencils, sure, but a roof?" She tugged at her hair. "And, given it's almost June, we need to fix it before winter kicks in."

"Where do I come in?" Pippa reached for another biscuit.

"Fundraising." Erin's eyes widened. "I have many strengths. Teaching. Identifying the title of an episode of Friends before ten seconds in. Making the perfect Negroni. But fundraising events?" She shook her head frantically. "No. Not me. You, on the other hand …"

Pippa's hand froze, biscuit midway to mouth. "Me?"

"I bet you'd smash this!" Mae declared. "You turned Goodman's around. It was going down the tubes before you came along!"

"I don't know about that…" Pippa chomped on her biscuit but then she thought about the state of the accounts when she finally got her hands on them. Why was she downplaying her role in the farm's success?

"We need to set up a big fundraising event," Mae went on. "Like Erin said, it has to happen before winter, so, sooner rather than later."

"The great news is we finally found a roofer able to do the job," Erin went on. "And as we are a school, he'll give us a lovely discount but only if he can do it during August as he had a cancellation. That's perfect, as it'll be finished long before the bad weather starts. He needs an upfront payment of fifty percent for materials four weeks before the start date."

Pippa consulted her internal calendar. "It's almost June now," she said. "That means we have to pay him in July." She gulped. "Are you telling me that we need to get this event up and running in less than a *month* so we can pay him?"

Mae grimaced. "See why we need you? I offered to help with my local business contacts but I'm way out of my depth when it comes to, like, everything else."

Pippa took a contemplative bite of her biscuit. "And you say we need eight grand?"

"Yes, we do," Erin answered. "It's a lot, I know, but that's cheap for the work that's needed, believe me." She worried a loose thread from her pink blouse. "If there was anything in the budget, we'd be making use of it, but we need to find this money and fast. I do have some pin money for start-up costs but not much. So, we need to do something cheap and easy to set up, but something that will also yield a ton of cash."

"Come on, what do you say?" Mae nudged Pippa's arm. "Please say yes."

Erin fluttered her eyelashes. "Please. For the kids, Pip. Think of the kids."

Mae affected a wide-eyed, mournful expression. "The kids will shiver through their lessons this winter if you don't do this."

"All right, all right!" Pippa waved her hands. "I'm in. If only to shut you up."

Erin and Mae squealed in delight.

"Thank you!" Erin cheered, pulling her in for a hug. Pippa squeezed her back, her mind racing with possibilities. Although Pippa wasn't a fundraising expert, she knew how to organise and work to a budget. She knew how to negotiate as well as manage people. As she looked at her friends' expectant faces, a familiar feeling swelled within her: purpose. And with it, a speck of pure happiness. As she leaned out of Erin's embrace, she started mulling over possibilities. "Have you had any ideas?"

Erin blushed. "No. Honestly, I'm so overwhelmed."

Pippa thought for a moment. "I'd say we need an event, right? Something that makes people *want* to hand over their money."

"You mean like a party?" Erin said. "Or maybe, a costume ball?"

"That could work." Pippa opened the notes app on her phone. "Any other ideas?"

"Sponsored walks are always good," Mae suggested. "Erin, get the kids doing a sponsored walk, it'd be so cute."

"Never thought I'd hear the day *you'd* describe kids as cute," Erin said with a chuckle.

"I like kids!" Mae protested. "From a distance. Walking. Preferably away from me. In fact, I'll happily throw money at them to walk away from me."

"I can't see us raising that amount from a sponsored walk alone," Pippa said. "We have to do something with scale, that appeals to lots of people." She stood, beginning to pace. "Also, something that doesn't need a great deal of budget to initiate." She came to a halt by the kitchen window and looked out across the garden. "The sort of event that businesses would happily sponsor the set-up costs in return for exposure." Her eyes drifted to the old shed, where, through the open door, she could see the wheelbarrow hanging. The idea was so obvious Pippa almost laughed out loud. She whirled on her heel to look at her friends. "We can resurrect the Summer Fair! The Wheelbarrow Races!"

"Oh my God!" Mae clapped her hands. "Yes!"

Erin laughed. "What, like the old days?"

"Why not?" Pippa said. "It's perfect! Remember the crowds it used to pull? The races alone used to be oversubscribed, and I bet we'd get so much interest if we resurrected them again. Charge for admissions to the races … get people in fancy dress. I'm sure local news would be interested. That might pull in some donations too."

Erin's face twisted in doubt. "Do you really think we can pull it together? We don't have long."

Pippa thought for a moment. "If we have to pay upfront in July then we need to have money in our hands in four weeks at least. If you can hand over money by July 31st, let's say?" Erin nodded. "Then the event needs to be, like, July 20th at the latest. Give us time to get all the money in and ringfenced."

Erin's face began to dissolve into panic. "That seems so tight. I don't know…"

Mae grabbed Erin's arm. "If anyone can do this, Pip can."

A warm glow spread through Pippa at Mae's confidence in her. "We can do it, but it will have to be a team effort. We'll all need to pitch in."

"I'm sure I can get the teaching staff to help," Erin said, confidence slowly restoring her smile. "But we need a clear action plan."

"I think the most pressing issue is start-up costs," Pippa

said. "Mae, reach out to your contacts to see who would sponsor the event and to what extent."

Mae saluted ironically. "No problem. I'm off to the local business association meeting tonight as it happens – the perfect opportunity."

"That's great!" Pippa said. "We can offer extensive advertising opportunities like billboards, leaflets ... the original fair used to attract hundreds upon hundreds of people – the exposure will be huge. We can invite vendors – food carts, ice cream trucks and the like, set up a little market and make them all pay for pitches. The races themselves are easy enough; we just speak to the council to close the roads—"

"I can do that!" Erin interrupted excitedly. "I have to work with the council quite a lot, so I know exactly who to pester."

"Great. I presume we'd need some kind of insurance; you should ask them to advise on that." Pippa felt as if she was coming alive. The fair was taking shape before her very eyes, and they'd only just started.

Mae raised a hand. "I have a great broker for my insurance. Let me speak to her about it."

"Perfect." Pippa beamed. "Maybe I can ask Wolfie if we can hold the prizegiving ceremony at Squires, like they used to?"

"Ask him? You've seen him then?" Mae asked, in hallowed tones. Pippa nodded.

"Wolfie Squires is a total mystery," Erin added. "I know I'm one to talk having lived abroad for so long, but I can't even remember what he looks like."

"Well he's here a lot nowadays." Pippa filled Erin in on the pending sale and she was gratified to see her friend's face drop in horror, like hers.

"I still can't believe it," Mae said.

"I only wish he could see how special this place is," Pippa mused. "If this house got some proper love and care, it'd be like it used to be."

Mae threw her hands in the air. "Well, the races are the perfect opportunity, aren't they? Get the whole community out here! He'd have to be blind not to see how much this house is loved."

"I'm not sure the Summer Fair will be enough of a demonstration, to be honest. He's so bloody grumpy," Pippa huffed. "I so much as mention the significance of this place and he shuts down." It was increasingly clear that the house was not just a source of irritation as she'd initially presumed, but actually one of outright pain. "Seriously," she went on. "I don't know how I'm going to even talk to him about this place, let alone convince him not to sell."

"I'm sure you'll find a way." Mae stood and walked to the window. "God, what a view. How anyone could walk away from this I do not know." She squinted. "Is that a veg patch?"

Pippa joined her. "Yup. Thinking about doing it up and giving gardening a go," she said. "Any tips?" Mae's pub garden was her pride and joy, an explosion of lavender and climbing plants.

"Yeah. Manure!" she replied firmly. "I have to time when I use it so as not to damage trade, but you find yourself a good supply of shit and you've got it made."

Pippa pointed. "Well, I do live next door to a pig farm. I could have a constant supply of shit, if I wanted."

Mae laughed. "Oh, I bet the smell must be heavenly."

"Nah." Pippa shrugged. "He stores all the muck on the other side of the farm until he sells it, so I never catch wind of it."

"God, can you imagine if you did?" Erin shuddered. "Wouldn't be quite so idyllic, would it?"

Erin's words sparked an idea in Pippa, and she grinned devilishly. "No, it wouldn't," she said.

Chapter Twelve

The next day was greyer and cooler, with a brisk wind rolling in off the hills. Rain was a promise. After waking early to get started on Fair organisation, Pippa was nearing the end of an epic dusting session. It had taken the entire morning, but every flat surface was sparkling. From the hallway, she heard chatter. She recognised the voices and peered out from the dining room to have her suspicions confirmed. Call-Me-Stef and Toby from *Top Stay* were back, only this time they had a lanky, shabbily dressed youth with thick glasses and a vivid orange neck tattoo. Her mood hit the floor; they must be seriously interested in buying the place.

"This is Ezra, our Vibe Consultant," Steffany was saying proudly.

Wolfie's face remained as impassive as ever, but Pippa thought she'd known him long enough now to recognise incredulity beneath the surface. His restraint was admirable.

"Did... did you say *vibe*?" Wolfie shook the man's hand politely.

"Yep! Clients bring me in to help them determine if a location fits their, like, well, their vibe," Ezra explained. "I've done branding for a number of corps, and I am never wrong."

Toby lifted a hand. "It's unusual terminology I know," he said. "But we consult Ezra when we have multiple options for a new location. Helps us narrow down our choice."

Steffany brought out a tablet from her leather bag. "It's like this. We want to get a sense of the place for ourselves, what kind of *Top Stay* experience do we want to create?"

"Same as all the others?" Wolfie replied acidly.

"Oh no!" Steffany turned her tablet to him. Pippa could just make out the images. "Look at the Leamington Spa site." Steffany swiped through a series of photos depicting a neat, Spartan space in the trademark coral and turquoise. "Relaxing, no? With a chic touch for the city slicker needing a break. But then you look at our Dorset location." She flicked to photos seemingly identical to the first set. "As you can see, the Dorset vibe is much more patrician, an understated elegance designed with the older, discerning day-tripper in mind."

Wolfie blinked. "Seriously?"

"Oh, yes." Steffany nodded enthusiastically. "I mean, look at Swansea." She swiped more. "A cheeky, slightly sexy hotel for the naughty weekend-away types, know what I mean?" She attempted a humorous elbow nudge, but she may as well have done it to a stone, such was the response.

If Wolfie thought it was bullshit then he hid it well. "Right." He gestured behind him. "How do you see this place then?"

Steffany and Toby turned to Ezra reverently.

Ezra narrowed his eyes. "I'm still vibe-ing," he said in all seriousness. "But I'm thinking eco-tourist, hiker, cool dudes. Flowing air, bring nature inside. You know?"

Wolfie stared at Ezra, agape. Then his mouth snapped shut. "Right. I suppose you need a tour?"

"Yes, a tour!" Ezra enthused. "Tell me everything about this place."

"You know what?" Steffany said. "Let's start with the USP. That view?"

Pippa stifled her giggles behind her hand. That meant they were visiting the garden, and she knew for a fact there would be something out there not to their liking. She was unable to resist following them through the house.

The execs and Wolfie traipsed to the kitchen, whereupon the view of the moors revealed itself through the large windows. The *Top Stay* execs murmured in delight, Steffany wittering about the 'oxygenation of the great outdoors'.

"Ah, this is top," Ezra enthused. "Big time."

"Please, follow me." Wolfie led them to the kitchen door and the group filed outside. Pippa remained hidden behind the door, holding her breath as she waited for the inevitable. And seconds later, there it was. Steffany let out an ungodly shriek as her colleague burst out with some very un-corporate invectives. Pippa counted a few seconds and then rushed out after them, desperate to see the effects of her handiwork.

"What's wrong?" she cried, only for the stench to hit her in the face harder than expected. "Wow." Pig shit really was vile.

"What *is* that stink?" Ezra demanded, looking positively green.

"Do you mean the smell?" Pippa fought to keep her face nonchalant. "We get that a lot when the wind blows a certain way. I'm so used to it I barely notice." She hoped they didn't clock her subtle retch at the end of the sentence.

"Where's it coming from?" Steffany was almost in tears.

"Could it be that?" Toby was pinching his nose with one hand; the other was pointing towards the perimeter fence. There, piled up against the boundary fence, was what could only be described as a giant pile of shit. Atop it, a peg clipped to his nose, was Todd, merrily forking away at it and it seemed with every twist of his tool that more scent was unleashed into the air.

"Todd?" Wolfie stalked over to the fence. "What is the meaning of this?"

"Ah, greetings, neighbour!" Todd waved. "A relatively recent initiative for Johnson farms. Manure!"

"I can see and smell that it's manure," Wolfie snarled. "But why is it up against my fence all of a sudden?"

"Good question," Todd said cheerfully. "It's a safe space away from the other animals; contains a *lot* of nasty bugs does pig shit. Had to move it over here. Against regulations to store so much shit so close to my beehives."

"Regulations?" Wolfie snapped.

"Yeah. Total bugger. You know," Todd leaned on the fork handle, "it's excellent fertiliser and the rose gardeners at Sumpter Hall pay through the nose for it."

Wolfie levelled him with a stare and Pippa could only marvel at Todd's composure in the face of it. "Are those noses immune to the stench?"

Todd blinked. "Excuse me?"

Wolfie took a deep breath. "Far be it from me to limit your enterprise," he said, "but I'm trying to sell this place and you're stacking pig shit right against our shared boundary. Forgive me if I seem a little perplexed!"

Todd shrugged helplessly. "I do apologise for that," he said. "The only thing is, I just learned that legally if I'm to store it I have to keep it a certain distance from my bees."

"You've really got used to this?" Steffany murmured to Pippa. The exec clutched her tablet to her chest, face drained of colour. Pippa wondered what zany 'vibe' she'd attribute to the scene before her. *Turd chic*, she thought absurdly. *Faecal eleganza*. She couldn't stop the snort that escaped, but instantly wished she had, as more stink rushed up her nose and her mirth turned into a gag.

"God yeah." Pippa styled out the gag as a chuckle. "Barely notice it."

Steffany heaved. "Are you telling me this is what *Top Stay* guests can expect to smell every morning?"

"No way in hell." Wolfie turned his electric eyes on Pippa. "Did you have anything to do with this?"

"Why would I have anything to do with it?" Pippa said, nose pinched. It was hard to hide her smirk because of course she'd suggested this tactical relocation of the manure pile and Todd had been only too happy to oblige.

Wolfie didn't answer. He merely narrowed his eyes then turned back to the visitors. "I can only apologise for this," he said to them. "Rest assured, this is some kind of misunderstanding that I will resolve."

"How about we go inside?" Ezra suggested. "I think I've seen enough."

With a final suspicious glare at Pippa, Wolfie shepherded his guests back into the house. As soon as the door was closed, Pippa whirled around to face Todd.

"That was epic!" she squealed.

"I think that tattooed kid was about to faint," Todd said. "What a wuss. It's just a bit of shit."

"That's more than a bit, Todd," Pippa corrected him. "It's a fuckton of shit."

"Ah, yes, the metric fuckton, that oft-forgotten unit of manure measurement." Todd grinned.

"Seriously, though, I have to move. It's so vile." Pippa backed away. "And well done for assembling it late-notice. Just hope it works."

"Me too." Todd's face turned sombre. "I would hate for my animals to endure construction work. Pigs are so sensitive."

His concern made Pippa's heart twist. "You never know," she said, "we might yet put all the developers off and he'll sell to someone nice who just wants to live here and take care of the place."

"I wish you'd stay here," Todd blurted. "I think we'd have a cracking time being neighbours for life."

Pippa was warmed by his compliment. "If only," she said. "Do you have a cool million you could lend me?"

"And the rest," Todd said. "Pat was speaking to a friend of his who heads up acquisitions for a property group. They looked at Squires briefly. Anyway, she told Pat the whole plot was up for over two million five."

"Forget that then." That was more money than she'd ever earn, even if she lived five times over. Conscious of the all-pervasive smell, she gave Todd a hasty goodbye and hurried back inside to carry on working. This afternoon she had to wipe down the oil paintings. Well, the few that were left. There were some rather harrowing looking family portraits that populated the living room, and they needed a gentle wipe once a month. The binder dictated warm water with olive-based soap and a cotton cloth. In the utility cupboard Pippa found a Tupperware box marked 'painting care' in what must have been Grantham's spidery writing.

Pippa made her way to the living room. In there she could hear Wolfie discussing the house with the *Top Stay* team from where he was in the library. Trying not to worry about the fate of the house, she lifted the first painting down. It was of a woman, with flowing red hair and a luminous quality to her skin. It was her eyes that made Pippa stop; they were identical to Wolfie's. Large and deep blue, all at once wondrous and haughty. Pippa deduced this person must be an ancestor and, sure enough, the brass plate on the frame identified her as Caroline Emilia Squires.

"It's bath time, Caroline," Pippa advised the painting and she got to work. The cloth lifted a noticeable amount of grime and Pippa was delighted to see a marked improvement after just a couple of minutes. As she worked, she became aware of a damp smell. Although the house was plagued by damp spots, this seemed new. Pippa paused in her task and looked around the room for tell-tale dark patches, but she couldn't see anything. It was entirely possible that there was a leak somewhere behind the walls, and Pippa made a note to call her plumber friend, Linda. It seemed as if the smell was strongest in the right-hand side of the room. There wasn't much there apart from a corner table with a decorative glass carafe sitting on top. As she investigated, she noticed some damage to the wooden panelled wall; an indent about head height that could only be seen when viewing from a certain angle.

Pippa moved to view the curious mark, but her hip bumped the table, sending the carafe flying to the ground! Horrified, she could only watch as the slender neck of the vessel snapped in two.

"Nooooo!" Pippa dropped to her knees. This was the exact opposite of what she was meant to do. She was meant to care for this place, keep it safe, and yet here she was, damaging a no doubt priceless piece of crystal. Mortified and very aware that the heir of the property was yards away, Pippa reached for the broken pieces, clinging to the faint hope that she could perhaps glue them together so skilfully that no one would notice her error. "Ouch!" Pippa yelped, whipping her fingers to her mouth. The swan-like neck of the carafe was more jagged than she had thought, and the cut had lanced deep. Crimson blood beaded and swelled, and a thick tendril of it snaked down her finger.

She clamped her other hand around it, feeling a little woozy.

"What happened?" Wolfie skidded through the large archway in alarm. Clocking Pippa on the floor, he hurried to her, eyes wide.

"I'm sorry!" Pippa pleaded. "I didn't mean to break it, I'll pay for it, I—"

"You're bleeding." Wolfie knelt by her side. "Let me see."

"It was an accident," Pippa babbled. "My stupid hips. I was looking at that mark on the wall, it looks like the wood is damaged, and I was—"

"It's okay. Calm down." Wolfie took her hand with surprising gentleness. "Show me."

Wincing, Pippa released her grip on the wound, only for the blood to flow afresh. She felt distinctly nauseated. "I'll pay for it."

"Nasty cut," Wolfie murmured. "Hold it again." Then he frowned. "Pay for what?"

"The carafe," Pippa explained, nodding at the broken glass.

Wolfie gave her an odd stare, then jumped to his feet and left the room, returning moments later with a first aid kit.

"I mean it," Pippa insisted, wondering if perhaps Wolfie didn't understand what she was saying. "It's probably very valuable."

"It's a bit of fucking glass," he snarled as he unrolled a length of bandage. "There are loads of that sort of thing lying around this place. You only have one finger."

"Actually, I have ten," Pippa giggled, feeling a little light-headed.

Wolfie gave her an exasperated glare. "You know what I mean." He pulled away her hand from the wound and wiped the area with an antiseptic cloth. He then quickly bound and affixed the bandage. "I don't *think* you'll need stitches," he said. "But keep that clean and see a doctor as soon as you can."

Pippa watched him tidy away the kit, his capable efficiency oddly soothing. "Thanks," she said. "It already feels better."

"I've seen much worse injuries than that," he muttered.

It was then that Pippa remembered what Grantham had told her. "When you were in the army."

"Yes," Wolfie said tightly. If he wondered how she knew, he didn't show it.

"Did you serve for long?"

Wolfie hesitated, as if debating with himself. Then he spoke. "Long enough. I joined at eighteen. You sure that bandage feels okay?"

Pippa ignored his question. "You were a *child*!"

Wolfie's mouth twisted. "I was old enough, Pippa Munro. Old enough."

"That's so young," she said.

"I know." Wolfie settled back on his heels and glanced towards the damaged wall. He seemed to be mulling over his answer. "It just seemed like the thing to do."

"You must have had plenty of options. Why that?" Pippa knew Wolfie had had the best education money could buy and although the military was a very respectable career

The House Sitter

choice, it was at odds with the solitary, music-loving boy she remembered from all those years ago. Enlisting so young seemed to her a drastic act of rebellion.

"Why *not* that?" He rose to his feet, eyes fiery, and Pippa got the sense that the topic was very much off limits. It seemed as if he might say something else, but then a voice piped up from the library, calling his name. "Shit." Pippa realised the *Top Stay* team were still here. Wolfie extended a hand and helped Pippa to her feet. "You feeling okay?"

Pippa nodded. She felt a little woozy but now the injury was bandaged tight it was better. "Nothing a glass of water can't fix."

As Wolfie hurried back to the *Top Stay* visitors, Pippa made her way to the kitchen and poured herself a large glass of water. Her hand throbbed in time with her beating heart, and she hoped the injury wouldn't leave a scar. As she drank, Pippa found herself replaying the brief discussion with Wolfie. Once more, she'd got a glimpse of something real underneath that aloof carapace. Why did he need to guard himself so carefully?

Pippa heard the *Top Stay* team leaving and after finishing her water, she gathered a dustpan and brush, plus some kitchen towel to tidy up the shards of glass safely. As she passed the library, she heard Wolfie's voice reverberating through the hallway.

"Listen, it's what needs to be done," he was saying. Instinctively, Pippa held her breath and softened her steps, somehow understanding he wouldn't want her hearing this.

"No, I know." Wolfie was soothing whoever was on the

other end of the phone. "I know you think that, but I want to do it."

Pippa's insides churned. The tenderness in Wolfie's voice, the kindness with which he spoke, it was so at odds with the man she knew that it stopped her in her tracks.

"If I could give her the moon on a plate, I would. You know that." Wolfie sighed, almost dream-like. "She gets the best. I'll do anything for her."

Pippa had to turn away. That call could be interpreted many ways, but it did sound like Wolfie was selling the house to please someone – a woman – he loved. His girlfriend? Maybe there were no debts and Mae's assumption was wrong. Maybe the money was intended for something else, something that was none of her business. Grumpily, Pippa wadded the glass up with paper towel, and stomped out to the bins to dispose of the broken glass. If Wolfie was selling such a beautiful house purely to impress a woman, then there was something truly wrong with this world.

Once outside, Pippa took deep breaths and looked out across the driveway to the moors. The rolling green looked vivid under the overcast sky, and she wondered if it might rain. The beautiful scenery calmed her, as it always did, but her fingers twitched with the need to be busy. Glancing back at the house, she saw Wolfie's silhouette pacing past the window and Pippa knew she couldn't go back in there and listen to him smugly boasting about how he was going to callously have Squires razed, all to please some selfish gold-digger. No, Pippa craved the fresh air, and it was then she remembered the vegetable patch. Instantly soothed by the thought of it, she hurried round to the back of the house, determined to put all things Wolfie-related firmly behind her.

Chapter Thirteen

The next day was even cooler than the one before, with blustery winds bringing the rich smell of heather in from the moors. Pippa found herself rushing through the day's tasks – intensive bathroom cleaning – purely so she could spend some more time in the garden. She told herself she'd have just an hour or so outdoors then she could spend the rest of the day planning the Summer Fair.

She braved the grimy greenhouse with its army of beefy-looking spiders and found some twine, using it to fix the raspberry plants to the half-buried canes, and they were now looking a little happier. Some new weeds had already sprung up and she gleefully ripped them out. Then, using a small gardening fork, she poked holes in the soil. The Merry Garden Girl – her new favourite blogger and gardening expert – recommended doing this for an untended bed. Todd had kindly donated a small tub of his stinky mulch and even though the stench of it turned her stomach, Pippa slopped it on top.

"There you go, little plants!" she cooed excitedly. "Drink up the delicious shit—"

"Are you seriously talking to vegetation?"

Mae's voice from behind her startled her so much that the tub of mulch slipped out of Pippa's hands and fell to the ground, splattering her leggings all the way up to the thigh. "Damn!" She instinctively swiped at the mess, forgetting it was animal faeces, only to almost pass out when she realised her hand was coated in it.

"Sorry!" Mae flapped around her. "Didn't mean to startle you and oh—!" Her eyes watered and she took a large step back. "Wow, that's ... ripe."

Pippa grimaced. "Don't worry about it. I'd hug you but I'm afraid you'll catch, like, cholera or something."

"Isn't it ringworm you can get from that stuff?" Mae covered her nose with a sleeve.

"To-may-to, to-mah-to," Pippa chanted but then retched again. "At any rate, a multitude of gross germs are currently swarming all over my favourite leggings. Oh God."

"Favourite leggings?" Mae eyeballed them incredulously. "Love, I know you never had much time for fashion but come on. Those leggings are the clothing equivalent of a lobotomy. We *must* take you shopping."

"Frankie does keep threatening to do that." Pippa had always found it hard to really care too much about fashion. "You know, not everything I wear has to be worthy of Vogue." For a brief moment she thought of the lovely white dress she'd worn to please Alex that awful night he dropped the bombshell regarding Kent. No, it really didn't matter what you wore, Pippa thought.

"Hard disagree. Anyway." Mae lifted an accordion file above her head, eyes bulging at the weight. "Ready to do some organising?"

"Absolutely." Pippa glanced down at herself and grimaced. "Let me clean up first."

Whilst Mae settled herself at the kitchen table with paperwork and a cup of tea, Pippa hastily showered and changed into clean clothes. As she started to head downstairs with her trusty old laptop, she heard the pipes rattle. This wasn't unusual in itself, but this did seem louder than normal. She made a mental note to tell Grantham. Or Wolfie, seeing as he'd stayed over the night before.

But all thoughts of noisy pipes left Pippa's head when she saw the swathes of paper spread out on the kitchen table.

"Wow." Pippa slid into the chair opposite Mae. "We're going to need pints of tea to get us through this."

Mae let out a harried sound. "There is a lot," she agreed. "How are you getting on?"

Pippa couldn't contain her proud smile as she opened her laptop. "Well, as you can see, I've confirmed the following sponsors." She pointed to her chart.

"What, in the past twenty-four hours?" Mae looked at the figures and gasped. "They're donating *that* much?"

Pippa nodded. "Yup. They're all run by people who remember just how good the fair used to be and the crowds it used to draw. Killer advertising opportunity for them. So, thanks to these guys, we have some great seed money to help organise the event." She flicked to another part of the document. "Now we need to sell pitches to vendors – food trucks and that."

"You must have some good contacts from the Goodman's days," Mae suggested.

"Maybe a few." Pippa swallowed. Working on a farm had embedded her and Alex in the local retail economy. Once upon a time, her social and professional network had been filled with all sorts of interesting and talented people; cheesemongers, butchers, craftworkers and the like. But they had known her as Alex's girlfriend. Many had assumed she would one day be his wife, often making jokes about being their official wedding suppliers. The very notion of approaching them now, in her current state, made her want to curl up and die. "I don't know if I can ask them."

"Why not?" Mae screwed up her face. "What, because they were mates with Alex too?"

Pippa shrugged helplessly. "I just don't know if I can face it."

Mae levelled Pippa with a fierce stare. "You, my friend, can do anything. You have every right to meet with those people in your capacity as Fair organiser."

"I know that!" Pippa said heatedly. "Intellectually, I know that. But the thought of actually seeing them after what Alex did..." She shuddered. "It's humiliating."

"Listen." Mae took Pippa's hand. "I can't imagine how hard it's been rebuilding your life after what Alex did. Hurst Bridge is a small town. People know your business and that's the way it's always been." She squeezed tight.

"So bloody well call them, meet them and show them you're a goddamn queen."

Pippa swallowed tears. "Thanks."

"Thank me by nailing this fair," Mae shot back with a wink. "I need my Pip, not some wet blanket."

Pippa swiped at her eyes. "You have her." Mae was right. Pippa's experience at the farm had not only imbued her with useful skills but plenty of contacts that could really be beneficial for the fair. So what if she'd endured a painful break-up? Mae was right – everyone in Hurst Bridge knew about it by now, so why hide? It would only be to her detriment and Alex had done enough damage without Pippa heaping on more. "I'll start reaching out."

"Great. I'll have a think too," Mae said. "For my part, the advertising has gone out, and I've applied to the council for the roads to be closed for the races." She winced. "We're a bit tight for time but Rick – my mate in the council – thinks that as it's such a good cause they'll rush it through."

"Great." Pippa went through the checklist. "Insurance?"

"This is where I'm struggling." Mae's face fell. "We must have at least two first aid stations as well as on-site medics to get coverage. Problem is, I'm struggling to find available medics at short notice. It's summer, so they're booked up with festivals and such."

Pippa frowned. "There must be *someone* out there qualified and available!"

Mae threw her hands up. "You would think. I even asked Finn Goodman if he knew anyone through the university, that's how much I've been struggling." She winced. "Hope that's okay."

"What, that you spoke to my ex's brother?" Pippa said. "Of course it is. Desperate times and all that."

And so the organisation went on. They reviewed the trophies – Erin had some on order from a place that made the school sports day trophies – and Mae had been networking with local bands who'd gigged at her pub to see if any would provide entertainment.

"Did you speak to Wolfie about doing the prize-giving at Squires?" Mae asked, a wistful smile spilling across her face. "It used to be one of the best things about the fair, hanging about those gardens in the sunshine, sneaking a cheeky fag in the maze…"

"Not yet." Pippa pulled a face. She really couldn't judge how he would react to such a request and there hadn't been an opportune moment. "Let's just hope he doesn't raze the place to the ground first."

Mae rolled her eyes. "Must really need the money."

"Maybe." Pippa told Mae about hearing Wolfie on the phone, the devotion in his voice. "He was almost … *gooey.*"

"You really think he's selling up to spend all the money on a woman?" Mae said.

"I don't know," Pippa said. "A girlfriend would make sense, right? After all, someone as good-looking as him must have…" she trailed off, distracted by Mae's knowing grin. "What?"

"That's the first time I've heard you even compliment a man that wasn't Alex." Mae rested her chin on her hands. "You might be ready."

"Ready for what?" Pippa was unsettled by Mae's glee.

"Ready for a new penis in your life," her friend shot back.

"Shut up." Pippa's treacherous memory tantalised her with the image of Wolfie's naked chest and she squirmed in her seat.

"No, listen!" Mae wagged an authoritative finger. "A significant stage of recovery is the first post-break-up shag."

"*Mae!*" Pippa's cheeks were on fire. The thought of being intimate with another man was bringing her out in a sweat.

"Look at me." Mae's voice was low, tender. "I only say it because I care." Mae stroked Pippa's hand. "I care that you get some new penis because honestl— Oi!" Mae didn't get to finish her sentence because Pippa had thrown a biscuit at her head. Mae swooped up the biscuit, taking a triumphant bite. "Trust me. You need to get out there, embrace singlehood."

"Easy for you to say," Pippa said. Mae was a prolific dater.

"It's just a matter of confidence!" Mae scoffed. "Seriously, Pip. I really think you could benefit from inviting some new penis into your life."

"Right, okay. Let's discuss this, if only to stop you from saying 'new penis' for the billionth time." Pippa rose from her seat to stretch. "Tell me, where would I find some of that? I've been off the shelf so long I wouldn't even know where to begin! Let's face it." She threw her hands up into the air. "Mae, when it comes to getting laid, I'm utterly clueless." Instead of offering a sympathetic smile or indulgent giggle, Mae was stock still, her dark eyes fixed on something behind Pippa. Something creaked. Leather. *Oh fuck.*

Pippa turned slowly and, sure enough, there was Wolfie, standing in the doorway wearing his motorcycle leathers. All the blood in Pippa's body went straight to her cheeks. She opened her mouth to greet him casually, as if she hadn't just announced she was a terrible shag, but nothing came out. Feeling wobbly, Pippa lowered herself back down to the table.

"Am I interrupting something?" Wolfie asked. He strode to the sink to pour himself a glass of water, which he knocked back in three large gulps. Despite her furious embarrassment, Pippa couldn't help but notice the way his throat moved as he swallowed, and how his large hands dwarfed the pint glass in his hands. And how the leathers showed off every line of the powerful body she knew full well was under those clothes.

"Nope!" Pippa squeaked. As Wolfie filled up his glass again, Pippa glanced at Mae, who made a *talk to him* gesture.

Pippa shook her head frantically. And say what? It seemed like every time she crossed paths with Wolfie, she was making an idiot of herself, like being covered in filth or smashing valuable glass trinkets. Her latest gaffe just completed the trifecta of awkward. Pippa snatched up her pen as if to carry on notetaking for the fair, but the lines on the page blurred before her eyes.

"Hi, I'm Mae," Mae said, kicking Pippa under the table.

Wolfie removed his moto jacket to reveal a faded T-shirt damp with sweat. "Nice to meet you."

"I'm this one's best friend," Mae said. "She's currently forgotten how to talk, but we're organising a Summer Fair. You know, like the ones that used to be here?"

Wolfie remained unmoved. "I see," he said.

If Mae was fazed by Wolfie's glacial demeanour, she didn't show it. "Yeah, it's to raise money for the school roof. Pip didn't mention it?" Wolfie's eyes slid to Pippa.

"No. She did not."

Pippa couldn't imagine a world where she could just 'mention' her everyday minutiae to Wolfie. She took a deep breath. "It doesn't interfere with my duties here," she said. "I've been asked to pitch in, that's all."

"Pitch in?" Mae patted Pippa on the back, hard. "She's practically organised the entire event single-handed in a matter of days. In fact, Pip just had the most amazing idea... Maybe we could host the prize-giving here for the Wheelbarrow Races?"

"I'm not sure we have the space anymore," Wolfie said stiffly. "You must have noticed our garden is much smaller nowadays."

"We don't need vast acres." Pippa found her voice. Talking business was oddly soothing. "There's still plenty of room."

Wolfie snorted but didn't elaborate.

Mae glared curiously at Pippa, and she met her friend's eye helplessly, as if to say *See what I'm dealing with?* "It'd just be for a couple of hours," Pippa persisted. "The green will be chock full of food stalls and whatnot, so we'd like to have an open space for the prize-giving."

Wolfie shrugged. "What do I care? If people want to trek

up the hill to receive a little plastic trophy, then they can knock themselves out."

"I can't tell if that's a yes or if you're actively wishing unconsciousness upon the people of Hurst Bridge," Pippa said, fighting hard to quell her irritation.

Wolfie sighed audibly. "It's a yes."

"And if you know any professional medics who could man the first aid support for the fair, that'd be great too!" Mae chirped. Wolfie eyed her strangely.

"*Mae!*" Pippa growled.

"What?" Mae gesticulated innocently. "Desperate times, you said it yourself." She turned to Wolfie. "Without qualified first aiders, we can't insure the event. And we need insurance in case some nitwit burns their tongue on an extra hot coffee or, like, has a heart attack pushing their mate around in a barrow."

"Without insurance, the event can't go ahead," Pippa added. "But we'll sort it, I'm sure." For some reason it felt important that Wolfie understood Pippa wasn't entirely useless.

Wolfie blinked. "I see." Just then a loud screech tore through the house, followed by the unmistakable sound of spurting water. "Fuck." He slammed down his glass and sprinted towards the sound. Pippa was close behind him, her heart racing. What on earth had that been? The noise was coming from upstairs and the three of them hurtled up towards it. It soon became clear from where the disruption emanated: the cupboard on the landing that housed the ancient boiler and water tank. Water was spilling out onto the hallway floor via the gap under the door.

Wolfie raced over to the cupboard and yanked it open, cursing as more smelly water bled out into the hallway. He turned to Pippa. "Run downstairs and turn the water off. Stopcock under the kitchen sink."

"I'll do it!" Mae yelled, already sprinting back down the stairs.

Pippa joined Wolfie at the cupboard entrance. It seemed like the pipe from the tank had burst at the join. There was some clutter at the bottom of the cupboard; mostly dusty boxes and as Wolfie pulled them out, Pippa had an idea. She hurried to the bathroom and fetched old towels from the storage bin in there, placing them at the foot of the leaking tank to protect the floor. But then a large pipe that ran parallel to the boiler began to make ominous noises too and Wolfie winced.

"That's a wastewater pipe," he said with a groan. "If *that* goes ..."

"Here." Pippa advanced with a stiff bath sheet poised to tie around the shaky wastewater pipe joint. "We can just—"

"Whoa!" Wolfie held her back.

"What?"

"You have an open cut on your finger," he said impatiently. "If any dirty water gets on it, you could get an infection."

"It's fine!" Pippa said dismissively. She'd wrapped several large plasters around the bandage he'd given her to protect herself when gardening. "I was muck spreading this morning and it's totally secure."

"Muck spreading?" Wolfie grimaced as he took the bath sheet and wadded it around the noisy pipe.

"Just a little garden project." Pippa tried to be nonchalant about it, but she couldn't hide the glow of excitement.

Wolfie nodded, somewhat disconsolately. "I see."

"That is okay, isn't it?" Pippa panicked at the idea she was over-extending her welcome. "You didn't seem to mind me having a go at sorting the maze…"

"Do what you want," he said. "It was Joan's patch, that's all. I swear she could turn one tomato plant into a thousand. Chuck us another towel, would you?"

"Here." Pippa handed him a towel. "Speaking of tomatoes, do you remember the Bloody Mary things Joan made for one of the fairs? My dad got so tiddly on those."

"Remember?" Wolfie said. "I had so many of those cocktails I threw up. I'm still not a fan of tomatoes even now."

"You threw up?" His confession made Pippa oddly happy. She realised she wasn't the only person to make a fool of herself from time to time.

"It *was* my fault," he went on. "I had no business drinking them at fifteen. God, she was cross."

"Did she make a lot of things from the vegetable patch?" Pippa asked.

His eyes brightened as he wadded more towels around the pipe. "Tons. Feeding people was her passion. And my grandfather loved her like a sister, so he let her grow whatever she wanted out there." A soft smile spread across his face, making his chiselled features less severe. "I remember she would always have heaps of courgettes every season, more than she knew what to do with."

"My mum was the same!" Pippa laughed. "As a kid I ate so many stews with courgette as the main ingredient, I'm surprised my skin didn't turn green."

"Joan was genius with them though," Wolfie said. "She ended up making courgette cakes with them, way before it was fashionable. God, they were good."

It didn't escape Pippa's notice that Wolfie was talking about Joan the way she spoke about her mum. "Sounds like Joan means a lot to you."

"Yes. Well." Wolfie folded his arms in a clear attempt to maintain composure, but Pippa could see the wounded look in his eyes.

"Parkinsons is a bitch," Pippa said sympathetically.

"It is," Wolfie agreed. "The dementia is just starting to kick in now..." He exhaled, eyes shining. "Not sure what's worse."

"My uncle had dementia."

Wolfie looked at Pippa sharply. "He did?"

"Yep."

Wolfie swallowed. "How did it...? I mean, how did it go, in the end?"

"It was a bad time. Early onset, you see." Pippa had the strangest sensation that Wolfie was very much hanging on to her words and it was as intoxicating as it was discomfiting. "I was only a teenager – it's all kind of fuzzy now – but it was so awful to feel that helpless as someone you love just ... vanishes." She ducked her head. It wasn't *entirely* fuzzy. It had been quite simply one of the most horrendous times of her life. Uncle Jack reduced to a shell and needing round-the-clock care. Aunty Pauline barely able to get out of bed, such was the weight of her grief. And *Frankie*. His suffering had been seismic.

"I'm so sorry you went through that." A corner of his mouth lifted. "But it's nice to talk to someone who understands."

Pippa had never considered that she might have something in common with the likes of Wolfie Squires, but here was an area of commonality where she'd least expected it.

"You can talk to me any time you like," she said softly.

Wolfie nodded his thanks and his bright blue eyes flicked to her mouth yet again. Instinctively, Pippa licked her lips and Wolfie's gaze tracked her tongue. Pippa knew she wasn't imagining the way his breath sped up, the charge in his eyes, just as she knew she wasn't imagining the heat pooling deep within her, the low ache between her thighs. Wolfie took a step towards her, something unnameable burning underneath that intensely still face. He opened his mouth and—

"Has it stopped?" Mae reappeared at the top of the stairs, causing Pippa to jump so hard she winced. "That stopcock took an age. It was a bastard to twist, but the water should be off now." Pippa turned back to Wolfie but he'd moved away to inspect the pipes.

"Looks like it," he replied. He withdrew from the cupboard and gestured to the floor. "I'll clean this mess up. Can you call a plumber?"

"O-of course. I know exactly the woman." Pippa fought to get the words out. Linda Cornish had fixed most of Goodman's Farm's ancient pipework; she was more than qualified. Once back in the dry sanctuary of the kitchen, Pippa began searching her phone for Linda's number.

"Are we going to talk about what just happened?" Mae asked archly.

Pippa composed a hasty text to Linda and shoved her phone in her pocket, avoiding Mae's stare. "It's an old house, Mae. Plumbing emergencies are to be expected."

"Give over." Mae tilted her head, snagging Pippa's attention. "You know that's not what I mean."

"I really don't," Pippa said innocently.

"Oh Pip, come on! I left you and Wolfie alone for two minutes!" She smirked. "I come back upstairs and the pair of you were like, seconds from tearing each other's clothes off."

"No we weren't!" Pippa retorted.

"You were panting," Mae said wickedly.

"That's an exaggeration!" Pippa blushed.

"No, it's not," Mae asserted. "What's more, that man was looking at you like he wanted to ravish you. Trust me on this."

Pippa shook her head. Now the heat of the moment had passed, she wasn't sure if what she'd felt was real. If she'd imagined the intensity of Wolfie's gaze. "He'd just told me something really personal," she said. "I was merely trying to be a friend."

"A friend? To Wolfie Squires?" Mae was disbelieving. "The man who makes Dobermans look approachable?"

"He's not that bad," Pippa protested. "He wanted to make sure I didn't get my injured finger exposed to wastewater, that's all." She showed off her bandage.

"Oh, did he?" Mae gave her a knowing look. "How very Knight in Shining Armour of him."

"Shut up," Pippa groaned. Her phone began to vibrate in her pocket. Expecting to see Linda's name on the screen, she pulled out her phone. And then dropped it on the table.

Alex Goodman.

Mae clocked it and pulled a face, jabbing at the red call-end button as if poking a venomous snake with a stick. "What the fuck?"

Pippa thudded down into her chair. Why was he calling? It had been months of radio silence and it had started to feel like she had turned a corner. But now, Alex was for some reason, forcing his way back in. The phone started up once more and Pippa watched, paralysed with indecision.

"Why is he calling?" she croaked. "What does he want?"

"You won't know until you talk to him," Mae said softly. "Which, personally, I don't advise."

Pippa's insides churned. The anguish of those early post-breakup days reared its head again and it was then she realised how far she'd come. How little he'd crossed her mind of late. Losing Alex had been like losing her rudder and the mere visual of his name on her phone brought that loss screaming back. She couldn't bear it. "What do I do? What if something's wrong with him?"

Mae threw up her hands. "Then he'll have to handle it like a big boy. Which, God knows, he never had to do that when you were around." The phone stopped ringing and Pippa felt like she could breathe again. They waited, eyes glued to the phone. A voicemail notification popped up.

"Shall I listen?" Pippa asked.

"Up to you." Mae's eyes darkened. "I know what I'd do."

Pippa pulled the phone towards her and pressed play.

"Pippa. Please. Call me."

Pippa gaped. "Is that it?" True, Alex wasn't the chattiest of men, but after everything they'd been through together, Pippa felt she merited more than four words on a voicemail.

"What are you going to do?" Mae asked.

Pippa thought for a moment, then leaned over and hit *delete*.

Chapter Fourteen

The month of June advanced relentlessly and Pippa's days were full of caring for the house and garden as well as organising the fair. She was grateful. It stopped her from dwelling too much on Alex's unilluminating voicemail. But today, she'd checked the calendar and realised that he'd called on the anniversary of their first ever date. Coincidence? She wasn't sure. But just as she'd felt she was turning a corner; Alex had reared his head again, threatening the peace she'd so valiantly created for herself. Those four words on the voicemail strummed through her mind, mocking her. Months without contact and that was all she got? An instruction to call like she was some kind of employee.

Her phone buzzed and she checked it anxiously, sighing with relief that it wasn't Alex, just a text from Frankie. She had hoped that it was Mr Rogers from Pigs in Clover. She had been pursuing the upmarket butcher to purchase a stall for the Summer Fair, with little luck so far. They would be a perfect candidate for a premium spot on the green, but Mr Rogers wasn't returning her calls. Pippa couldn't deny a twinge of guilt though, as Juniper was fast becoming one of her favourite sights around the garden. The sassy swine had taken a liking to breaking into Squires's Garden and was especially fond of rootling around Pippa's fledgling vegetable garden for treats. Pippa was tackling it as best she could; however, there was scant advice out there on how to protect them from half-ton rare-breed pigs, even in the dusty old gardening books she'd rescued from Squires's library. She'd ended up cobbling together something from old chicken wire found in the shed and fallen branches harvested from the wreck of the maze.

So far, it was working. Hilariously, it seemed like Juniper had taken her efforts to protect the vegetables as a personal challenge and visited more often than not, butting her snout into the wire mesh petulantly. Whilst the vegetable patch was doing very well, the maze was another story. Pippa had attempted to clear the weeds there several times, but the task seemed never-ending, with the weeds regrowing quicker than she was able to keep on top of them.

Wolfie hadn't been around much in the past week either. The last time they'd spoken, he'd muttered something about being needed in London and Pippa could only presume that he was with his girlfriend, the one he was selling this place off to please. So, it was a little surprising to hear Wolfie's voice that morning as she knelt in the dirt, pulling up the pesky weeds that had sprung up overnight. Wolfie emerged into the garden, accompanied by a short, ruddy-faced man in a shiny suit.

"...so, yes, on a good day you can see clear across the moors," Wolfie was saying as they approached Pippa.

"Simply stunning," the man commented. "You can't buy a view like that. Well,"—he elbowed Wolfie with a wink—"obviously someone can."

"Quite." Wolfie agreed. "As you can see Clough Hill is nearby. A local landmark – great hikes." Pippa rolled her eyes. Funny how Wolfie could be so complimentary about the place when he was looking to sell up.

The visitor caught sight of Pippa and snorted. "Speaking of stunning views..." He ambled over. "Lovely to meet you, my dear. Percival Smart."

"Hello." Pippa rose to her feet and shook his hand, cringing at how it managed to be both rough and clammy all at the same time. "Pippa Munro," she said. "Are you looking to buy this place?"

"Oh no." Percival flicked back his oily grey hair. "I'm the surveyor."

A chill ran through Pippa's bones. A surveyor. Could that mean a sale was agreed? She caught Wolfie's eye, and he had the decency to look a little regretful. "I see."

"Yes. I do a lot of land surveys." The man preened. "For some of the biggest and best corporations in the country."

"And who is today's client?" Pippa asked boldly. She caught a warning glare from Wolfie, but she didn't like the way Percival was eyeing up the property. Like it was something to be torn apart and devoured.

"Ah, confidential." Percival tapped his nose then his eyes widened. "I say, is that a maze?"

"It is," Wolfie said. "Unsubstantiated rumour is that my great-great-grandfather copied a Capability Brown design."

"It's not an actual Brown maze, is it?" Percival barked.

"No." Wolfie shook his head.

"Phew." Percival pretended to mop his brow. "Because if so, it would be protected, and you don't need me to tell you why that would be a disaster. By the way, that gravel driveway out front ... I have some concerns about the aggregate underneath. Looks like some sagging."

"I'll look into it," Wolfie said sombrely.

"And those trees worry me." Percival clearly meant the towering Cypress trees that lined the front drive. "Their root systems can be extensive and damaging – need to tear 'em down. But no matter!" He bared large yellowing teeth in what might have been a smile. "All fixable issues."

Pippa thought she'd explode with the heartbreak. Percival was casually discussing the total destruction of this beautiful old place, dissecting it like it was devoid of any worth aside from the scenery. Furthermore, because she'd not known about this visit, she hadn't been able to prepare another off-putting stunt like the manure heap, which Todd had reluctantly moved after Wolfie threatened him with lawyers.

Just then, Percival started, his eyes bugging as he looked at something behind Pippa. "What on earth is that?"

Pippa turned and couldn't hide her laughter. Good old Juniper was bearing down on the vegetable patch with such determination she looked almost human. "It's only Juniper," she assured the man. "She doesn't mean any harm."

"Can they not keep that blasted pig in a sty?" Wolfie groaned. "Damned thing treats my garden like her own private space." But Pippa swore she could see a glint of amusement in those eyes of his. Percival, however, was less relaxed about being so close to a hungry Tamworth and was backing away. Juniper, oblivious to Percival's fear, made her way towards the corner of the vegetable patch he was next to. This had a dramatic impact on Percival. Throwing his hands up in the air, he let out a deafening bellow.

"Shoo!" Percival yelled, running away. "Shoo!" The noise clearly startled the poor pig, who let out a panicked squeal and began to run. Unfortunately for Percival, her flight interrupted his trajectory. Man and pig collided. Juniper, being almost a half-ton of solid flesh, was thankfully unscathed but Percival flew over her and landed square in the middle of the vegetable patch, bringing Pippa's makeshift pig-guard down around him. Furious, Percival jumped to his feet, ripping up two of the raspberry canes and brandishing them before him in a demented attempt at defence.

"Hey!" Pippa had never moved so fast in her life. "Put those down! She won't hurt you!" She manoeuvred herself between Percival and Juniper.

"What is the meaning of this?" Percival roared at her. "Wild animals roaming the place? Attacking innocent bystanders?"

"Does she look like a wild animal?" Pippa scolded. Juniper plodded around her to reach the now churned-up vegetable patch and began to placidly nose at the earth. "You scared her!"

"She's vicious. You saw that!" Percival gestured at Wolfie. "Come on, back me up here! The pig went for me."

Wolfie regarded Percival with his trademark assessing stare, then flicked his gaze to Pippa who met it defiantly. Wolfie folded his arms. "Juniper is trespassing, I grant you that, but she meant no harm."

Percival's face turned bright red. "Trespas—! Of all the nonsense." He swiped at his clothes in a feeble attempt to rid them of stinking mulch, but he was coated. "I can't possibly recommend this location for development if there are wild pigs roaming around. I could be sued."

"For the second time, she's not wild!" Pippa snapped. "She's free-spirited."

Percival tossed his head back regally, a move incongruous with his now dishevelled state. "This place is a nightmare."

"Steady on," Wolfie said. "Let's get you cleaned up so you can finish."

Percival waved a hand. "I think I've seen enough," he sneered. "Let's not forget I'm an expert. I know what my recommendations to the client will be. I'll see myself out." And with that, he stormed off.

Wolfie levelled Pippa with an icy gaze. "Well, that was quite something."

"What was?"

Wolfie's lips thinned further. "I don't even want to guess at how you trained that pig to come charging at us like tha—"

"Wait, whoa, I didn't train her to do anything!" Pippa interrupted. As if anyone could train Juniper to do anything that wasn't her own idea. "He scared her, you saw."

"I know you don't think I should sell up, but seriously?" Wolfie's voice was tight with exasperation. "Do you honestly think these childish games will stop me from getting what I want?"

There was a sensual menace laced through his words that Pippa found hard to dismiss. Pippa lifted her chin and met his gaze, squarely. "It's not childish to struggle to understand how someone could dismiss something so beautiful as if it means nothing." She sounded angrier than she had intended and Wolfie looked at her in alarm. Pippa took a breath. Maybe after everything Alex had put her through, she was overly sensitive. But Pippa knew she had a point, one that was shared by most of the citizens of Hurst Bridge.

Now it was Wolfie's turn to look vulnerable. "God, all I hear is how beautiful this house is. How meaningful." He shook his head, jamming his hands in his pockets. "Beautiful doesn't mean perfect, you know."

"I never said it did," Pippa retorted.

"It's a house," Wolfie went on. "A simple house. Nothing special about it."

"Maybe not to you." Pippa shrugged. "But perhaps if you opened your eyes for a moment, you might see what I see. You might see what's special."

Wolfie's lips thinned but he didn't reply. He merely stood, staring as if waiting for her to say more. Pippa didn't trust herself to meet that intense gaze of his, so she turned to inspect the vegetable patch, where Juniper was happily nuzzling around. Pippa looked at the bruised leaves amidst churned-up soil, the exposed roots with raw green flesh poking through torn skin. It had taken Percival mere seconds to damage days of hard work. Pippa's throat clogged with emotion.

"I mean, take that Percival guy," she blurted suddenly, startling Wolfie. "There's someone who doesn't stop to think about what's important. So quick to lash out he didn't even think about the devastation he left behind." Pippa knew she was ranting about more than just the vegetable patch, but it was like something had unlocked inside her and the words poured from somewhere deep and painful. "A person puts in all that effort, all that sacrifice, and it ends up being treated like total crap."

Wolfie stepped forward. "I'm not sure I un—"

But she wasn't done. "And a voicemail. A fucking voicemail after all this time. He thinks that I'll let him back in, after giving over a decade of myself and waiting for my life to truly begin *like a sap!*"

"I'm not sure what's going on here, but you aren't a sap," Wolfie said softly, his well-meaning tenderness like salt on a wound.

"Well, Alex treated me like one." The adrenaline ebbed away, leaving Pippa breathless and red-faced. But it had felt good to say the words out loud, to send them soaring across the open skies of the moorland where they could dissipate. It was a freeing, *final* feeling. After all, if Alex hadn't done what he did, would Pippa still be stuck in a cycle of work and elder care without a moment for herself? Was it entirely possible Alex had done her a favour? Pippa laughed, causing Wolfie to look more alarmed.

"You all right?" he asked.

Pippa nodded, dazed. "I think I feel ... the best I have in a long time," she said. Excusing herself, she hurried inside to get her phone. Frankie needed to hear all about this.

Chapter Fifteen

"It's settled," Frankie crowed down the phone to her. "Let's party! The sun is shining, we're young and carefree ... plus, you know there's no better place to pick up men than The Halfpenny."

"Hey, I said I want to have some fun, not pick up men!" Pippa repeated yet again. After her revelation about Alex, Pippa was in the mood to let her hair down and so Frankie had promptly invited her out on the town with him and Theo that very night. Although Frankie seemed to think that Pippa's emotional breakthrough indicated she was ready to hook up with a new man, which was not the point. "Like I said, I'm feeling like I've made some progress on myself, not that I'm ready to start a new relationship yet."

"Who's talking about relationships?" Frankie snorted. "I'm suggesting a casual snog, maybe some PG-13 over-the-clothes dry-humping. Surely, you're ready for a gentle, non-accidental boob-graze? How long has it been since you had some action?"

Pippa tried very hard not to picture Wolfie in that instant. "Never you mind," she said. "I was with the same guy for, like, ever. I wouldn't even know how to pick up a man if he stood naked in front of me and offered me the keys to a forklift."

"Have you seen yourself?" Frankie demanded. "You are a five-foot-two *bombshell*. Just stand in the middle of the room, you'll soon have men crawling all over you."

"Maybe that's how *you* pick up men," Pippa shot back. "Us mere mortals have to make some effort."

"Are you wearing that booby dress?" Frankie countered.

"Don't call it that," she hissed. But for want of a better word, yes, Pippa was wearing the white sundress Alex had once made fun of, back when she was his to be mocked. It was a little fancy, but perfect for a sun-drenched evening enjoying drinks with friends. It seemed apt to wear it, the way she was feeling. "I'm in the booby dress," she said.

"And wear some lippie," Frankie advised.

"You aren't the boss of me," Pippa grumbled, but she picked up her ancient lipstick and swiped some creamy pink across her lips. The amount of time she'd spent in the outdoors recently had dusted her skin with a healthy glow, making her pale eyes pop. She'd slid a couple of grips into her unruly waves to hold them back from her face and by the time Pippa had slipped on her soft leather sandals, she felt like a different woman. She felt womanly, and for the first time in ages, sexy. "This could be fun," she said.

"Can't wait," Frankie said. "You catching the bus?"

Pippa checked her watch. "Shit." The bus to Sheffield would be leaving soon, so she needed to move. She bade goodbye to Frankie and excitedly made her way downstairs.

As she approached the bottom of the staircase, Wolfie strode in from the hall, staring down at his phone. At the sound of her footsteps, he glanced up.

"Ah, Pippa, did you—" He halted in his tracks.

"Something wrong?" Pippa hurried down the last few steps.

"Ahm. No." Wolfie gulped. "Everything's fine."

"Okay. Great." Pippa waited for him to say something back but he seemed stricken, as if caught in headlights. That or he was about to be violently sick. "Anything else?"

His eyebrows jumped. "Well, um, actually..." He cleared his throat and cricked his neck. He opened his mouth then shut it. Pippa was wondering if he was quite all right when he suddenly blurted somewhat loudly, "Did you manage to water the plants in the pots out front? They looked a little wilted earlier."

Pippa was bewildered. Did he really need to yell? "Yup," she said. "I did them twice today. Because of the sun."

"Great, good." Wolfie nodded. He seemed to be waiting for something. Pippa arched an eyebrow to urge him on; she had a bus to catch after all. "You, ah, you look nice."

"Oh." Pippa blushed, smoothing down the skirt fabric and ignoring the warm glow that a compliment from Wolfie gave her. "Perhaps it's a little much for a few drinks in Sheffield."

"No, no," Wolfie corrected her with a small smile. "I'd say it's just enough, Pippa Munro."

"Enough for what?" she replied with a grin, then clamped her lips shut. Was this flirting? Was that what they were doing? "I mean, thanks," she said stiffly. The man had a girlfriend, for crying out loud. "I've got to get the bus," she babbled. "Have a good evening."

"You don't want a lift?" Wolfie called after her as she reached the door.

"Are you offering me one?" Pippa imagined being alone in a car with Wolfie Squires and the air suddenly got that little bit more difficult to breathe. She fought to keep her breathing regular as a corner of his mouth quirked.

"Yes," he said patiently.

"Why?"

Wolfie rolled his eyes, exasperated. "I'm looking out for you, that's all. A pretty girl, out on her own, wearing a nice dress ... it can attract the wrong kind of attention."

He thinks I'm pretty, was the first thought that danced across Pippa's mind. But his protectiveness chafed, and she pushed away the languorous wave of delight his words elicited. "I'll be all right," she said. "The purity police aren't patrolling tonight – I checked."

"Haha," he said dryly. "I mean, there are idiots out there."

"Thanks for your concern," Pippa said politely. "But I can look after myself."

"I know that. I saw the way you handled Percival Smith." Irritation creased Wolfie's face and Pippa silently fumed. That Smith man had been odious, and she wasn't about to apologise for standing up to him. Although it seemed Wolfie wished she would. He glared at her. "Look, do you want a lift or not?"

Pippa lifted her chin. "Thanks, but no thanks." And with a prim nod, she scurried outside into the sunshine.

"I literally don't get that man!" Pippa signalled the barman again. "He offers me a lift whilst being a dick about the way I behaved with the awful surveyor man today."

"He sounds pretty chivalrous to me," Theo said, finishing the dregs of his pint. He looked especially gorgeous, showing off his muscular body in a fitted shirt and jeans. "And he's not wrong. Pretty lasses have been known to get bothered on public transport."

"Well, not me." Pippa shrugged. "I had a perfectly uneventful journey." She finally got the barman's attention and ordered the same drinks again. The Halfpenny was packed, with gentle soft-rock music coming from a three-piece guitar band in the corner. Despite the crowd, the friends had found seats at the bar where they could talk in comfort.

"Hang on, I think we're missing the critical point here," Frankie said. "Wolfie said you were pretty, right? He then offered you a lift into Sheffield. Hello?" He gaped, his hands spread wide. "The man clearly has a crush!"

"God, you sound like Mae," Pippa groaned.

"Oh, well, case closed." Frankie dusted his hands with a smirk. "If Mae's noticed something then I must be right."

Pippa gulped her wine. Wolfie had definitely reacted

when he'd clocked her coming down the stairs, there was no doubt. "I'm always dressed like a slob or covered in cleaning products when he sees me," she said. "He was probably shocked I even owned a dress like this, let alone had occasion to wear one."

"I don't know," Theo said. "Frankie makes a compelling case."

"Thanks, babe," Frankie cooed.

Babe? Pippa mouthed at her cousin. When had Theo progressed to 'babe' status? Frankie merely smiled secretively. "Well, it's all moot," she said, shooting Frankie a look that said *this isn't over*. "He's got a girlfriend."

"You've met her?" Theo asked.

"No, but, I'm fairly sure—"

"Ah!" Frankie pounced. "Fairly sure isn't sure. You could be wrong."

"I heard him on the phone." Pippa's cheeks heated. "He was all gaga, talking about how he wanted to sell Squires to please her, that she deserved it."

Frankie took a contemplative sip of his wine. "Could you have misunderstood?"

"I don't see how," Pippa answered. Frankie's knowing grin riled her and so she sat up straight. "What does it matter anyway?" she huffed. "He's selling the place no matter what. I'll be homeless again and out of his life soon enough."

"Such a shame he's selling," Theo sympathised. "You'll have to let me visit sometime before that happens."

"For sure!" Pippa enthused. "As payment, I'll rope you into helping organise the Summer Fair."

"Hey, anything for Frankie's family." Theo winked at her, then excused himself to go to the bathroom. The moment he was out of earshot, Pippa whirled on Frankie.

"Okay, you have a minute to explain."

Frankie assumed an air of innocence. "Explain?"

"Um, *babe*?" Pippa repeated. "Got something to tell me, *babe*?"

"Oh, that." Frankie was enjoying himself. "Yeah ... we might be kind of seeing each other."

Pippa grabbed his arm in delight. "Finally! How did it happen?"

Frankie preened. "Oh, you know, I was merely my usual charming self." Then he softened. "Actually, I cooked him a roast dinner one weekend. Sank a bottle of red and then, well, things kind of happened. He's *soooo* funny, Pip. And clever. You know he got his Master's at Oxford?"

"You don't need to sell him to me," Pippa said. "I like him. I do! Although he *is* your roommate. Isn't that a bit risky?"

"Maybe." Frankie's smile was uncontrollable. "But he's put an offer in on a house up Hunter's Bar, so he'll be moving out soon anyway. That takes the pressure off a bit."

Pippa gave his arm another squeeze. "I've never seen you so dreamy over a man," she said.

"Well, most of my previous love interests have been severely lacking on the interest side," Frankie said.

"Oh, I don't know, the fellow who practised taxidermy on roadkill was interesting," Pippa mused. "Not to mention the guy who listed weapons as a hobby." She glared at her cousin. "Weapons! And yet you still swiped right."

"You know what I mean." Frankie rolled his eyes. "Theo is different. It feels different."

"I'm only teasing," Pippa told him. "I'm really happy for you."

"Me too." Frankie studied her over the rim of his glass. "Now, anything new with you besides seducing handsome and mysterious mansion owners like something out of a Brontë novel?"

Pippa chose to ignore the jibe about Wolfie by sticking out her tongue. "No, my life is still an utter shambles." Then she froze, her glass halfway to her mouth. "Actually. Something did happen. Alex called me," she said.

Frankie's face hardened. "He did *what*?"

"He tried to call me. I didn't answer." Pippa's hand strayed to her bag where her phone waited, as if it would ring again. She relayed the exact message Alex had left.

"What, that's it? No apology? No explanation?" Frankie growled as Pippa confirmed with a nod. "Prick."

"It did throw me for a loop," Pippa admitted.

"And how do you feel about it now?" Frankie asked. "Because when you called earlier you sounded like … well, the old Pippa." He beamed. "Like, full of verve the way you used to be."

"I think I'm okay," she replied honestly.

"Promise?" Frankie set his glass down. "Because it was only a couple of months ago that I couldn't prise you off my couch thanks to that waster."

"Really promise." Pippa felt lighter just saying the words. "I'm not saying I'm 100 per cent over what Alex did, but I'm moving past it. I can see my life without him in it now. And I'm happy about the way it looks."

Frankie looped an arm across her shoulders and dropped a kiss on her forehead. "Then I'm thrilled."

Theo reappeared. "Another drink?" he asked.

"Absolutely!" Frankie cheered. "She's back on the market!"

"No, that's not what I'm saying." Pippa tutted as Theo tried to catch the barman's eye. "And only one more for me," she went on. "I have to be up early for a meeting about the Summer Fair."

"Boring!" Frankie chimed.

"No, it isn't." Pippa nudged him. "It's fun!"

"If you say so." Frankie teased. "Now drink up and let's see how many phone numbers you can score."

Chapter Sixteen

Pippa slid out of the taxi with a very unladylike hiccup. The 'one more drink' had turned into three more drinks and she'd left Theo and Frankie to head on to a nightclub together. It was past eleven and, if she was to meet Erin and Mae for breakfast, then sobering up and sleep was needed.

"Water," she told herself as she opened the front door. "Pints and pints of water." As she locked the door behind her, she was aware of beautiful music echoing through the house. Pippa cocked her head. Was that ... piano? Curiosity thudded through her as she recognised the tune as a classical piece, one she'd heard recently on a TV advert. Forgetting her need for water, Pippa followed the sound, creeping across the hall to the library.

The room was dim, lit only by a small lamp in the corner that cast a soft golden light around it. The tarp covering the piano had been tossed to the floor and there, hunched over the keys, was Wolfie, playing a solemn melody that was all at once dark and lovely, like a letter to someone long lost. Wolfie's body was tilted away from her and so Pippa leaned against the doorway, taking the opportunity to observe him unseen. He was completely abandoned to the music, his blond thatch of hair rumpled, like he'd run frustrated hands through it many times. His T-shirt was so thin she could see the muscles in his back rippling as his hands played up and down the keys, his head bobbing in time. There was something about the intensity of his movements, the way he swayed with the rhythm; it was as if the music was being pulled from somewhere deep and painful within his soul. The music trailed off and he reached for a whisky that rested atop the piano. After a large gulp, his long fingers returned to the piano and started a different tune.

"Oh, I know this one!" Pippa blurted and with a discordant blare, Wolfie's fingers slipped off the piano. He turned to glare at her. "'Ain't No Sunshine'," she said weakly. His eyes were almost black in the half-light. "Sorry for disturbing. You're really good," she went on. "Like, professional level."

Wolfie pulled his gaze away from her and picked up his drink, swirling what remained of the amber liquid. "Fun night?"

Pippa grinned. "Yeah, it was. How about you?"

Wolfie considered her question. "I had about as much fun as one can, rattling around this relic by myself."

Pippa's buoyant mood instantly crashed in the face of such grumpiness. Fuelled by her multiple wines, Pippa spoke without filter. "Don't you get fed up being so miserable?" she asked.

The House Sitter

Wolfie blinked. "Who says I'm miserable?"

"Well, your face, for one thing," Pippa retorted.

"Charming," he tutted.

"Look. I'm sure your life is all hearts and rainbows away from this house." She pushed back the flare of jealousy at the mere thought of the woman Wolfie was selling the house for. "But when you're here you're always so gloomy."

"So, because I don't skip around this house full of nostalgic joy about my childhood, I'm 'gloomy'?" Wolfie cracked.

"Well, yeah." Pippa nodded. "For someone who hates this place so much, you sure are here a lot."

Wolfie gazed at her intently. "Well, that's because..." He let out a long sigh and shook his head. "Listen. I'm selling the place. So of course I'm here more than normal. I have to oversee everything."

Pippa wrinkled her nose. "There are these people called agents, you know. You pay them to take that responsibility off your hands."

"True." Wolfie regarded her stonily. "But for some reason I feel compelled to take on that responsibility."

"Because you care so much about this place?" Pippa rolled her eyes. "Please. You didn't bat an eye when that surveyor bloke trampled all over the garden and ruined all my hard work."

A muscle flickered in Wolfie's cheek. "I consider it a duty," he said.

"A duty to, what, stamp and moan like a spoilt brat?" The words left her mouth before she could stop them. Before she could apologise, Wolfie let out a bark of laughter.

"A brat? You think I'm a brat?" He stood, flexing his arms. "Let's see. My father gambled away much of the money my grandfather left us and didn't even have the decency to keep his paws off my mother's own inheritance. He then had the temerity to bloody well die before sorting out his debts. Meanwhile this place?" He waved around him. "Is falling down around my ears and my salary, good as it is, barely keeps the lights on. We need the money more than we need to worry about the hurt feelings of a few local people." Wolfie snickered. "My father was not a good man, and because of him, this house was never a home, at least not to me."

He swallowed the last drop of his whisky and stalked towards her. As his powerful form approached, Pippa felt every hair on the back of her neck rise, every nerve and every cell spring to attention. Her breath sped up; her heart thudded. Wolfie stopped in front of her, his eyes boring into hers. He smelled of whisky and leather, of clean cotton and fresh lime. It was intoxicating. "Tell me, do you understand me now, Pippa Munro?"

Pippa's lips were suddenly dry. When she licked them, Wolfie's gaze followed the motion yet again. Was she imagining a hunger in his eyes? Or had the copious wines she'd consumed in town begun to cultivate delusions?

"I'm not sure a woman could ever fully understand you," she said shakily, although in that moment she fervently wished to be the one that did.

Wolfie dragged his stare away from her mouth. "Trust me when I say a woman like you wouldn't be able to."

His tone was so acidic that Pippa actually had to take a

step back from him. "And what does that mean, *a woman like me?*"

He scowled at her. "Well, for one thing, I'd love to know when you intend to take those rose-tinted glasses off."

Pippa knew she'd drunk a lot that evening, but his words made no sense. "Rose-tinted...? What do you mean exactly?"

"This place! This *town*!" Wolfie gestured around him. "You talk as if it's made of gold or something. Like it's perfect."

"Nothing's perfect," Pippa said. She'd learned that much about life. "But as a place to live? Yeah, I think Hurst Bridge is the best. Beautiful town with lovely people ... what's not to like?"

"It's a small town, with a small-town mentality," he spat.

"Care to explain what *that* is?"

"The people here live for the gossip, the excitement, don't they?" His handsome face twisted in what looked like grief. "But they don't care what's beneath. What's really going on."

He has no idea, thought Pippa. If Wolfie spent any time with the people of this town he'd know he was wrong. He possessed a wilful ignorance about it. "Grantham cares about you, doesn't he? Joan too." Wolfie stilled, allowing her a tight nod. "So how can you say people don't care?"

"That pair aside, trust me when I say that people, as a rule, don't," Wolfie uttered darkly.

"Well, they probably would if you actually let them in," Pippa said. "You might be surprised."

Wolfie lifted fathomless eyes to hers. "And also, I might not."

Pippa didn't know what to say. All her life, she'd looked at this house, at the family name and wealth, and imagined a life that was so perfect it could only be unreal. Yet it was all too clear looking at this beautiful, broken man before her that that perfection had been a long-running and ugly facade. But Pippa couldn't be the one to fix that damage for him. She suddenly felt very tired. "You know what? I had the worst kind of heartbreak forced upon me this year," she said, her voice hoarse. "I lost everything. My home, my love. All of it. For the longest time I hid at my cousin's place—"

"You were hiding?" Wolfie interrupted.

"Yeah!" Pippa nodded. "I didn't know what the point of anything was. I had no future. It was like being on a long, painful road with no destination in sight and I couldn't face walking down it. But eventually I did. I had to." Pippa's own words resonated around her brain. Because despite the wine fog, she knew she was right. "And I'm so glad I did."

"Why?" Wolfie asked.

"Because it led me here," she said. Wolfie frowned and Pippa hurried to elaborate. "Every day has been hard. The trying, you know? But the trying is what got me off that stupid, pointless road and onto, like, a nice road. One with flowers and stuff. A road that's actually got a hope of leading me somewhere good." Wolfie's face remained impassive and Pippa suspected she sounded a bit waffly. "I'm happy," she clarified.

"Good for you," was all Wolfie said.

Pippa sighed. Maybe there really was no getting through to him and never would be. "If I were you, I'd appreciate all that you have in this moment. Because take it from me, there might come a day when it's all snatched away from you."

Wolfie stared at Pippa for one long second, his jewelled eyes unreadable. Just when she thought he might say something, his shoulders slumped, and he turned away from her. Dismissed, Pippa left the room and stomped up the stairs, frustrated and ready for bed.

From the depths of the library, the piano music resumed.

Chapter Seventeen

Pippa's head was sore, and the cockerel was not forgiving, his morning shrieks relentless. She'd lain painfully awake since dawn, desperately trying to get back to sleep but her throbbing head, along with the joyous cockerel, wouldn't let her. Had she really charged into the library and drunkenly forced Wolfie to open up about his torturous past? And what had all that nonsense about a road been? She shoved her head under the pillows, begging for peace, but her mind still churned with the memory of his pained face, interspersed with the occasional reminder of the way he looked when soaking wet and clad only in a towel. With a groan, Pippa wrested herself to a seated position and checked her phone, letting out another moan when her diary flashed a reminder for her meeting with Mae and Erin about the Summer Fair in a couple of hours. It was probably sensible to get caffeinated if ever she were to survive the day.

Conscious that Wolfie might still be lurking around the

house, Pippa made sure to brush her hair and teeth before venturing downstairs in sweatpants and a thick hoodie. She might have been desperate for a coffee, but she was just as keen not to look as hungover as she felt. As she trudged downstairs, she wondered if her drunken outburst had offended Wolfie. What if he asked her to leave as a result? She hoped she hadn't upset him too much, especially after he'd divulged some home truths about his father.

Pippa entered the kitchen, beelining straight for the kettle. As she touched it, apprehension took over; it was quite warm, clearly recently used. Her hackles went up; Wolfie was around. She fetched a mug and made coffee as quickly and quietly as possible. If she could just get her drink and hibernate upstairs until she felt ready to face him, that would be ideal. But as she turned to leave, movement in the garden caught her eye.

There, in the glory of the early morning sun, was Wolfie and he appeared to be … gardening? Pippa almost dropped her mug in shock when she realised that whatever it was that he was doing, he was doing it on her vegetable patch. He wore a mucky vest and tatty sweatpants, with dirt streaked through his hair. His task was clearly infuriating him; his cheeks were red, and Pippa could lipread the curses from where she stood. All thoughts of coffee forgotten, Pippa darted out of the kitchen and flitted across the lawn that was still damp with dew.

"What are you doing?" she demanded.

Wolfie started at the sight of her, dropping the huge fork with which he was wrestling.

"Morning!" He raked a hand through sweaty hair,

leaving trails of mud across his forehead. Panicked, Pippa looked down at the vegetable patch, praying he hadn't added to the damage that Percival had inflicted. Following her gaze, Wolfie was quick to explain. "Thought I'd try and make up for what that Smith fellow did. Repair the damage."

"You're *gardening*?" She choked out the words in surprise.

"Yes!" he said, then shrugged modestly. "At least, I'm attempting to."

"I didn't realise you knew anything about gardening," Pippa said curiously.

"I would have thought it's very obvious that I don't, despite Grantham's best efforts," Wolfie replied sheepishly. "But how hard can it be?" He reached into his back pocket and pulled out a battered old paperback. "Found this in the library and stayed up half the night reading it for tips." Pippa took the book from him. It wasn't one she'd read during her garden research.

"Mrs Meekin's Wartime Garden?" she read. "How to grow your own and defeat the enemy from the safety of home!"

Wolfie picked up the fork and plunged it into the soil. "I admit it's a little dated. But there were some useful tips in there. Great chapter on radishes."

Pippa wasn't sure if he was mocking her or not. "Why?" was all she could say.

Wolfie gulped. "Because I wanted to show you how sorry I am."

"Sorry?" she repeated.

"Last night." He folded his arms, hugging himself. "I was an arse."

His apology brought forth the crashing memory of their altercation in the library in all its glory and Pippa cringed so hard that she thought she'd turn inside out. "No, *I* should apologise," she said. "I should not be talking to you in that way."

"Why not?" Wolfie leaned on the fork. "You were merely speaking the truth. I appreciated your candour."

Pippa suddenly really wanted that coffee she'd abandoned in the kitchen. "By candour do you mean rudeness?" When Wolfie laughed, she pressed on. "Look, I'm sorry. You have valid reasons for wanting to get out of here and it's not my place to nag you about it."

"You gave me a lot to think about, Pippa Munro." Wolfie grinned and Pippa couldn't help but smile back, encouraged by the rare openness of his expression. The gaze held for a little too long and, conscious of her tired, make-up-free face, Pippa sought distraction.

"So, explain exactly what it is you've been doing here then?" she asked.

Wolfie coloured. "If we're being truthful, I'm not sure." He pointed at the raspberries. "Did I fix those canes right?"

Pippa nodded. "You did." Behind the canes she spied a snarl of chicken wire. "But that was serving as a cover to protect the berries from birds. That needs to go over the top."

Wolfie's face fell. "I thought so but I couldn't wrangle it into shape. It's pretty bashed up, I'm afraid."

"Let me have a look." Pippa picked up the twisted, filthy

wire. Thanks to Percival's panicking, it was virtually unusable. "Damnit," she whispered. Now she'd have to source something else to cover up the fruit.

"I was also a bit worried about those plants there." Wolfie gestured to the courgettes. Some of the leaves were bruised and torn.

"Hm." Pippa hovered over the plants. Her mother always used to praise courgettes for their ease of growth. Yorkshire provided plenty of rain and, thanks to Todd, they'd had lots of fertiliser. "We'll see, but I think they'll be fine. I bet there will be tons when it comes to picking them."

"That'll be soon, right?" Wolfie asked. "Joan always used to get a bumper crop around this time of year."

"I want to give them another week of fertiliser and hopefully more rain." Pippa pointed at the sky. "They've had a lot of sun. Then I'll pick a few, see how they're doing."

Wolfie leaned heavily on the fork, resting his head on his forearm as he gazed down at her. "And once they're out, then what?"

Pippa's mind went blank. She really hadn't considered what she would do with the fruits of her labour. She'd been so focused on getting the garden functioning and healthy, she hadn't actually imagined enjoying what came of that effort. "Um. Eat them?"

Wolfie laughed heartily. "I guess we'll be researching courgette cake recipes then."

Pippa laughed along with him, thrilling at his use of the word 'we'. "I'm not much of a baker, Wolfie."

"Maybe you don't get to lick the spoon, then." Wolfie's

lowered voice sent a thrill down Pippa's spine. She sat back on her heels, not breaking eye contact.

"You were right about one thing last night," Pippa said.

"And what's that, Pippa Munro?"

"I'm not sure I'll ever understand you," she replied.

A silence fell between them, punctuated by the haunting melody of curlews in flight. Wolfie didn't reply. He just dipped his head down, but not before she saw the shy smile and the spots of pink on his cheeks. She really wanted to know what was going on in his head. What he made of her. Why was he taking such an interest in the garden, all of a sudden? After all, he wanted to sell the whole property off to the highest bidder, right? Yes, he'd said he wanted to apologise for being harsh with her, but this sweet gesture was at odds with the grouchy man she'd encountered the night before.

The sound of her name being called startled Pippa and she looked over to see Todd frantically waving over the fence. The desperate look on his face had her up on her feet and over to the fence in seconds.

"What is it?" she called out.

"Juniper!" he declared. "Please tell me you've seen her."

"She's not in the garden." Wolfie had followed Pippa and was now standing behind her, and it took all her willpower not to lean back against his solid warmth.

"Has she escaped again?" Pippa tried to focus on her friend's distress and not Wolfie.

Todd's head bobbed up and down. "Ploughed right through the special fence I erected. I'm a bit worried she's headed out into the wilderness." He indicated up towards the moors.

"She's probably gone foraging or something," Pippa said calmly.

"Maybe." Todd wrung his hands. "But I woke up to find her pen empty. I'm not sure how long she's been gone. Could have been all night!"

"Okay, we need to look for her then," Pippa offered. "She can't have got far." But then she remembered the speed at which Juniper had raced around the garden yesterday and she shot Wolfie a look, hoping he'd see the concern in her eyes. It was entirely possible Juniper had travelled quite a long distance with such a head start.

"Thank you," Todd accepted. "Pat's checking the roads. I'll try the southern perimeter, but maybe you could check north?"

Pippa grimaced. "And north would be...?"

Wolfie, the former soldier, stepped in. "That way." He pointed downwards, towards the maze and to the moors beyond.

"Juniper loves a good rootle!" Todd called after them as they hurried off. "Look for disturbed earth!"

"Copy that!" Wolfie shouted back. He lowered his voice. "You promise this beast isn't vicious?"

Pippa laughed. "My experience of Miss Juniper is that, whilst she is feisty, she isn't aggressive."

"Got it." Wolfie didn't look convinced, however. It took merely a few seconds to see that Juniper hadn't ventured into the chaotic tangle of the maze, so they decided to head out to the open moorland. Wolfie led Pippa to the bottom of the garden where a high wall separated the Squires's property from the moors. A heavily cobwebbed and rusty door barely visible amidst the ivy creeping across the wall led directly onto a small trail that soon split off into various directions. They stopped and looked around. No Juniper in sight. Wolfie huffed. "Where do we think this pig will be then?"

Pippa thought. "Todd said she likes to rootle, which means ... soft soil, right?"

Wolfie shrugged. "She'll not find too much of that here." He stubbed the ground with his foot. "Ground is rock solid." But then his face brightened. "There is a little stream over that way." He pointed right, down a gentle heathered slope. "Maybe the ground will be to her liking there?"

"That's sound logic," Pippa said. "Let's try."

It didn't take long to traverse the slope. The air was sweet with the smell of heather and warm earth. A gentle breeze ruffled their hair. Soon the merry sound of trickling water became audible and, sure enough, they came across a sliver of a brook wending its way across the land. The ground was boggier and softer here, but there was no sign of a pig.

"Damn!" Pippa said. "Now what? Should we follow the water?"

"I think we need to put ourselves in the mind of a pig," Wolfie said in all seriousness. "Ask ourselves, what is Juniper's motivation?"

"Her motivation?" Pippa repeated in bemusement.

"You know. Food. Safety. Shade." He closed his eyes in apparent concentration and rubbed his temples as if trying to read Juniper's mind. "Where would I go, if I were Juniper?"

"Are you really trying to be at one with a pig?" Pippa asked.

"Well, someone has to *do* something," he deadpanned, but his mouth twitched.

"You're so weird when you want to be," Pippa said. She'd never seen this silly side of his humour before, and it looked good on him. "But seriously, where else might she go?"

Wolfie stopped still, rubbing his head. He looked around, thinking. "There's a little patch of birch trees further along," he said. "If we follow the stream this way, we'll find them. Probably all sorts of goodies there for a pig like that." He started walking and Pippa scurried to keep up.

"You really know your way around," Pippa said as they walked beside the stream. "Is that from all your running?"

"I suppose," Wolfie said. "But even as a child I'd spend all my time out here. Running, climbing, daydreaming. Anything to get away from my dad." He jammed his hands in his pockets. "I'm sure you got drilled on the dangers of the moors as a child, but I've always felt safe out here, then and now."

Pippa looked at him in surprise. "I had no idea."

He smiled down at her. "What, that I like the great outdoors?"

"No." She had to watch her step as the ground was a little marshy. "That there's at least one thing you like about this part of the world."

"I'm not a total monster," he said. "Oh, mind that bit." He pointed to a boggy patch, and they skirted it. "Look, there are the trees." He nodded ahead to where a cluster of birches huddled against the exposed moor. "Mind if I ask a question?"

Pippa gulped, her cheeks heating. She hadn't expected an interrogation. "If you'd like."

"Why *do* you love this town so much?" he asked. "You keep banging on about how special it is, and how Squires is the heart of it…" He shrugged. "Help me understand."

Pippa allowed the gentle breeze to cool her flaming cheeks. In all her years living in Hurst Bridge, she'd never had to clarify why she loved the town so much and being asked left her feeling raw. But something told her that Wolfie was exactly the person she should talk to about this. "I told you about my uncle, didn't I?"

"The one with dementia?" Wolfie asked. "Yes, you mentioned him."

"He died. Young." Wolfie didn't comment. "My Aunty Pauline fell to pieces. She couldn't even talk. Took to her bed for weeks. Mum and Dad were worried sick. And my cousin, Frankie…" Pippa's heart ached as she thought back to those days, to darling Frankie as a frightened teenager who had needed his mum more than he ever had before and she simply wasn't there. "It was an awful time, but this town rallied around him," she said. "Around both of them, actually, and it was like a miracle. My family obviously supported Frankie loads but my dad worked, and Mum had her hands full with Aunty Pauline. So, the neighbours stepped in. Made sure Frankie never had to worry about food or company. People would take turns to visit and do the laundry, run a hoover around. That sort of thing. For a time, he was a proper terror; skipping school and acting out. But this town showed him so much love. Even our teachers! They were so patient, visiting him at home, giving him free tutoring." Pippa stopped walking and raised damp eyes to Wolfie's. "This town saved my cousin in every way he needed to be and it's the most wonderful thing I've ever seen. Ever since then I've felt – I've *known* – I had to give something back."

Wolfie went very still. "I–I didn't realise," he said, so quietly Pippa could barely hear.

Pippa rubbed her eyes. "And Squires, yeah, I know it's only a house, but every summer the community would gather here and be happy and it always made me feel so secure, so grounded. Like, anything could happen, and this town would make it all right. Who wouldn't want to grow old and raise their kids in a town like that?"

"You want children?" was the quick question.

For some reason, Pippa wished she hadn't divulged that last bit about children. It felt so personal, putting out her fondest wish, one that had seemed certain to come true when she was with Alex. But Alex had rejected that life for something else and the fear that children might never happen was now very real. Facing that had sent her adrift and for a crazy moment she wished she could grab Wolfie's hand, so she could touch something solid and true. "I'd like to, one day," she admitted. "You?"

Wolfie was silent for a few moments. "I can't say I've given it much thought," he replied eventually.

Pippa didn't say anything. It didn't shock her. The biological clock moved at a different pace for men.

"Your parents emigrated, didn't they?" Wolfie changed the subject and Pippa was impressed with his memory.

"Yes," Pippa said. "They retired to Florida. Something my dad always wanted."

"So, *they* left." It wasn't a question, but entirely understandable given Pippa's devotion to the town.

"They did," she said. "Thing is, they had me young. They didn't have much money and it was tough; my dad worked all the hours. That meant no big holidays, no adventures. It was always my dad's dream from a young age to live abroad, so they made up for the lack of holidays when he retired."

"Was it your mum's dream?"

Pippa exhaled. She'd never even considered that aspect. Her parents were so in sync, so loving, that when they announced their emigration, Pippa had presumed it was a wholly mutual ambition. "Honestly, I don't know. But she really enjoys living out there. I suppose when you love someone enough, all you need is to be where they are." And the irony of her words hit Pippa squarely in the gut. Her legs became heavy, and her heart thudded in her chest as she inwardly repeated her own words back to herself.

"What's wrong?" Wolfie's face contorted in alarm, and he gripped her shoulder. "You've gone terribly pale."

Pippa searched Wolfie's face. How was it that after all this time apart from Alex, she had only now stumbled upon the truth of their break-up? The thing that twisted her conscience every time she thought of him. Why hadn't she seen it? She and Alex had created a home together and that should have been enough for him. Yet the reality was it also hadn't been enough for *her*. Because surely, if it had, she would have followed him to Kent. She would have found a way to stay with him. Waves of an unnamed emotion washed over her. Relief? Pity? Pippa didn't know. She also didn't know why those roiling emotions ebbed away when she looked at Wolfie, leaving a welcome stillness.

But Wolfie wasn't looking back at her. He had turned towards the trees, his face lit up. "Hang on, isn't that our missing pig?"

Pippa was glad then that he wasn't looking at her. Because that earlier need to reach for his hand was intensifying into something more urgent and Wolfie might have recognised it. And that prospect was terrifying. She tried to calm her ragged breathing and followed Wolfie's gaze. Sure enough, Juniper could be seen gambolling amongst the trees, stopping every now and then for a root.

"Thank goodness!" Pippa pulled out her phone, glad to find something to do with her hands. "I'll text Todd." She sent a quick message, dropping a pin in her map application to indicate their location to send to him. But the phone beeped – no signal. "Ha, one thing not to love about this town," she remarked. "Patchy signal!"

"Let's try up here." Wolfie gestured up the slope towards Squires. Raising her phone, Pippa followed Wolfie, waving the device about in the mission for bars. "Watch your step!" Wolfie urged but just as he said it, his foot plunged into a slurpy patch of boggy ground, knocking him off balance. With a yelp, he suddenly pitched forward, crashing into Pippa, his weight knocking her down and sending the two of them into a tumble down the slope, landing square in squelching, cold, mud.

Pippa took a few seconds to catch her breath, only to find herself strewn across Wolfie's lap, her bum and legs caked in mud. Wolfie hadn't fared much better. Before either of them could say a word, Juniper was there, snuffling around them with great curiosity as if to say, 'Who are you?'

Pippa looked over at Wolfie, expecting to find him outraged, but he was chuckling away as Juniper's huge snout nudged at his side.

"There you are, old girl." He patted Juniper's coarse head. "You've got a fair few people worried about you." Juniper grunted and Wolfie nodded as if in conversation. "All right, I'll get up." With some difficulty, Wolfie pulled himself to a standing position, lips pursed in concentration as he navigated the slippery ground. He then reached a hand to Pippa. "Staying there all day?"

Pippa grabbed his hand, and he pulled her up as if she were lighter than air. She stammered a thanks and as she did, her phone indicated the text to Todd had finally got through.

"Suppose we'd best get back to Squires and clean up," Wolfie said. Pippa noticed he hadn't let go of her hand. Irritated at how giddy that made her feel, she whipped her hand from his grasp. God, she was such a schoolgirl about him. But being in a relationship for more than a decade with Alex had rendered her totally useless at reading signals from any other man. Her instincts were screaming at her to show some kind of encouragement towards Wolfie, but she didn't know how. Besides, she still wasn't sure if he had a girlfriend or not. If he did, then he had no business holding her hand like that. Trembling, Pippa stepped back, smiling weakly as Juniper busied herself with the ground around their feet.

"Good idea. I have company coming over," Pippa said.

"You do?" Mild concern flickered across Wolfie's face.

"Yes," she said. "Don't worry. I'll get to my tasks for the day soon enough."

"Take all the time you need," Wolfie said. "I expect the sale to go through soon, so you don't need to worry too much. It'll be someone else's problem."

His voice was so cheery that Pippa had to turn away. "Okay."

Todd's voice suddenly echoed down from the top of the slope. "Juniper! Thank heavens!"

Relieved that she was no longer alone with Wolfie, Pippa waved to her friend. "She's fine, Todd."

Todd sprinted down the hill with remarkable agility, throwing his arms around an utterly nonplussed Juniper.

"What are you like?" he scolded her, before raising his head to Pippa and Wolfie. "A million times thank you," he said. "I can't believe she— Did you guys have a mud bath with her or something?"

Pippa laughed. "Or something," she said. "I'm glad she's all right."

"Can you manage to get Juniper back by yourself?" Wolfie asked politely.

"Gosh yes." Todd produced a lead from his pocket as

well as a small bag. "I've got a new weapon. Roast chestnuts! She'll practically stand on her head for one." As if on cue, Juniper charged at Todd's ankles, her little tail flicking gleefully from side to side. He beamed. "See? I'll lure her back with no problem."

"All right then." Pippa waved goodbye and strode off, Wolfie following her. She sensed he wanted to chat, but her every nerve felt exposed. The feelings she had for him clouded her every thought, her every breath. If she even attempted any kind of conversation with him, surely he would see her torment?

They made it back to the house in no time and when Pippa glanced at the clock, she realised she had forty minutes until the girls arrived for their meeting.

"Do you mind if I shower first?" Wolfie asked. "I have some calls this morning before my meeting in Rotherham."

"Go ahead," Pippa said, keen to be clear of him so she could digest everything she had just experienced. As Wolfie went upstairs, she hurried to the kitchen for a drink, downing several glasses of cold water to clear her head. Logical thinking and planning were needed as a matter of urgency. She had to focus on the facts: Wolfie was selling up and he would leave Hurst Bridge. So regardless of what Pippa felt, she had to plan for the reality that should the sale go through as Wolfie expected, she would be back at square one: homeless and jobless. Frankie might put her up for a few days, but she couldn't prevail upon him for too long, not again. Mae had limited space at the pub, but maybe she could bed down there and take on some shifts? That could only be a short-term solution however, and what lay beyond that, Pippa really didn't know. "I need to sort my shit out," she uttered miserably.

The sound of the gate's buzzer pulled her from her reverie. Glancing at the clock, she saw it was still thirty minutes until the girls were due, but perhaps they were early. She looked down at her mucky clothes with a sigh. She could at least settle them with a cup of tea whilst she quickly cleaned up.

As she reached the button to release the gates, she noticed with dismay that she had tracked dirt across the wooden floors she had waxed only a few days ago. Cursing, she bashed the button to let the girls in and raced back to the kitchen, picking up a cleaning cloth and disinfectant spray.

The doorbell rang as she was hastily wiping up the last of the muck. She ran to the front door. "What time do you call—"

"Pippa, hi." Alex stood there, hands jammed in his pockets, those once so familiar twinkling eyes uncharacteristically sombre.

"—this?" Pippa blurted out the end of her originally intended greeting because all other words failed her.

"I hope you don't mind, but Finn told me you were here," he said.

"I'm here." In the immediate aftermath of the break-up, Pippa had run through endless combinations of what she might say to Alex when she saw him again. She'd rehearsed devastating put-downs and some emotional home truths. But now he was standing there before her, Pippa had nothing to say. Alex had once been the centre of her world.

She'd trimmed his hair, chosen his outfits for special occasions, nursed him through multiple episodes of man-flu. She'd even had to tie his shoelaces for months when he broke his leg in a skiing accident. He'd once been as essential to her as oxygen. Yet now, it was akin to seeing a stranger wearing his face. Had he always stood like that? Was that shirt new or was it an old one he was wearing differently?

"I'm sorry to show up like this," Alex said. "May I come in?" Because she didn't know what else to do, Pippa stepped back to allow him in. The moment Alex entered the hallway, his gaze turned upward, taking in the high ceilings and the covered chandelier. "Crikey," he breathed. "Look at this place." He sniffed. "Do you have mice?" He cast an expert eye around and Pippa recalled the mouse infestation they'd once suffered in the milking sheds several years ago.

"Probably," she murmured, drinking in the sight of him whilst his attention was diverted searching for rodents. She tried to pinpoint how it made her feel. He looked good – if a little tired – and his hair was longer, more rakish. She'd always wanted him to grow it out but, ever practical, Alex had kept it neat. Now it seemed wilder, highlighting his square jaw and rosy skin. She kept waiting for the urge to bury herself in his embrace, for the old desire to lure her in. She waited. And waited. But all Pippa felt was lost. And so very confused.

"Why are you here?" she asked.

"I want to talk." Alex stepped forward, his eyes searching hers. "I miss you."

There they were. The words she never thought she'd

hear again but in the early days of the break-up had longed for. Pippa hugged herself. "And Kent?"

Alex huffed. "Kent is... I don't know. All I know is, I'm nothing without you." He took her hand, not even bothering about the dirt coating it. "Pip, I want you back. I need you in my life."

"And it took you this long to work that out?" Pippa tore away from his grasp. "Give me one good reason why I shouldn't throw you out right now."

"You're right, you're totally right!" Alex waved his hands placatingly. "I let you down and I hate myself for it. Please, can we talk?"

"Talk? And say what?" Pippa demanded. "You left me homeless and unemployed. You didn't just leave me Alex; you ended my life as I knew it."

Alex's eyes filled with tears. "I know. I get that, I do, please..." His voice gave out and he dropped to his knees. "*Please*. Give me a chance to make it up to you."

Pippa looked down at him. To see the man she'd once adored so vulnerable was unsettling. "Get up," she muttered.

Alex did as he was told, his gaze yearning. "God, I've really missed you."

Pippa inched away. Anger frothed inside her. She missed him so much in those horrid, early weeks. Back then, she would have killed to hear him say those very words. In fact, she would have probably crawled across broken glass to get her old life back, but Alex had gone, and she'd had no choice but to forge a new life from the scraps he'd left her with. He looked so wretched, standing humble and teary-eyed before her. Pippa forced herself to speak. "I missed you too." She ground each word out in a strangled voice.

Alex dipped his head for a kiss and Pippa recoiled. He flinched. "Sorry."

"What the fuck?" she yelped.

He gestured helplessly. "I–I thought— You said you missed me."

"Yeah, missed as in, *past tense*, Alex!" She couldn't believe how dense he was being. "I had weeks … months, of missing you. And now, when I've finally learned to live without you, you turn up here thinking I'll welcome you back with open arms?"

"Of course not!" He reached for her hands again. "We had something so special, and I ruined it." His eyes searched hers. "Pip. We spent nearly half our lives together. I know I have no right to ask anything of you, but please hear me out."

Even as outrage racked her body, Pippa could see his point. She took a deep breath, then pointed towards the sitting room. She probably should listen to what he had to say at least, if only to get closure. "Go and sit down. I'll put the kettle on."

A glimmer of hope shone from Alex's eyes. "Okay. Great. Thank you." He caressed her cheek, briefly, then headed to the sitting room. Pippa scurried to the kitchen and as soon as she was out of sight of him, she allowed the tears to fall. She turned on the kettle then bolted out to the back garden, where she cried openly, painfully. Deep, racking sobs took over her body, leaving her breathless and weak-kneed. What was she to do? On the one hand, it was *Alex*. One-time future husband, the man she'd constructed her entire life and purpose around. Learning to live without him had been like growing a new limb, yet she'd done it. But did he really believe that waltzing back into her life with a hangdog expression and some meaningful handholding would remedy all the ills between them? Anger, frustration and misery jostled with each other for dominance.

Pippa took a deep breath and another, allowing the fresh breeze to dry her skin. Alex would no doubt come looking for her if she dwelled too long out here and she didn't want to give him the benefit of seeing her cry. No, she had to have this talk. Their relationship had meant too much for her to dismiss him entirely, Alex was right on that score. But as for taking him back... Pippa looked inside herself for the answer. However, the overwhelming 'yes' that would have been there months ago was absent. In its place was something fiery and tenacious that felt an awful lot like hope. Instinctively, Pippa knew that she wanted to nurture that feeling, keep it for herself. Keep it from Alex.

Resolved, she let herself back into the house and rinsed her face at the sink, then made the teas, texting Mae as she did so to postpone their fair meeting. Then she carried the teas through to the sitting room.

Alex stood with his back to her, his hefty frame a dark outline against the large window. His feet were placed wide, one hand jammed in his rear jeans pocket. Pippa was struck by a memory so strong it almost made her cry out; of him piggybacking her through the farmyard on the first day of autumn, both of them laughing so much it made their throats hurt. She'd been so sure of their love that day, so certain that they were sharing the same vision of the future. It killed her to think how wrong she'd been.

But then it hit Pippa; *Alex* was the one crawling back, not her. She had nothing to be ashamed of. Taking strength from that, she strode into the room and handed him a mug. Alex reached out his other hand tentatively and stroked her upper back.

"Thanks," he said softly.

Pippa edged away from his touch and nodded towards the sofa. "Let's sit," she said. As she lowered herself to the sofa, she realised how filthy her clothes were, so she hurriedly grabbed some newspaper from the side to protect the furniture.

Just then, Wolfie's feet thudded down the stairs and he emerged into the hallway, phone glued to his ear. Pippa's mouth went dry at the sight of him. Alex shifted position and his legs jammed against hers.

"Is this the elusive Wolfie Squires?" Alex asked her. His voice was loud enough to distract Wolfie from his call. His eyes tracked from Pippa to Alex and back again as he listened to whatever his caller was saying. It occurred to her then that he must be assuming Alex was the company she had mentioned to him out on the moors earlier that morning. Pippa had a sudden urge to vault over the sofa and make it clear that wasn't the case.

"It is," Pippa confirmed to Alex, subtly moving away from him as she spoke.

"Don't mention it," Wolfie cooed down the phone even as his eyes bored into Pippa's. "Please let me."

Pippa averted her gaze and looked down into her mug. The girlfriend, had to be. Pippa took a scalding sip of tea, hoping the temperature would burn away the misery she felt in that instant.

Wolfie finished the call, placing the phone in his pocket. "Hullo," he said as he entered the sitting room.

"Hi." Pippa greeted him as cheerily as she could, as if everything was totally normal and her world wasn't crashing around her ears.

"Alex Goodman." Alex jumped up, hand extended. "Nice to meet you."

"I see." Wolfie shook Alex's hand, his gaze coolly assessing. He turned to Pippa. "Everything okay?"

"Fine," she assured him.

"It's nice to finally meet you," Alex said. "Pip was about to fill me in on everything she's been doing here." He squeezed her shoulder.

Wolfie's eyes flicked to where Alex touched her and Pippa subtly brushed off his hand, annoyed. Alex hadn't earned the right to touch her so familiarly.

"She's doing a terrific job," Wolfie said eventually. "It's a shame I'm selling the place, as she's been an excellent custodian. Rampaging pigs aside."

Pippa stifled a laugh. Alex frowned down at her. "You didn't mention the place was for sale." Alex spoke as if he and Pippa had been having multiple conversations recently, like there had been no rift between them. Pippa ground her teeth at the cheek of it.

"It's not for sale anymore," Wolfie said brusquely, and Pippa's heart briefly soared, before he clarified, "it's been sold." He jammed both hands in his pockets. "Nothing's been signed yet, but I expect the paperwork very soon."

"And what happens to you when this place sells?" Alex asked Pippa, his handsome face creasing with worry.

Pippa forced a casual smile. "I'll work something out."

"Right, wow! Who's the lucky buyer?" Alex asked.

Wolfie's stare was unforthcoming. "When it's official, it'll be public knowledge." He turned to Pippa, a sliver of concern warming his face. "Please don't worry," he said. "I won't throw you out on the street."

Pippa's heart did a funny little skip at his tenderness. What on earth did *that* mean?

"Anyway." Wolfie turned to leave. "I should leave you both to ... whatever this is."

Pippa leapt to her feet, desperate to ensure Wolfie knew the truth. "Alex isn't staying," she blurted.

"None of my business," Wolfie shot back as he left the room.

"I can't believe he's selling this place," Alex said once Wolfie had gone. "The town will be in uproar. He must be so dense not to know that."

"It's really none of the town's business," Pippa echoed Wolfie's words, although the hypocrisy of her statement was not lost on her. After all, had she not made the sale her business the moment she'd learned about it? But now she knew a little more about Wolfie's motivation, she felt supremely defensive about anyone else weighing in on the decision. In fact, knowing what she did made it all the more obscene for Alex to pry. "You don't know him, so don't act like you do."

Alex's mouth twisted, the way it always did when he was thinking.

"What?" Pippa asked.

"Are you really just the custodian?" he asked.

"What's that supposed to mean?" Pippa turned on him.

"Hey, whoa, calm down." Alex put his hands out to placate her. "It's an obvious question. You're here, by yourself. He's also here and, come on, I mean, the guy looks like he models underwear as a side hustle."

"It may seem an obvious question to you, but you don't have any fucking right to ask it!" Pippa cried. God knows what Wolfie thought about Alex being here, but for Alex to start throwing accusations around about a situation he literally knew nothing of made Pippa want to scream.

"You're right. I'm sorry, okay?" Alex said.

Pippa eyed him murderously. She ran a hand through her hair, suddenly needing Alex to be very far away. "Look, I have a lot of work still to get on with and I desperately need a shower, so can you say what you have to say and then go?"

"Crikey." Alex looked down at his feet and shook his head. "You never used to be so blunt with me."

Pippa lifted her chin. "Well, you never used to make huge life-changing decisions without me, so I guess we're even."

Alex winced at her tone. "Fair." He set his mug down on the coffee table and gathered her hands in his. "Let me show you how much I've missed you. We'll spend quality time together. Dinner ... coffee ... we could even take a trip to that lovely B&B up in Lancaster again ... however you want to do this."

"Do what?" Pippa asked.

Alex's mouth flapped and he waved an arm between them. "This. Me, you. Getting back together. Whatever it takes."

Pippa gazed at the man she'd once loved with all her being and a trickle of revulsion curled around her heart. "Do you really think after what you did that a few dinners, and a weekend in a bed and breakfast somewhere will make up for it?" Her voice was icily calm.

"I know. I was a total idiot," Alex said, his eyes red. "Blinded by ambition and my stupid self-centredness. I know I can't demand you take me back, and I get that there are no guarantees but please, let me try. I'm willing to stick around for however long I need to."

Pippa looked at him curiously. "What about Kent?" Surely, he was needed there.

Alex shifted. "It can take care of itself for a while," he said. "You're more important. I'm not leaving here until—"

"No." Pippa lifted a trembling hand. "I can't give you what you want," she said. "You almost destroyed me and there's no coming back from that."

"You say that now," he assured her. "But if you could just let me show you how sorry I am, you might feel differently."

"You can show me all you want," she said softly. "But it doesn't mean—"

"You're worth the shot, Pip," Alex interrupted tearfully.

"I wish you'd realised that before you decided to leave," she whispered.

Alex exhaled tearily, managing a bashful smile despite his emotion. "You and me both." He stood. "Look, I think I'd best leave you to your day, but can I call you later, set up a lunch or something? There's so much more I want to say."

"I don't know." Pippa didn't see the point in lunches or prolonged conversations. Her mind was made up. "Thing is, I don't get a lot of free time. Between the house and the Summer Fair organisation... I'm pretty busy. It's not fair on you to suggest otherwise."

Alex gulped. Nodded. "Wow. Okay." He turned as if to leave but then stopped. "By the way, I've been hearing lots about the Summer Fair. Sounds great. If you need any help, please let me. At least let me do that."

"Thanks." Despite the agony of seeing him again, Pippa had to admit that they could do with an extra pair of hands. "If you really are hanging around, I'm sure we can find something for you to do." She walked him to the door and opened it.

"Bye, Pip," Alex said. Too choked to reply, Pippa simply offered a wan smile. Alex turned to leave then stopped and squeezed her hand. His solemn eyes met hers. "Pip. I need you to know... If I had my time with you all over again, I'd never let you go."

A little later, once Alex had left and after a shower, Pippa was relieved to answer the door to Mae, who brandished a good bottle of red and a stormy expression.

"The NERVE!" Mae barrelled into the house, a whirl of righteous fury. "The total fucking AUDACITY of that man."

"I see you got my text." Pippa led her to the kitchen.

Mae waggled the wine bottle. "Why do you think I have this?"

"It's 11am," Pippa said, scandalised.

"Well, we won't drink all of it then." Mae wielded the corkscrew attached to her keychain.

Pippa rubbed a palm over her eyes. "Fuck it. After what I've been through, I think morning wine is a good idea."

"I'm full of them." Mae giggled. The cork popped out and she grinned gleefully. "Glasses?"

Pippa found tumblers and accepted one full to the brim, filling Mae in on the conversation with Alex. "I don't know what to make of it," she said, as they settled at the kitchen table. "It was as if I was talking to a stranger. I loved him once. There was a time I wanted to marry that man and yet ... every time he touched me all I wanted to do was push him away and scrub my skin clean."

"Yikes," Mae said, swallowing a particularly big mouthful.

"Massive yikes," Pippa groaned. "He just kept talking, demanding forgiveness, begging me for a chance. But the more he talked the angrier I got, you know? Like, we used to love each other, know everything about each other, but nothing he said made me think he truly understands what he did. And then, he got all weird around Wolfie."

Mae squinted. "Weird?"

"Like, possessive. Hovering over me as if I was still his girlfriend."

"Ah." Mae waggled her eyebrows. "Alex may be a colossal twat but he's a twat with functioning eyes."

"What do you mean?" Pippa gulped, because she already knew what Mae was insinuating.

Mae took a sip of wine and smacked her lips. "Well, he obviously picked up on the raging pheromones that start flying around when you and Wolfie Squires exist in the same space."

Pippa straightened her shoulders. "Don't know what you're talking about." More than anything, she wasn't ready to admit to the emotions Wolfie was arousing in her. It was all too much to process, especially after Alex's unexpected arrival.

"Only saying what I see!" Mae cackled. "Wolfie has a thing for you."

"Shut up!" But Pippa was curious. "What do you mean by *a thing*?"

Mae hiccupped. "I refer you to our earlier conversation about new penis."

"Oh God," Pippa said. "You have to stop that."

"He's into you," Mae said bluntly.

"You don't know that." Pippa didn't dare to breathe, as if Mae naming the mysterious emotions Wolfie inspired might jinx them.

"If you say so." Mae rolled her eyes. "But if Alex genuinely wants you back then he's bound to be threatened by rich, handsome, mysterious Wolfie Squires."

"But Alex hasn't got the right!" Pippa cried. "To upend my life and saunter in, all *Oh Pip never told me about the house sale...*" She lifted her nose and squared her shoulders in an imitation of Alex.

"Bang on," Mae smirked. "If you do end up jobless then maybe consider a career as an impressionist."

"That may happen sooner than you think, because the sale is definitely happening." Pippa updated Mae on what Wolfie had told her. "Everything is a mess!"

"Oi." Mae pointed at her. "No, it's not. You're going to be fine. And as for a mess, well, I must disagree. The fair is in great shape and that's largely thanks to you. I knew you'd organise the shit out of this thing, and you have."

"We still don't have medics!" Pippa wailed. "We have to have—"

Mae raised a hand. "You might be wrong there. I got a call only an hour ago from a private hire medical group who are interested. They tend to a lot of large-scale concerts and celebrity events, but they are available on the day. Could be our saviours!"

"They sound expensive," Pippa fretted. "We have to spend—"

"As little as possible, yes, yes." Mae flapped a hand. "Thing is, apparently they're looking to do more charity projects. For free. Sort of, marketing themselves a bit."

"At a small country fair?" Pippa was taken aback. "Bit weird."

"I know," Mae agreed. "I kind of got the impression they were, I dunno, connected somehow."

"Connected?" Pippa repeated.

"Yeah." Mae nodded. "The person I was talking to said something about *'our urgent need had been impressed upon them'* which made me think maybe someone from round here asked them to volunteer, even though they're based down south-east way."

Pippa sighed with relief. "Listen, if they're kosher, I don't care where they come from. They could be from bloody Mars! Let's check them out and—"

"Yes, yes, yes, I'm on it!" Mae declared. "You're going through a lot right now and working hard enough." She fixed Pippa with a determined stare. "We're going to have an amazing event and raise heaps of money for our friend's school. Yeah?"

"Yeah." Pippa tried her best to match Mae's enthusiasm, but it fell flat. How could she be happy and carefree when the man who'd broken her heart was back in town?

Chapter Eighteen

Pippa yawned. She'd barely slept the night before, thanks to Alex's unexpected appearance. Her mind had refused to relax, instead analysing every second of their reunion, examining each word, each gesture. Should it trouble her that she hadn't been a weeping, raw mess after his visit? In fact, the overwhelming sensation remained irritation. No, Pippa was resolute. Alex could beg all he wanted; it could never mend the damage he had caused.

Her meeting with Mae the previous day had done little to soothe her busy brain, although the red wine had definitely helped. The fair was in good shape, that much was true, but there was so much yet to be done: the barriers to secure the roads, a load of signage needed printing and then there was the mystery medical company that had volunteered their services – would they be able to save the day? Had someone from Hurst Bridge called them in? If so, who?

Overnight, heavy rain had fallen and, when Pippa

opened her bedroom curtains, the lush green hills were spread out before her like a bejewelled carpet. Although grey clouds continued to loom overhead, pockets of bright clear blue remained. Pippa opened all the windows and allowed the fresh air to rush in. It smelt so enticing that she decided to take herself on a walk later that day.

As she leafed through the binder of chores over coffee in the kitchen, she heard Wolfie's deep voice echoing through the house. It sounded like he was at work in the library. Today's task was to dust down all the shelves in there, but if he was planning to be in the library all day, she'd have to choose a different job. Pippa steeled herself, tried not to think of Mae's 'new penis' catchphrase, and headed to the library.

Poking her head round the door, it was clear that Wolfie was finishing a video call. He closed the window down as she entered the room, but she recognised Steffany from *Top Stay*, as one of the other people on the call. It must be their offer he'd accepted. So that was that, then, Pippa surmised. A hotel. A bland, corporate block of bricks instead of this beautiful building. It beggared belief.

Her emotions must have been writ clear across her face because the moment Wolfie clocked her expression he grimaced. "Good day to you too," he said crisply, writing something in a notebook.

"You're selling to *Top Stay* then," Pippa shot back.

"Until the contracts are signed, I'm not confirming anything," Wolfie said, leaning back in his chair. "But the sale is proceeding. Papers are being drafted and reviewed by my lawyer as we speak." He leaned back in his chair. "If you're concerned about having somewhere to live, please don't be. We'll work something out."

"I'm not worried about me." Pippa ignored the way her body was responding to the way his arm biceps strained the sleeves of his T-shirt. Some things were more important.

"Oh yes, the people of Hurst Bridge. How *will* they cope without their beloved Squires?" He rolled his eyes.

It was as if their conversation about Hurst Bridge yesterday had never happened. Pippa understood he had reasons for not loving the house himself and she totally respected them. But did he have to be so callous about the importance of the house to the people who lived near it? "Don't be like that."

"Like what?" Wolfie said. "I know your feelings on the matter, but I have to be practical here."

Pippa wondered where the Wolfie of yesterday was, the outdoorsy, laughing man who'd tried to fix the damaged garden and helped to find a runaway pig. "What's wrong with you?"

"Nothing." He shrugged. "Taking care of business, that's all."

"Is this because of Alex?" Pippa asked suddenly.

Wolfie's lips thinned. "Who? Oh, your boyfriend."

"Ex-boyfriend," she corrected him.

"He seemed pretty chummy with you," Wolfie said. "Look, if you two are getting back together and you need to move out, that's more than fine by me."

"More than—" Pippa swallowed. "You'd really be all right with me leaving?"

Wolfie nodded nonchalantly. "I'm sure I can manage this

place alone until the sale." He snickered. "It's not like you do that much, is it?"

Pippa was stunned by his coldness towards her. Had she imagined the spark between them? She felt like she was going mad. "Have you seen the binder?" she said. "It's a fucking Bible."

"No matter." Wolfie ran his thumb over his lips. "Entirely manageable."

"Seriously, what's going on?" Pippa edged towards him. "I thought we—" She took a deep breath. "We were getting along."

"Who says we aren't?"

"Alex and I are not back together," she said.

"Like I said, not my business." Wolfie started to swivel back towards his laptop. "So, if that's all…?"

Pippa's eyes blurred with tears. It wasn't so much his odd demeanour, but the fact that she'd been such an idiot to allow herself to remotely entertain feelings for this man. "I understand now," she said.

"Understand what?"

"I think I understand a man like you," she said.

Wolfie froze, turning in his chair to face her. "And what do you think you understand?"

"I'm sorry you were let down by the very people who should have looked out for you," Pippa said. "That must make it really tough to trust anyone."

He remained very still. "You don't know what you're talking about."

"Oh, but I do." A tear traced down her cheek and she swiped it away. "You know what Alex did to me. And maybe I'm an idiot for turning him away because of it, time will tell, but unlike you, I'm not turning *everyone* away as a result."

"That's not what I'm doing," Wolfie protested.

"Isn't it?" Pippa cried. "I don't know what this is between us – and there *is* something—" she declared boldly before he could deny it. "But you don't get to put the walls up and treat me like I'm disposable just because you're scared."

"Scared?" Wolfie attempted bravado, but Pippa could see the hurt flash in his eyes.

"Yes." She steeled herself. "You saw me with Alex and assumed I was going back to him. That I'd leave this house and leave you; leave you or hurt you like everyone else did."

"Right, so you're an amateur psychologist now?" he spluttered. "Give it a rest."

Pippa clenched her fists. She'd had just about enough of men who didn't listen to her.

"Fine," she said. "Have it your way. Maybe I'll succumb to the inevitable and move out now. You know, let you live out the rest of this house's days skulking around like some lonely beast. No friends, no—" Pippa stopped herself from saying *love*. She could feel more tears threatening, and she was damned if she'd let this obnoxious idiot see them. She turned to leave, then stopped. "You know what," she went on. "You can sneer all you want at this town and the way the people here love this house. I'm sorry you had a less than brilliant childhood, and that it stops you from seeing what's right in front of you." Wolfie tried to speak up, but

Pippa was in no mood to listen. "Maybe it's for the best. Sell up. Escape. Then you can forget all about the little, insignificant people of Hurst Bridge." And with that, Pippa powered back to the kitchen, her mind in utter turmoil. Perhaps it wasn't too wise to sound off like that, but she'd felt like she had no choice. Had she been wrong about the connection between her and Wolfie? Pippa knew she wasn't the most experienced when it came to relationships but surely she hadn't imagined the lingering looks, the way her body seemed to awaken in his presence? Wolfie's indifference seemed to indicate she had, and the humiliation was painful. How could she face that man ever again?

Wolfie yelled her name. Panicking, Pippa slipped out of the kitchen door and into the garden. Wolfie called for her again and so she darted round the side of the house, out of the main gate and onto the road. Pippa didn't know whether she would yell at him or fall at his feet in a mess of embarrassed tears; at any rate, she couldn't spare Wolfie any more emotional energy. She needed space from him and so she kept walking. The fresh air felt so good pouring into her lungs that she decided not to stop, and to give in to that earlier desire to get up into the hills. She was only clad in slip-on shoes and leggings with a T-shirt, but it wasn't particularly cold. Besides, if she wanted more sensible footwear she'd have to go back to the house and that wasn't happening.

Pippa knew there was a footpath into the hills just off the main road that she was now travelling on. It was identifiable only by a narrow cut in the drywall, with a worn wooden sign that once upon a time probably proclaimed the actual name of the route. Locals didn't need any such direction though – they said they were 'going up Clough'. It didn't take long to find it – a little more overgrown than the last time she'd ventured up there – but the air smelled so green and lush that she happily forged on. Only a few steps in and a peace descended upon her; to the extent that even the cars passing on the road behind her were reduced to a mere hush. Soon enough, her muscles began to relax, her mind slowing.

The path led her to a steep bank where evergreen trees valiantly pushed up towards the sky. The way here became rocky, some of the larger stones slick from the overnight rain. Undeterred, Pippa forged on. Despite the shelter of the canopy, the wind began to whistle relentlessly through the wood and Pippa pulled the sleeves of her T-shirt down. Soon, the incline became steeper, forcing Pippa to use the trees around her as leverage. The earth was wetter and sludgier here, causing her shoes to slip and slide. Up ahead the incline levelled out, and she dragged herself onward, knowing the view was worth it.

"There it is." Finally, Pippa emerged from the treeline and before her lay the loveliest, lushest meadow, sprinkled with wildflowers and lichen-patched boulders through which a well trampled path weaved its way to Clough Hill. As small children, she and Frankie would hide amongst the boulders, graduating to climbing them as they got older, much to the chagrin of their worrying mothers.

Eyes misted by nostalgia, Pippa picked her way through the meadow, shivering as more clouds began to gather overhead. Everywhere she looked she saw memories: the ditch where Frankie had found a rat's nest; the rock shaped like a hedgehog that she'd fallen off on her tenth birthday, breaking her wrist; that time they did a school trip up here to examine the wildlife and Pippa had snuck a baby frog into her backpack. That had earned her a week of detention. Then there was that sponsored hike across the moors to raise money to fix the fences protecting the duck pond on the green. Vincent Squires had hosted a mulled wine and parkin fuelled celebration in his gardens for all the hikers, which had been featured in the local newspaper. Pippa still had the clipping from that day somewhere. She'd kept it because there was a lovely photo in which she, Frankie and Mae lolled in the bottom corner, their thirteen-year-old smiles clagged with sticky, fragrant parkin. It hadn't just been a day that mattered to her, it had mattered to everyone.

The memories were so intense that she didn't clock the boggy patch ahead and with a sudden, vicious swipe, Pippa found herself flat on her back. Winded, she couldn't move for a moment, conscious of a sharp pain in her ankle and her lungs wheezing for air.

Gradually, the shock subsided, and Pippa gathered enough strength to manoeuvre to a sitting position. Above her, the sky grew even darker, the fat clouds from before now ominous grey weights settling solidly into place. A storm was imminent. She had to get to low ground, fast.

Pippa tentatively put her weight on the throbbing foot and instantly regretted it as a spike of pain shot up her entire leg. Breathing heavily, she gave her ankle a poke and stifled a shriek.

"Shiiiit." Wincing, she massaged her ankle as best she could then tested the weight again but once more she buckled and collapsed back down. From far away came the faint rumble of thunder. Panic flashed; was she due to be stuck up here, lame and alone during a thunderstorm? Pippa eyed the path back down towards the road; could she slide down through the mud on her bottom away from the high ground?

As fat raindrops began to plop on her head, Pippa made the decision to at least reach the shelter of the wooded incline, hoping that she could wait out the worst of the rain before attempting to walk back. With the most unladylike of grunts, she scooted forward, grimacing as cold mud slushed up her backside and under her top. The lazy plops became more insistent, thrumming hard against her skull and plastering her hair to her scalp. Pippa braced her weight on her hands and slid, over and over, her ankle complaining at the smallest movement. The rain was relentless, the drops bouncing painfully off her skin, and it didn't take long until she was soaked to the skin, right down to her underwear.

"What was I thinking?" She cursed herself for imagining that she could attempt such a trek, especially in her flimsy shoes that were useless in the face of this weather. How long had she lived here? How many times had she seen with her own eyes how the weather could turn on a whim?

Many long minutes later, she had only managed to slide a few metres down the track; the trees might as well have been miles away. Miserable and shivering, Pippa tried once more to stand. Breathing hard through the pain, she managed to achieve a lopsided stance but one look at the slope ahead that she had yet to navigate had fresh tears of frustration springing. Small streams of water began to pour down the rocky path. Was this the end? Pippa wondered. Was the whole moorland going to become a giant lake in which she was to drown?

"Pippa!" A familiar voice echoed through the trees.

She froze. Had she imagined someone calling her name? No, because there it was, her name being shouted again and again. It was Wolfie. Frantically, she tried to regain some dignity by standing up straight. Yet again her injured ankle betrayed her, and she was back down, her spine aching from the fall. Wolfie could not see her like this, weak and helpless after she'd run away from him so dramatically. But suddenly, he was by her side, his T-shirt soaked to the point of transparency. "Pippa?" Rivulets of water ran down his angled face. "Thank God. Are you all right?"

"I fell." The rain was so loud she had to shout. Self-consciously, Pippa tried to swipe wet hair off her face, cringing as she felt a thick smear of mud transfer from hand to cheek.

"Come on." Wolfie extended a hand. "This storm is set to last for hours. It's not safe to be out here."

"I can't walk," she admitted, allowing him to pull her up to a precarious one-legged stance. "My ankle."

He glanced down. "Can you put any weight on it?"

She gingerly attempted a step. Pain knifed its way up her leg. "No. Not really."

"Right." Wolfie put his arm around her shoulders. "Lean on me."

Pippa did just that, trying not to react to the sheer wall of muscle she found herself propped against. As her ankle throbbed angrily, Pippa forced herself to concentrate on using his strength as a crutch. Together, they edged their way through the boulders and into the trees, where the sound of rain on leaves was deafening.

"Careful here," Wolfie yelled. The sloping path before them looked incredibly slippery, with little streams rushing between the pebbles. Pippa gulped.

"I don't think I can get down there," she said. Even with a human crutch, the wet rocks seemed too treacherous.

Wolfie growled in exasperation, but just as it seemed he was about to respond, white light flickered through the trees, soon followed by a roar of thunder. His face tightened. "We need to get to lower ground," he said. "Now."

Pippa gestured helplessly at her ankle.

"Ah," Wolfie said. "Sorry about this, then." He ducked to her waist, arms encircling her body.

Pippa shrieked. "What are you—?"

Her words were cut off by her being suddenly flipped over his shoulder, fireman-style. He straightened up and Pippa squealed as wet branches scraped her shoulders.

"Keep your bloody head down!" Wolfie ordered, and Pippa was too shocked to do anything other than as she was told. Clinging onto Wolfie's back, she kept her head as low as possible, all the while very conscious that her bum was nestled up against his cheek, her thin leggings soaked through to the skin and coated in mud. Her cheeks burned at the idea of what she must look like.

And yet she felt safe. Pippa realised she completely trusted the hands that gripped her close to him, even as he navigated their way down the precarious slope. Despite the uncertain terrain and her extra weight, Wolfie was sure-footed and calm. The thunder crashed so loudly it felt like the world was falling around her, but Wolfie remained steady. His every muscle was tense, each step carefully considered. Pippa craned her neck to look at the back of his head, an odd wave of emotion taking over. How many men would run out in a thunderstorm and carry someone to safety, putting themselves at risk the way Wolfie was right now? With every fibre of her being, Pippa knew Alex would probably have baulked. At least, he would have done pre-break up, back when he took her for granted. Because, as Wolfie worked the last few steps of the slope, it was clear to Pippa that Alex had taken her for granted their entire relationship. She'd been *his* crutch, his support. The farm's success was purely down to her. It hadn't been a joint dream they were building together; it was her vision for the future that had suited Alex fine until it didn't.

Wolfie reached the lower, flatter path with an audible sigh of relief and he crouched, letting her slide off his shoulders. He straightened, pausing when his face became level with hers.

"Do you want to lean on me from here?" Raindrops buffeted his face without mercy.

Pippa was mesmerised by a single drop of rain tracing its way over one of his exquisite cheekbones. She nodded, dreamlike. "Yes. I do." She reached around his waist and the weight of his arm was across her shoulders once more. The duo began the slow journey down the path. Although Wolfie's assistance made it easier to move, every step sent agonising jolts up her leg and when she saw the drywall, the gap leading out to the road, she wanted to cry in relief.

Once on the road, the pavement was easier to traverse, though the rain slammed relentlessly against it, splashing up their legs as it did. But soon they were back at Squires, collapsing through the front door.

"Christ!" Wolfie shook himself like a dog, droplets spraying everywhere. Pippa giggled, but she was shivering so much that the noise was oddly strangled. Wolfie sprang to action, disappearing briefly into the living room and re-emerging with a throw.

"Here." Wolfie wrapped the blanket around her, rubbing her arms. Pippa let him, stunned by his tenderness. His face was inches from hers, intent with the need to make sure she warmed up. Pippa's gaze was inexorably drawn to his full lips and sharp white teeth. A kernel of electricity began to pulse within her. "Are you feeling any warmer now?"

"Yes," Pippa croaked, her mouth dry. Wolfie glanced up at her and his face creased with concern.

"You're very pale," he murmured.

Pippa couldn't reply. Her body trembled, but it wasn't the cold. It was the magnitude of everything falling into place, of Wolfie being so close, holding her tight. Did he not see how she was coming apart before him? Then Pippa frowned. She wasn't the only one who was soaked to the skin. Wolfie's lips were almost blue.

"You're cold." She touched his slippery arm.

"I'll be fine. Show me your ankle," he ordered gruffly. The nearest place to sit was the stairs and, with Wolfie's help, Pippa manoeuvred herself in an ungainly fashion down on to one of the lower steps, stretching out her injured leg. His face set with concentration, Wolfie knelt before her and cupped her calf with one hand, the other gently pushing back the hem of her sodden leggings to prod at the sightly puffy skin. Pippa reeled. Because the moment Wolfie's fingers brushed her bare leg, she wanted him with a need so strong it made her dizzy. The desire was a force that threatened to take her apart, sinew by sinew, bone by bone. The only thing that could bring her back together was his touch. Wolfie grinned shyly. "Is this really the second time I'm performing emergency medical care on you, Pippa Munro?"

He was clearly expecting her to laugh, but that was the last thing Pippa wanted to do. When her face stayed serious, his stilled. "What is it?"

Pippa's gaze drilled into his with urgent command. "Kiss me."

Stunned, Wolfie's eyes dropped to her lips. "You want me to kiss you?"

Pippa nodded slowly. "I do."

Wolfie reverently lowered her foot, and for a devastating moment, Pippa thought he was going to walk away. But then he leaned over her, a hand either side of her hips on the step and brought his face close to hers. "Thank fucking God," he murmured.

With a ferocity she hadn't known she was capable of

until that moment, Pippa grabbed his face and pulled his mouth to hers. Wolfie met her lips with a kiss of equal fervour. He tasted like rain, his large hands raking through her hair to gently tug it away from her face. Pippa didn't want gentle however; this was not the time for restraint. Pippa wanted him to unleash that force she knew lurked beneath the proper demeanour. No. More than wanted; she needed. She burned for it.

"Don't hold back," she panted against his mouth. She knew if he didn't ravage her with every ounce of the power he had within, she would surely combust out of sheer frustration.

"You sure?" His lips brushed against hers.

"I'm sure." Pippa's tongue snaked its way across his Adam's apple, and he gulped. He pushed himself between her knees, hands sliding to her rear so he could pull her against the firmness of his body. Pippa moaned. She wanted him so badly, she didn't care that her wet hair was plastered to her skull, or that she was coated with dark mud. Pippa didn't even care that her ankle hurt like blazes; all she cared about was Wolfie and what his mouth was doing to her, what it could do to her.

She trailed a hand down Wolfie's chest, to the hem of his shirt. He batted her hand out of the way and pulled his top off. Fat drops of rainwater trickled over his bare chest and Pippa leaned in, doing what she had been dreaming of since she'd seen him in his towel: she reached out her tongue and licked his wet skin. Wolfie shivered. His hands went to her hair again and dragged her mouth back to his. His kisses hard, he pushed Pippa back against the stairs, his full, delicious weight upon her.

Impatiently, Pippa slid her hand down to the fly of his trousers and her mouth went instantly dry at the size of what waited for her there. Wolfie glanced down at what she was doing.

"Are you sure about this?"

Pippa tugged at his belt. The prong slipped from its notch. "Does it seem like I'm not sure?"

His answering grin was wicked.

Hours later, when they'd finally made it off the stairs and up to Wolfie's room, they lay in his bed, tangled in sheets as the rain still hammered down outside. As she lay on her back, trying to catch her breath, Pippa felt totally at peace. Making love to Wolfie had been unlike anything she'd ever experienced. True, her frame of reference was incredibly limited, but that hadn't mattered. As a lover, Wolfie was all at once tender and ravenous, exhausting her body whilst blowing her mind. And yet, it all felt so right. Natural.

When her heart rate had returned to a normal pace, Pippa rolled onto her side to face him. Wolfie's long fingers reached for her hair, smoothing it back off her face. She ran her hands over his broad chest and the tattoo that was emblazoned across his pectorals. Wolfie followed her gaze down to the dark script that read *'Fortune Favours the Brave.'*

"The motto of my regiment." Wolfie pre-empted Pippa's

question as her fingers brushed the two red poppies entwined amongst the text.

She looked closer. "What are those for?"

"Two of my men that never came back," he replied hoarsely.

"God, I'm so sorry." Pippa's hand stilled. She couldn't imagine what that must have been like. "Did you injure your chin out there?" She brushed her lips along his scar's silvery path.

"That?" Wolfie rolled his eyes. "No. Although it's kind of connected to me being in the army."

"How?"

Wolfie propped himself up on his elbows and cleared his throat. "You know that dent you noticed on the living room panels?"

Perplexed by the sudden topic change, Pippa nodded curiously.

"My father. He caused that damage," he went on. "He did it when I told him I wanted to study music in London instead of something 'masculine' like business or law. He threw his glass at me, but he was so blotto it missed. It hit the wall and smashed and a shard of glass hit my chin." Wolfie worried the scar with his thumb. "That's when he told me no son of his was to study music as that wasn't what 'real men' did. Trouble was that, apart from music, I had no interest in school or academia. I loved – *love* – music. For years it had been my escape and he—" His mouth twisted ruefully. "At any rate, I enlisted the next day. Shipped out just a few months after that."

"Your father hurt you?" He was so calm, Pippa thought.

So measured.

"My father *tried* to hurt me," Wolfie corrected her gently. "He almost always failed. That time was the first and last time he was successful."

"What about your mum?" Pippa demanded. "Why did she let him treat you like that?"

Wolfie hesitated, his serene composure slipping. "Mum was ... she was just as much a victim. He never hit her, but he inflicted mental violence on her every day. She was helpless against him. I'm working on forgiving her for that, believe me. It's what she deserves."

"God." Pippa sat up. She felt sick. All those years dreaming about the perfect Squires family, their dream house, but the whole time Wolfie was living an utter nightmare. No wonder he'd spent much of his adult life far from here. And then she'd come along, squawking about how he didn't appreciate what he had, how he owed it to the town to keep the house in the family ... a town full of people ignorant to the horror going on within said house. "I had no idea. Why didn't you tell me sooner?"

"Pippa Munro, we've known each other for a few weeks. It took me *months* to tell a therapist all that stuff." Wolfie's smile was small, but shaky.

"You're in therapy?" Pippa said.

"All the best people are." His attempt at a breezy tone made Pippa's heart ache. She'd long noted his calmness – it was one of the things she found most attractive about him – but now it was downright admirable how he achieved such a demeanour in the face of such trauma.

Pippa lowered herself back down and wriggled so her

gaze was perfectly level with his and he could see her sincerity. "No judgement from me." A smear of mud on the pillowcase caught her attention. "God, sorry. I'll do a laundry load."

"We'll take care of that later." Wolfie snared her waist. "Stay with me." His teeth grazed her shoulder and Pippa's insides turned over as his hands began to wander south. But the sight of the mud had triggered a question and as much as she was enjoying what his hands were doing to her, she had to ask.

"Wolfie. Why did you follow me up Clough Hill?"

He paused, brushing a lock of hair off her face. "I wanted to apologise for talking to you the way I did. Everything you said was true and I realised if I didn't tell you right there and then I never would and I'd miss the chance to ... well, you know." He grinned bashfully. "So I followed you out to the road, but you were stomping away at speed like a rampaging beast—"

"Rampaging?" Pippa echoed with a giggle.

"I said what I said." He nibbled her shoulder again. "I did consider leaving you alone to ruminate on how much of a bastard I am. But then the heavens opened, and I got a storm alert on my phone."

Warmth bloomed through Pippa's chest. "And then you came after me," she said.

His eyes locked with hers. "And then I came after you."

Something tilted inside Pippa as she held his gaze and pure contentment flooded her veins. "Thank you."

"Any time, Pippa Munro," he murmured, leaning in for another kiss. "Any time."

Chapter Nineteen

Pippa opened her eyes. The room was dim thanks to the closed drapes but she could tell that the rain had stopped. Disoriented, she sat up. It took a second for it to sink in that she was in Wolfie's room and the delicious ache spreading through her body was thanks to him. She wasn't sure where her clothes were – no doubt scattered up the stairs and along the landing, if memory served. Wolfie wasn't next to her, but the bed was still warm. He hadn't been gone long. Wrapping a sheet around herself, she moved to the window. The sky remained an ominous grey, casting the moorland in shadow.

Hearing movement downstairs, she decided to go to her room and dress, then noticed a note on Wolfie's pillow.

PM,
Doing a conference call downstairs. Didn't want to wake you.
Yours, W.

Pippa traced the writing with her finger. Like Wolfie, it was elegant and efficient. And despite the spare detail, the sign-off made her tummy flip. *Yours,* he'd written. Was there a more beautiful word?

As Pippa made her way back to her room, she realised she'd not asked Wolfie about the girlfriend she'd suspected him of having. She dressed blindly as her mind tumbled over all the possibilities. It had to be that her assumption was wrong. Perhaps she'd misheard the call where he'd pledged to spend the Squires sales profit on this woman. Surely Wolfie wasn't the kind of guy to bed someone whilst he was in a relationship? The way he'd kissed her, the way his eyes had connected with hers as he moved inside her, Pippa had felt like the only woman on the planet. There was no way she could have misread that.

She took some care brushing her hair and spraying perfume, but there was nothing to be done about her puffy lips and sleepy eyes. Pippa grinned as she examined herself in the mirror. There was no disguising it; she looked exactly like someone who'd spent much of the day having the best sex of her life. Pippa headed downstairs, her breath quickening at the thought of seeing Wolfie again. She'd just spent the afternoon naked with the man yet was wracked with anticipation. What would she say to him? The anxiety couldn't mask the joy, however, and soon she was smiling to herself like an idiot. As she rounded the bottom of the stairs, her phone pinged with a call from Frankie.

"Hi!" he cooed. "We're outside."

"*We?*" Pippa repeated.

"Yeah, me and Theo," Frankie said. "I'm dropping off

my car for you to use for the fair organisation this week, remember? You asked?"

Pippa groaned. "Duh. Yeah. Thanks for that."

"Can't believe you forgot after all the nagging," Frankie mused.

"Um. Maybe I've had a lot on my mind," Pippa said, as casually as she could manage.

"Right. Anyway, Theo's in his car behind me." He paused and Pippa could sense the huge grin on his face. "We're off to dinner with his friends shortly."

"Oh, we're at the dining with friends stage, are we?" Pippa teased. "Should I buy a hat?"

"You don't have the head for hats," Frankie shot back. "We discussed this after the trilby fiasco of 2017. Anyway, seeing as we're here, I wondered if Theo could get that quick tour of the house you promised."

"Well..." Pippa thought for a moment. She wasn't sure how she felt about her cousin potentially encountering Wolfie when things between them were so new. So new she couldn't put a name to it and right now, didn't want to.

"Pllllleeeeaaaase," Frankie wheedled. "I really want to impress Theo. He's, like, so curious about Squires."

Pippa considered. Wolfie had said he had a work call. From previous experience she knew he could potentially be locked away in the library for hours, so if they stayed quiet, what harm could it do? "Fine," she huffed. "But tell him to keep the gasps of awe to a minimum please – Wolfie's working."

Moments later, Frankie and Theo were in the entrance hall, Theo's handsome face lost in wonder as he drank in the interior of the house. Pippa could hardly contain her glee at the sight of her cousin gazing dreamily at his new boyfriend, his eyes glazed with happiness.

"What do you think?" she asked Theo.

"Stunning example of early Victorian architecture," he breathed. "The parquet flooring..." He gestured down. "Worn by foot traffic but I bet it buffs up a treat."

"I thought you worked in ecology?" Pippa said.

"Yep." Theo nodded. "But I consult for a lot of trusts and stately homes. I'm something of a nerd when it comes to old buildings." His lips thinned. "This house must have been glorious once upon a time. I can tell it's suffered serious neglect."

"It has," Pippa said. She didn't bother to add that the neglect was due to Carmichael Squires being a colossal waster who spent money destined for the house's upkeep on his own private vices.

"Please may I wander?" Theo asked.

"Of course," Pippa said. "If you could avoid the library though because Wolfie's working in there."

Theo threw his head back. "A library! This house." He stroked Frankie's arm. "You coming?"

"I've had the tour," Frankie said. "You go ahead." The men exchanged sweet smiles and Theo ambled off, his face aglow with curious excitement.

"Okay, I have to admit it," Pippa said, once Theo was out of earshot in the living room. "He's perfect."

"Isn't he? Here are the car keys, by the way." Frankie dropped them on a small side table. "Sometimes, we're hanging out and I look at him wondering what the hell a god like that is doing with a mere mortal like me."

"Hey." Pippa nudged him. "Don't talk about my cousin like that."

"You know what I mean." Frankie blushed. "I keep thinking, this must have been how you felt when you got with Alex, right? Exciting and new but meant-to-be all at once."

Pippa shrugged. She'd been a teenager when Alex had become her boyfriend. *Everything* was heady and dramatic back then. "That was a long time ago," she said. "A lot has changed since then."

Frankie's face twisted in sympathy. "It must have been a real head fuck to see him again."

"It was unreal," she said.

"You know he's been sniffing around the pub, asking Mae what he can do to help with the fair." Frankie squeezed her shoulder. "I think he's trying to impress you."

"He can do all he wants to help. Won't make a difference." Pippa exhaled heavily; her thoughts chaotic. It felt wrong to be discussing Alex when she could still smell Wolfie on her skin.

"Amen to that," Frankie snorted.

Just as he said that, Wolfie emerged from the library. He was stretching, his T-shirt riding up to show his rock-hard torso. He saw Pippa and broke into a stupefied smile, quickly rearranging his face when he clocked Frankie standing behind her. Even though it had been very little time since she'd last seen him, Pippa felt a rush, like it had been too long. In the half-light of the hallway, she saw a line of sinew stretching down his neck and she thought how she'd like to run her tongue down it. She noticed Frankie watching her curiously and rearranged her face into what she hoped was a neutral, non-lust-dazed expression.

"Hi." Wolfie walked over to shake her cousin's hand. "Wolfie Squires."

"Pippa's cousin, Francis Munro." Frankie grinned. "But call me Frankie. I hope you don't mind my boyfriend geeking out about your house?"

"Geeking professionally," Theo corrected Frankie as he wandered back into the hallway. "I love the view from the living room," he called over to Wolfie.

"Er, thanks," Wolfie said, bemused.

"Theo does a lot of work with old buildings," Pippa explained quickly. "He's been dying to visit, and I thought you wouldn't mind."

"You thought right, Pippa Munro. How's the ankle by the way?" Wolfie's attempt at nonchalance failed; he was thoroughly unable to hide the hunger in his eyes. Pippa stifled a grin, not daring to look at Frankie, although she knew full well her cousin's stunning skills of perception would see right through hers and Wolfie's lame attempt at subterfuge.

In reply to Wolfie's question, she wiggled her foot. The joint was a little sore, and she'd have to watch her step, but it didn't seem that bad. "Well, I can walk on it, so that's an improvement." She couldn't resist teasing him. "I think being on my back for hours really helped."

Wolfie's lips twitched. "Glad to hear it."

"You hurt your ankle?" Frankie asked her, his gaze

darting quickly between the two of them.

Pippa nodded. "I'm fine, don't worry." She met her cousin's eye and inwardly groaned as suspicion bloomed across his face, soon followed by glee. He'd totally guessed.

"Great, great. So, Wolfie." Frankie's tone was mischievous. "You're selling up?"

Wolfie dragged his gaze from Pippa's mouth to Frankie. "I am."

"That's a shame," Frankie said. "I bet you're really, really going to miss this place. And certain people."

"Frankie..." Pippa warned. "Leave it."

"I'm only saying." Frankie's eyes were wide with affected innocence. "I'd have thought there's plenty of reasons for a man like you to stay in Hurst Bridge." He slung an arm over Pippa's shoulders, ogling her blatantly. "Isn't there?"

Pippa wanted to crawl into a hole with the embarrassment. As powerful as her feelings for Wolfie were, things between them were too new for any suggestion of him staying in Hurst Bridge. And there was the real possibility that Frankie's goading could push Wolfie away. "Ignore him, Wolfie," she said quickly. "Frankie just loves to stir."

"No, it's okay," Wolfie assured her. "Um, I haven't really thought about what happens after the sale. But...." He bit his lip and Pippa felt every inch of her strain in anticipation of what came next. He offered a tentative grin. "You never know."

"You don't?" Pippa squeaked. What did *that* mean? Her phone rang and she reached for it, glad for the distraction.

In her haste, her thumb slipped and hit the speakerphone function.

"Hi, love." Alex's voice echoed through the hall. Although Pippa wasn't looking at Wolfie, she could sense his face falling.

"Alex? Wha—?" Clumsily, she jabbed at the screen until the speakers were off. Cursing Alex for his habitual affectation she moved away from Wolfie, forcing herself to sound calm. "What is it?"

"You have a moment?" he asked. "I need to confess something."

"Oh God." Pippa wasn't in the mood for any more revelations from him.

"Don't panic, don't panic," he chuckled. "I hinted at it when I came up to Squires the other day, but I thought you should know I've decided to volunteer with the fair."

"Oh?" Pippa tried to sound surprised.

"Yes," he said. "I want to help. It's important to you."

Pippa was torn. On the one hand, they did need all the help possible. On the other, she had very little desire to rub shoulders with Alex on a regular basis, especially if he thought his volunteering might result in them reigniting their relationship. "I see."

"That's okay, right?"

Pippa took a deep breath. It was the best thing for the fair. And surely Alex would be on his way back to Kent soon. It would be temporary. "Fine. I did say you could help."

"Great." He sounded relieved. "Just as well, I've already been quite busy."

Pippa frowned. "What on earth are you on about?"

She could practically feel his smugness radiating down the phoneline. "Well, Finn called me several times the past few weeks to ask for advice on what we could do for the fair as he and Julie have been pitching in. So, I'm kind of up to date on everything. Anyway, I spoke to Mae and Erin—"

"Yes, I heard you spoke to Mae," Pippa couldn't hold back her incredulity. "Well done on remaining alive."

Alex whistled. "Yeah, she was particularly outraged."

"Was there shouting?"

"There was a *symphony* of shouting," he confirmed. "But no less than I deserve. Anyway, once I convinced Mae and Erin I genuinely wanted to help, they grudgingly allowed me to only if you permitted me."

"Fine." Pippa knew she couldn't deny the extra aid just because it came from Alex. "And what do you mean by busy?"

"I've been able to put my contacts to good use," he said with a little laugh. "Which I am sure you will find will *really* get this show on the road."

Pippa thought for a moment. What was he on about? But then it hit her. The mysterious benefactor. "The medics? That was *you*?" She wanted to weep. *Of course* it had been Alex. He'd said he was willing to do whatever it took to get back with her, and he must have worked out what she needed after talking to Finn.

"I—"

Pippa didn't let him finish as gratitude overwhelmed her. "You literally saved our skin!" she cried. "The event would have actually been cancelled had you not done that."

"Um. Don't mention it," he said hoarsely.

"We wondered who had hooked us up with them." She remembered Mae mentioning that the organisation was based in the South East. She groaned. Kent was South East! How had she not noticed that? "I can't thank you enough."

There was silence for a while but then Alex spoke, his voice stronger. "You don't need to thank me. I know this fair means a lot to you. And you mean a lot to me. I'll do whatever it takes – I told you that."

It took all of Pippa's strength not to ask where this energy had been when he'd made the choice to leave. "Well, the gesture's appreciated." *Albeit totally futile,* she thought as she glanced over at Wolfie, who was engaged in conversation with Frankie. Although he wasn't looking at her, Pippa had the strange feeling he was keeping tabs on her every movement through his peripheral vision. His quiet possession of her sent a delicious shiver through her body.

"Anyway," Alex was saying. "What I also wanted to say was I've managed to get a cracking deal on bunting from a mate. It'll take some effort, but I reckon I can string it up across the green and make it look really festive."

"Lovely," Pippa said. Bunting flapping in the fresh breeze coming off the moors would be a nice touch for the festivalgoers perusing the food trucks and stalls on the green.

"Thanks," Alex said. "Will I see you at the set-up day tomorrow?"

"Tomorrow," Pippa echoed. God, tomorrow was the

penultimate day before the fair and she'd barely thought about it for the past day. A flurry of images assaulted her memory: Wolfie's lean body, his mouth leaving burning trails across her skin... No wonder the fair hadn't been her foremost concern that day. "Look, I'd best go," she said. Wolfie had vanished into the library and Frankie was glaring at her, arms folded and toes tapping. "Thanks for everything." Before Alex could comment further, she hung up.

"You sly minx." Frankie nudged her shoulder.

Pippa looked around for Wolfie, clocking almost straight away that the library door was closed. "What?"

"Something happened with Tall, Blond and Brooding, didn't it?" Frankie giggled. "The way he looked at you when he came out ... I swear, I could have started playing naked Twister whilst singing '99 Red Balloons' in the original German and he wouldn't have so much as glanced my way."

"Don't be so silly," Pippa said. "Your singing voice is perfection, Frankie, of course he'd have glanced."

Frankie didn't waver. "You're not denying it."

Pippa blushed. "Denying what?"

"You and Wolfie!" Frankie cried. "What's happened? Did you kiss or—" He clocked her burning cheeks, and the resulting shriek could probably have been heard at the top of Clough Hill. "You *didn't!*"

"I couldn't possibly say," Pippa said, but under Frankie's relentless gaze, she caved. "Okay yes. Something happened this afternoon."

"Something?" Frankie repeated.

"*Something.*" Pippa's tone left no doubt as to what she meant.

"YES!" Frankie whooped.

Pippa sighed. "Yeah, but I think Alex's call just now gave the wrong impression. Wolfie disappeared pretty quickly, didn't he?"

"Well, he needs to stop being a baby." Frankie pulled a face. "Alex is out of your life, right?"

"Big time!" Pippa exclaimed. She was mildly annoyed that Wolfie could believe anything else, after their afternoon together.

"You'll set Wolfie straight," Frankie said. "But more importantly"—he gripped her shoulders— "Tell. Me. Everything."

Chapter Twenty

Wolfie didn't emerge from the library, not even to say goodbye to Frankie and Theo. Pippa had spent the past couple of hours in an anxiously frustrated state. He'd clearly reacted to Alex's poorly timed phone call, but Pippa was damned if she was going to run around appeasing Wolfie with regards to Alex's status. If today hadn't made it abundantly clear where her heart lay, then she wasn't sure what would.

Pippa took her mind off her frustrations by running through her outstanding tasks: cleaning, dusting and polishing various pieces of furniture throughout the house. By early evening, she was scrubbing the kitchen sink to a high shine, when her phone began buzzing in her back pocket.

"Mr Rogers!" she greeted the caller. "Thanks for calling me back."

"Sorry it's taken an age to get back to you." The

butcher's voice was rasping, but kindly. "It's been rather a frantic few weeks."

"I'm sorry to hear that." Pippa dropped her cleaning cloths in the sink. "I hope everything's all right?"

"Don't worry," he said. "My daughter's going through a divorce. Long story," he advised hastily as Pippa made sympathetic noises. "And so we've been preoccupied with that. Glad to report business has been booming however."

"That's great to hear," Pippa replied. "And apropos of the offer I was hoping to make."

"Yes, I did see your emails," Mr Rogers said. "And I heard the voicemails. The Hurst Bridge Summer Fair! What a blast from the past."

"Indeed," Pippa said. "I was very much hoping Pigs in Clover would still be interested in hiring out a stall on the green. We have one space left." Pippa had been holding out against a couple of last-minute offers from other businesses, hoping she could get the famous butcher to come on board. "It's a premium spot," she said. "And your fee would go towards a worthy cause."

"I know. I was going to refuse," Mr Rogers said, and Pippa's heart plummeted. "But Iris – my daughter – insisted I take part."

"Really?"

"Yes. She reminded me just how lovely the fairs were once upon a time. And," he conceded, "I checked the accounts for the last ones we participated in, which was some time ago, mind. The numbers don't lie – the fairs were always good business."

"As will this one be," Pippa said confidently. "We fully

expect the same level of footfall, if not more, now that we have improved bus routes from across the region."

"You can stop the pitching," the man laughed. "I'm in, at the price you quoted."

Pippa had to stop herself from shouting in delight. For Pigs in Clover, she would have been willing to negotiate, but the fact she didn't have to was a huge bonus. "You won't regret it."

"I'm sure I won't," he said. "I'll sign the agreement and email it over. I say, the prizegiving isn't at Squires, is it?"

"It is," Pippa said. "Just like the old days."

"Marvellous," Mr Rogers remarked. "You know, Iris applied for the housesitting gig there."

Pippa froze. "She did?"

"Yes," he replied. "She fancied a clean break after leaving Dan but didn't even get invited for interview."

Pippa's mind was a whirl. Wolfie had told her that no one else applied for the role. "You're sure Iris definitely applied?" she asked dumbly. "For Squires?"

"Yes. She had an interview booked in for the Wednesday and then got a call Tuesday night saying the position was no longer available." He chuckled lightly. "You must have an excellent interview technique." Pippa gaped. Her interview had been on a Tuesday, hadn't it? But why would Wolfie lie about not having had any interest in the role? Unless her sob story about Alex had moved him to the point he had felt obliged to offer her the place. "Anyway, Iris is sorted with a great job now, so everything worked out," Mr Rogers went on amiably. "Look, I'd best dash, but I'll email over the agreement, yes?"

Pippa ended the call as politely as she could, her head spinning. She had to grip the sink to remain upright. She had been something of a wreck at that interview, hadn't she? The need for a home and a job had probably radiated off her like a small screaming sun. Could it be that Wolfie, with all his baggage, had recognised her pain and that was why he'd offered her that lifeline? Something occurred to her, then, something Wolfie himself had remarked on when they were hunting for Juniper out on the moors.

She pulled out her phone again.

"Hello darling!" Eileen Munro was sunning herself, wet hair raked back into a scraggly topknot. "This is a nice surprise."

"Hi Mum," Pippa said. "Not disturbing you, am I?"

"Not at all!" Eileen pulled on sunglasses. "Just had a dip in the pool. We're hosting the neighbours for a potluck this evening so I'm relaxing before the chaos starts."

"Sounds fun." Pippa missed her mum's dinner parties.

"Should be. So, what can I help you with?" Eileen asked tenderly. Pippa's eyes unexpectedly filled with tears and Eileen bolted upright in alarm. "Oh God, what's wrong? Is it Alex? Are you pregnant?" Her face became infinitely more hopeful at the last sentence.

"No, it's not Alex and calm down, I am definitely not pregnant." Pippa swiped at her eyes. "I'm not sure why I'm crying, it's only that..." She took a deep breath. The moment felt strangely significant. "I have a question for you."

"Ohh." Eileen pursed her lips in intrigue. "Go on."

"What made you move to Florida?"

Eileen let out a sharp laugh. "Why do you ask?"

Pippa felt as if her entire future hinged on what her mother said next. "Can you just tell me?"

Eileen smiled softly. "It's quite simple. I love your dad."

"But you loved Hurst Bridge," Pippa said.

Eileen's eyes moistened. "True. I mean, still do. I miss it. As I miss you. But ... from day one your dad told me his absolute dream was to retire in Florida. I always knew it was part and parcel of being with him."

"And you didn't even try to convince him to stay?" Pippa asked incredulously.

Eileen laughed gently. "Of course I tried! But at my core, I knew what would make him happy and, honestly, when the time came, it felt right." Her warm eyes reached across the miles as she looked into the camera. "Let me tell you, when you love someone enough, you can make big sacrifices like that and still be blissfully happy."

"You loved Dad enough to leave," Pippa said.

"Quite simply, yes." her mum beamed. "We had the means and the freedom. You were – or so we thought – settled, so our job was done when it came to you. Ultimately, my home is with that man, which means wherever he goes, I follow. It's the same for him. If I'd put my foot down about living somewhere, if it was for some reason important to me, Pete would do it."

"And you were always sure of that?" Pippa asked.

"Surer than anything in this world," her mum said firmly. "Apart from loving you, of course."

Pippa blinked away fresh tears. That was it, right there. It was clear that certainty had never been there with

Alex, not when it mattered. She heard footsteps in the hallway.

"I'd best go," she murmured.

"Is everything all right?" Eileen demanded.

"Absolutely," Pippa smiled mistily. "I'm just working some things out."

"Well, I'm always here if you need me," her mother told her, face shining with adoration.

"Love you," Pippa said.

"Back atcha." Eileen waved and the call blinked off.

Exhaling slowly, Pippa lowered the phone. In the reflection of the window, Wolfie appeared, leaning against the doorway to the kitchen. Pippa returned to her task of cleaning the sink, reeling from the powerful emotions that raged through her. Finally, she felt brave enough to speak.

"I know that call earlier sounded bad," she said, her words tumbling over each other, "Alex calling me *love*, but he isn't … if it hasn't been clear this entire time, he and I aren't together anymore."

"All right," he said softly.

Pippa scrubbed furiously at an old coffee stain. "So why hide yourself in your study all afternoon then? Because I did nothing wrong and if you think that—"

Wolfie was at Pippa's back before she could even finish her sentence, his hands circling her waist.

"I'm sorry," he said. "It's just … he was a significant part of your life for so long and you have so much shared history I find it quite daunting. I know I'll have to get used to that, but I really don't like him."

"I don't expect you to like him." Pippa squirmed against

Wolfie. He smelled so good. "I mean, he's my ex who broke my heart in a terribly cruel way."

"That and he seems like an insufferable douche," Wolfie muttered.

"Okay, okay, but please, the next time you're freaking out about something, tell me. Don't shut yourself away." She met his eyes in the reflection of the window, squinting thanks to the fiery brilliance of the sunset. "You can be open with me, I hope you know that."

Wolfie pondered this. Then he nuzzled into her hair. "Come with me."

"Where?"

Moments later, they were outside and stood by his motorbike, a helmet in Wolfie's outstretched hand.

"Are you fucking serious?" Pippa gingerly accepted the helmet as if it were a bomb. "Me? On that thing?"

"This *thing* as you call it, is an MV Brutale Dragster." Wolfie patted the leather seat. "Lightweight but an absolute beast."

"Beast?" Pippa repeated. "Okay, yeah, now I'm *really* comfortable getting on it."

Wolfie sighed good-naturedly at her sarcasm. "I want to show you something," he said. "But we have to move quickly because the sun is setting." He plucked the helmet from her hands and eased it onto her head. "You just need to trust me. I've been riding for years; you'll be perfectly fine."

His face was so open with hope, Pippa couldn't refuse him. "Okay," she relented. "But if I die, I'm coming back to haunt you so much your grandkids will be calling in an exorcist."

"Nothing will happen to you, Pippa Munro." His lips curled sensually as he checked the helmet was secure. "Well, nothing you don't want, anyway."

"How dare you," she said, weak with desire. "I'm a lady."

He winked at her. "You won't hear any argument from me on that score." He helped her climb on, then effortlessly slung his leg over the bike in front of her. "This thing can reach over 200 kilometres an hour, so you'd best hold on."

"Yeah but, you don't ever ride that fast, right?" She chuckled into his shoulder. When Wolfie just laughed softly in response Pippa shrieked and wrapped her arms around him like a vice. "Remember I am prepared to haunt the shit out of you."

Wolfie turned the key, the engine revving throatily. "Then may I suggest not letting go?" With a smooth, sudden leap, the bike took off. As soon as the bike hit the open road, Wolfie applied more speed and with it Pippa's adrenaline soared, her thrilled scream stolen from her mouth by the sudden velocity. Gripping Wolfie's back, she looked out across the hills as they whizzed by, their beauty kissed by the glow of the setting sun. She had never felt so vital; exposed and vulnerable on the back of a speeding bike, the cool wind darting under her dress and up her bare legs. Her head was filled with a whooshing sound that almost drowned out the aggressive roar of the engine beneath her, every muscle engaged to ensure she didn't slip off. They were travelling well over 100 kilometres per hour, of that she was sure, with the merciless drop of the hills to their right. One skid and they'd be plummeting to the rocky valley below. Pippa should have been terrified. But she wasn't. It was the most exhilarated she'd ever felt in her life.

The road evened out as they reached the top of the hill, but Wolfie didn't slow down. He pitched a left, cutting across open moorland on the narrowest of lanes, before heading down the other slope towards Hadley Gorge. Hadley Gorge had been one of Pippa's favourite places as a child, a narrow, tree-lined valley with a crystal-clear stream at its base that ran through fairy-like mossy grottos of ancient woodland. Before they descended towards the trails, Wolfie turned down a little track hidden almost entirely by dense trees. At a sheltered spot, he killed the engine and parked. He then jumped off the bike and removed his helmet, eyes shining.

"How was that?" he asked, helping her dismount.

Pippa pulled off her helmet, taking a second to catch her breath. "No words," she said honestly.

Clearly proud, Wolfie weaved his fingers through hers. "This way then," he said.

Pippa allowed him to guide her further down the little track, which soon became so narrow they had to walk single file. Trees closed in overhead like a vaulted ceiling akin to a church. It was utterly peaceful. Ahead of her, Wolfie peeled off through a cluster of evergreens, holding back branches so they didn't hit her in the face. And then, they emerged onto a rocky outcropping, high above Hadley Gorge.

Pippa's breath was stolen for a second time. The spot Wolfie had chosen was perfectly positioned to deliver the most stunning view of the sunset. The dazzling sun was currently sinking between two high peaks, its rays beaming directly into the valley and turning the stream into a streak of fire that blazed the whole length of the dark-emerald valley. Overhead, the deepening sky was clear, except for swirling skylarks and the occasional bat. The silence was total.

"Wolfie..." Pippa was so moved by this new and beautiful view of her home county that tears sprung to her eyes. "I don't think I've ever seen anything so beautiful."

He raised a finger to wipe away a tear sliding down her cheek. "Same."

She tore her gaze away from the panorama to look at him. "Thank you for showing me this."

"Grantham was the one who brought me here," he said roughly. "As a kid. Whenever things were difficult at home, he'd bring me up here and we'd talk. Or not. Sometimes, we'd just sit quietly and say nothing. Whatever I needed." Pippa sensed she didn't need to say anything. She gripped his hand and let him speak. "That man taught me to drive," Wolfie went on. "He helped me open my first bank account and showed me how to sign a cheque. He showed me what it meant to be a man. Joan too. I would be nothing without them."

"I don't believe that," Pippa said.

Wolfie shook his head. "Well, I do. I owe them everything. And that stubborn old coot won't let me help him."

"Let you help him how?" Something about the total frustration on Wolfie's face made things click into place for

Pippa. "Wolfie, you aren't just selling Squires to pay off Carmichael's debts, are you?"

His eyes reddened. "No."

"You're selling for..."

"Joan," he said softly. "She needs very specialised care. And it's, well..."

"It's expensive," Pippa finished.

"Extremely." He grimaced. "I told Grantham I would use whatever profit remained from the sale of Squires to fund it. I did the maths and there'd be a sizeable sum left once Dad's debts are paid off that could cover at least a couple of years of care. But he won't let me. I've been hoping I could convince him as the sale goes through, but he won't take a penny off me." He scuffed the ground with his feet.

Pippa could barely catch her breath at this revelation. This man, whom she'd once dismissed as grumpy and uncaring, had been willing to give up everything to ensure the wellbeing of a person he loved. Despite the harshness of his childhood and the trauma he'd had to work through, love had won out. With Wolfie, it always would. Pippa knew that here was a man she would do anything and go anywhere for.

"Thank you for telling me," she said, her voice soft. "And you never know, Grantham might come round. But if he doesn't, you can be there for him in other ways. Money isn't always the most important thing in these types of situations." After what Frankie went through with his dad, Pippa knew that better than anyone.

"I know, I know," he said. "I just... I hate not being able to fix things."

Pippa stroked hair back from his face. "I get that," she said. "But I was a little confused. You know I thought you had a girlfriend?"

Wolfie's face contorted. "What? No, I don't have a— I mean, there's you, now, but no one else. Why would you think that?"

Pippa laughed, half in embarrassment, half in nervous relief. She explained the phone calls she'd overheard him having. "I made assumptions that you were trying to impress a heartless gold-digger," she finished, blushing hard.

Wolfie groaned with laughter. "Well then, that makes sense now. Why you got a bit cagey with me sometimes."

"Cagey?" Pippa repeated.

"Oh, I just thought it was my complete inability to flirt." He brushed a stray tendril of hair off her face. "Whenever I attempted to sweet talk you, you'd look at me with such confusion. I put it down to my absolute lack of game, but now I get it. You thought I already had a girlfriend."

"I wasn't sure, that's all."

He pulled her close to him, brushed his lips against her cheek. "Are you sure now?"

"I'm sure you shouldn't even need to ask me that." She cleared her throat and looked up at him. "But can I ask you something?"

"Anything."

"When I interviewed for the job, you made it seem like no one else had applied." It may be entirely unimportant,

Pippa considered, but she had to know. "Thing is, I found out today that at least one other person did."

"Ah." He laughed throatily. "Busted."

"Was it because I was a pathetic homeless mess?" Pippa asked. "You took pity on me, is that it?"

"No." Wolfie looked appalled. "God, no."

"So, what then?" she asked.

"You might think this is a bit silly," he said.

"Go on."

"I gave you the job because ..." He wavered, deliberating. Then he gave a minute nod of resolve. "Because, the day you came to meet me, when I saw you standing on my doorstep, beautiful and determined and, let's be honest, a little bit sassy, I had the strangest feeling."

"God, what?" Pippa's insides clenched.

He smiled softly. "For the first time in my life I knew what it felt like to come home."

Pippa's throat closed with emotion. "Home?"

"Yes. Does that sound weird?" He hummed a laugh. "I told myself that hiring you, the first person to interview, was the simplest way of solving the house sitter issue, but that wasn't the case." His face stilled. "You're not mad I lied, are you?"

"Wolfie, I..." She experienced many feelings in that instant, but mad was the least of them. It was then Pippa knew she was falling in love with Wolfie Squires. It was that simple. Maybe she had started that descent the moment she met him; she wasn't totally sure. There was something so *fierce* about the gift of Wolfie's emotion. He hid it away, like a guarded treasure behind high walls, but when the defences came down, when he entrusted a person with his heart, it was possibly the strongest force Pippa had ever encountered. She laughed quietly and shook her head. "Just when I think I have you figured out, you say stuff like that."

Wolfie looked adorably blank. "Say what, the truth?"

"I mean, I can tell you're going to keep me on my toes," she said. "Always guessing."

His smile turned devilish. "Oh, you won't need to be guessing *everything*." His purposeful gaze dropped to her mouth, and her knees weakened.

"Is that right?" She teased as he loomed over her, his nose brushing her own.

"You'll never need to wonder whether I'm yours." Wolfie put his hands on her hips and pulled her flush against him, where she could feel every inch of his desire for her. "Are you mine, Pippa Munro?"

Lust flooded Pippa's body to the point she could barely form words. "Y-yes."

He gently guided her towards the trees until her back hit the broad trunk of a mossy oak. "Because, if it isn't clear, I consider you mine."

She met his eyes boldly. "Then you'd better take me."

His kiss was determined and strong, leaving her breathless, the tree's bark digging into her back. And then Wolfie's knee was easing her legs apart, his hand trailing up her bare skin towards her core. As his mouth moved to her neck, his fingers began confidently probing their way in between her thighs.

"Tell me you're mine," he commanded. Pippa struggled to get her mouth to form words. She wanted him more than she'd ever wanted anything or anyone, but she was very conscious they were outside. Yet within seconds his insistent, sensual touch forced her to abandon all rationality. Soon, she didn't care about where they were, she just didn't want him to stop doing what he was doing.

"I'm yours," Pippa moaned. She reached down to the fly of his jeans, wanting to return the gift that he was giving her so expertly, but his strength held her in place. He gently chided her with a nibble to her earlobe.

"Not yet," he said rearing back so he could watch her face. "Let me see you. Show me." His fingers moved faster, firmer. "Do you like that?"

Pippa could only nod as she gripped onto him for dear life. Tremors of pleasure soon wracked her body, surging to an intense wave that peaked so brilliantly the world briefly went white and all she could see during that temporary, insane blindness was the blue heat of her lover's eyes.

Chapter Twenty-One

"Do you have to go?" Pippa kissed her way down Wolfie's throat. They'd spent several hours on that private hillside spot, returning to Squires long after the sun had sunk below the horizon. The dawn was breaking and although they had hardly slept, she still couldn't get enough of him. Thankfully, it seemed as if he felt the same. Barely a moment went past when his hands weren't on her, or his mouth wasn't trailing across her skin. Pippa never wanted his attentions to stop. The man hiding behind those high walls was a never-ending maze of delight and she was utterly, pleasurably lost in him.

"I have an early appointment in Liverpool," he groaned regretfully, glancing at the clock on his bedside table. "Client emergency." He gripped her chin, tilting her face to look into his eyes. "But if I promise to break all the speed limits on the way there and on the way back, I should be home before lunchtime. Anyway, don't you have a busy day yourself?"

Pippa rested her chin on his chest. "Yeah." Tomorrow was the fair and there was a lot of preparation to do. It promised to be a gruelling day. "I may regret not getting any sleep."

"I don't remember you complaining at any point last night." He grinned wickedly as he pushed her snarled hair back from her face. "But, like I said, I shouldn't be away too long. Maybe I can help?"

Pippa pushed herself upright. "You?" She widened her eyes in a theatrical display of disbelief. "*You* would help with the fair?"

A strange smile flitted across his face. "Stranger things have happened."

The image of Wolfie pitching in with the volunteers and engaging with the people of the town tugged at Pippa's heart. "That'd be great."

He bundled her into him, planting a deep kiss on her mouth. "I'd best get in the shower then."

Pippa stretched. "Should I make you a coffee for the road?"

Stark naked, he reached for a dressing gown that was hooked across the enormous wing-back chair that took up a corner of the room. "No, don't worry. Stay where you are," he said gently. "Try and get some rest."

As she watched Wolfie's magnificent form strut off to the shower, Pippa vowed to stay awake until he returned, but she dozed off and when her alarm went off at eight, he'd already gone. He had texted a farewell:

Didn't want to wake you. See you later. Yours, W.

There it was again, that wonderful word, *yours*. Despite the weariness in her bones, Pippa fairly danced her way to the shower, not even noticing her tender ankle giving intermittent protests at the effort. She was so happy she didn't care when the shower water came out cold and intermittently trickling, nor did she care when she spilled her coffee all over the kitchen table, or that Wolfie had clearly stuck the butter knife in the jam and left crumby streaks in the jar. Nothing could touch her mood.

As she drove into town, Pippa mused on the day ahead as the radio blared out retro tunes that she couldn't help but sing along to – tunelessly. Luckily the storm of the previous day had passed and although the sky was overcast, Pippa could sense the sun waiting to break through. She pulled into the Hand and Flower car park, where Mae had established a rudimentary command centre. The town centre was a hub of activity too; the green was freshly mowed and someone from the council had obligingly repainted some of the yellow lines and parking spaces in the vicinity to ensure drivers knew exactly where they could and couldn't park.

As Pippa got out of the car, she waved to Erin who was pacing around the car park on the phone, finalising the monitors for the races: responsible individuals who would be dotted along the racecourse with walkie-talkies to ensure safety for the participants. She'd largely recruited from the parents of the children she taught, bribing them with the promise that their kids would be pushed to the front row of all the pictures taken for the papers. Mae had been polishing the race trophies and boxing them up so Pippa could take them back to Squires with her ready for the prizegiving. As Pippa locked Frankie's car, Mae emerged from the pub, box of trophies in hand.

"Morning!" Mae beamed. "You ready for this?"

"As I'll ever be." Pippa stifled a yawn. "Sorry."

Mae raised an eyebrow. "Wow, late night?"

"Not as such, I got to bed relatively early." That at least was true. Pippa pointed to the box in Mae's arms. "That ready to go?"

"Yup. Will you need help carrying it?" Mae hefted the box into Pippa's arms.

"Nah." Pippa clutched it tight. "I've got quite strong since taking on the job at Squires. All that housework and gardening, who knew?"

"Yeah, you're looking fit." Mae flashed a wicked grin. "I hear Wolfie thinks so too."

As Pippa's face flamed crimson, Erin pulled away from her call with an excited gasp. "Sorry Mrs Murgatroyd, one sec!" Covering the phone with her hand she went on. "You and Wolfie?! Is it true…?"

"How the—?" Pippa tutted. "Frankie. God, he's got a mouth."

"It's all over his social media." Mae roared with laughter when Pippa lowered the box she was holding and dove for her phone. "I'm joking! I spoke to him this morning and he spilled."

Pippa groaned. "I'm going to kill him."

"He's happy for you." Mae gripped her shoulder and eyeballed Pippa earnestly. "As am I. New penis, Pip. You did it!"

Erin cleared her throat. "Sorry Mrs Murgatroyd, I'm just going to move somewhere quieter." She shot a warning glance at Mae.

"All right, enough with the new penis." Pippa laughed.

"Sorry, sorry." Mae didn't look the least bit sorry. "But at least it explains why you look completely wrecked this morning. You clearly got some serious action last night!"

Pippa affected primness. "I couldn't possibly say," she sniffed.

Mae elbowed her. "Maybe *you* can't, but that love bite on your neck says plenty."

Blushing, Pippa adjusted the collar of her top. "That's ... a bruise."

"What, you walked into Wolfie's mouth by accident?" Mae giggled mercilessly. "Listen, we have a busy day ahead and we need to crack on. But at some point, you need to tell me *everything*. And I mean everything. Was it hot? I bet it was hot. Frankie said Wolfie was looking at you like he wanted to eat you alive."

Pippa smiled wryly, bumping her hip against the car boot so the electronic keys could open it. "Maybe, maybe."

Mae arched an eyebrow. "Is it ... serious?"

Pippa put the box in the boot and closed it, gnawing her lip. "I want it to be," she said. "Which is mad, I know, so soon after Al—"

"Nope, not mad." Mae shook her head firmly. "If you like Wolfie enough, it isn't mad."

"He makes me feel safe," Pippa blurted. "Isn't that funny? Living here, I didn't think I could feel any safer. But he does that."

"I'm glad to hear it." Mae's walkie-talkie on her hip crackled and she rolled her eyes. "Timing." She listened for a few seconds and groaned. "Sounds like an issue with the portaloos. I'll sort it."

"You crack on," Pippa declared. "I have my duties." Mae blew a kiss at Pippa and stormed off towards the green, barking orders into her radio. As Pippa locked the car up, her phone buzzed. Reaching for it, she hoped it was Wolfie calling, and was very glad to see it was indeed him. It had been only six hours since she'd watched him walk to the shower, but it had felt like years.

"Pippa Munro," he greeted her softly. Pippa's tummy tilted. She loved the way he said her name.

"Hi," she said. "Everything go okay with the client?"

"It did," he replied. "Already on my way back to you."

To you, he'd said. Not *to Squires* or *to Hurst Bridge*. To *you*. "That was quick," she remarked. "It's only just gone ten."

"Well, I made it to his house in record time for 7am," he said, as the car's indicator clicked down the line. "And we restructured his security operation within an hour. Had to get finance and legal on the phone to finalise but … all done. Roads are really quiet, so I'll be with you very soon."

"Great." Pippa couldn't wait. "And you still want to help with the fair?"

"Absolutely," he said. "If you need me."

"We'll find you something, I'm sure," she said. "We might have to make sure the doctor is on call in case people drop from the shock of seeing you in the town, like, socialising. Talking to people."

"I know it's a little uncharacteristic. That's entirely your fault," Wolfie said.

"Excuse me?" Pippa said with a laugh.

"I hold you entirely responsible for changing everything," he said solemnly.

"You're going to have to explain," Pippa said. There were a few silent seconds as she could practically hear him labouring over what words to choose.

"I told you what my childhood was like," he said eventually. "You grow up with a father like that and *home* becomes a dirty word. Something you run away from." He trailed off, swallowing audibly. Pippa didn't speak. She feared that if she did, it would break the spell they were under and Wolfie might not reveal what was on his mind. "So that's what I did. I ran and kept on running."

"I think most people in your shoes would do the same," she said, softly.

"Maybe," he allowed. "I always felt like I had to keep moving, never stopping, never settling. That way, I could escape the memories. And then you came along." Pippa could hear the smile breaking through his voice. "You made my world slow down, Pippa Munro. In a good way. It was the thing I needed most, and I didn't know it. What I'm trying to say, in a rather roundabout way, is that if you need me to, I don't know, build a flipping coconut shy with my bare hands, then I will. For you."

Pippa was struck dumb, filled with a whirl of emotions that she couldn't name. She stood staring into space, scarcely able to breathe.

"You still there?" He asked after a few seconds of silence.

"Yeah, sorry." She needed to see him, to hold him. Right now. "Get back here to me."

"On my way." There was such promise in his voice that it made her weak. For a moment, Pippa didn't care about the fair or her hometown. She longed to be alone with Wolfie again, tangled up in bedsheets and cut off from the world.

"Pip!" Mae yelled from across the car park. "Get your bum here now!"

"I think that's your cue to hang up," Wolfie said with a laugh.

"It is." Pippa waved at Mae *one minute*. "Come to the town," she said. "I'll be at the pub or somewhere near the green."

"I'll see you presently," Wolfie said.

Once she'd they'd said goodbye, Pippa took a moment to even out her breathing. She wasn't sure she'd be able to wipe the grin off her face and, sure enough, as she neared Mae, her friend took one look at her and groaned.

"You're going to be useless today, aren't you?"

Pippa lifted her chin. "Shut up. What's the problem?"

"My dad has had to pick up a shift," Mae said. Wally Grant had been managing the team that was marking out the pitches on the green for all the trucks and stalls. "So he's got to go. Thing is, some of the trucks start arriving this afternoon."

"I can finish for him," Pippa said.

"Thanks." Mae was relieved. "You sure?"

"Yup." Pippa nodded. "Then once I've done that, I can drop off the trophies and make sure Squires is decorated for the prizegiving. When are the race barriers getting set up?"

"They're getting delivered tonight," Mae told her. "But we can only erect them tomorrow when the roads are actually closed. We've got some of the teachers pitching in to do that though."

"Got it." Pippa hugged Mae, wincing at how tense her friend was. "It's all in hand." She then hurried down to the green, finding Wally in one corner with the line marker machine. He and Grantham were studying the plan Mae had given them, showing where each vendor was to be.

"Pip, love!" Wally hugged her, enveloping her with his familiar smell of cigarettes and chewing gum. "Sorry about this."

"That's all right," Pippa assured him. Wally was Head Porter at Chesterfield Hospital, a job he took very seriously.

"One of my team's going home with the flu," he explained. "I need to pick up his shift."

"Don't worry." Pippa gripped the handle of the marker machine.

"I know you've got a lot on your plate," he went on apologetically.

"Wally, it's fine." She gestured around the green. "You've done so much already. It's nearly finished."

"All right, love." Wally gave her a fatherly pat on the shoulder, then permitted Grantham a nod. "See you."

Once he'd gone, Grantham clapped his hands. "Let's crack on, shall we?" The two of them began to mark out the remaining vendor pitches, Grantham guiding Pippa as she marked out the rectangles, then he painted the corresponding vendor number in the centre of each pitch. The painting was laborious, but it meant that as each vendor arrived, they could go straight to their assigned spot without any confusion.

Just as they marked out the final spot, noise at the top of the green caught Pippa's attention. "Oh good!" A flat-bed truck had reversed onto the green and two men were busying themselves unloading its contents.

"Hay bales?" Grantham observed.

"Yeah, cheap seating!" Pippa confirmed. "Mick Dunstan donated them. He— Oh." One of the men heaving the bales around was Alex.

Grantham noticed her troubled expression. "I can finish up here," he said. "If you need to go."

"Thanks Grantham." Pippa handed the marker machine over. "Can you take this back to the Hand and Flower? The hire company is coming for it this evening."

"No problem," he said.

"Thanks." Before she ran off, Pippa stopped. "How's Joan? Sorry, been so manic of late I haven't been able to ask."

To her alarm, Grantham's eyes watered. "She's not so well, I'm afraid. I can't keep her at home anymore." He forced an exasperated smile, but Pippa could see the pain behind it.

"Oh, God, I'm sorry." Pippa put all thoughts of Alex and Wolfie out of her mind. "Is there anything I can do?"

"You're doing it now," he said gently. "It helps to talk about it."

"Any time," she promised him. "Please, let me know if there is anything else."

"Maybe I'll take you up on that," he said. "Now, let me finish up."

Pippa kissed his cheek then strode across the green. Alex had left his colleague to move the bales around as he was unspooling bunting from a paper sack. She had to admit that the bunting was perfect: all the colours of the rainbow.

"That'll look good hanging from the trees," she said by way of greeting.

Alex beamed, eyes crinkling as they always did. Pippa felt a glow of satisfaction at the revelation that his grin no longer had the same effect on her as it once did.

"How's it all going?" he asked.

"We're getting there." She nodded at the bunting. "Thanks for your help."

"You're welcome." He stood, hands on hips. "You look good."

Pippa glanced down at herself uncertainly. Baggy jeans and an old band T-shirt that had been washed so many times it was an indiscriminate shade of grey where once it had been blue. "Thanks."

"Do you remember when I bought you that top?" Alex stepped closer. "We saw that band at The Grapes."

"I do." It had been a fun night. The band were kind of terrible, off-key and shrieking, so Alex and Pippa had turned to beer to drown out the noise.

"I laughed so much." Alex smiled.

"Me too," Pippa said. "They really thought they were the next Arctic Monkeys."

"That they did." He tilted his head. "We had fun, didn't we?"

"We did." Pippa couldn't deny that fact.

Alex's eyes teared up, but he made no move to wipe them. He held her gaze. "I miss that."

Pippa folded her arms. "I know."

"Anyway." Alex sniffed, conscious of being in public. "I'll get this all set up. Erin said something about some signage; I can get to that afterwards."

"Great." Pippa remembered the medics. "I really do owe you a huge thank you." She grimaced. "As hard as that is for me to admit."

"Excuse me?" Alex's mouth quirked.

"You know!" Pippa said. "Without the medics, we couldn't be insured. Without insurance, well, you can imagine, this whole event wouldn't be able to go ahead. So thank you, for pulling whatever strings you did to get them here."

"But I —" Alex stopped, locking eyes with her. "You're welcome. I mean, whatever you need, I'm here for you."

"I appreciate that." Buoyed by his generosity and her recent happiness, Pippa felt a wave of magnanimity. "I really hope we can get through this awkward bit, you know?"

He arched an eyebrow. "You do?"

"Sure." Pippa couldn't hold on to resentment forever, she realised. Alex may have left town, but his family were here. He would never be fully out of her life as a result, so they had to find a way to keep things civil at the very least. "I'd like to stay friends, if we can."

"Friends?" Alex repeated dully.

"Yeah." She nodded.

"*Friends?*" He spat the word this time. "What, that's it? Decision made? You're really not going to change your mind? After all this time alone, you really don't want me anymore?"

Pippa stared at him, infuriated by his arrogance. "Was I not clear?"

Alex growled. "We were together for over ten years, Pip. We had something special! You can't just dismiss that!"

"You did when you left me," Pippa said imperiously. She wondered how he had the nerve to make such accusations. "You can't blame me for moving on with my life."

"Moving—?" Alex tilted his head, gazing furiously into her face. "There's someone else, isn't there?"

Pippa couldn't halt the rush of blood to her cheeks and he reared back in horror. "That's ... that's neither here nor there," she croaked.

Alex threw his arms up, running his hands through his hair. "No. *NO.*" His eyes filled with tears. "This can't be happening."

"I'm sorry," Pippa said truthfully.

"I can't accept that." He was suddenly holding her arms, pulling her close. "Tell me it's not true."

"Alex!" She tried to extricate herself, but his grip was strong. "Let me go."

"You *have* to let me fix this," he declared. "Remember what we meant to each other. Don't you dare throw it all away."

"Alex, for the millionth time, I'm not the one who threw our relationship away." Pippa tried to remain calm.

"You have to remember," he cried. "Please, you have to."

"Alex. Come on, stop," Pippa chided gently. It was only right she tell him about Wolfie, she decided. Because he was due here any moment and if the first Alex learned of their relationship was to see them together, he could cause a real scene and Pippa didn't want that. "Look, you should know —" Her words were cut off by Alex's lips suddenly landing on her own. The husky strength of his body pressed against hers and for an infinitesimal second, she froze, dominated by the overwhelming familiarity of it. It was like some sick muscle memory that demanded she yield. But sense prevailed and she recoiled, pulling away. "No!"

Alex leapt back as if scalded. "Sorry. God. So, so sorry."

"What do you think you're doing?" Pippa wiped at her mouth.

"I wanted you to remember how it used to be," he said defensively. "I thought ... if I reminded you, maybe—"

"What, one kiss would undo the horrible damage you did?" Pippa felt sick.

Alex's head shook. "No, no, that's not what I mean, you know that." He raked his hands through his hair. "Are you sure you know exactly what you're saying no to? What you're throwing away."

"What *I'm* throwing away?" she echoed furiously. "We have nothing *left* to throw away! You made sure of that. You broke what we had, *you* did, not me, and we can't go back. Not ever." Pippa couldn't bear to hear any more. She had to tell Alex about Wolfie, if only to make her point absolutely clear. But Alex had turned ashen, and he looked like he was about to vomit. "What is it?"

"The business is failing." His voice was so low Pippa thought she'd misheard.

"What?"

"The retail park. I'm struggling." He ran a hand over his face, hair dishevelled. "I'm losing money hand over fist."

The irony was too much. Could it be that just as his project failed, Alex had realised what he'd lost when he left her? She wondered if his desire to win her back was rooted in the need to restore his fortunes, and fury gave way to a bleak pity.

"That's not what Finn said," Pippa remarked acidly. "Does your family know?"

Alex grabbed her hands. "No. Please, Pip, if you could—"

"Stop." Pippa shook her head. "Just. Stop." There was silence for a few long moments. A large truck rolled past, and fair volunteers hailed the driver with waves and laughter. As Alex wilted before her, his chest heaving with emotion, Pippa thought of Wolfie and felt free. She couldn't share Alex's misfortune as it was no longer her own. She took a deep breath. "Alex. I'm genuinely sorry things didn't turn out the way you wanted." She gestured around her. "But you made your choice, and now I've made mine."

He lifted a tear-soaked face. "Pip—"

"No." Pippa took a step back, then another. "If you want to stop helping us with the fair that's fine. Feel free to leave. But don't for a second think I'm ever taking you back." She allowed herself to look upon him properly, just briefly, to allow the significance of the moment to sink in. "Goodbye, Alex."

And with that, Pippa turned her back on the man who had once been her entire world and strode away. As she walked, she looked out across the Green then checked her phone. No word from Wolfie. She sent a text to see where he was, but he didn't reply. He must be on the road still, she thought, and decided to check in with Mae.

As she crossed the car park, Grantham emerged from the pub.

"Hire company said they'll be sending someone over to collect the paint machine," he said.

"Great," Pippa said. "Mae in there?"

"Yes, on the phone." Grantham peered around her. "Wolfie not with you?"

"He's on his way." A warm glow spread through Pippa's chest. "Wants to volunteer his skills."

"I thought he was here already." Grantham frowned. "I mean, I saw his car."

"You did?" Pippa couldn't see him anywhere.

"Yes, he was parking up just as you were speaking to Alex," Grantham said. "I'm surprised you didn't see him; he wasn't far from you."

Pippa gazed to the part of the green where she and Alex had been. Wolfie's car wasn't parked anywhere nearby. "Are you sure it was him?"

"Completely." Grantham shrugged. "I wonder why he didn't stay?"

A sick feeling began to develop in Pippa's gut. She could

guess. If he'd shown up just as Alex was throwing himself at her, Wolfie may well have got the wrong impression. In fact, given how vulnerable he was when it came to his emotions, Pippa could almost guarantee it. "I need to get back to Squires," she choked.

Grantham regarded her with wise eyes. "Got something you want to tell me?"

"No." Pippa checked her phone; no reply from Wolfie still. There wasn't time to brief Grantham on their relationship. "I mean, not now." She scurried back to her car, all thoughts of fair prep dismissed.

You back yet? She messaged Wolfie again, keeping one eye on the screen as she buckled herself in. No answer even as she gunned the engine. Grantham knocked on the window and she wound it down.

The old man leaned on the door and fixed her with a gentle smile. "When it comes to Wolfie," he said. "Persistence is key. That boy has a big heart but a stubborn mind."

Pippa gulped back hot tears. She was aware of those traits and loved Wolfie for both of them. "Okay."

"He's been in some dark places." Grantham's lip trembled. "But I think that's how he recognises when something really shines. That he has to hold on to it." He nodded at her. "I'm glad you're in his life."

"Thank you," Pippa said. As much as she appreciated the old man's words, she was desperate to get back to Squires.

Grantham gave another satisfied nod and, with a tap on the door, he stepped back, allowing her to set off. Minutes later, Pippa pulled up to Squires and she could have wept with relief when she saw Wolfie's car parked outside the house. Grabbing the box of trophies, she let herself into the house, heart soaring when she ran into Wolfie in the entrance hall. But then she saw the freshly packed overnight bag waiting by the door.

"What...? Where are you going?" Pippa lowered the box to the ground. "Work?"

Wolfie shook his head tightly. "No."

"What is it?" His arched tone sent a chill down Pippa's spine, and she knew his walls had gone right back up.

"*It* is what I saw." Wolfie let out a strangled laugh. "You and Alex all over each other in full view of the town."

Pippa briefly closed her eyes, fighting to maintain composure over her internal rage towards Alex. "It wasn't what it looked like. He tried to kiss me; he certainly wasn't *all over me*. Did you not see me push him off?"

"No." Wolfie's eyes reddened. "From where I stood you looked pretty happy."

"Well, that's not the case. He and I are totally finished, I promise." She reached for Wolfie, but to her anguish, he veered away from her touch.

"I know. You told me. But I saw you with him, the way he looked at you," Wolfie shot back. "You have all this shared history binding you together, everyone in this town thought you were going to get married. What will they make of me, giving you a job and then all of a sudden taking his place at your side? Seeing you there, with *him*, merely reminded me how much I don't belong here."

Pippa could barely believe what she was hearing from

him. Only last night he'd made her swear she was his as he gave her the most intense orgasms of her life. And she'd sworn exactly that, meaning every ounce of her vow then as she did now. She fought to retain her composure.

"Wolfie, don't do this. Of course you belong here. You belong with me."

He shuddered. "I close my eyes, all I can see is you and him. Staying here, I'll see that for the rest of my life and I can't do it." Wolfie bent down to pick up his bag. "I have to … I need to get out of here, okay?"

"No, it's not okay!" Pippa snapped. "Please, stay. Talk to me. You can't let Alex's behaviour ruin everything between us."

But Wolfie was immune to her words. "It's my niece's birthday tea this evening so I've decided to drive over to Cumbria and surprise her." He pointed to a fat envelope lying on the hall table. "That's the signed paperwork for the sale of the house. Courier comes tomorrow afternoon around 3. Once those papers leave, that's it, sale done. I'm out of here."

"Wolfie, wait—"

"If you're worried about where to live, Top Stay have agreed you can stay here for another six weeks or so whilst they coordinate their plans," he went on stiffly.

Panic threatened to overwhelm Pippa. How could he do this to her? "Wolfie, I don't care about where I live. Please, talk to me." But it was like she hadn't spoken.

"I'll aim to be back to make sure the contracts get picked up, but if I'm not, I trust you can hand the envelope over?"

"No." Pippa shook her head.

"I'm selling," Wolfie said. "It's happening. Once those papers have been sent off, I'm washing my hands of this place. I'm gone."

"I'm not talking about the papers!" Pippa thought she might be sick with fury. How could Alex's presumptive behaviour have led to this? "Get them picked up by private jet for all I care." She moved closer, forcing him to meet her eye. "It's you I care about. Only you. I thought we had something really special, but if one misunderstanding is enough to make you jack it all in then I suppose you really should get out of here."

Wolfie spoke in barely a whisper. "Will you be around for the pick-up?"

Hot tears flooded her eyes. "It's the fair tomorrow. I'll be out of the house for much of the afternoon."

"Then I'll let Grantham know he might need to be here."

"Wolfie, *please*." Pippa laid a hand on his arm, totally unable to believe this was the same man who'd made love to her as if she were the only thing that mattered in his life. Who'd made her feel truly alive for the first time in years. And yet he was ready to destroy all that over something so pointless. "Alex threw himself at me, you must believe me. He thought that just because he helped us out of a pickle by arranging the medics and chucking up some bunting, that I'd come running back to him, but I set him straight."

"The medics?" Wolfie stopped dead, his eyes boring into hers. "That was Alex, was it?"

Pippa nodded. "Yeah. And don't get me wrong, it was a much-appreciated gesture, but not enough for me to change my mind."

Wolfie swallowed. "Right. I see. So, tell me, when you were 'setting Alex straight' did you see fit to tell him about me? About us?"

Pippa gulped. "No." Her heart lurched with horror as Wolfie shook his head and reached for the door handle. "I tried to, I was literally about to, really I was but then he—"

"I'm sorry." Wolfie opened the door, his voice cracking. "But I can't do this." And with that, he left.

Chapter Twenty-Two

The day of the fair was as perfect a day as Pippa could have hoped for: an azure sky with just a few clouds and the freshest, sweetest breeze flowing in off the moors. Mae, always the early bird, sent a 5am selfie of herself on her yoga mat in her garden, face bright with excitement. Yet Pippa couldn't share her friend's jubilation. She'd lain awake most of the night, despite working herself into the ground after Wolfie's departure to finish the set-up. She had hoped the labour would exhaust the agony that made her body physically hurt. Yet even after all the exertion, sleep had eluded her and she spent the night staring at the ceiling, replaying Wolfie's anguished words over and over in her mind. She raged at Alex for taking such liberty and cursed bad luck that he chose to do it just as Wolfie pulled up in his car. But most of all, she was angry at herself. Angry for not seeing how vulnerable Wolfie truly was and what a gift he was giving her when he'd entrusted her with his heart. Angry she'd not been able to reassure him that

Alex now knew with total certainty that she was never taking him back.

At some point in the early hours, Pippa had abandoned all pretence of sleeping and dragged herself downstairs, filling herself up with as much coffee as was humanly possible. As soon as her eyes felt capable of reading, she pored over the fair plans, checking the timings and logistics one last time until she was confident there were no gaps. Around 6am Mae texted a confirmation that all the roads in Hurst Bridge would be closed for the afternoon, with traffic routed in a loop around the town. Local police would be on hand to guide any emergency or essential traffic through closed roads and Pippa texted Erin to make sure she'd checked all the race monitors were aware of this. She then heaved herself into the shower, blasting herself with icy water to try and lift the fog.

Unfortunately, the combination of coffee and cold water didn't work the necessary miracles. Pippa stared at her reflection in the mirror. Her face was drawn, her eyes sunken. "I look like shit," she hissed at herself. Which, considering she had a high profile as one of the fair organisers, was not great. She dug out her cosmetics bag and rifled through it, wishing she was the type of person who cared about quality makeup and knew what to do with it. She did the best she could to cover the eye bags and add some colour to her cheeks, but there was no makeup in the world able to disguise the misery in her eyes or the heartbroken downturn to her mouth. In an attempt to cheer herself up, she put on her favourite dress Wolfie had admired. It didn't work. As she checked her reflection, it was all she could do not to tear the outfit off and crawl back into bed. However, the constant flurry of texts from Mae and Erin reminded her of her duties, and so Pippa tossed her hair back and stood straight. They needed her. The town needed her. She just had to get through today and then she could mope to a professional standard for as long as she wanted.

Pippa drove herself down to the green, where Mae and Erin were mingling with the vendors setting up their stalls and trucks. Erin was deep in conversation with the very handsome owner of the Vietnamese salad truck, so Pippa went over to Mae, whose eyes bugged at the sight of her.

"Wow!" Mae hugged Pippa tight. "You look incredible. Should I change?" She looked as effortlessly chic as ever in a patterned tea dress and a headscarf. Pippa felt reasonably sure she'd look like a dowdy housewife from the 1950s if she wore such a thing, but Mae's cropped hair and tattoos just made it look damn cool.

"Shut up, you look amazing," Pippa mumbled.

"Did you hear from Frankie yet?" Mae pulled back from Pippa with a grin. "He and Theo will be swinging by later." She cast a glance behind Pippa. "Lover Boy not coming?" It was all Pippa could do not to burst into tears and Mae's delight descended into horror. "What?"

"Wolfie's gone," Pippa said. "He saw Alex making a pass at me and assumed we were back together. He freaked out and took off."

"You are kidding me!" Mae guided Pippa over to a hay bale and made her sit. "Did you explain?"

"I tried." Pippa wrung her hands. "He just wouldn't

hear it." Pippa considered quoting Wolfie's exact words, but she knew getting them out would be impossible. "And now, because of Alex's hideous timing, he's scared. He's gone."

"You told him, though, right?" Mae demanded. "You told Wolfie that Alex was ancient history?"

"Repeatedly." Pippa nodded. "It wasn't enough to make him believe me. He struggles to trust anyone and what Alex did shattered whatever faith he had in me. In us." She stopped short of divulging anything about Wolfie's past and the reasons behind his trust issues. It felt disrespectful.

"You really like him." Mae tucked an errant curl of hair behind Pippa's ear. It wasn't a question.

"I do." Pippa's entire being ached. She lifted her eyes to Mae's. "I think ... I mean, I *know* ... Mae, I'm in love with him."

"Oh, babe." Mae stroked her arm.

"But he went to Cumbria overnight to see his niece. Won't answer my calls or my texts." Pippa buried her head in her hands. "I wish I knew how to make him hear me!"

Mae sighed. "Is he coming back?"

Pippa lifted her anguished head. "He said he might come back today around three to ensure the documents for the house sale get picked up."

Mae stood, her face deadly serious. "Then you must be at Squires when he gets there. Make him see sense."

Pippa gestured around them. "How can I with all this going on?"

Mae waved a hand. "Bah. We've organised the shit out of this fair. You and Wolfie are more important. Erin and I can take care of everything."

"But what if he doesn't show up?" Pippa felt sick as it occurred to her she might never see Wolfie again. "What if he actually sends Grantham?"

"Or, what if Wolfie *does* show up?" Mae said. "You have to take that chance."

A lump lodged itself firmly in Pippa's throat. "I'm not sure he'll listen."

Mae snorted. "I've been in the same room as the pair of you. I've seen the way you look at each other. The man is obviously crazy about you and has been for some time. I'd put money on him *wanting* to listen, except he's scared to try. You're the master negotiator, Pip. *Make* him try." She leaned down and stared Pippa squarely in the eye. "Don't let that man leave your life without understanding what he's throwing away." The unspoken comparison to Alex stirred something in Pippa's gut. Grantham's warning about persistence swam through her mind and she knew Mae was right.

"Okay." Pippa nodded, determination burning deep within. "I'll head up to Squires before three. But I'll stay here until then."

"That's my girl." Mae winked. "In the meantime, we need to get over to the pub because some of the race monitors haven't checked in and I was lying my arse off about being able to handle everything without you."

Pippa reached for Mae's hand and pulled herself up. "Lead the way, pal." As they made their way over to the pub, two private ambulances trundled past. Pippa wanted to groan. As good as it was to see them, the medics were inextricably bound up with Alex, which just made her want to throw up. Mae looked at Pippa in concern.

"Do you want me to handle them?"

Pippa lifted her chin. Alex was not going to strip her of her ability to organise the hell out of everything. "I've got this," she said. "You get started with the monitors and I'll come and help you once I've checked this lot in." Mae dropped a kiss on Pippa's head and charged into the pub. Taking a breath and wishing she could somehow inject coffee into her veins, Pippa headed over to the medics, who had parked up in the pub car park and were jumping out. She was impressed to see their smart grey and mauve uniforms, ironed with military precision, buttons gleaming and shoes shining. A tall woman with fierce red curls and lime green glasses was clearly in charge, directing her crew as they assembled outside their vehicles. At the sight of Pippa, the red-haired woman smiled warmly.

"Mae Grant?" she asked.

"No, Pippa Munro." Pippa extended a hand in greeting. "I work with Mae. She's handling an issue with the race monitors, but I can check you in."

"Nice to meet you. I'm Sue. I head up this team." The women shook hands and Sue reeled off the names of her colleagues, all of which an exhausted Pippa instantly forgot. "Right, where do you want us?" Sue finished, rubbing her hands expectantly.

"We've identified a couple of key locations." Pippa reached into her bag and handed over some photocopied maps of the town. "You should have a set-up on the green and one by the finish line of the race."

Sue perused the map and nodded in agreement. "Makes sense. I'd also like to station some of the team at a couple of strategic points along the route of the course."

"Absolutely." Pippa exhaled in relief. "Honestly, I'm so glad you're here. Feels great to have some professionals taking care of us all."

"A pleasure!" Sue beamed, showing perfectly straight white teeth.

"Come with me to the pub and we'll get you sorted with walkie-talkies," Pippa said. "We want to be able to communicate with you."

"Lead the way." The women fell into step as they headed to the pub.

"Is this your company, then?" Pippa asked. Sue was so bubbly and warm, she instantly wanted to know all about her.

"It is," Sue answered proudly. "I finished medical school, thinking the whole time I was going to become an A&E doctor but then Iraq invaded Kuwait and..." She shrugged sheepishly. "Something didn't sit right with me there."

"You enlisted?" Pippa gawped at the older woman with respect.

"Yes." Sue grimaced. "Well, tried to. Back then, women were only allowed to serve in support roles, so I never got to face actual combat. At any rate, I got shipped into a lot of different warzones to staff hospitals, then moved into training. I still train a lot of servicemen and women in emergency aid, for when they're in combat."

A suspicion began to take hold in Pippa's mind. "Sue, do

you mind if I ask who got in touch with you about this job?"

Sue halted. "Why do you want to know?"

"Just, tell me." Pippa couldn't hide her impatience. "Was it a man called Alex?"

Sue shook her head in bemusement. "No. It was one of my old students. I taught him before he shipped out. He's quite simply one of the bravest and most brilliant men I've ever met so it was an absolute pleasure to come here. Wolfie. Wolfie Squires. Do you know him?"

Chapter Twenty-Three

Hours later, Pippa's voice was hoarse from constantly cheering; the fair had kicked off promptly at midday and so far, it had been a true success. Pippa and her team of volunteers had handled everything with aplomb, and the ebullient crowds were not only having a blast, they were also spending plenty of cash on everything. So far, so perfect, and Pippa fairly brimmed with pride. It was almost exactly how she remembered the fair as a child. The air was full of delicious smells emanating from all the food trucks and a local band rocked out on the green, where guests of all ages danced, chattering and laughing. A miniature fairground taking over the entire High Street added to the genteel chimes of carousels and cheers from the coconut shy as excited kids raced from ride to ride, faces smeared with ice cream or barbecue sauce.

But underneath Pippa's pride lurked a heartbreak so painful that on the occasions it managed to briefly surface past the distractions, it left her breathless. Wolfie had yet to return any of her calls or texts but there was simply no time to dwell on his absence. There was so much Pippa needed to say to him, starting with a huge apology for crediting Alex with finding the medics. How could she have thought her ex was responsible for finding the medics? She'd spent her entire adult life watching that man do the bare minimum so her belief that he could have researched companies on her behalf and convinced them to work the fair was entirely stupid on her part. Luckily for Alex, he seemed to be staying away from the fair. Pippa was relieved; she was so angry at him for his lies that there was no telling what she might have said to him.

The children and teenager wheelbarrow races had recently finished, and next up were the adults, then finally, the pinnacle of the races: the costume endurance race. This was only for the fittest of competitors; a gruelling two-mile route that had to be completed in costume. Pippa had seen some of the contenders already. She'd counted a witch, two dinosaurs and a fully kitted-out Darth Vader, complete with a lightsabre. Pippa couldn't wait to see how that worked out.

A trepidatious gnawing in her gut had grown steadily by the hour, driving Pippa to check and re-check the time as it marched relentlessly on. But soon the moment came to set off to Squires. As all the roads were closed to traffic, Pippa wanted to allow plenty of time to walk up there. She fired off a quick text to Mae and Erin to let them know she was stepping away; Mae replied instantly with a barrage of love heart emojis.

Pippa began to make her way through the throngs of

people. Thrilled as she was to see the crowds, it made her movement slow. Mr Dmitri stopped her to press some free ouzo upon her, just as Mrs Mayhew demanded a hug as a reward for all her hard work. As much as Pippa loved the happy attention, it delayed her progress and by the time she made it to the bottom of the hilly road that led to Squires, she was running out of time and what's more, her ankle was starting to complain again. As she hurried up the hill towards Squires the pain soon became almost intolerable, but Pippa forged on. She had to get to the house in time to see Wolfie. She had to make him see the truth.

By the time Pippa made it to the house, her ankle was throbbing. Falling through the front door, she glanced at the hall table, and, to her horror, the envelope wasn't there. She checked her watch. It was 2.45pm. The courier must have come early, and she'd missed Wolfie. Slamming the door behind her, she rested against it. Her heart sank to her toes. "That's that then."

Wolfie's head popped out from the library. "What's what?" Pippa almost dropped to her knees due to the sheer force of love that bowled into her at the sight of him. He looked as immaculate as ever in an elegant suit cut to flatter his physique and his thick blond hair gracefully tumbling over his forehead.

"You're here!" she cried.

"Yes." He nodded abruptly. "I decided to be here for the courier after all, so I left Emilia's early because I knew about the road closures." He gestured vaguely. "I had to come the long way round from Hadley Gorge and down the—"

"I know you organised the medics for the fair," Pippa

interrupted desperately. "I know it was you and not Alex." She limped towards him. "Why didn't you tell me? Why did you storm off letting me think he arranged them?" When Sue had revealed her connection to the fair, everything had slotted into place for Pippa. If ever there had been a sign that Wolfie was right for her, there it was, loud and clear.

"I wasn't sure if it would do any good," he said, with uncharacteristic meekness.

"Well, that's bollocks," she shot back. "I think you wanted a way out. You saw an opportunity to walk away, and you took it."

Twin spots of pink appeared on his cheeks. "That's not true."

"You're scared," Pippa said. "I think what we have scares you." For a moment it looked like Wolfie was going to deny her claims and Pippa couldn't bear it, so she kept on talking. She simply had to get the words out. "I know you have bad associations with this town, with this house, and I don't blame you. I can't imagine what it must have been like to see Alex and me, how it must have looked. So, I get it. I get why you want to leave this place in the dust. But … I'm here now. And not to sound like an egotistical prick, but you're not a stupid man, so please don't ignore what could be the best thing to ever happen to you." Wolfie's eyes moistened, and he dipped his head down. Pippa took two more determined and painful steps until she was right in front of him. She lifted her hand to his face and tilted it so he could see the sincerity in her eyes. "Sell the house, don't sell the house. Whatever. You deserve to be happy, Wolfie, and if selling this heap of bricks does that, then please do it. Burn it to the ground, sell it to the highest bidder, I don't care." Her thumb stroked his temple. "What you saw, with Alex? I swear that was not what it looked like. I told you last night and I'll tell you every night for the rest of my life. I'm *yours*." Pippa's heart was thudding so loudly it actually hurt.

"Mine." Wolfie said the word slowly, as if tasting it for the first time.

"Yours," she pushed on. "In all the ways you want me to be."

The tiniest crease of a smile flickered across his face. "Mine."

She stroked his cheek. "But seriously Wolfie, why didn't you tell me you were the one who found the medics?"

He blushed disarmingly. "When Mae told me about the problem you had, you looked so worried. I wanted to help, so I did. I was going to tell you, to make sure you were okay with it and that I hadn't overstepped, but I never seemed to find a moment. Then I started having feelings for you." He blushed even harder. "And I thought it might seem like I was trying to impress you and I didn't know how you'd react to that. Although I did really, really want to impress you." He frowned. "God, I'm so bad at flirting, aren't I?" His hands slid down to her waist.

"You're just good enough at it, Wolfie Squires." Pippa ran her thumb over his lips. "Because I don't know if you've noticed, but I've developed feelings for you too."

"There were a few signs, yeah." He chuckled softly,

pressing his forehead to hers. "I'm so sorry for running off like an idiot."

Pippa was so relieved she thought she might faint. "Kiss me then, idiot."

Wolfie leaned in, then froze, millimetres away from her lips. He blinked. "Fuck," he said.

Lips parted, Pippa sighed. "What?"

He pulled back and looked at her. "I can't sell this house." Like a man possessed, he disentangled himself from her grasp and ran to his bag.

Pippa wasn't sure she had heard correctly. "Are you serious?"

Wolfie rifled through his bag and pulled out his phone. "Completely."

She went to his side. "You don't have to, not for me."

"For you, for us, it's the same thing," he said. "Shit! It's not there!" He tapped the phone against his lips, the cogs in his mind clearly whirling.

Pippa was steadily fighting the urge to combust out of sheer joy. "What isn't?"

"I was hoping I had the courier's mobile number in an email so I could call him and get the papers back," he said.

"Is there a head office number?" Pippa asked, reaching for her own phone so she could google it.

"No, it was the solicitor's courier," he answered, thumbing at the phone. "I don't know what company they used."

"Call your solicitor!" Pippa urged.

Wolfie lifted his phone, from which a voicemail message emanated. "It's Saturday. No one's there." He hung up with a huff. "They should use a different company. The driver was beyond rude, cursing left right and centre because of all the road closures. He was whinging about—" His eyes widened.

"What?"

Wolfie advanced towards Pippa. "He had to get to the SPAR in Hurst Bridge to pick up some packages from the collection point there."

Pippa saw what Wolfie was getting at. "He can't get to the town centre directly from here because the road has closed. He'd have to take the big diversion which means—"

"It means if we leave now, we could run down the hill and maybe catch him at the SPAR!" Wolfie looked down at his watch. "He won't get there for at least another ten minutes by my estimation. We can intercept him in that time!"

"Can we really make it?" Pippa worried.

Wolfie pointed at her. "You and I can do anything, Pippa Munro." He reached for her hand again and Pippa felt like she might burst with elation as his warm grip enveloped her fingers.

"You're damn right we can," she said, determinedly ignoring her ankle's persistent twinging. They left the house and exited the main gate onto the road. Wolfie pointed north towards the moors.

"The courier will have had to go all the way up past Foxhouse, and then back to the A road so he can come back into the other side of town where the SPAR shop is." He then indicated downhill, where just a few feet away the barriers closed off the road to traffic. A monitor in a high-viz jacket leaned against them, staring down the hill to where ant-sized wheelbarrow racers were beginning their ascent. "So if we go down this hill it takes us directly to the shop. Do it quickly enough, we just might beat the courier."

Pippa looked down the cordoned-off hill. There was a little pavement that started further down it, but it was crowded with spectators. "But what about them?"

"Well, we'll just go on the main road," Wolfie said. "It's closed to traffic, after all."

"Yeah, no cars!" Pippa yelped, gesturing at the army of competitors advancing along the road towards them. "We just have to make sure we don't get run over by that lot. That's quite a spectacular way to die." *If my ankle doesn't fall off first,* she thought.

Wolfie shrugged. "I've had a good life."

"Death by wheelbarrow." Pippa laughed. "I'm all in then."

Luckily, the race monitor was Mrs Allen's son, who instantly recognised Pippa, and despite all his pre-race safety training, allowed her and Wolfie past the barricade and onto the road itself. Once through, Wolfie and Pippa took off as fast as they could down the hill. It wasn't long however before the pain in Pippa's ankle became overwhelming and soon the joint was alarmingly puffy. Pippa and Wolfie's pace slowed, whilst the racers got closer and closer. Pippa tried to brazen it out, but her breathing became reduced to impatient hisses. Wolfie looked down at her and frowned. "Your ankle."

"Yeah. It hurts." Pippa gasped with frustration as their

pace became a crawl. "I don't want to slow you down. Go on without me."

"And leave you on the road like an injured badger?" He shook his head. "No way! We need to find you a medic. They're on the green, right?"

"Yes but— Oh GOD!" Pippa squealed as Wolfie swept her up in his arms, carrying her like a large baby. She frantically adjusted her dress for modesty as the first racers zoomed past them, more than one of them sending curious glances at the couple making their way downhill against the flow of the race. Although their initial pace was quick, it was hard for Wolfie to keep it up and their progress slowed down once more.

"Wolfie, you'll never get to the SPAR in time," Pippa groaned. "Seriously, leave me on the side of the road. Get to the contracts!"

"Sod the contracts." Sweat beaded on Wolfie's face. "Let's get your ankle seen to. Sue can sort you out."

"It's just a sprain," Pippa insisted. "I'll survive. Let's weigh the importance of that against getting the legal documents back, shall we?"

"Everything all right?"

Pippa blinked. A seven-foot neon-pink dinosaur skidded to a halt before them, speaking with Todd's voice. Sure enough, Todd's face peered out from the mesh window in the dinosaur's neck. Sitting in his wheelbarrow was Pat, dressed in chef whites with a comically enormous fake moustache. "Um, no," Pippa admitted. "Wolfie needs to get to the SPAR right away, but I'm slowing him down." She pointed down to her ankle.

Todd's little dinosaur arms waved anxiously. "Oh, love, are you okay?"

"I'll be fine," she said. "Thing is, we must get to the village and stop a courier van leaving. Like, now."

"I'm trying to do a big romantic gesture," Wolfie explained. "But she's really hurt."

"That ankle looks nasty." Pat frowned. "I think there's a medic station on the green if you—"

Todd attempted to clap his hands through his costume. "I bloody love a romantic gesture! Take the barrow!"

"What?" Pippa said faintly, hoping she'd heard him wrong.

Pat's head tilted comically back to look up at his husband. "Hang on, what about the trophy?"

The dinosaur propped its arms on its hips. "Some things are more important than trophies, Pat."

Pat sighed. "That's not what you were saying over breakfast." Then he slid out of the barrow. "But seeing as my darling can't resist a romantic gesture, please, help yourselves."

"Seriously." Todd nodded at the sturdy and thankfully clean barrow. "Take it. This was bought especially for the race. No pig shit has graced it thus far."

"Wolfie, go on ahead," Pippa begged. It had been humiliating enough being carried down the hill like some kind of invalid, but she'd gone along with it for the sake of love. What Pat was proposing was beyond absurd.

Wolfie's eyes blazed down at her. "I said I won't leave you here and I meant it." With that, he heaved Pippa into the barrow, where she sprawled ungracefully in the bottom like a discarded sack of potatoes. "Thanks, chaps."

"It's like something out of a movie!" Todd thrilled, clapping his hands together.

Pippa scowled up at him. "I'd like to know just what kind of movies you're watching that involve women being thrown in wheelbarrows against their will!"

Wolfie peeled off his suit jacket and wadded it into a ball. "When this day is over, I'd very much like to hear about the thinking behind the costume theme," he said to the couple. "A dinosaur and a chef?"

Pat grumbled, "Todd was *supposed* to be a frying pan but oh no, he just *had* to go rogue."

"My niece loves dinosaurs!" Todd had the decency to sound at least a little apologetic, but then he flapped his dinosaur arms manically at Wolfie and Pippa. "Never mind that now, you go!"

Wolfie didn't need telling twice. He lobbed his jacket at Pat, lifted the wheelbarrow handles and began to run. All Pippa could do was cling on and hope she made it to the SPAR alive. The hill's incline steepened, allowing them to pick up some speed. Air rushed past her skin, roaring loudly in her ears and she felt every bump in the road as Wolfie jolted over them. Racers ran past them in the opposite direction, some calling out in jest about their lack of costume, or sense of direction. The crowds watching the race cheered them on, too, their curiosity plain to see.

But Pippa didn't care about any of that. She didn't even care about her sprained ankle anymore. As she gazed up at Wolfie's face, she felt an overwhelming sensation of total, secure, contentment. Despite her ungainly position, despite the possibility she'd done real damage to her ankle, Pippa knew that she was exactly where she was meant to be; that everything would be okay. Sure, she had no plans beyond the housesitting gig and yes, if Wolfie did end up selling Squires then she would technically be homeless. But none of that mattered. All that mattered was this moment.

The wheelbarrow rounded the corner and Pippa realised with a start that they had made it to the bottom of the hill. Craning her neck, she could see the green and, sure enough, there was Mae, cheering the racers along with everyone else. When Mae noticed the wheelbarrow travelling in the wrong direction, she opened her mouth to protest, at which point Pippa cheekily offered a royal wave and Mae's eyes bulged.

"Pip?" she shrieked. Then Mae clocked who was pushing the wheelbarrow and her jaw literally dropped. Mae went on to yell more, but her words were lost in the general cacophony of the cheering crowds.

"There it is!" Wolfie panted, his face pink with exertion. The SPAR sat at the other side of the green, its storefront covered with brightly coloured bunting. As they approached, a white transit van appeared from around the corner and parked outside. "Shit!" Wolfie picked up his pace. "That's him."

Pippa shouted, "Hurry!"

Wolfie dug in, wind whipping his blond hair madly and sweat patches blossoming across his chest. Pippa twisted, keeping her eyes on the van. A sturdy, tired-looking man in a

Pearl Jam T-shirt slid out of the vehicle and marched into the shop. Wolfie peeled down the road circumventing the green, and when they reached the fence lining the racecourse, a bemused monitor let them through. Pippa sighed with relief that they were no longer on the racecourse, but then had to start hurling apologies to fairgoers walking around the pedestrian area who were forced to jump out of their way.

Wolfie was now yards away from the SPAR. The driver came back out, a small stack of parcels in one hand. He glanced towards the bustling green and the closed roads all around and shook his head ruefully. Wolfie's face turned bright red as he pushed to reach the man before he got into his vehicle.

Pippa began to cry out. "Stop! Stop! Stop!"

The driver halted, glancing around before realising Pippa could only be shouting at him. "What, me?"

"Yes." Wolfie stopped, lowering the barrow handles. "You. Hi."

Recognition dawned across the driver's face. "You're the bloke up at the house," he said. "The fancy one."

"Hang on," Wolfie wheezed and bent over, breathing hard.

"Give him a moment," Pippa said, awkwardly wobbling in the now stationary barrow. "He's just pushed me through the town in this thing."

The driver waited. Wolfie coughed, trying to catch his breath.

"Will this take long?" The driver edged towards his van. "It's just I have a tight schedule so..."

"The envelope I gave you..." Wolfie coughed again and straightened. "I need it back."

The driver's lips thinned. "No can do. When I take receipt, I log it in, so now I'm legally bound to return it to the courier hub, whereby we coordinate delivery to the intended recipient."

"You don't understand," Wolfie said. "Those documents were for the sale of my house. I am no longer selling my house."

The driver's gaze flicked towards Pippa, who remained prone in the wheelbarrow. "So, between the time of you handing me those documents and now, with, whatever's going on here"—he nodded at Pippa—"you changed your mind about the sale?"

"Yes," Wolfie said.

"That's mad," the driver said.

"No. It's love," Wolfie said.

"What?" said the very confused driver.

"What?" Pippa echoed with a yelp from the wheelbarrow.

Wolfie turned and looked down at her. "Yeah. Is that okay?"

"More than okay." Pippa could barely breathe at the epic 'okayness' of what he had just said.

"I'm staying in Hurst Bridge," Wolfie went on, "and so I won't be selling."

"Are you sure?" Pippa said. "I don't want to make you stay if—"

"I'm staying, Pippa Munro." Wolfie grinned. "I'm staying at Squires. And I'm staying with you." His eyes snared hers and in them she saw no guile, no uncertainty. He looked at her like she was a treasure the world had been denied for far too long.

"As romantic as this is, I do have to go." The driver's irritated voice broke the spell. Pippa and Wolfie's heads whipped round like they'd forgotten he was there. "Like I said, I can't help. If you need the envelope back, you'll have to take it up with the intended recipient. If they refuse the delivery and request return to sender, then we can return it to you." He coughed. "Subject to fees, of course."

"Please!" Pippa said. "Are you sure you can't make an exception in this instance?"

"No," the driver said wearily. "I've scanned the package in. It's logged. It can't be un-logged."

"This is really important though," Pippa insisted.

"Actually, what's important is, I don't care." The driver shrugged and trudged to the back of the van to open the doors.

"Come on, help us out!" Wolfie said. "I made this big romantic gesture to take the documents back."

"He pushed me in a wheelbarrow!" Pippa piped up. "He ran down the hill in leather brogues, for crying out loud! You can't get more dramatic than that."

"Churches brogues as well!" Wolfie pointed down to his smart shoes which were now scuffed and one of the laces had become frayed. "Ruined!"

The driver blinked. "Was I not clear on how much I don't care?"

Wolfie threw his hands up in exasperation. "I know you

don't! Come on, surely you've been in love? Done something crazy to impress a woman?"

The driver stifled a belch and shoved the parcels he was carrying into the van. "No. But if I was still married, I can tell you my wife would not find me losing my job due to breaking protocol remotely romantic."

Wolfie dug in his pocket. "I have some money. I could—"

"Hey, no." The driver backed away, hands raised. "You think a few quid is acceptable for me getting sacked?" He sighed, defeated, and reached into the cab of his van to pull out a small flyer. "Call the head office. The number's on there and it's manned 24/7. We can hold the package at the hub if you raise a dispute. Say you gave me the wrong envelope and they'll suspend delivery. That'll give you time to fix this, right?"

Wolfie took the flyer. His eyes flicked up to the driver. "I pushed this woman through town on a wheelbarrow when I could have just called this number?"

The driver tutted. "Yes. You did. Now, if you'll excuse me, I have to drive twenty miles out of my way to get to my next pick-up because of these chuffing road closures."

As the courier drove off, Wolfie turned back to Pippa, who still lay in the wheelbarrow. He ambled over and looked down. "So. What now, Pippa Munro?"

She eyed him cheekily. "Do you think he meant your house was fancy or that *you* were fancy?"

"Come here," he growled.

With a rush of happiness, Pippa stood up in the barrow, flinging her arms around Wolfie's neck. The barrow wobbled precariously due to the sudden movement, but she didn't care.

Wolfie snaked his hands round her back and pulled her tight to him. The barrow almost tipped, but Wolfie's grip kept her safe.

Nose to nose, Pippa whispered. "Ask me your question again."

Wolfie arched his head back so he could look at her. His eyes shone and Pippa had never felt surer of anyone's love.

"What now, Pippa Munro?" he said.

Pippa smiled as she leaned in for a kiss. She didn't have the answer to that question, not in that exact moment, but she knew she had everything she needed to work it out. And for the time being, that was all that mattered.

Chapter Twenty-Four

Pippa gazed upon Squires with a fierce glow of satisfaction. Squires's grounds were full of happy fairgoers, with sugared children chasing each other around the lawn as the racers waited anxiously for their prizes. A local brass band oom-pah-pahed gently to one side, whilst a few pensioners danced along, cheeks flushed, whether from sun or the delicious Pimm's cocktails Mae's pub had sold en masse that day, Pippa wasn't sure.

"Who's the chap with the ouzo again?" Wolfie was beside her, sniffing his cup suspiciously.

"Mr Dmitri," Pippa said. "He used to run the pharmacy before he retired. Now he makes lethally alcoholic spirits but calls them artisanal so he can justify whacking the prices up."

"He's funny," Wolfie said, knocking back his drink and failing spectacularly not to cough. "Christ!"

"I did warn you!" Pippa laughed.

"Wolfie, Wolfie!" Todd appeared at their side, cheeks flushed with excitement. "We hear the sale is off!"

Wolfie eyes narrowed. "Wow, word really does travel fast in Hurst Bridge."

"Well, you two did put on quite the passionate performance in front of the whole town by all accounts, so you can't blame the gossip mill for going into overdrive," Todd said. "We're very happy for you."

Pat arrived, handing his husband a bottle of water. "We really are. Wolfie, listen, please could you allow me to introduce you to my grandmother Agnes?" He waved at an elderly lady so tiny and wrapped up in so many woolly layers that she resembled a tea cosy. "She's desperate to meet the owner of this house. She worked here as a teenager before she got married and moved away."

Wolfie's eyes widened. "It'd be an honour." He looked down at Pippa. "Is that okay?"

"Sure!" She nudged him. "Go and mingle."

He thanked her with a blazing smile, then followed Todd and Pat, chattering easily with them as they walked.

"You have to tell me everything." Frankie suddenly grabbed her arm from behind. "The whole town is abuzz with the goss about you and Wolfie Squires."

Pippa rolled her eyes, thoroughly unsurprised. "I'm glad everyone's focusing on that and not on the success of the fair."

Frankie laughed. "Do you really need anyone telling you what an amazing feat you pulled off?" He motioned around them. "I mean, look at this crowd. Surely you've hit the fundraising target?"

Pippa felt a surge of pride as she nodded. Mae had confirmed as such only minutes ago, via an emoji-riddled text that was almost certainly champagne-fuelled. "And more besides."

"Perhaps this will become an annual event again then?" Frankie asked hopefully. "Like, forever?"

Pippa looked over at Wolfie. "I hope so."

"Anyway. Enough boring chat." Frankie elbowed her. "Are you going to tell me?"

Pippa arched an eyebrow, enjoying the tease. "Tell you what?"

Frankie practically screamed. "About why Wolfie Squires pushed you through the town in a wheelbarrow and *why* were you seen snogging each other's faces off outside the SPAR? I hear Mrs Allen had to take an extra dose of angina medication because it was so raunchy!"

"Mrs Allen should mind her own business," Pippa retorted with a giggle.

"Pip." Frankie glared.

"Fine." Pippa couldn't hold back the wave of joy. "We're together. He's not selling the house."

Frankie clutched her arm, eyes bulging. "Are you serious?" She nodded and he frowned. "But what about the money issues? Doesn't he have to pay off his dad's ancient debts or something?"

"Yes." Pippa sobered. She'd been so wrapped up in the romance of the moment that she'd forgotten the practical reasons behind the sale. How was Wolfie going to solve the old debt hanging over his head? "We've not gone into detail, but I'm sure he has it all in hand. We'll sort it out."

"No time like the present." Frankie pointed at Wolfie.

"What, now?" Pippa groaned. "Can't it wait until the prizegiving? I haven't even finished my Pimm's!"

"You can drink and talk!" He glanced fondly back at Theo, who was laughing companionably with Erin and some of her schoolteacher friends. "Take it from me, it's best to lay all your cards on the table from the get-go."

Pippa sighed. Frankie was right. After all, hadn't she and Alex fallen foul of that snag? If she'd known what Alex really wanted from his life, maybe she wouldn't have clung on to that relationship beyond its expiration date. She squeezed Frankie's arm and then headed over to where Wolfie was ensnared in deep conversation with Pat's grandmother. The elderly lady had his hand gripped in her tiny ones and her eyes sparkled when they alighted upon Pippa.

"You must be the woman I've been hearing so much about!" Agnes greeted her.

"You've been gossiping about me?" Pippa said to Wolfie.

"He literally mentioned you once," Pat reassured her.

"Yes, but the *way* he mentioned you..." Pat's grandmother wagged her finger, "was practically an essay. She's every bit as beautiful as you described."

"Agnes, now I thought all that was between us," Wolfie gently chided the woman.

"You know, I was just saying, I knew his grandfather and he was a true gentleman," Agnes went on. "Charming, just like you, young man. I think this town is lucky to have you."

Wolfie swallowed, visibly moved. His hand found

Pippa's and squeezed it tight. "Grandpa was a good man," he replied hoarsely.

Pippa tugged on his hand. "As are you," she said. Wolfie smiled at her, and Pippa was awash with love. The way Wolfie looked at her, the way he touched her... It was incomparable. She thought she'd known love with Alex, but just being in Wolfie's presence made her feel as if a million fireworks raced beneath her skin.

Todd cleared his throat. "All right, lovebirds," he said. "When is the prize-giving?"

"Whenever the mayor shows up," Pippa said with a laugh.

"Um, I last saw our mayor necking Dmitri's ouzo," Wolfie said. "We may be waiting a while for her."

Pippa texted Erin for an update on the mayor's presence and was told *ten minutes*. She let out a sigh of relief. "Not long now," she assured them all. "I just need to borrow this man for a moment." She pulled on Wolfie's arm.

"A pleasure to meet you." Wolfie stopped and shook Agnes's hand. "Hope to see you again."

"Anytime!" Agnes smiled.

"What's up?" Wolfie asked, as soon as they were out of earshot.

"I need to ask you something," Pippa said. "And it's—" She was interrupted by Mae's sister, Katie, demanding to know where Mae was. "She's at the gates," Pippa informed her. She turned back to Wolfie, only for the winners of the Teens Wheelbarrow Race to interrupt with their clamouring to find out when the trophies would be handed out. "Ten minutes," she told them, trying not to show her frustration.

"You won't get a minute of peace!" Wolfie's eyes darted around. "Follow me." He led her down to the bottom of the garden. A cordon had been erected here to stop people wandering into the overgrown maze. Wolfie lifted it and guided Pippa through. "Come on."

Thanks to Pippa's efforts, the path to the centre was a little less overgrown, however not yet ready to be walked through. But Wolfie persevered in clearing a path, and soon, the cacophony of the crowds magically hushed as they finally made it to the middle of the maze where the bench still rested.

"So, what's up?" Wolfie asked again.

"As thrilled as I am that you aren't selling up," Pippa said, "I just want you to be certain about what you're taking on here. You still need to clear Carmichael's debts."

"You don't need to worry about that," he said.

"Wolfie." Pippa grabbed his chin. "All cards on the table. It's the only way forward."

He nodded soberly. "Fine, fine. The truth is, I'm not sure. I'll work something out." He pulled her down to the bench next to him. "Selling Squires wasn't my only option, to be fair; it merely seemed the most attractive option at the time. But I'll work something out."

"Are you sure?" Pippa said. "Because please don't let your financial situation go to shit just because of me. Sell the house if it's the best thing to do."

He looked at her with a laugh. "The best thing for me to do is to stay here with you. Don't you get that? I'm good with money, I'll think of something."

"Wow." Pippa shook her head in disbelief. "You're really not going to sell up and take the easy way out?"

Wolfie shrugged. "Doing the right thing isn't always easy but deciding to do it, is." He met her eyes earnestly. "I'm willing to put in the work, if you are."

Pippa remembered something Frankie had told her that bleak day she'd moved her meagre possessions into Squires House. He'd said that sometimes, the worst thing to happen to you can turn out to be the best. Well, the best thing was right in front of her, and Pippa truly thought she might explode with the love she felt for this man. "Wolfie," she said seriously. "I'd move to Kent for you."

He let out a puzzled laugh. "What?"

"Look, this town is my home and I love it," she said. "So much so that when Alex wanted to take me away from it, I refused to follow him. But you? I'd follow you. To Kent. Or Rome. Or Siberia. Doesn't matter where."

Wolfie straightened his shoulders. "You'd follow me? Tell me, why is that?"

Pippa smiled the kind of smile that put the sun to shame. "Because I'm in love with you, Wolfie Squires."

Wolfie grabbed her hand and raised it to his lips. "Right back at you, Pippa Munro."

Epilogue

ONE YEAR LATER

"Why can't I take it off?" Pippa scratched at the blindfold.

"Because I said so," Wolfie said haughtily. "Mind your step."

They were outside, Pippa knew that much, somewhere in the garden at Squires. The evening was cooling, and she could sense the sun slipping down behind the hills.

"I'm exhausted," she said. "Can we not just get a takeaway and watch some shit on TV?"

Wolfie spluttered. "Be still my beating heart."

"Well then you're going to have to explain pretty quickly what's happening here," Pippa said.

"Excuse me for thinking the one-year anniversary of our first kiss should be special," Wolfie said, his lips moving close to her ear. Pippa's heart sped up; she'd never stop finding this man irresistible.

"I'm suddenly very much on board with the blindfold," she said, reaching for him.

"Uh-uh-uh," he tutted cheekily. "All in good time, Pippa Munro."

Pippa couldn't fight the smile. She still loved hearing him say her name like that. Wolfie's hand slid to her lower back and she leaned into his touch, letting him guide her. It had been a manic year, starting with Wolfie's bold step of selling off much of Carmichael's precious wine collection, defying his late father's wishes. "He won't be here to drink it, will he?" was Wolfie's rationale and he'd suffered no resistance from his mother or sister. The funds raised from the sales had wiped out virtually all Carmichael's debts and allowed them to stay at the house, where they were embarking on a new dream together.

Squires B&B was to open to the public the very next day and Wolfie and Pippa had worked all the hours possible to turn the old house into a chic yet cosy boutique hotel. Thanks to Pippa's business acumen and Wolfie's extensive contacts, the summer was already looking to be incredibly busy with masses of bookings. So long as their joint business followed projections, it seemed as though their big gamble might just pay off, and handsomely so. Despite this, Wolfie had been forced to keep his job as a security consultant whilst the renovations were ongoing – they needed every penny they could scrape together – so Pippa had had to manage a lot of the works by herself. But he hoped to wind his consultancy down soon enough, should the venture succeed the way they believed it would. Theirs had been a true

Epilogue

partnership, light years away from what she had shared with Alex.

"How was Joan today?" Pippa asked, gladly pushing all thoughts of Alex far from her mind.

"Good." Wolfie's tone dipped, as it usually did when talking about Joan. She had moved into a special care home that Grantham was proudly funding himself, although he did permit Wolfie and Pippa to visit whenever they wanted and bring whatever treats they wanted to help cheer her up. Pippa fell more deeply in love with Wolfie every time she watched him with the woman. On her bad days he would feed Joan soup or comb her hair. She had sadly lost the ability of speech and could often be found staring into space, but Pippa swore her eyes lit up when Wolfie walked in, that her mouth quirked in a half-smile whenever he talked about Squires or its gardens. "She ate some of the carrot cake you made," he went on. "Think she liked it too."

"Aw." Pippa grinned. Her carrots had been particularly good this summer.

"Right, watch yourself." The air suddenly became a little more hushed and Pippa knew she was amongst the high hedges of the maze.

"What are we doing?" she asked. The maze had been a laborious project of theirs but an important one. Pippa had an instinct that it would be a unique selling point for any guests that came to Squires. After all, how many B&Bs had their own maze with a view of the Yorkshire Moors? But the neglect had been extensive and fixing it properly had ended up being costly and time-consuming. Due to Wolfie's work keeping him busy, Pippa had really struggled to complete

Epilogue

the final tidy up of the maze and unfortunately, it wouldn't be available to visitors until at least a few weeks after the hotel opened.

"You'll see," Wolfie said. "Come along." They walked a few more paces, twisting and turning. Pippa knew he was leading her to the heart of the maze. Soon enough, they stopped.

"Can I take it off now?" she begged. As an answer, Wolfie tugged at the fabric and pulled it away from her eyes. "Oh, my."

The maze had been transformed. The tatty, ragged hedges of before were now healthy and vibrant, filling the air with a fresh green scent. The grass beneath Pippa's feet was lush and even, with patches of fragrant verbena and striking foxgloves dotted about. Festoon lighting had been strung around the hedges, casting the space in a golden glow. It was magical.

"Wolfie," Pippa giggled. "You finished it. How did you—?"

Wolfie grimaced. "Don't ask. Let's just say I owe Frankie and Theo several rounds of drinks."

Pippa shook her head in disbelief. "And your piano? Why is that here?" The huge piano from the library was inexplicably placed right in the centre, stool and all.

Wolfie pointed to the old bench, lovingly restored with a simple brass plaque that read 'Joan's Bench'. "Sit."

"Okay." Full of questions, Pippa did as she was told.

Wolfie took a seat at the piano and cleared his throat. As he stretched his fingers over the keys his hands trembled. "Pippa Munro," he said softly.

Epilogue

Curiosity gave way to anticipation swelling in her chest. "Yes?"

"You ready for a song?"

"Always." It had been a real joy over the last year to watch Wolfie slowly come back to music, taking precious spare moments to play whatever music was on his mind.

"Good. Because I wrote a little something." He blushed. "A song of my own."

"Oh." Pippa sat up straight, intrigued. She hadn't known he was writing his own songs. They'd talked about him providing some kind of musical entertainment for guests at the B&B, but Wolfie was still too shy to commit to that, restricting the gift of his music only to people he trusted.

"Yep." His fingers skittered across the keys. "I'd like to sing it for you now, if I may?"

Pippa nodded, thoroughly intrigued. "By all means."

Wolfie cleared his throat again, blond hair falling adorably into his eyes. Then, with a nervous breath, he began.

First came deep notes, ponderous and slow; soon followed by a gentle melody infused with joy. Then, a brief pause and Wolfie began to sing:

I thought I knew what life was, I thought I knew what love was.

Thought life was only for running and love was for everyone else

But one girl, with faith, one girl, she said...

She said she'd move to Kent for me,

Epilogue

And then I began to see...

Here, he smiled at her, and Pippa shimmered with admiration. All this time and she'd never once heard him sing. His voice was clear and strong, despite the nerves radiating through each word.

But here's what I would do for her
 Literally anything, because I'm sure,
 I'd carry her through the storm, race down that hill
 Turn my life upside down to give her a home
 I'll be her home, because she is mine.
 But now I have to ask this girl, what is it you could do for me?

Here Wolfie stopped and swivelled on his seat to look at her. He lifted an eyebrow. Somewhat discombobulated, Pippa touched her chest in a 'who me?' gesture. He nodded as if to say, 'yes, you'. When Pippa didn't answer immediately, he gave her a mysterious grin and turned back to the keys.

It's quite simple, haven't you heard?
 All I need from you, Pippa Munro, is one word.

In one fluid motion, Wolfie was out of his seat and on his knees before her. From his pocket, he produced a small velvet box.

Pippa clapped her hands over her mouth, barely able to believe what she was seeing. Wolfie flipped the lid of the box, and nestled on a cushion was the most elegant diamond ring. Slim white gold, with a perfect, round solitaire.

"One word," Wolfie repeated, breathless. "All I need."

For a brief, beautiful moment, Pippa couldn't speak. Happiness soared through every inch of her being. "I – I had no idea you were planning – why..." Sheer joy stole her breath away and her words gave out.

Wolfie raised an eyebrow. "Are you seriously going to leave me hanging?"

Pippa laughed. Heart bursting, she held out her hand, nails ragged and work-worn. One word was all Wolfie needed from her, and she was more than happy to give it to him. It seemed a fair exchange for all her tomorrows. "Yes," she barely squeaked. Wolfie beamed with a mix of relief and joy as he slid the ring onto her finger then raised himself up to bring his face to hers. Before he could kiss her, Pippa placed her finger over his lips. "I hope it's very clear now that I consider you mine."

Beneath her fingertips, Wolfie's mouth curved into a true smile. "Yours," he said softly. "Always."

Acknowledgments

I've been told by more than one writer friend (ooh, look at me, writer friends, plural) that book two is always the hardest. And boy, they weren't lying. Of course, having my second child during the heights of the pandemic and returning to work when said child was five months old definitely didn't help the writing process. Forging this story from my time-poor, post-partum brain was gruelling. And it's for that reason that I'm immensely proud of it, no matter what. The story began when I read an article about house sitters, and I instantly envisioned a beautiful old house suffering neglect, with a handsome, Mr. Darcy-esque character rattling around it. And it got me thinking about the concept of home. Is home a place or a person? Can love transcend where you live?

I grew up in an area not a million miles away from where *The House Sitter* is set, and every summer during my childhood I would attend the local wheelbarrow races, sometimes participating alongside my school friends. The memory of the village all coming together is one I will never lose and an apt demonstration of the power of community. Pippa is the embodiment of that power, the perfect companion for a man like Wolfie, who has lost all faith in the notion of home.

Thanks a million to Jennie Rothwell and the OMC team for being so supportive and encouraging, not to mention patient (hahaha that July deadline!) and of course my wonderful, award-winning agent Hannah Schofield at LBA. I would also like to mention a fantastic human being named Erin Mitchell, whose winning bid in the 'Promises for Bibi' auction won her the prize of having a character named after her. 'Promises for Bibi' was an auction held to raise funds for Beatriz Maia-Farmer, who is suffering from high-risk neuroblastoma. Her parents Laura and Thiago are fighting like hell to get her the treatment she needs that is currently not available on the NHS. As a parent, I cannot imagine what this must be like. To learn more about Bibi, please check out: https://www.solvingkidscancer.org.uk/children/bibi/

Special thanks must go to my besties Sarah Salmon and Kerry Cookson for being my constant cheerleaders and showing up at my little book launch for my first novel. It meant so much to me and if every woman had friends like you the world would be a better place. This book would also not have been completed were it not for the support and understanding from my amazing husband Neil, but it might have happened faster were it not for the interventions of my daughters Lila and Beatrix. Good job I love you two, isn't it? If you could just let me sleep you'd be perfect. And to everyone who read/bought/reviewed my debut novel, *The Reunion*, words cannot express how grateful I am. If you enjoyed my first book I fervently hope you like this one just as much.

Finally, this book is dedicated to my parents, Ruth and

Nigel Harrison. Dad, you once called me your little dreamer and all I can say is, it takes a dreamer to recognise a dreamer. From a young age I hoped I would one day see the stories floating around my head in print and I still can't quite believe I've achieved that. Mum, thanks for giving me a love of books and for being an excellently tough but fair critic. It's no exaggeration to say I would not be where I am without you both.

ONE MORE CHAPTER

YOUR NUMBER ONE STOP
FOR PAGETURNING BOOKS

The author and One More Chapter would like to thank everyone who contributed to the publication of this story...

Analytics
Abigail Fryer
Maria Osa

Audio
Fionnuala Barrett
Ciara Briggs

Contracts
Georgina Hoffman
Florence Shepherd

Design
Lucy Bennett
Fiona Greenway
Holly Macdonald
Liane Payne
Dean Russell

Digital Sales
Lydia Grainge
Emily Scorer
Georgina Ugen

Editorial
Arsalan Isa
Sarah Khan
Charlotte Ledger
Bonnie Macleod
Jennie Rothwell
Caroline Scott-Bowden
Kimberley Young

International Sales
Bethan Moore

Marketing & Publicity
Chloe Cummings
Emma Petfield

Operations
Melissa Okusanya
Hannah Stamp

Production
Emily Chan
Denis Manson
Francesca Tuzzeo

Rights
Lana Beckwith
Rachel McCarron
Agnes Rigou
Hany Sheikh Mohamed
Zoe Shine
Aisling Smyth

The HarperCollins Distribution Team

The HarperCollins Finance & Royalties Team

The HarperCollins Legal Team

The HarperCollins Technology Team

Trade Marketing
Ben Hurd
Eleanor Slater

UK Sales
Laura Carpenter
Isabel Coburn
Jay Cochrane
Tom Dunstan
Sabina Lewis
Erin White
Harriet Williams
Leah Woods

And every other essential link in the chain from delivery drivers to booksellers to librarians and beyond!

ONE MORE CHAPTER

YOUR NUMBER ONE STOP FOR PAGETURNING BOOKS

One More Chapter is an award-winning global division of HarperCollins.

Subscribe to our newsletter to get our latest eBook deals and stay up to date with all our new releases!

signup.harpercollins.co.uk/
join/signup-omc

Meet the team at
www.onemorechapter.com

Follow us!
@OneMoreChapter_
@OneMoreChapter
@onemorechapterhc

Do you write unputdownable fiction?
We love to hear from new voices.
Find out how to submit your novel at
www.onemorechapter.com/submissions